Praise for *Word Gets Around*

"Wingate's sweet writing style incorporates the best of romance, friendship and small-town life. The characters resound with down-home charm and light up the pages with touching spiritual insight."

—*RT Book Reviews*

"Each character is lovingly crafted. . . . Wingate's idyllic small-town atmosphere in this sweet romance makes for a charming read."

—*Booklist*

Praise for Lisa Wingate's Novels

"Full of suspense, mystery, and romance, *Wildwood Creek* is a must read."

—*RT Book Reviews* Top Pick

"Versatile and prolific Wingate weaves a story of deception, secrecy, and scandal. . . . fans of women's fiction will find this novel . . . deeply satisfying."

—*Booklist* on *Firefly Island*

"Wingate pens a light and entertaining story of life in a small town with Texas-sized charm."

—*Publishers Weekly* on *Talk of the Town*

Word Gets Around

Word Gets Around

Lisa Wingate

BETHANYHOUSE

a division of Baker Publishing Group
Minneapolis, Minnesota

© 2009 by Wingate Media, LLC

Published by Bethany House Publishers
11400 Hampshire Avenue South
Bloomington, Minnesota 55438
www.bethanyhouse.com

Bethany House Publishers is a division of
Baker Publishing Group, Grand Rapids, Michigan

Printed in the United States of America

New paperback edition published 2019

ISBN 978-0-7642-3302-9

The Library of Congress has cataloged the original edition as follows:

Library of Congress Cataloging-in-Publication Data
Wingate, Lisa.
    Word gets around / Lisa Wingate.
      p. cm.
    ISBN 978-0-7642-0491-3 (pbk.)
    1. Horse trainers—Fiction. 2. Texas—Fiction. I. Title.
    PS3573.I53165W67   2009
    813'.54—dc22

Scripture quotations are from the King James Version of the Bible.

Cover design by Paul Higdon

Cover illustration by Paul Higdon and William Graf

19 20 21 22 23 24 25   7 6 5 4 3 2 1

For my two small-town boys
who know that moms (and writers) need quiet time,
and that trips to town to deliver forgotten ball gloves,
left-behind track shoes, lost band instruments,
and trash bags full of sweaty football pads
are a great way to get it.
Thanks for looking after my peace of mind,
and for making every day an adventure.
What a blessing!

Acknowledgments

In considering this second visit to Daily, Texas, I'd be a pretty poor neighbor if I didn't thank all the people who made the first visit such a hoot. To all the readers who became honorary Dailyians last year when *Talk of the Town* hit the shelves, thank you for taking time to send notes, e-mails, cards, letters, Texisms, historical snippets, book club reviews, and little stories that might be useful for the installment. Your companionship on these journeys completes the circle of blessing in ways that are truly amazing. Because of you, the population of Daily is growing by leaps and bounds, the stories keep flowing, and Imagene and the girls are up to their elbows in small-town mischief again. I can't wait for you to drop on in and see what's happening now!

I'd also like to thank a few "hometown" friends who've helped with technical details and other research for *Word Gets Around*. First of all, thanks to A-number-1 coach, Bennett Fields, for sharing the Bigfoot story in the teachers' lounge, and for letting the folks of Daily borrow your mysterious creature for a bit. In some cases, truth is even more fun than fiction. Thanks to film producer and screenwriter, and generally sweet and funny person, Cynthia Riddle, for introducing me to the world of moviemaking, and for hanging on the phone through endless silly questions. Thanks to Sharon Mannion for proofreading, Janice and Lawrence Wingate for helping with books and feeding wandering Wingate boys, Teresa Lohman for helping with online scrapbooking, and Ed Stevens for getting me going on Youtube and for being the world's best encourager. How in the world did I ever get so lucky as to have all of you?

Lastly, I'd like to thank the folks who do all the hard work that turns ideas into books. Thank you to my agent, Claudia Cross at Sterling Lord Literistic. A special measure of gratitude goes out to the amazing folks at Bethany House Publishers, who make this process such an incredible joy. In particular, thanks to Dave Long for always giving invaluable input and support, to Julie Klassen for astute (and fun—who would have thought?) line edits and suggestions, and to the amazing crew in marketing and publicity, who bring the books to the hands of readers with enthusiasm, innovation, and tender loving care—Steve Oates, Jim Hart, Brett Benson, Debra Larsen, Carra Carr, and Noelle Buss. Thanks for welcoming me and my crazy cast of imaginary friends into the BHP family!

Chapter 1

Lauren Eldridge

They say you can't go home again, but the truth is, if you're a small-town Texas girl, you can never really leave. The town travels with you like an extra layer of skin—something flamboyant and tight fitting. Even though you may hide it beneath the trappings of sophistication, it's right there under your clothes, your secret identity. Whether you admit it or not, you have an affinity for big hair, shirts with pearl snaps, cowboy boots, and faded blue jeans. Even in the most upscale restaurants, you secretly search the menu for comfort foods like chicken-fried steak and catfish, especially on Fridays. Any Texas girl knows it's not Friday without all-you-can-eat catfish.

The world would be better off if everyone ate fried food at least one night a week, and drank coffee you could cut with a knife, and lingered with their neighbors. We'd understand each other a little better, and maybe we'd understand ourselves. Perhaps we'd ponder, over the plastic basket with the grease-stained tissue paper, the need to run so far, so fast—to have, to do, to achieve, to gain, to win—to be *all that* and make sure

11

everybody knows it. A pecan pie does not toil, nor does it spin, but it sure tastes good, and it makes a fine conversation piece.

In the right setting, you can talk for twenty minutes about the merits of a good pecan pie. You can discuss the pecans—paper shell, Stuart, native, chopped, broken, whole. You can talk about the fact that farm-fresh eggs make a better pie than store-bought. You can theorize as to why that might be. One thing that's wrong with society today—too many chemically altered chickens living in giant egg factories, toiling mindlessly, uninspired by their work.

There's a whole world out there that doesn't know one egg from another, and for some reason, that world had always held an attraction for me. My limited contact with the strange and wondrous realms outside our little town of Daily, Texas, was the subject of my earliest childhood fascinations. That world seemed like the place to be, even when I was too young to understand it.

In the farthest reaches of my memory, there are hippies. They're sitting on a street corner in Los Angeles, shaking tambourines, playing guitars, railing against nukes and advocating love. It's a nice song, I think, and I'm enthralled by their swinging leather fringes, and the fact that they're dancing half-naked on the sidewalk. We don't see things like that back home in Daily, Texas.

Aunt Donetta grabs my hand and drags me across the street and we go find my father, who is delivering a herd of our ranch horses to their winter jobs at a movie studio. The horses have been ferrying city kids and troops of Girl Scouts out at Boggy Bend Park all summer, so they're *dog gentle*, says my father as he and the studio wrangler, Willie Wardlaw, watch the herd exit the trailer and blink in the bright California sunlight. The wrangler, my dad's old rodeo buddy, laughs. "Just because Girl

Scouts can handle them horses don't mean movie actors can,"
he says.

Standing there in my new pink cowgirl suit, proudly wearing
my latest goat slapping championship belt buckle, I catalog
that information in my six-year-old brain. Movie actors are
worse horse riders than Girl Scouts. Even at six years old, I have
suspected as much from watching TV westerns, but my theory
is confirmed when Willie grins and says, "You know they only
ride for the camera. Other than that, not a one of 'em knows
the head from the hind end."

Then Willie walks away with his clipboard, leaving me to fret
about abandoning our remuda in movie land. I've been worried
about this all along, because the horses are my personal friends
and favorite playmates, except in the summer, when the camp-
ground at Boggy Bend fills with yammering city kids who are
fun to play kickball with, but painfully ignorant about horses.

I cling to my father's assurance that he has a *sweet deal*
worked out to lease our horses for the winter, then bring them
back to Daily in time for summer campers. He cannot believe
the amount a movie studio is willing to pay for this. It's well
worth the long haul from Texas in the rebuilt Ford pickup he
has lovingly pieced together from spare parts.

Aunt Donetta isn't worried about the paycheck or the horses,
but she does have something on her mind. She tells my father
about the dangerous hippies in the street. They're everywhere—
singing, carrying anti-government signs, smoking and being
s-e-x-u-a-l (she spells this word then blushes) in public. Los
Angeles is one big, full-scale hippie convention. "It's hardly a
proper place for an impressionable child," she says and frowns
because, thanks to my father's part-time rodeo affliction, my
brother, Kemp, and I are often in improper places. We love those
places, but Aunt Donetta feels the need to protect us, being as

we have no mother to do it. She demands that my father take us home to Texas *immediately*. No—she does not want to see Hollywood Boulevard or Grauman's Chinese Theatre.

Our trip to California is ruined. Daddy and Aunt Donetta pack my little brother and me into the truck and we head home, and I never go back to California again, even though my dad helps support his rodeo habit for years by supplying Willie Wardlaw with movie horses. In fact, our existence is all about horses. My father is certain that, since Kemp's only interest is sports, I'll be the one to take over the ranch, eventually.

The day I gave up horses for a graduate teaching assistant-ship at Kansas State University and left Daily, Texas, for good became the biggest disappointment of my father's life. At twenty-nine, I needed a clean break from the hometown, and even though my father knew the reasons, my leaving was hard for him to accept. For two years afterward, he pretended he didn't have a clue *what* I was doing, *way up north* in Kansas.

When he finally managed to navigate the university phone system and call my office, I knew something big was up.

"Hey-uh, Puggy, what ya doin'?" My father has forever in-sisted on calling me *Puggy*, despite the implied unattractiveness of it. In my family, you're saddled with a nickname the minute enough relatives make it to the hospital to establish a quorum. After that, you're stuck with it. My name is Lauren, but to my dad, I am forever *Puggy*.

"Eating a breakfast taco and grading anatomy finals," I re-plied. "It's always entertaining. I wonder if some of these kids ever come to class. If they did, they'd know that a fracture of the first phalanx in a racing greyhound would be in the foot, not the mouth. We tried offering an anatomy course in summer minimester this year, but it's looking like it was a mistake."

"I read where kids startin' college are even dumber than

we used to be." Dad seemed surprisingly willing to talk about campus life. This was a first. Normally when I brought it up, he changed the subject. "Them SAT scores are down three percentile points overall. Read it in the *Wall Street Journal*."

The Wall Street Journal? *My dad?* "Well, it's a good thing the *Wall Street Journal* is not here grading these tests, because this kid has the jawbone connected to the leg bone."

Dad hooted as though I'd said something hilarious. "Woohwee, that'd be interesting, now wouldn't it? Don't reckon that dog'd hunt. I took anatomy once. Don't remember much. Think that mighta been the year I broke my shoulder." It was a well-known fact that my father's undergraduate career involved more college rodeo than actual coursework. When he broke his shoulder and couldn't continue to compete, he quit school, went home to Daily to work in my grandfather's auto shop, and never returned to academic life. According to him, it was probably for the best.

"So, how's the teachin' business?"

"It's fine, Dad. It's good. I'm a little behind in getting some things graded. I'll catch up now that the minimester course is over." Ah, heaven—the lazy hours of midsummer, when the campus was quiet and the student population reduced by half.

"Got a lot to do this weekend?"

"A bit, but I'll get it finished. We're off tomorrow, so it's a long weekend for us, and I'm not teaching anything else this summer, which means I don't have to prep until closer to fall." Something began to needle the back of my mind. These were strange questions, coming from my father. Dad didn't like to talk on the phone. When he did call, we conversed about ranch business, or the latest happenings in Daily, or how my brother, Kemp, was doing now that he'd moved home and taken a coaching job at Daily High. "What's up, Dad?"

"Well, nothin', nothin' . . ." His pregnant pause shifted my attention from the anatomy test to the conversation.

"Dad, is something wrong?"

"Well, no. No, a'course not." He diverted the dialogue with a short dissertation about a local girl having made it big in a TV-show talent competition a few months ago. Amber Anderson's second-place finish on *American Megastar* last April was the biggest thing to hit Daily, Texas, in years. Aunt Donetta made sure I tuned in for the big Hometown Reveal segment, when Amber was announced as a finalist. It was strange, seeing Daily on the screen—all the familiar places, all the same people. The town seemed to have remained frozen in time during the two years I'd been away. Watching Amber's hometown show, I basked in the transient warmth of memories. And then, during a scene at the rodeo arena, completely without warning, there was a big roan horse with a Hash-3 brand on its hip. I remembered the day the horse was born. I remembered Danny and me helping it into the world. I remembered when the Hash-3 was the two of us—young, married, living in a crumbling ranch house on the back side of my father's place, with a mile-high stack of impractical dreams.

The history of that life, and its abrupt and painful ending, had flashed through my mind, and I couldn't breathe. My body felt heavy and numb. I turned off the TV, walked to the bedroom, crawled into bed, and cried until I fell asleep. The next day, I called in sick and let another GA teach my classes. I was careful not to turn on week two of the *American Megastar* finals. . . .

Dad's voice brought me back to the present. "So, anyhow. You'll never guess who's here. Ol' Willie Wardlaw. You remember him? You met him when you was just little. Remember? The year you and Aunt Netta rode along to deliver the horses at the movie studio?"

16

Ah, the infamous year of the hippies. "Sure, of course I remember." My one and only Hollywood experience, when I didn't get to meet either Mickey Mouse or the cast of *Little House on the Prairie*—my two fantasies at the time. "Wow, that's something. I didn't know you two kept in touch anymore."

"Well, we hadn't talked in a while. Few years. Boy, between the movie business and race horses, Willie's kept busy. All that time when we was bringin' him our park horses, he was charging the studio *four times* the lease fee he paid us per animal. Old scoundrel. And here I thought we was gettin' rich. You should see the pictures of this place he runs out in California. It's like the Tash-mer-hall for horses—thirty-stall barn, all the pastures mowed like golf course lawns, exercise track with a startin' gate, white fence runnin' as far as the eye can see. Got an indoor workout arena, too. Air-conditioned. I mean, Willie's got hisself a horseman's heaven."

Well, that's it. Dad's moving to California to train racehorses with Willie. He's trying to break it to me gently. "It sounds wonderful, Dad. I'm glad you and Willie are having a good visit. What's he doing in Texas, anyway?" *In Daily, of all places.*

My father went right on talking. "Yeah, old Willie's done good. Stands some big time runnin' horses at stud, right there on the place. Got three hot walkers, and a full-size arena out back. Keeps horses for some movie stars, too. Lord a'mercy, these pictures got girls ridin' in bikini bathing suits. Willie's got him a cute little girlfriend, too. She's upstairs gettin' ready to go to breakfast at the cafe. Wooh-wee, Daily ain't ever seen anything like her, I'll tell you. She dresses like that Pamela Hilton."

"Paris Hilton?"

"Yeah, her."

Dad has fallen for Willie's Malibu Barbie girlfriend. He's

*headed to California to find one of his own. That's why it's him
calling, not Aunt Donetta. She's too mad to talk.* "Well, now
there's a picture." *Paris Hilton on the streets of Daily. Look
out.* "Has Aunt Donetta seen her yet?"

"Oh, you bet. This afternoon, Aunt Netta's gonna take her
down to Boggy Bend to get some sun at the RV park pool."

*Aunt Donetta is hanging out with Willie's bikini-babe girl-
friend. At the Boggy Bend RV park. Wonder if Paris knows
that, by* swimming pool, *they mean a hollowed-out section of
the creek with bluegill, perch, and an occasional diamondback
water snake living in it. The first time a fish nips her toes, she'll
freak.* "That's nice."

"Yeah. Willie and me have some business to tend to. He's got
a heck of a sweet deal goin' on right now. Willie's the wrangler
for that new movie they're makin' from that book that was on
Good Mornin' America a few years back. You remember—*The
Horseman?*" Dad lowered his voice, saying the title as if he, himself, were the show's announcer. "Remember how right after
that book come out, all that horse whisperin' was a big deal?
Every yay-hoo around was gonna be a horse whisperer, like the
fella in the book. Anyhow, now Willie's got the contract to do
all the horse wranglin' for the movie. Big job for one man."

*My father has gone Hollywood. He's hiring on with Willie
Wardlaw to help make* The Horseman. *Willie will rent him
out for four times what Dad's getting paid.* "Sounds like it,"
I agreed.

"It'll be worth the work, though. This thing's gonna go all
the way to the A-cademy A-wards, I'll guar-own-tee. They're
gonna make it sure-enough authentic—change it up a little from
the book, make the horseman a little older, so it'll be believable
that he'd have all them insights about horses and people."

My father has been asked to play the horseman. He's going

to be a movie star at sixty-six. "That makes sense. Sounds exciting, Dad. I bet it'll be a big success."

"Sure is. They got star power, too—that there Justin . . . uhhh . . . Justin . . . well, you know, that there Justin fella that's so famous. The fella Amber Anderson got to be friends with while she was in California singin' on *American Megastar.* Justin . . ."

"Shay?"

"Yeah, sure, that's him. Justin Shay. Willie says he'll be good for the part. He's real popular. Just needs a little coaching in the horse whisperin' end of it."

My father is going to train the Hollywood horse whisperer— Justin Shay, pop-action-thriller star who undoubtedly doesn't know one end of a horse from the other. I'm offended. For years, I tried to bring my father in tune with modern, kinder, gentler methods of training horses. He had no interest. He wanted to do things the old-fashioned way. "A horse ain't broke until you break it," he'd say.

"Well, Dad, there are definitely some things to know about resistance-free training. It isn't all intuitive, even for people who have been around animals all their lives. You have to understand why the animal does what it does—what the body language means and what actions on the part of the trainer cause those reactions. It's all about action and reaction."

"Exactly. That's right. See, you know all them modern terms for that stuff. Back in my day, we just put a horse in the pen and got him broke, but now everyone's gotta whisper. It's a whole new science."

Good gravy, Dad has just admitted that resistance-free training is a science. What is going on? "There is some behavioral theory behind it. . . ."

"Well, sure. This movie'll really be good for the whole horse whisperin' industry."

"Could be." It was strange to be talking about horses after not having been near one in two years. I felt like a reformed smoker discussing the taste of cigarettes.

"They got star power on the horse end, too. The broke-down racehorse is gonna be played by Lucky Strike hisself—you remember, that big bay that was on the way to a triple crown a couple years ago until he snapped his leg? Willie bought into the stallion syndicate on that horse, big time. Got him cheap, but it turns out they can't get hardly anything bred with him. Not enough huevos in the burrito, so to speak."

"Mmm-hmm." Growing up in the ranching business, you think nothing of discussing reproduction and who's capable of it. This is acceptable dinner conversation.

"The Lucky Strike syndicate owners are hopin' that getting him on camera in a western-type setting will help make him popular with quarter horse breeders. Thoroughbred registry, of course, they'll only allow live breedin', but with the quarter horse registry, they can do it in a lab. It could be a whole new market for a horse like Lucky Strike."

Hmmm . . . my father has bought syndication shares in a very expensive reproductively challenged racehorse. He's calling to see if I want to buy in, too. "Seems like the financial potential there would be limited." *Not to rain on your parade, or anything.*

"Lucky Strike's gonna be a bigger star than that Arab horse that played the black stallion, what with that Justin . . . uhhh . . . Justin . . . Shay playin' the horseman, the sky's the limit, I guar-own-tee."

"So, they're going to combine an actor who's not really a horse trainer with a five-year-old racehorse stallion and try to make a movie? That doesn't seem very wise."

"Oh sure. Sure." Dad swished off my comment like a pesky

gnat. "Amazin' thing is, they're gonna film the movie right here in Daily. After that Justin fella was here with Amber last April, he bought the old Barlinger ranch. He says he wants to film the movie there."

"In Daily?" I imagined my little hometown, which was only now recovering from the excitement of Amber Anderson's big second-place *Megastar* finish, caught up in another dose of glitz. Suddenly, I was glad I lived two states away.

"Sure 'nuf."

"At the Barlinger ranch? That place is a wreck. It's been abandoned for years." Back when I was in high school, we held spook houses at the Barlinger ranch. The sprawling limestone homestead had been trapped in probate for as long as anyone could remember.

"Wooh-wee, not anymore." Dad whistled appreciatively. "They got all kinds of crews out there workin'. You oughta see it. Amber and that Justin fella are gonna turn the ranch into some kind of camp for foster kids, eventually. But right now, they're gonna film the movie there. A'course, first they show the bigwig directors and movie-mogul types the project—sell 'em on it, so to speak, then the movie gets made. We gotta take a few days to get the horse calm and bring ol' Justin up to speed on lookin' like a horse whisperer."

In a few days? Good luck. "Sounds interesting. Are you going to help Willie with that?"

Dad paused, and my attention drifted to the window, where a student was loading her suitcases into her car and hugging her boyfriend good-bye in the parking lot. I checked my watch. Time to get back to work if I was going to have the grades in before I went home. I was really looking forward to taking Friday off, rather than coming in to check leftover exams.

"Well, Puggy, you know I'm not any good at that kinda

thing," Dad said. "I'm just an old cowhand. I only know how to break a horse one way." He held an extended pause. I didn't notice at first, because I was watching the girl on the sidewalk cling to her boyfriend like she couldn't bear to let go. I hoped she was smart enough not to elope, leave school, and ride off into the sunset on the back of his rodeo pony.

For a moment, I saw Danny and myself all those years ago, standing on a sidewalk at Texas A&M. *"Come on,"* he said. *"Let's just do it . . . take a year and travel hard, hit all the big rodeos. Grad school's not going anywhere. . . ."*

"I was thinking you could come do it." Dad's voice seemed far away at first.

"What . . . Dad. I got distracted. What did you say?"

"I thought you could come here and help teach this Justin . . . uhhh . . . Justin . . . what's 'iz name to work with the horse."

"Huh?" was the only answer I could come up with.

Dad huffed impatiently. He'd soft-pedaled as long as he could. Now he was ready to put this mule in the chute. "You know, come down here, help out with the project. There's never been anyone could work a horse like you could, Puggy. Everybody knows it wasn't Danny who trained Mo and Blue. It was you. All Danny could do was throw a rope and tie a calf. Only reason he made it as far as he did was because you trained the horses for him. Surely you can help this Justin fella get on with Lucky Strike."

The instant he said *Mo and Blue* and *come down here*, an invisible fist seized my lungs and squeezed tight. I couldn't breathe. The room seemed airless. Training Mo and Blue was the greatest regret of my life, because of what it led to. "Dad I . . . I can't, I . . . have tests to grade." The words were wooden, robotic.

"You just said you had a long weekend startin'. This'll only take a few days."

"I have to log the scores . . . for minimester finals."

"Bring that stuff along. You can do paperwork anyplace, right? You can stay down at Aunt Netta's hotel if you don't want to bunk out at the ranch with Willie, Mimi, and me. Come on. Folks around here think you've gone and moved to Timbuktu."

"Dad, I can't just drop everything and run off to Daily. I'm sorry." A rising tide of nervousness mingled with guilt and made the words sound harsh. I closed my eyes, thinking, *Calm down, calm down. He can't force you to do anything . . .*

Dad's voice was gentle. "It'll be good for ya, Puggy. Been an awful long time since you seen the hometown. You won't hardly recognize it. Road's been repaved and we got souvenir shops with Amber Anderson T-shirts, coffee mugs, bumper stickers, and CDs."

"I can't come, Dad." That much was true. *I can't.* Perspiration beaded on my forehead, and I mopped it away, focused on my reflection in the window. The woman there was pale, frightened, her eyes, green in this light, hiding behind a mop of dark curls that, by this time in the morning, needed a barrette. She looked tired, afraid, worried, older than thirty-one.

Dad sighed. I pictured him stroking his long gray mustache, analyzing the situation.

Pressing a hand over my stomach, I gulped in a breath, let it out, took in another, quelling the fear-induced adrenaline. *You're having a panic attack. Stop it. Right now. Calm down. You're a grown woman. He can't make you do anything.*

"Lauren Lee." When my father took that tone with me, I felt ten years old. "You can't spend the rest of your natural life hidin' from the past. You can't. It's been over two years. Nobody blames you for what happened. We all just want you to come home."

We all just want you to come home. . . . I gripped the side of the desk. "I'm sorry, I just . . ."

"You gotta face this thing, baby girl. It's time."

I deflated into a chair with my head in my hand. A curtain of hair fell across my face, catching the light from the window and turning a soft coffee color. "I know, Dad." What had gone unsaid between us for so long was finally out in the open. "I'll work toward it, I promise. But not right now. Not this way."

"Why not? Why not now? This movie business'll be a good distraction—help keep yer mind off . . . things."

Things . . . what a strange way to put it.

"Come on, puddin'-pie. Pack up your suitcase and get on the road home."

Now he was using childhood endearments to try to talk me into it. I'd become so pathetic my father was cooing to me at thirty-one years old. "No, Dad. No. All right? I'm not interested in helping some neophyte actor—who, by the way, is known for having a lousy attitude—play cowboy with a horse that's also known for having a bad attitude. I heard Lucky Strike almost killed one vet, and he was so prone to kicking the stall, they had to reset his leg a dozen times."

Dad clicked his tongue—a gesture of regret, of finally hitting the brass tacks. "I promised I wouldn't tell anyone, but Willie's got lung cancer. He don't want people to know. He hasn't even told his girlfriend, Mimi, because as soon as he does, she'll hit the road. She's thirty-six and she wants to be an actress. She ain't gonna stay around for some old man with lung cancer, even if he does have a ponytail and a twelve-hundred-dollar cowboy hat. Willie's son from his second marriage died a few years back in a motorcycle accident. He don't have anyone else."

"I'm sorry . . ." A kernel of sympathy sprouted in my chest, and I pictured Willie Wardlaw, the once-strapping movie studio wrangler, who in my memory still stood laughing on a backlot with my father, now washed up, aging, with a few bad marriages, a superficial girlfriend, lung cancer, and a son who'd passed away prematurely. I thought of the times that checks from Willie's studio had bought extra Christmas presents, helped pay the bills at our ranch, or financed a new truck or tractor. I remembered Friday nights, curled up on the couch between Kemp and Dad, watching *The Texan* on TV, pointing out Willie working as an extra in the background—a tall man on a tall horse.

This wasn't a fitting way for a childhood icon to end up.

Another part of me, my self-defense mechanism, said, *For heaven's sake, don't go sappy. You barely know this man. Dad hasn't seen him in years. Now suddenly everyone's supposed to drop everything?* "Dad, I don't see what I can—"

"This movie deal's gotta work with Lucky Strike, Puggy. Willie's got everything tied up in the syndicate on that horse, and he's got some partners turning impatient." Dad's tone was low and somber, laced with a weary disappointment. Disappointment in me. In my weakness. In my selfishness. In my lack of willingness to do for him what he had done for me two years ago. Drop everything, give all. "I need you here, Puggy. I got money tied up in this thing, too."

"What money? What are you talking about?"

His hesitation indicated that I wasn't going to like his answer. "I took out a loan to help Willie. I put the shop building and the ranch up against it."

My mind went blank. "You did what? Dad, why would you do that for someone you haven't seen in years?"

"I owe a debt," he said, as if it were that simple, as if it made sense to have mortgaged everything he owned for an old rodeo buddy. "Willie helped me out when I had to have it, Pug. It was Willie that paid for the surgery on Kemp's arm when he got hurt pitching his junior year. Without that operation, Kemp wouldn't have been able to play college ball. Willie never would take a dime back, until now. It's time to repay."

Not this way, I thought. How dare Willie Wardlaw drag my father into his problems. My father had fixed cars, scrimped, and saved for years to take care of the ranch left to him by my grandparents. His shop building was part and parcel with the building that housed Aunt Donetta's beauty shop and the Daily Hotel. The building owned by Eldridges for over a hundred years. How could my father be so foolish as to gamble it on some ill-conceived film project? He could lose everything. Aunt Donetta could lose everything. Where was Kemp while all this was happening?

"Don't sign anything else." The words seemed to come from somewhere outside my body. "I'll be in Daily tomorrow afternoon."

Chapter 2

Nathaniel Heath

There are days when it just doesn't pay to wake up. There shouldn't be days like that in a million-dollar house in Malibu, where the surf is as blue as liquid sapphires and the would-be actresses come out early to jog and comb the beach, getting workouts and tans on the way to their day jobs in sunless confines of upscale restaurants and stores. They see me on the deck and they slow down, their curious and slightly forlorn glances saying, *Come on, notice me. Offer me my big break.* If they've studied the star maps, they know this is Justin Shay's beach bungalow. They've heard he likes girls in bikinis. He's been known to invite them in and keep them for days—take them around town and show them all the hot spots. Sometimes they make the tabloids. Once in a while, one of them gets discovered. They probably think I'm his manager or a producer. I'm really just the last guy who can stand to hang out with him. And that's only because we've got history together.

It's hard to turn your back on someone you've got twenty years of history with. Every once in a while, I swear off trying to fix Justin and tell myself that the next time he calls, I won't answer. I won't drop everything and come to the beach house,

27

or the LA compound, or the Moroccan desert, or wherever he is. He can crash and burn without me—paint the town, live the good life while I head for the mountains, promising myself that the next thing I create won't be a Shay special. No more straight-from-the-can action flicks. I'll write something meaningful—the next *On Golden Pond* or *To Kill a Mockingbird*.

I sit in a rented cabin in Tahoe, Mammoth Lakes, Truckee, or some other quiet place, staring at the computer screen as it goes into snooze, framing the reflection of the guy with the shaggy brown hair and unshaven writer chin against fathomless darkness, which seems appropriate. The guy in the screen waits, blinking bleary eyes that disappear into the fog, to take on its color, turn from brown to black and surrender. The words won't come. Finally Justin shows up with a hot new car and a screenplay he needs me to work over so that it *fits* him— sometime before next week. I take it on and tell myself, *I'm a guy who writes movies no one will remember next year. I'm a script doctor. There are worse things to be in life. At least the money's good.*

But no matter what you tell yourself when you're hanging out in Shay-ville, it usually feels like the best thing might be to stay in bed and never get up. If you rise and start the day—at noon, or whenever The Shay decides to roll out—you can pretty much figure the hours ahead will be weirdness, piled on insanity, stuck together with an act of pure stupidity or two. Sprinkled through all of it will be lots of hooch, weed, and girls in tight clothes.

Eventually, sometime before the age of thirty-eight, that stuff gets old. You get . . . tired somewhere down deep inside. You start thinking, *There must be more to human existence than this. . . .*

But old habits die hard. One cryptic Shay phone call, and

there I was, standing on the deck of the Malibu house, taking in the ocean view, and waiting for The Shay to roll out of bed. I was probably up about three hours too early. He'd buzzed in last night on a late flight from somewhere, long after I'd driven down from the cabin in Mammoth Lakes and sacked out in one of the guest rooms.

There was a blonde wandering around inside this morning. As usual. In a minute or two, she'd come out and ask why there was no food in the house. Unless she wanted beer, wine, or Weller and water for breakfast, she'd be out of luck. I'd offer to drive her to the Coffee Bean. She probably didn't have a car here. On the way, she'd try to figure out if I was anyone who could do her any good, in terms of getting work in the industry.

We'd hang out until noon or so, making awkward conversation, waiting for Justin to hold court.

He wouldn't like it that she'd just poured a perfectly good bottle of wine down the sink. . . .

I moved closer to the patio door, watched her dump out the contents of the bar and pile the empties on the counter. She noticed me coming in from the deck. She smiled and waved, then pulled out a Hefty bag and snapped it open with the efficiency of a truck-stop waitress.

Where did Justin find this chick? She looked about seventeen— petite and slim, even in baggy sweats. I hoped she was more than seventeen. Justin had enough trouble with *adult* females. The pantry door was still hanging off its hinges, thanks to his last live-in, who had tried to rip it down when she found him in there with a former co-star.

The door came loose in our newest house guest's hand before I could get inside and tell her it was broken. She caught it against her shoulder and stood momentarily trapped.

"Here, let me give you a hand," I said, crossing the room.

"I got it." She shoved it into place with the strength of a welterweight female wrestler. "Ye-ew got a screwdriver and some wood gle-ew? I can fix this thang so it won't fall on any-buddy."

I was temporarily stunned by the thick accent. The words sounded like a foreign language playing on a draggy tape recorder. She quirked a brow over her shoulder.

Eighteen . . . maybe nineteen . . . hopefully. Justin had brought home a very young, strangely perky at early hours of the morning, door-fixing chick who sounded like the Dukes of Hazzard. She was cute, in a down-home way, but kind of . . . well . . . plain, for Justin, wearing an oversized T-shirt with a faded high school logo on the front, her hair pulled up in a ponytail, no makeup, and a smattering of freckles over her nose. She looked vaguely familiar.

"Could'ja gimme a hand a mean-ut?" The last word was a mystery. She frowned at me like I was daft. "Ye-ew all ri-ight?"

"Sorry." I realized who she reminded me of. She looked a lot like Justin's ex-wife, Stephanie—the one he married before all the money, dumped for some British model after his career took off, married again and had two kids with, then lost a second time. I'd always liked Stephanie. She was a genuinely nice person, kind of wholesome and midwestern. She wanted Justin to lay off the partying and stay home.

The Stephanie look-alike inspected the broken hinges. "Ye-ew got a Phillips hay-ud? Not too big, all ri-ight?" Even the real Stephanie didn't know how to repair broken hinges.

I took the door from her hands and propped it against the wall next to the opening. "Let's just leave it for now. I'll get somebody out here to fix it." Mental note. Track down Justin's personal assistant of the week, Marla-of-the-tight-skirts, and provide notification that the beach house needed some repairs. Justin would never remember to have it done. *Leave it be, Nate,*

I thought. *Dude, just get in the car and go home. When Justin calls to see why you weren't here this morning, tell him you're going to sit this one out. You're too old for this stuff.* The muscles in my shoulders tightened and my head cramped like I had a hangover.

The Stephanie girl turned to me and stuck out her hand. "Ye-ew must be Nate," she said. "It's so good to meet ye-ew. Justin's just told me so much good stuff. He says you te-ew are just li-ike brothers."

"Just like," I said, but it came out sounding sardonic. She didn't seem to notice. She just smiled at me in a warm, genuine way that made me feel bad for being cynical and grouchy. Go figure.

Why did that smile look so familiar? It was more than just the resemblance to Stephanie. I'd seen this girl somewhere before. . . .

I studied her as she peered into the pantry. "I was gonna make some bee-us-cuits, but there's no flour in here or anythin'."

Ahhhh, the part in which the morning girl tries to make Justin a home-cooked breakfast, on the theory that his heart and his stomach are somehow connected.

"He doesn't stay here much. Actually, he doesn't stay any-where much." *Or with anyone. Do yourself a favor, sweet thing, and move on. The man isn't relationship material.*

"I been figurin' that out." With an exasperated eye roll, she shook her head. "Between all he's got goin' on, and then I been tourin' since the show got over, I haven't hardly seen Justin these last couple months. If it wasn't for the project down in Daily . . . well, I don't know if we'd ever git the chance to talk at all."

Tour . . . show . . . project . . . Daily . . . My brain revved from dot to dot. Who was this girl? Justin hadn't mentioned her on the phone last night.

"Where is Justin this morning, anyway?" As if I didn't know. Sacked out. Probably hung over.

She shrugged toward the master suite hallway. "Oh, I don't know. I was down in one of the guest rooms."

Guest rooms . . . excuse me? Justin brought home a female friend and put her in one of the guest rooms?

The Stephanie girl turned toward me, her smile fading. "Justin and me aren't a couple. That's just stuff the tabloids say. We're friends, but nothin' more. I'm engaged to some-buddy. He goes to film school in Illinois." She held out a hand with a tiny engagement ring on it.

Tabloids . . . friends . . . not a couple . . . The light went on in my brain, the line raced from dot to dot and everything made sense. Amber Anderson. This was Amber Anderson, the little Texas girl who made it all the way to runner-up on the spring season of *American Megastar*. She looked different without the stage makeup. Even younger. The tabloids had been having a field day with the romantic hookup between her and Justin for a while now. Apparently, you can't believe everything you read in the tabs.

Maybe she was the little sister he'd never had. Maybe Justin was back in one of those sappy, slightly depressed phases in which he showed up at my door, cried on my shoulder, and sounded like a beer commercial. *You're my family, man. You're the only one who gets it. You're like a brother to me, dude. You're all I got. . . .*

Two months before we were going to get married, Nicole said if Justin crashed a date one more time, and I let him, she was out of there. He did. I did, and she was. The split wasn't really Justin's fault. He was just the catalyst for something set to blow anyway.

". . . and Justin tells me you're gonna do the scree-upt,"

the girl, Amber, was saying. I'd missed a sentence or two—
something about having stopped by a grocery store last night.
She was pulling bacon and eggs out of the refrigerator.

"Script?" I repeated, only half listening. A homeless man
was walking by on the beach, his trench coat flapping in the salt
breeze. The trench coat was coal black, new and slightly shiny.
He probably had cameras and an assortment of long-range
lenses hidden in his duffle bag. "Don't go near the window," I
said, motioning toward the wall of glass that fronted the deck.
"You'll be in *Celebs Inside* next week."

Amber scowled toward the door. "I hate those people."

I'll bet you do, I thought. Amber was almost as popular
with the tabs as Justin—quite a feat, considering that he'd had
twenty years to achieve show-biz notoriety, and she'd only had
a few months.

Outside, the homeless man pretended to watch the surf.

Amber cracked some eggs into a bowl. "Scrambled or fried?"

"Not much of a breakfast eater."

She smacked her lips playfully. "I can see yer not a farmer."

"Really?" I said, holding up a flip-flop clad foot, and she
chuckled.

"You know anythin' about horses?"

It was an oddly off-the-wall question. I shook my head. "Not
a thing."

"Huh . . ." she muttered, a wrinkle forming between her
eyebrows as she mixed the eggs. "I can't wait to git on back
to Texas and have some garden vegetables and farm-fresh hen
eggs. I bet these chickens never saw a worm or a grasshopper
or a rotten tomato in their whole lives."

I squinted into the bowl. I'd never really thought about where
eggs come from, or what chickens eat to produce them.

"Ye-ew just wait'll we get to Texas," Amber went on, pulling a couple frying pans off the overhead rack. "You'll see what a rea-ul farm breakfast looks like."

"What's in Texas?" I was almost afraid to ask. This sounded like another Shay special. The last time I got hooked up in one of those, I landed in a hut in Morocco with a hopelessly lousy script, no air-conditioning, an impossible deadline, a director breathing down my neck, and sand fleas in my bed.

Amber seemed surprised I'd missed the memo. "Way-ull, the ranch, of course. Justin wants to do the movie there, and then, when we're done, we're gonna turn it into a place for kids."

Kids . . . Please tell me Justin isn't planning to start yet another family. He's paying enough child support already. . . .

I considered telling Amber exactly that, but I've always been a firm believer in live-and-let-live. Before you try to be someone else's moral compass, you'd better make sure your own points north.

Amber went on chattering, "I've wanted to do that for a long time, but I didn't figure I'd ever be someone who could. You just never know, though. God can do anythang with any-buddy. I always did believe that." She nodded earnestly. "Who'd ever think a girl from little ol' Daily, Texas, would wind up travelin' all over the place, singin' and stayin' in big motels and stuff? And now, gettin' to sing some of the songs for Justin's new movie. Well, that's just past amazin', huh?"

"Way past." I put a hand over my eyes and squeezed my skull, hoping the pressure would block out all other conscious thought. This was overload so early in the morning. Any minute now, The Shay would pop around the corner and say, *Ha! Gotcha, dude. Had you going there for a minute, didn't I? I swear, Nate, you're so easy . . . .*

"Hey, Nater, you pack your cowboy boots?" It was The Shay's voice, but not the words I'd imagined. "Amber fill you in on all the details yet?" Justin was sauntering up the hallway, looking surprisingly sober in sweats and a T-shirt. He had a towel wrapped around his neck, as if he'd been down in the fitness room. Hardly likely at eight-thirty.

"Yeah, not quite," I hedged. *Good to see you, too. How long's it been . . . six months? Come to think of it, your company still owes me a couple checks from that Moroccan project—the one that tanked when you plowed your car through the basket factory and got us thrown out of the country, remember that?* "What's up?"

Justin peered into Amber's grocery sack and came out with a banana, then proceeded to peel it and take the first bite of food I'd ever seen him consume before noon. Non-processed food, at that. Something that actually grew on a plant somewhere.

"Dude, you don't look so good," he pointed out.

"Jet lag." As usual, Justin didn't get the joke. I'd driven down from the mountains, of course.

He tossed the banana peel back into the grocery sack. "So, you got your stuff ready, Nater?"

"Ready for what?" *Although, really, I'm afraid to ask.*

"For Texas, dude. You bring your stuff?" Justin shook the sweat out of his dark hair in one of his typical pretty-boy maneuvers, sending a fine spray across the kitchen. Amber, the girl who'd been worried about the grasshopper content of the eggs, frowned into the bowl like she was wondering what might have landed there.

"That looks good, babe." The Shay's dark eyes glittered with more enthusiasm than he'd shown for anything in a long time.

Hold the phone, Justin's in love. I know that look. The only thing that made Justin light up that way was a new woman.

He turned back to me, his face still basking in the soft glow of amour. It was a little creepy. "Man, Nater, wait till you see this place. Two thousand acres of hills and trees, creeks and grass. It's so quiet, you can hear the train go by in town, seven miles away. We would have killed for a place like this when we were kids."

I scratched my head, trying to root out this strange new unreality like a flea. When we were kids, we were sneaking out of Mama Louise's foster house, hanging out on street corners, playing quarters with the girls, and lifting candy bars from convenience stores.

"You wouldn't believe how cheap you can buy land down there. Under four mil for the whole thing. Of course, there's a bunch to do on the buildings, but that's the beauty of it, see? We do the film there, and we bill some of it off as production cost. Then we roll the whole place over into the Anderson-Shay Foundation, hire someone to run it all, and let the kids come in. And, we put a percentage of the proceeds from the film into the foundation—good PR, see?"

"Justin can use some good PR after gettin' arrested last spring and all," Amber put in, her enthusiasm jingling like a wind chime. "And the ranch is gonna do such great stuff. Kids who don't have anywhere to be can come there and stay together with their brothers and sisters, and kids who are split up in foster care can come for a couple weeks in the summer. Isn't that just awesome?"

Both Amber and Justin looked expectantly at me, their eyes shining with the dreamy glitter of unbridled optimism. I felt like the only black cloud in the room. The token pessimist. "So, you bought two thousand acres in Texas, and you're going to turn it into some kind of charity home for kids . . . after Justin does a film there?" *And Amber's going to sing the songs for the sound track. Don't forget that part.*

I swilled a mouthful of coffee, trying to think. What kind of

Justin Shay flick could possibly be filmed on a ranch in Texas? Justin's films were all about chase scenes, high-tech planes, trains, and automobiles, falls from tall buildings, and bad guys with state-of-the-art weaponry.

The Shay struck a pose with his arms over his chest. Sometimes I wondered if, in his mind, the cameras were rolling twenty-four hours a day. "Not just any film. We're doing *The Horseman*."

The coffee reversed in my throat and went up my nose, and I spewed into the sink, choking on a combination of liquid, air, and a laugh. "Oh, come on." Any minute now, he'd tell me I was on *Candid Camera*. The screenplay for *The Horseman* was a notorious dog that had been wagging its tail around Hollywood for several years now. Bestselling book, poorly rendered for film by the author, who knew nothing about screenplays but owned the rights and insisted on creative control. The media glow surrounding the book had come and gone, and the time for bringing it to the screen was long past. Aside from that, westerns, particularly contemporary ones, weren't selling. Audiences wanted flash, action, exotic locations, and political intrigue. *The Horseman* had none of those things. A man-meets-animal piece, heavy on the emotion, was the last thing Justin needed. "It's a dog, Justin. Everybody knows that project's a dog."

Justin bounced an answer nonchalantly in my direction. "It won't be when you get through with it."

"Not interested. Not my kind of job." The words were out of my mouth before I realized what I'd done. I'd said no to The Shay. Actually, it wasn't that hard. *No. I don't want to be involved in your latest tip-of-the-brain idea. I have a life of my own (sort of) and I'm going back to it.* Everyone has to grow up sooner or later.

Justin stopped foraging in the grocery bag. "Come on, Nate.

Don't chap my a—" Glancing at Amber, he revised. "Stop holding out on me."

Amber's big blue eyes widened, pleading with me. Her lips fell into an unconscious pout, like she might cry.

Not even for you, sweetheart. I'm not going to Texas to pen cowboy stories. A man can't write what he doesn't know. I know cars, planes, trains, and bad guys named Guido with big guns. Sensitive man-bonds-with-animal-and-meets-girl stuff is not for me. It's not for Justin, either. This thing'll flop harder than a fifty-pound mackerel. What producer in his right mind would look at Justin for a part like that?

"Who's behind this thing, anyway?" *Did I say that? Was that me keeping the dialogue going?* "I heard that the last guy who attempted to put it into production went bankrupt trying to find backing for it." *Stop. Halt. Alto. Cease. Don't ask any more questions. Leave gracefully. Get in the car and drive north while there is still time.*

"I am." Justin had the chutzpah to appear proud of the fact. "I've got the rights, and I've got the creative control. You can do whatever you need to with the script, Nate."

A string of expletives pulsed through the space between my ears. I threw up my hands, crossing the room. "You've got to be kidding. What? Have you lost your mind?"

Justin met me as I opened the back door. Pressing his hand against the frame, he pushed it closed again. "Come on, Nate. Hang with me here. Just come and see the place. Take a look at the script. The plane's ready. We'll fly down to Texas, take a long weekend, and check it out. If you don't like it, you can bail. No hard feelings."

"Yeah, right." I muttered something for which Mama Louise would have made me scrub the kitchen with a toothbrush, and then, "How much are you into this thing for?"

"Enough." Justin's gaze lifted and met mine, and I knew what was next. "Come on, Nate. You're my family, man. You're as close to a brother as I've got. I bought this project for us." For a rare moment, I sensed the guy behind the mask, the one who hid from the cameras, who hid from everyone. Sometimes I thought there was more to The Shay than people saw. Sometimes I was convinced he was as one-dimensional as the roles he took on. "I'm sorry about the thing with the car last winter."

"You almost got us both killed, Justin."

"It was a bad day. I didn't mean it. Come on. We need this project. We need something that . . . matters."

"Right," I muttered.

Amber crossed the room, her flip-flops slap-slapping until she put a hand over my fingers, and then Justin's, linking us like the wire on an electrical circuit.

"It'll be good, you'll see," she pleaded.

Her voice was an annoying buzz outside the rush of my own thoughts. "I didn't bring any clothes." I'd thrown shorts and a T-shirt in the car, toothbrush, razor, boxers, and that was it. One change of clothes, on purpose. A measure against exactly what was happening now.

"There's clothes here. Heck, there's more stuff in that closet than Macy's. Take any of it." Justin knew he had me hooked. Any minute now, he'd strike a pose, then swagger back to the kitchen.

"This is gonna be so much fun," Amber bubbled, throwing open the door to see the school of dolphins that were cavorting close to the shore. On the beach below, the homeless man produced a long lens and pointed it our way. "You just hadn't been anyplace until you been to Daily, Texas."

Amber tripped on the stoop and landed against my chest.

Justin reached toward me as I caught her, and for a moment we hovered in an unsteady tangle.

That'd look great in the tabs tomorrow.

Unfortunately, Justin and Amber weren't concerned about the tabs or anything else. They were more interested in breakfast, which Justin consumed with great abandon, while Amber blushed at his cooking compliments.

Justin and I were still lounging at the table when Marla, Justin's lovely assistant, showed up at the gate to take him to do some promotional spots for a film that had been stuck in editing for a couple of years. *Broken Streets* was a futuristic flick about undercover cops trying to track down the ultimate terrorist. Not a bad project, really—lots of action, scant dialogue, big special effects budget. Perfect for Justin. Justin's manager, Randall Patterson, was confident the film would reenergize The Shay's career.

Marla breezed in the door with the usual bag of tricks—pharmaceuticals, aspirin, eye drops, and a properly-chilled Red Bull.

She was surprised to find Justin in relatively good shape and fully dressed. For once, she wasn't going to have to roll him out of bed, feed him Diazepam and Rolaids, and load him into a limo like dead weight. Marla was pleased, until she saw Amber outside tossing crumbs to seagulls.

"Hey, babe." Justin was completely oblivious to Marla's sweeping death ray, as always. "Is it that time already?"

Marla nodded, still trying to vaporize Amber. "It's time." She cast a wide, flirty smile that wasn't lost on Justin. "You look good this morning."

The Shay took that as more of a given than a compliment. Leaning back, he rubbed his stomach. "Most important meal of the day."

Marla took in the leftovers in a way that said, *Eeewww. Trans fats.* "You didn't tell me you were coming out to the Malibu house. I was looking for you in town. Randall's not happy."

"Tell him to chill." Tossing his napkin on the table, Justin stood up. "I'll be there when I get there."

Marla watched him disappear down the hall, then swiveled toward me. "What's he up to?"

"Not quite sure yet." It was always hard to decide whether to keep Justin's secrets or report him to the adults. On the one hand, he had a right to his own life. On the other hand, he usually did stupid things with it. On the third hand, I'd never seen him out of bed, dressed, sober, and happily eating real food so early in the morning.

"What's *she* doing here?" Marla's laser beamed the deck again.

"Still trying to figure that out."

"What's that?" She pointed to the script Amber had plunked on the table along with breakfast—the one that had spoiled my appetite. *I read some of it this mornin'*, she'd said. *It's real good . . . mostly.*

"Something I'm looking at."

Marla twisted to read the title, then gave a rueful snort. "You've *got* to be kidding. Even *you* aren't *that* stupid, Nathaniel. *The Horseman?* You didn't bring that thing to Justin, did you?"

"Nope." Typically, with Marla and me, the less said, the better. Too bad she didn't keep up her end of the deal.

"Did he bring it to you?"

"Nope." *Technically, Amber did.*

"You're not trying to get him to attach his name to that thing, are you?"

"Nope."

Her eyes flashed, then turned icy. "Well, don't. Randall's got a new Davis VanHarbison project for him, and if Justin can keep his act together a few more days, we'll ink the deal. He doesn't need you distracting him, and he doesn't need that." She pointed at the script, and then at Amber, who'd just noticed we had company. "The last time he got mixed up with that little bimbina, I had to bail him out of jail in some disgusting town in the middle of nowhere, Texas. VanHarbison's people are concerned about Justin's insurability for a new film. If he screws up before we ink this deal, he's dead. Get her out of here."

I rubbed my head. Amber's nonstop chipper chatter might have been a bit much first thing in the morning, but talking to Marla was like being trapped in an elevator with a dentist's drill. "Fortunately, I'm not in charge of her. You'll have to talk to Justin about that one." *The man is capable of making his own decisions. Sometimes.*

"I'll talk to her people." Marla lowered her voice because Amber was trying to open the door. "Her handlers don't want her within *fifty feet* of Justin. I bet they don't even know she's here."

"Good luck." I meant it, and then I didn't. The kid in me was rooting for Justin and the intrepid Amber, and their Hansel-and-Gretel plan to run away to the gingerbread ranch. The adult in me knew that the Davis VanHarbison project was the best thing that could happen to Justin. A tiny little bit of me thought about Justin with his eyes clear and his step steady so early in the morning.

Amber finally wrestled the door open just as Marla was turning to leave. "Hey, Marla. Guess what," she said, and for a minute I was afraid Amber was going to spill the beans. "They finally fixed that culvert by the Daily jailhouse where you got your car stuck. They cee-mented it in and put up a red post with a big ol' reflector on it, so no one else'll back off into the ditch like you did. Isn't that ni-ice?"

Marla's face puckered inward around her surgically-perfected nose. She looked like a rat sniffing for something tasty to nibble on. "Your people are probably looking for you, Amber. Did you sneak off the tour bus again?"

"Oh, no, ma'am. We finished the *American Megastar* tour yester-dey. We don't head into the studio for a whole 'nother week and a half. I'm just free as a bird."

Marla's lips expanded under pressure like an air raft wedged against a tree. "Well, Justin's not. We have meetings. Today, tomorrow, and all weekend." Marla shot a pointed look my way, hoping, no doubt, to turn me into a pillar of salt.

I lifted my hands. "Hey, he called me."

"He always calls you, Nate." Marla glanced toward the hall. "Every time he needs someone his own age to play with."

Amber sucked in a quick breath and braced her hands on her hips as if she were about to jump in on my side. Marla would chew her up and spit her out in wholesome little pieces.

"Let's roll," Justin called, coming up the hall. Marla moved toward the door, simultaneously providing the customary ego stroking, admiring Justin's wardrobe choice of a black T-shirt, jeans, and a blazer. "You look great." Her appraisal stopped where a pair of silver-toed cowboy boots occupied the spot that normally would have been devoted to some kind of custom-fitted Italian leather footwear. "What are those?"

"Cowboy boots." Dropping his sunglasses into place, he struck a pose. "I'm trying to get used to them."

By the table, Amber giggled behind her hand.

Marla vacillated in place. She, like all previous assistants, had learned not to speak negatively of something if The Shay liked it. "They work," she said finally, before smiling over her shoulder. "You two have a nice day. Make sure the security system is on when you *leave*."

"See y'all after a while," Amber called, and Marla stiffened.

Justin jogged back to the table and grabbed a piece of bacon, leaning close to Amber. "Have everything ready at five."

"I will. Don't worry."

"Later, Nater," he added before heading out, salt pork in hand.

"Later," I said, but I hadn't really decided if I was going to be there later.

Behind his back, he made the motion of an airplane taking off, then held up five fingers. Thirty seconds later, he and Marla were out the door, leaving Daisy Mae and me to pack the wagon, hitch up the team, and point 'em toward Texas.

Yee-haw!

Chapter 3

Lauren Eldridge

I couldn't stop myself from looking at the phone, replaying the conversation with my father and thinking I'd made a promise I couldn't keep. *I should call him back and tell him I'm not coming.* The idea came wrapped in a slick coating of guilt, so that I couldn't quite get a firm grasp on what I would say—how I would tell my father that now, when he needed me, I wasn't coming. Two years ago, when I lay in the hospital, it was my father who sat by my bedside for weeks. He was there for every minute of physical therapy, every doctor's appointment, every hopeless hour, each milestone on the road to recovery, all the dark nights of reliving the flood and the single careless act that changed everything. Through sympathy cards and funeral notices, breaking and healing, my father's love was steadfast.

If anything could pull me back to the place where my life fell apart, it was that love. My father knew it and I knew it, but my mind kept spinning through the list of excuses as the workday wore on. When the last finals were scored, I packed up the remainder of the minimester grades and decided to go home early.

On my way out, I poked my head into the office next door to tell Marshall I was leaving.

"I'm headed out. Lockup's all yours. Enjoy the day off tomorrow."

Marsh crossed the room, towering over the computer and the file cabinets. "Want to go grab a burger at P.B.'s?" he asked. "I've got Bella this weekend." The last sentence was hastily added so I wouldn't think he was trolling for a date again.

"I'd better not. Tell little Miss Bella hi for me, but I need to go home and pack. I'm heading to my dad's place in Texas for the weekend."

Marsh raised a brow. "Seriously? You're actually going to get in a car and drive somewhere . . . outside the city limits?" Marsh turned his head toward the slap-thud-slap-thud of Bella's little red cowboy boots coming up the hall.

Bella spotted me as she turned the corner. "Hey, Miss Lo-lo. Guess what?"

"What?"

"It's big, and white, and hairy."

"That describes a lot of things around here."

"It eats a lot."

I pretended to think for a moment. "Can't imagine."

Bell giggled, falling forward and slapping her knees. "Dad said I can bring Snuggles to the house and keep him in the yard this weekend." Snuggles was a miniature horse who had somehow found his way into the university horse program. He was completely useless, other than the cute factor.

"Cool," I said as Bella wrapped herself around my waist, vibrating like wiggling Jell-O. Sometimes, when Bella hugged me like that, I felt a painful yearning for what might have been.

"I wanna teach him some tricks," Bella said, smiling up at me. "Can you come over and help me?"

"I'm not a horse trainer anymore."

Bella leaned against the circle of my arms. "Dad says you used to be. He said I should ask you to help me with Snuggles."

Marsh blushed, and I felt a little pinprick, because I knew I'd never be what Marsh and Bella needed. I'd never be what anyone needed. There was no point encouraging either of them to hope. "I have to go on a trip for a few days."

"When're you gonna be back?"

"Next week." Next week seemed light-years away. I tried not to overanalyze my reasons for being relieved that I wouldn't be here to spend more time with Bella and the pony.

"Okay," Bella said, looking adorable and angelic as she let go of me and proceeded into her father's office. "I'm gonna miss you, but I'll have Snuggles." She spoke the words with complete simplicity, as if they made perfect sense. A girl must have her priorities in order, after all. Horses first, then people. I could recall being just like Bella. That girl, the one I remembered, seemed like someone I'd seen in a movie once, someone two-dimensional, whose head I couldn't quite get into, whose motivations I could no longer understand.

As I said good-bye and left the building, I tried to visualize that girl, that Lauren, going back—returning to the scene, as it were. Eight or nine hours of highway—through Wichita, through Oklahoma City, then Dallas. After the turnoff at Waco, she would leave the expressway, travel the two-lane into the hills, slipping soundlessly over clear-running creeks, beneath the thick shade of overhanging live oaks, and past fence rows laced with the scraggy cedar bushes my father hated. Things would start to look familiar, smell familiar, feel familiar. She'd remember driving those roads with Dad, with Aunt Donetta, with Danny. She'd feel the pull of all she had left behind in Daily.

She'd arrive in town, and then . . . what?

Every time I imagined the journey, it ended there, at the Caney Creek Bridge, just a few blocks out of town near the Buy-n-Bye. The place that had always been home now hung in shadow, in-distinguishable.

Sitting in my SUV in front of my condo with my fingers wrapped around the keys, I contemplated the idea of walking the streets of Daily, a stranger in the skin of a hometown girl. What would people say? Would they offer belated expressions of sympathy? Would they carefully avoid mentioning the night of the flood, skirt it like quicksand? Would they talk about old times, or ask about my new life? Would they whisper behind their hands that I was lucky to have survived when two others didn't?

Would they wonder about this stranger who looked like Puggy but wasn't?

I turned off the key, went inside, and started to pack. From the condo next door, some kind of head-banging music echoed through the wall. College kids celebrating the summer break.

The phone rang, and the noise drowned it out at first. The answering machine beeped, and something in the cadence of the voice on the message drew me around the corner. I knew who it was even before I turned up the volume. Aunt Donetta stretched words like taffy and began every conversation with southern endearments and the enticement of fattening food. In some way or other, pie was relevant to every conversation.

"Hal-lo-oh . . . Hal-lo-oh?" She paused, waiting for me to pick up, before finally covering the phone with her hand (which was never enough to mute Aunt Donetta). She talked to some-one else in the room—no doubt, she, Imagene Doll, and Lucy were all there in the beauty shop, where I'd passed long hours of my childhood observing haircuts and absorbing gossip.

They discussed my possible whereabouts while the answering machine recorded. Imagene theorized that I'd gone out to purchase some traveling necessity, like toothpaste, extra socks, or underwear.

"I doubt that'd be where she's at. Who goes out for underwear at four in the evenin'?" Aunt Donetta argued.

In the background, Lucy chimed in. She probably said something intelligent, but her voice was so soft, I couldn't make out the words—just the choppy ping-pong of her Japanese-accented Texas twang.

"I imagine she's got underwear." Aunt Netta's fingernails drummed the phone receiver in a rhythmic *click, click, click.*

"I don't know." Sometimes I wondered if Imagene and Aunt Netta argued just for the fun of it. "I was thinkin' I'd have to buy some when we go on that cruise. It's different when you're home all the time. You can just wash it out and hang it in the shower."

"I imagine they have showers on the cruise."

"You wouldn't want to leave your underwear, what with a maid and all . . ."

"A gal just thirty-one years old shouldn't *be* home all the time." The conversation hopscotched, as usual. "She should be out . . . livin' life."

"Well, maybe that's where she's at right now . . . out havin' fun."

Aunt Netta spat a puff of air, then returned to full volume. "Way-ul, I guess you're not there ri-ight now, sweetie. . . ." She waited, as if she knew I was standing with my finger just above the button, almost ready to push it.

Finally, she went on with plans. "Way-ul, anyhow, this is Aunt Netta and the girls. We just wanted to see what time you were gonna get here tomorrow. Now, you don't even worry about a thang, all ri-ight? Your old bed's still in the sewin' room, and

I'm gonna clean it out soon as I get home. And don't bring anythin', y'hear? I got a big ol' ham in the freezer from the FFA sale last Christmas, and I'm gonna slow roast him with some brown sugar and pineapple, and a little beer, but don't tell anybody—I did one for the church potluck and it was sure enough good. Uncle Beans's gonna fry some catfish out in the carport, and maybe we'll fire up the grill, too. I saw some good sausage down to the Buy-n-Bye. Imagene's gonna make us a pie . . . or two. Just come on, all ri-ight?" She waited for an answer, then added, "Okay, hon, you be real careful drivin'. Don't rush. Just be here when you get here, and we'll all have supper. Your daddy and his friend Willie, and Willie's girlfriend, and Lucy, and Imagene are gonna come over, too, and we invited Brother Ervin when he came by the shop while ago. It'll be a regular Daily event."

Aunt Donetta's voice jingled with the excitement of a big feed. In the background, Imagene and Lucy were already planning for more pies. "Night-night, sweetie. Love ye-ew." The voices of Daily faded into a series of beeps as Aunt Netta pushed the wrong button to turn off the receiver. "Ye-ew know, I hope her answerin' machine couldn't hear all tha-ut about the underwear. . . ."

The machine clicked, and the New Message light blinked. I pushed Save, then went to my bedroom, threw the last few things into my suitcase, turned off all the lights, and headed for the door. After so much time away, I wasn't prepared to roll right into a Daily gathering. If I tried to tell Aunt Netta that, it would hurt her feelings, and probably the ham's. By heading out now, I could drive straight through, get there sometime around two a.m., sack out in one of the empty rooms at Aunt Netta's hotel building downtown, and surprise everyone in the morning. . . .

Years of experience had taught me that the only way to defend against the combined social planning of Donetta Bradford and Imagene Doll was to arrive in town before the ham hit the oven.

Leaving Manhattan, Kansas, felt better than I'd thought it would. I was filled with the exhilarating sensation of breaking free, of finally taking action. The problem was that each passing mile brought me closer to Daily and all the things that were so much easier to forget amid the hustle and bustle of campus life. On campus, surrounded by hundreds of twenty-somethings who were progressing through weeks, and semesters, and years of higher education, it was easy to forget that while the students were hitting all the expected milestones, I was standing still.

Maybe I should keep going, I thought. *Skip the turnoff at Waco and head all the way to Mexico. Take a vacation, a hiatus, teach anatomy in Spanish somewhere below the border. Reinvent myself again and see if it turns out better this time.* I entertained a guilty vision of leaving it all behind, just driving and driving until I landed in someplace sunny, with a beach and palm trees, where nothing was the slightest bit familiar.

But then what would Aunt Donetta do with all that ham? The thought made me laugh. I pictured Aunt Netta bustling around the kitchen, the table so loaded it sagged in the middle like a swaybacked horse. She'd tell everyone not to bring anything. Everyone would bring food anyway. They'd clean out every Wal-Mart bakery, bulk barbecue joint, and roadside vegetable stand along the way. When the gathering was finished, Aunt Donetta would beg people to take food home, because she and Uncle Ronald didn't need it.

From his chair in the living room, Uncle Ronald would give her dirty looks and watch with great concern as future midnight snacks were evacuated in Ziplocs and cottage cheese containers.

My body warmed with the ethereal glow of childhood memory.

I hadn't let myself relive those gatherings at Aunt Donetta's in so long. It felt good to go back, even in my mind.

On the heels of that thought, I felt the loss of it all, the undercurrent that would be like an elephant in the room now. No one would talk about the night of the flood, the accident, the funerals, but we would all know. They'd give me sympathetic looks behind my back, fish for information about whether I was seeing anybody, pull out a few well-meaning anecdotes about grief and recovery, and life moving on.

I wanted to head for Mexico.

I wanted to go back to Daily.

I wanted Daily to go back to what it used to be.

As the sun slowly descended and the sky softened to evening hues near the Oklahoma border, I drifted far back in time, relived countless trips to Oklahoma City for the stock show and the National Finals Rodeo. In the early years, my mother was with us. I was never quite sure if I remembered all those times or if I only knew them because Aunt Donetta kept the stories alive, but I preferred to think I remembered the feel of being safely snuggled in the back seat while my parents chatted and the miles passed by.

Crossing the Red River as the moon rose high overhead, I heard the echo of my mother saying, *Hello, Texas! Four more hours to home. Let's play a game.*

One of my mother's games, which Aunt Netta later carried on, was Who's in Daily—a let's pretend exercise in which we predicted, as we drew nearer to home, what everyone had been doing while we were away. When we drove into town, we looked around to see how close we'd come to reality. We usually weren't far off.

I waited until I was looping Dallas before I began my own game of Who's in Daily.

When I left home, Amber Anderson was a skinny high-school girl trying to work up the courage to sing "Lion of Judah" with the Vacation Bible School kids. Now she'd hit the big time. Daily had become the home of a superstar, a developing tourist trap with a new claim to fame. My father was going into the movie business.

No telling Who's in Daily now.

Rolling down the window, I let the night air flow over me, soothing the knotted muscles in the back of my neck as the miles passed. The roads became familiar eventually, winding ribbons of asphalt known to the girl who'd grown up in Texas and thought she never wanted to leave. She'd planned to have a ranch, raise horses and kids, become a veterinarian, and take over for Dr. Potts, whose clinic was fifteen miles outside of town, next to the livestock auction barn at Hilltop.

The dream caught a breath as Hilltop came into view. Slowing the car, I gazed up at the tall false front of the auction barn. The place seemed to have waited patiently while I was away, the peeling-paint letters still advertising sheep, goats, cattle, horses on Tuesdays, swine occasionally. How much of my childhood had I spent out behind the sprawling silver barns, running up and down Caney Creek with my friends while my father did business inside?

I sank into the feeling of home. Even after two years away, I could have driven the road from Hilltop to Daily with the headlights turned off and my eyes closed. Each rise and fall, each hill, valley, and curve were familiar. Even the knotted juniper tree affectionately dubbed The Old Man in the Road was waiting, just as always. He waved a greeting in the headlights, then passed out of sight, his big-nosed silhouette a knobby profile in the rearview mirror.

Ahead, the ambient glow of town pressed back the night,

a tiny bubble of light against the darkened hills, a little bright spot you had to be looking for in order to find it. Overhead, the stars twinkled at full volume, unchallenged by the Daily illumination.

I let the SUV slow, enjoyed the swell of memories as I wound through the valley, then up the hill, around the curve by the bluffs above Caney Creek. There were so many good memories hidden beneath the painful ones. I'd tucked them all away in a box like old tubes of paint, and forgotten there were more than dark colors.

The live oaks parted, opening like a curtain around my hometown. Emotion welled in my throat, and even though my body was stiff and my eyes were burning after driving so many hours, I was glad I hadn't stopped to rest somewhere else. In the morning, I would just be here. Surprise! Puggy's back in town.

I pictured Aunt Donetta coming into the shop (after having tucked Mr. Ham safely into the oven with the timer on), and finding me there. Maybe I'd get up early, go downstairs and sit under one of the old sixties-style dryer hoods. See how long it took her to notice. When Kemp and I were kids, we loved to hide in closets, under the counter, in the dumbwaiter by the hotel stairway, then wait for Aunt Donetta, Imagene, or Lucy to come by. We'd pop out, and they'd jump and squeal. Every once in a while, we miscalculated and scared a customer. Once, we scared Betty Prine so bad she ran out into the street and almost became part of the postal jeep.

Aunt Donetta made us apologize, but Mrs. Prine didn't offer forgiveness. She said Kemp and I would probably end up in jail someday, and she wouldn't be a bit surprised, considering how we'd been raised—dragged off to rodeos and auctions constantly and all.

Aunt Netta felt so bad about what Mrs. Prine said, she took

us down to the Buy-n-Bye for an ice cream bar. Back then, the little cement-block store was the place where we bought sodas after biking around town on hot summer days. With our confectionary treasures in hand, we sat on the curb, shared Cokes, and tried to figure out how many licks it really took to get to the center of a Tootsie Pop.

Now it was the last place where everything was normal. The last place Danny and I had stopped the night the floodwaters changed everything . . .

Now I couldn't even look at it. I turned my head until I'd crossed over Caney Creek Bridge and the little store was safely dozing in the rearview mirror.

Main Street was quiet in its early-morning slumber. Rather than turning past the bank building to go to the back alley entry of the hotel, I drove through the business district, leaning near the front window, taking in the changes. The stores were still mostly empty on the side of the street by the washateria, but the pharmacy on the corner had reopened as the home of the official Amber Anderson Fan Club and gift shop. The windows were plastered with posters and T-shirts sporting everything from *Daily, Texas, Home of Amber Anderson* to the old tried-and-true *The Dailyians Have Landed*, with a glittering flying saucer below.

The McAmey dry goods shop, where my father had taken me for my first pair of cowboy boots, sat dark and silent, aging merchandise still visible in the streetlamp's glow, but a sign announced that it would reopen soon, and down the block, the old Texan Talkies theater, which once showed twenty-five cent movies on Saturday, had a message on the leaning marquee. *Way to go Amber. Welcome American Magastar fan!* Bodie Rogers never could spell.

Across the street, the Daily Café's neon sign blinked on one corner, and next to it, the Daily Hotel Building advertised *Daily*

Hair and Body, beauty salon, auto paint and repair, insurance welcome.

The alley behind the hotel building was just as it had always been. Traveling between the buildings of Main and B streets was like stepping back in time—pallet stacks behind the newspaper office, trash cans, rusting bread racks by what used to be the Watson's Grocery loading dock, bits and pieces of car bodies my father hoped to someday use, the remains of an old bicycle that had probably belonged to Kemp or me. Even the sign above the back door to the hotel was just as it had always been—a struggling neon *Hotel Welcome*. Two pallet stacks away, the rear entrance to my father's auto shop had an actual working light bulb, for a change. I parked beneath the light and found the key just where it was usually hidden, in the discarded bumper of a '59 Ford pickup. Half the population of Daily probably knew it was there.

As usual, the lock was stubborn. Dad never fixed it because he liked it that way. He said it kept out people who had no business coming around—mostly curious teenagers wanting to sneak into the hotel and investigate Daily's oldest ghost story.

Unfortunately, tonight the lock I could have opened blindfolded as a teenager was keeping me out, as well. After fifteen minutes of unsuccessfully trying to sweet talk it, and then resorting to threats and intimidation, I was marooned in the alley with my eyes burning, my body turning leaden, and the trip catching up with me.

"Please," I whispered, pushing the key into the lock again. The tumblers refused to turn. So much for Aunt Donetta's old theory that sweet talk could accomplish more than brute force. Right now, neither one was working.

Bleary-eyed, I watched the moon slowly descend behind the hulking gargoyles on the old bank building and tried to decide what to do next.

Chapter 4

Nathaniel Heath

As afternoon ticked toward evening, I'd mysteriously remained at Justin's beach house, sitting on the deck with the script occupying space beside me. I'd picked it up and looked at it, put it down, picked it up again—like weightlifting of a sort. Everything from the stilted dialogue to the lack of a perceptible three-act formula was worse than I'd imagined. The main character appeared to be more interested in waxing nostalgic about the cowboy life and hanging out with his ranch dog than he was in helping the female lead, her autistic son, and their broken-down racehorse—all that was left to her after her husband committed suicide amid a financial crash and left her penniless.

No wonder this thing had been stuck in development forever.

Run while you still can, the pages whispered as a breeze danced by. *Save yourself. This dog is already dead.*

Inside, Amber cleaned house and baked homemade cookies for our trip. In between batches, she stepped onto the deck to repeatedly remind me that as soon as Justin got there, we had to be ready to go.

I'd been with Justin long enough to know that was code

for *He hasn't told Randall and Marla he's taking off*. Another typical Shay maneuver—duck the entourage, trash all commitments, and do what feels good. If I involved myself in this, and Randall found out, the payback would be swift and decisive. If I ever wrote anything good, Randall and his cronies would make sure nobody touched it. I'd be finished. Completely.

I'd have to be an idiot to get involved.

"Tell me he's not taking off without the bodyguards again," I said to Amber, finally. The last time Justin had gone on the lam without security, he'd ended up with a cracked rib, and I'd lost a chunk of hair so big I'd heard it pop out of my skull. Whoever had grabbed it was probably disappointed when it was light brown, not dark, like Justin's.

"He won't need any bodyguards where we're goin'." Amber's twangy assurances weren't much comfort. "Daily's not li-ike other places. Folks there are real friendly."

Marla made it sound like a blast, I thought, then it occurred to me that Marla would be completely irked about the little Texas junket, which did make the trip more tempting, but not tempting enough. When Justin showed up, I'd tell him it was time for at least one of us to grow up; he was on his own with this one. I'd finally take the advice Mama Louise had given me when I flunked senior English after skipping school one too many times to get blasted with Justin. *"You're a good boy, Nate,"* she said. *"You've got a God-given talent, but if you follow where the world leads, you'll get what the world gives. That's the saddest kind of life there is."* Mama Louise knew all about sad lives. She'd taken in forty-two of them over the years. She told me I needed to let Justin find his own way.

Five o'clock came and went. Amber paced the floor, checking her watch and the driveway, her little pink bags packed and waiting on the entry tile.

I was standing in the kitchen, letting my mind wander out to sea, when the front gate buzzed. Justin squealed through into the portico in an SUV with tinted windows, high-chrome rims, low-rider tires, and an eagle decal on the hood. As the truck vibrated to a stop, Justin's personal trainer, Frederico, tumbled out the passenger-side door looking dizzy and slightly green.

"We're taking Fred's car to the airport," Justin announced, striding into the house. Frederico gaped, as if this was a complete surprise to him. It undoubtedly was. Justin's limo was probably parked in front of the gym, waiting along with several security guards and the obligatory group of Shay-obsessed fans and paparazzi. About now, they would be deducing that Justin had slipped out the back.

At most, we had a fifteen-minute window of opportunity before Marla tracked us down, bringing the limo, the body-guards, and the paparazzi to the gate.

"Let's go," Justin urged, and Amber trotted over to get her bags. To my complete amazement, Justin picked them up. He never even carried his own bags. "Got your stuff packed, Nate?"

"I never unpacked." *Too busy wrestling with my conscience all day, sorry.*

"You get some stuff out of the closet?"

I vacillated by the newly filled cookie travel container, trapped in my own personal dilemma. "Listen, dude, I think I'm gonna sit this one out. Got something in the works in Mammoth Lakes and all, you know?"

Justin stopped with one hand on the door. "Roll with me here, Nater. This project's got SAG nomination written all over it."

It was hard to know how to answer that, but I of all people was aware that Justin had about as much chance of getting a Screen Actors Guild nomination as I did of playing tailback for the Rams. Some dreams you just have to grow up and let go—realize life is what it is. Reality bites sometimes, but after a while there's no point denying it.

Justin stiffened, his chin going up as if he were about to flea-flick me off his shoulder and move on. The door vibrated in his hand, ready for a slam that would take the hinges off, but then he melted against it, his forehead resting on the cool wooden surface. "Come on, Nate, don't whiff on me now. I'll make this good for both of us. I promise." For a fraction of a second, he dropped the mask, and his face said it all. Whatever the reasons—career downturn, midlife crisis, new attempt at rehab—he needed me to believe in this project. He needed me to believe in him. "We been down the road a long time."

Survival instinct whispered in my ear, *Last time, the road had a nearly fatal experience on it. Sooner or later, Nate, you'll end up dead right along with him.* But then there was Justin saying, *"We been down the road a long time."* The road started the night of high school graduation, when we packed a '76 Comet and headed out of Joplin, bound for the big town. By the time I called to let Mama Louise know where we'd gone, we were sharing a cheap LA apartment with six other dudes of varyingly dubious reputation. Justin didn't want to call home at all. He figured a foster parent, even a nice one, didn't rate any explanations. A couple years later, he sent Mama Louise a new Cadillac to make up for the Comet. By then, I'd already paid the debt by waiting tables, but she probably enjoyed the Cadillac, too. Justin spent everything he made from his first bit part to buy it, which was stupid, because after that he didn't work for a year.

The dream never went quite like we thought it would. It was a wild animal with a will of its own—hard to tame, vicious sometimes, unpredictable and temperamental, yet irresistibly alluring.

"I'll get some stuff," I said, and seven minutes later, we were out the door, comfortably secured among the plush velour seats and red shag carpet of Frederico's SUV, ready for the trip to Daily, Texas, where the friendly folks lived and the culvert by the jailhouse had been newly cemented in Marla's honor.

Frederico made the sign of the cross over his spandex T-shirt, and Justin gunned it through the front gates. Things got crazy from there. With Justin, life is like a twenty-four hour movie marathon—there's not much difference between truth and pulp fiction.

By the time we made it to the airport, Marla was buzzing all the cell phones incessantly. I didn't have to listen to a half-dozen new voicemails to know what they said.

Before getting on the plane, we attempted to kidnap Frederico and bring him along to act as security. He said no because his twin sister was almost nine months pregnant and he was to be the godfather. Justin couldn't understand why that would be a problem.

"Dude, if she has it, you can just get on a plane and come back," he said, then offered another thousand.

Frederico shook his head, muttering in Italian and looking embarrassed.

"Dude . . ."

"Leave him alone, Justin," I said finally. "The man wants to be here when his sister's kid is born."

Justin frowned, the little computer in his brain trying to figure how the birth of a child could possibly rival a trip to the middle of nowhere with The Shay.

"You said we wouldn't need security when we got to this Daily place, anyway," I reminded him, although that was hard to believe. Justin needed security in the middle of the Moroccan desert.

Right now, he looked bummed that he couldn't buy Frederico.

"If we need security, we can just hire some when we get there," I pointed out.

"We could call and have the security team sent."

"Not unless you want Marla and Randall on your tail."

"True." Justin squinted toward Frederico again.

I grabbed my things and headed for the plane. By the time Amber and I got onboard, The Shay had wooed Frederico. They joined us, and Fred took a seat in the back. Amber sat in front to watch takeoff.

The Shay and I ended up in the middle seats, side by side. "You read the script today?" he asked.

"It's lousy."

"You'll fix it, Nater. You always do."

"I'm a writer, not a magician."

"That's pretty much the same thing, isn't it?"

Flattery. Go figure. "I don't know why you bring me along on these things. You know I'm not going to tell you what you want to hear." I leaned back and closed my eyes.

"You're my family, man . . ." I wasn't sure if Justin actually said it or if I just knew the line by heart.

The pilot told us we were in for some weather delays. No problem for me, since I didn't care if we ever left the ground. Relaxing in my seat, I got that floaty, drifty feeling. I gave in to it as we sat on the runway, waiting for the storm to pass. Sometime later, I was dimly aware of the plane careening toward takeoff.

When I woke again, we were on the ground in what looked like a livestock pasture. I could hear cattle mooing in the darkness beyond a runway that was probably just big enough to land a Gulfstream G550. A black and white cow walked by as we taxied toward a group of old hangars at the end of the field—the only buildings in sight. Leaning close to the window, I watched a man in coveralls chase the cow away with a stick.

I wondered if I was still asleep, having a weird dream we'd laugh about in the morning. *Hey, guess what—I dreamed we landed the plane, and outside the window, there was a cow, and a man in coveralls was chasing it . . .*

The plane stopped and the copilot came out of the cockpit looking a little pale, like he hoped he was having a weird dream, too. Wandering livestock and landing planes couldn't be a good combination.

The steps came down, and the coverall-clad man climbed into the cabin, his voice booming ahead of him. "How-dee! Welcome to Daily. Sorry about the livestock. Someone must've left the gate open." He grabbed the copilot's arm and shook him like an overstuffed rag doll. "That was just a joke about watch out for the cows, son. They can't git out on the runway on account'a the cattle guard."

The copilot backed out of the way, slipped into the cockpit, and sank into his chair.

In the back, Amber woke up with a squeal that was way too high-pitched and enthusiastic for two in the morning. "Mr. Ed!" she cheered, startling Frederico from a sound sleep. Fred rocketed from his chair, collided loudly with an air vent, then moaned and sat back down again, rubbing the goose egg that was sure to form and blinking as Amber wiggled past Justin and gave the airport man an enthusiastic hug. "How'r ye-ew?"

"Well just fine as frog hair, I reckon," Mr. Ed replied. "I didn't know you was comin' along with ol' Justin this time, Amber." The airport man reached around Amber and slapped Justin on the shoulder.

I glanced at The Shay. *Ol' Justin?* I'd never heard anyone, anywhere call The Shay *Ol' Justin*. The Shay had a reputation

for getting petulant and having service personnel fired from
their jobs.

"We just finished the *American Megastar* tour yesterday, Mr.
Ed," Amber answered. "Justin and me couldn't wait to get on
out here and see how the ranch was comin' along."

"Hear it's goin' real good. Dump trucks and lumber trucks
and all kindsa stuff head out that way, and I know lots of Daily
folk have been out there helpin' with the work. The churches
take lunch to the workers every day. Ty Baldridge was gonna
get on out there and mow the hayfield. He thinks y'all might git
eight hundred rounds or more." He nodded at Justin like that
should mean something, then stroked his chest hairs through
the open zipper of his coveralls. Clearly, our arrival had gotten
him out of bed.

"Awesome," Justin said. "That's a pretty good crop. At
thirty-five dollars a bale, it'll make . . ." Justin never was very
good at math. He only passed high-school algebra because the
teacher was sick of us, so she pretended not to notice him copy-
ing off my tests. Who knew he'd one day need that information
to calculate hay profits?

"Twenty-eight thousand dollars!" Amber deduced. "Justin,
that'll help pay for the new horse barn *and* the chicken house."

Justin winked at her. "We get this deal worked out for *The
Horseman*, babe, and you can build *three* horse barns and *ten*
chicken houses."

Amber giggled. "That'd be too many horses *and* too many
eggs."

I had that feeling again like none of this was actually happening. Any minute now I'd wake up back in Malibu, or better yet in Mammoth Lakes, having never heard from Justin
at all. I wouldn't even bother to write down this dream for
possible future material. This was one of those cases where

truth was too strange to be useful for fiction. Nobody would believe this.

I wanted to stay asleep and see what happened next. This was fun.

Behind me, Fred staggered to his feet, then stood blinking and rubbing his head. He leaned toward me and inquired, "Where have we come to?"

"Oz, I think . . . or maybe Texas. They're right next door to each other." I grabbed my duffle bag, which was heavy with the weight of Justin's lousy script. When this was all over, it would somehow be my fault that the foster children couldn't have a chicken house. Justin would wash his hands of the responsibility and say I should have told him this was a stupid idea.

Ahead, Amber and The Shay happily disembarked the plane with Mr. Ed. I followed, trailed by Fred. In the cockpit, the pilots were talking amongst themselves.

"I hate this place. One of these days, we're going to slide off the end of this cowpath and end up on our backs. I told him it's too short for a G550."

The pilot kicked up his feet. "Hey, no sweat. The cows'll break our fall."

"Where do you want to layover this time?"

"Let's grab a little sleep, then fly on up to Dallas and catch a Rangers game. The Yanks are in town. We'll keep her fueled. If he calls, we can be here in less than an hour."

"Works for me. Can we get breakfast at the café first? I like their waffles."

"Sure. Why not."

"How long's he plan to be here?"

"No idea . . ."

I moved out of earshot as we descended the stairs. On the tarmac, the air smelled strangely bovine as Mr. Ed ushered us away.

"The guy delivered yer new truck, there . . . uhhh . . . Justin." Mr. Ed motioned vaguely toward a metal building where a dim spotlight lit half of the word *OFFICE*, so that right now, the sign just read *OFF*, which seemed to fit. "She's gassed up and waitin' in the shed. I sent Julio around to get 'er. She's a dandy."

"You bought another new truck?" Amber gasped. "You just bought a truck when you were here last spring." Apparently, the realities of superstar life hadn't settled on Amber yet. Justin went through vehicles like most people went through shoes. Faster, actually. People don't wreck their shoes and leave them on the side of the road.

Justin shrugged off the question. "I gave the other one to the construction crew at the ranch."

"You gave the construction crew a *Cadillac SUV*?" Amber's hands fluttered emphatically in the dim light.

Frederico's eyes widened. No doubt he was hoping a discarded Cadillac SUV would roll his way, too.

Behind the office building, an engine roared to life. Justin turned an ear toward it, listening with satisfaction. "I wanted something closer to character . . . you know, for the horseman. The SUV wasn't right." His attention wavered as the engine noise grew louder, reverberating through the empty space between the office building and an arc-shaped hangar that looked like a holdover from World War II. Tires squealed, headlights appeared, and we were momentarily blinded.

"Mama mia," Frederico muttered.

We stepped back as a shiny new pickup rolled in on tires three times the normal size. The chrome, neon-lit running boards glittered at roughly chest level, illuminating a wild airbrush job that depicted a herd of running cloud-horses. Not bad artwork, if you were into tricking a ride.

"Whoa," Justin muttered. "It's better than the picture. How's that for the horseman?"

Amber started to giggle. To her credit, she didn't point out to Justin that, in the script, the horseman drove an '82 Ford flatbed pickup with peeling paint. Even I, who knew nothing about ranching, knew that this rig was a man toy, not a farm truck.

"Like it?" Justin asked Amber.

Amber just nodded. Sweet girl. "It's real pretty. It'd be a little hard to hook up a stock trailer, though."

Frowning, Justin checked out the back of the truck, then returned to stand beside us as Mr. Ed's assistant opened the pickup door and descended from on high. He handed the keys to Mr. Ed, who passed them on to Justin. "Reckon you folks are ready to git to the hotel."

"Awesome." Justin tossed up the keys and caught them in an enthusiastic sweeping motion. Whatever meds he'd procured from Marla had him bouncing off the walls, even though it was two in the morning. "Throw the bags in back."

As we loaded the luggage and Fred helped Amber in, it occurred to me that the truck was a three-seater, and already full.

"I'll ride in the back," I said, then climbed into the pickup bed. Threading my hands behind my head, I sacked out against the bags, listened to the rumble beneath me, and drifted back to a memory that was so deeply buried I hadn't known it was there. In the farthest reaches of my mind, before life in Joplin, before Mama Louise's, before foster care, before my grandparents got old and my mother married Doug, who didn't like kids—especially me—there was a sound like this. I was lying in the bed of a truck, floating over a gravel road. There were stars like these. A million stars, undimmed by the glow of city lights, fresh and clear, and close enough to touch.

Someone was beside me in the truck. My dad. He smelled

of wheat and axle grease, sweat and soil. I couldn't see him anymore. All the pictures of him had long since been lost in a series of moves to my mother's boyfriends' houses, and then to foster care.

I couldn't imagine my father's face or his form, other than that, in my mind, he was a big man. A good man, who put his hand on my hair, pointed to a sprinkled sky and said, *"Look up there, Nate. If you ever doubt there's a God, all you've got to do is look up on a clear night."* For my father, it was that simple. The awesome complexity of the night sky, the way grain sprouted from seed, the coming of the rains, and the changing of the seasons were concrete proof of God's existence. He'd inherited his views from my grandparents, from a simple life in a simple community. He believed easily, which might have been the reason he believed in my mother. When he saw her, brand-new in town, sweeping up hair in the barber shop, he fell like a tall tree on a windy day. I guess it never occurred to him that eventually she'd get tired of living on a dairy farm and being married to a man twelve years older than she was, and she'd move on to other things.

They say you can't die of a broken heart, but my grandmother described my father's death that way. The doctors said he was a big man born with a small heart. For the most part, I was just mad at him for leaving me stuck with my mom and an off-and-on string of guys. Eventually, we got a house in Joplin. Unfortunately, it was Doug's house, and he was still living in it.

Over the years, my dad and my grandparents and the farm faded until they were just a story I no longer bothered to repeat to people.

But now, lying in the back of Justin's pickup as the tires sang against the pavement and night slipped by overhead, they became real again.

By the time we reached civilization, I'd examined the memory of my father like a lost photo discovered behind a piece of furniture. I'd picked it up and looked at it from every angle, then tucked it away as streetlights dimmed the stars, the truck slowed, and we rumbled into town. The noise of the truck reverberated against buildings, seeming to rattle the glass and cause the neon sign on the darkened Daily Café to flicker as I took in the town—Justin's new home away from home, where we were going to make cowboy films, bale hay, and build chicken houses for foster kids.

It wasn't quite what I'd expected. Not much of a town, really—just rows of decaying brick and limestone buildings on either side of Main Street, a jail around the corner (I'd have to go by there and pay homage to Marla's culvert), a feed mill with tall concrete grain silos, a little park in front of the town hall at the end of the business district, and an old granite bank building with some interesting architecture and nifty gargoyles that had probably once been gilded and would have fetched a nice price in one of the antique auctions in southern Cal.

I checked out the gargoyles up close as we circled the block, turned the corner, and drove into the alley. The empty bank building would be good in a slasher movie—something in which an unsuspecting group of out-of-towners arrives in the middle of the night, thinking they've come to film a cowboy flick, but in reality, the town is empty, and the only real residents are bloodthirsty, man-eating zombies. . . .

One of them rounded the corner behind us in a police cruiser. He pulled up as Justin parked behind the hotel and turned off the engine.

"Well, hey there, Mr. Shay!" he said when Justin opened his door and descended to street level. "I didn't know who that was comin' around back of the hotel. Bein' as I'm the deputy on duty, I thought I better check up on it. Did ya git a new truck?"

Justin smoothed a hand along the doorframe of the Horsemanmobile. "Just picked it up at the airport."

The deputy whistled his admiration, then greeted Amber as she slid over and climbed down. "Well, hey, Amber! How's the singin' tour?"

"Just finished for a little while." Amber yawned, swaying on her feet. "Buddy Ray, would you mind drivin' me out to my peepaw's house? I don't want Justin to have to do it. Everyone's tired, and Frederico's sound asleep in the truck. I'm ready to be home in my own bed."

"Sure, Amber."

I handed Amber's suitcases down to Buddy Ray, who obligingly loaded them in the cruiser. Amber hugged everyone goodbye, then disappeared down the alley with her police escort.

I attempted to wake Frederico while Justin took a ring of keys from his suitcase and headed for the back door of the hotel. Fred didn't wish to be awakened, and he informed me of such. He wasn't moving again tonight and would be sleeping right where he lay. Since he was too big to carry, I left him there, snoring in the front seat.

"Hey, Nater, come see this place." Justin opened the hotel door like he owned the joint.

"Let's just take the stuff in and crash," I suggested. "It's two-thirty in the morning."

"In a minute." The Shay gave a peeved look over his shoulder. He was hours from being ready to crash. Right now, he was just ramping into party mode. He wanted to show me his new favorite place. "C'mon, Grandpa," he taunted, then disappeared inside.

I followed along and ended up in a darkened hallway that looked anything but welcoming.

Justin grinned at me as the door closed behind us. "Isn't it great?"

Following him past a storage room full of wigs and white foam heads, I reserved the right to remain silent. I looked around for the hotel desk, a night clerk, a caretaker, but the building seemed to be empty. The air was soundless, dimly lit by a lamp on a dresser beside a wooden staircase. "Are we about to get arrested for this?" *It wouldn't be the first time.*

"No, dude. It's cool. They know I come and go. Look, there it is! There's the cookie stash!" As giddy as a kid at Christmas, he lifted a white kitchen towel from a basket on the buffet and grabbed a cookie. He stuffed it into his mouth, holding the basket out to me, saying, "Hab one, 'ere goob."

"That's all right. I just want a bed right now," I muttered.

"You're so lame." Justin grabbed a key off the buffet and handed it to me. "Upstairs, to the left, last door on the right. I got you the Elvis room. I'm gonna go grab a Dr. Pepper." He headed back down the hall and turned into the room with the foam heads.

I looked up the stairs. The hanging chandelier was burned out, which was probably for the best. The place was old, with decaying plaster walls, high, wavy tin ceilings, and cloudy transoms over the doors. It smelled musty and ancient, like some of the apartment buildings my mother and I ended up in. Not exactly Justin's usual five-star accommodations.

Justin came back with a Dr. Pepper in one hand, a bag of chips in the other, and a case of sodas under his arm. "Hey, Nater, just bring my stuff up to my room." Setting down the chips, he grabbed a couple more cookies and tried to figure out how to carry everything at once.

"Bring your own stuff up to your room," I said, then headed for the back door. Sometimes he forgot I wasn't one of his little sycophants.

"Sorry. Geez," he muttered. Setting his stuff on the stairs, he followed me to the truck.

Back in the alley, I tried to wake Fred one more time, then gave up, climbed into the truck bed, and began tossing the bags down to Justin. As I was reaching for the last one, a flutter of movement drew my eye to the Dodge Durango parked next to Justin's new hot rod. There was something . . . someone inside. Leaning over the bed rails, I looked down into the partially-opened driver's side window. "Hey, Shay-man, check this out. We're not alone. There's something in there, and it looks like it's . . . either a dead body or . . . a girl . . . sleeping?"

Chapter 5

Lauren Eldridge

In my dream, the furniture store had sent over a red velvet sofa with matching pillows and a loveseat. I hadn't ordered a sofa. I didn't want the men to take away my old sofa and put the ugly red one in its place. As I protested, they began pulling sofas from their delivery truck and setting them all over the parking lot. The sun glinted against their truck, so bright it hurt my eyes.

"I didn't order anything!" I hollered, running down the sidewalk. "Go away. Get out of here!"

When I turned around, two more men had sneaked behind me and were moving the red sofa up my condo steps. "No!" I screamed. "No! No! No sofas!" I tried to make a dash for the door, but my legs wouldn't work.

On my porch, the men studied a clipboard, scratching their heads. Fragments of conversation drifted my way as I crawled toward the condo.

". . . think she's sleeping."

"That's better than dead."

". . . supposed to be here?"

"No one said anything. I called before we left. They told me there wouldn't be anyone here."

"You sure you talked to the right person?"

"Yeah. Donetta. She's the one I always talk to . . ."

"Maybe she left a note inside or something."

I blocked out the voices and tried to concentrate. This was Aunt Donetta's doing. For some reason, she had sent me a new sofa. Why would Aunt Donetta send me a sofa?

Rolling to one side, I squeezed my elbows over my ears. "Uddduhhh-ppp!" My voice reverberated strangely, as if I were inside a barrel rather than in my living room. The sound needled me as I attempted to sink back into sleep.

The delivery men kept talking. Couldn't they see someone was trying to sleep here? If they didn't hush, I was going to jump to my feet, grab the first dangerous object I could find, and start swinging until finally there was silence enough for sleeping. Dragging one eye open, I blinked through a dark, fuzzy curtain of bed hair, pointed at the two blurry figures that were . . . behind a partially opened car window? What happened to my living room? Was I in the delivery van now?

"I don't wanna urrr-red sofffa!" The protest came out sleep-laden and slurred. I was dimly aware that my lips were glued to my teeth.

The figures froze, the hair fell out of my face, and my eyes adjusted to the dim neon light outside the car. The sofas, the delivery van, the condo vanished, but the men in the window remained. My mind whirled like a hard drive caught in a loop, trying to make sense of something that wouldn't compute.

"Hello?" One of the men leaned closer, as if he were peering into a fishbowl, investigating some strange and potentially dangerous species. He looked familiar, like someone I should know. . . .

"I said—" my mouth was pasty and uncooperative—"I don't want a . . . red . . . sofa?" Okay, that didn't make sense, exactly.

He craned close to the opening, studying me with one eyebrow cocked. "Are you a . . . fan?"

"Whaaah?" I muttered.

Things began coming back to me—slowly, at first, then faster and faster, until the events of the past day rushed through my head like a pencil through a maze, then circled and came back again. My father's phone call, packing my suitcases, the Mr. Ham message, leaving town, driving for hours, the hide-a-key out back, the stubborn door, debating about surprising my father or Aunt Netta in the middle of the night, then deciding to sleep in my Durango until morning . . .

It wasn't morning yet. It was still dark outside.

A hot flush burned into my cheeks and traveled down my neck. I'd just been found sleeping, and even worse, muttering irrationally, in my car in an alley—by two people I didn't know. How humiliating.

I recognized the dark-haired man from somewhere—the outline of his face, the perfectly placed hair . . . Where had I seen him?

He curled a hand over the edge of the glass, and I scooted toward the console, feeling vulnerable.

"Come on, honey." He sighed, thumbing over his shoulder. "Start it up and drive off. No photo ops tonight. Move on."

I sat gaping at him, my rear end in the cup holder. Who was this lunatic and what did he want?

The back door of the hotel was open. Maybe I could dive out the passenger door and make a run for it. But there were two of them. I'd probably never get there before they caught me.

"Just clear out and I won't call the police, sweetheart," he said. "You don't want that kind of trouble."

"Just clear out and I won't call the police, sweetheart . . . you

don't want that kind of trouble" . . . I'd heard those words before. Those exact words. In the same voice, with the same intonation, from a guy who looked just like that. It had happened someplace else—someplace in the Middle East . . . some exotic location . . .

The strangest sense of déjà vu slipped over me, and I squinted at him, trying to separate dream from reality. I'd never been to the Middle East, but I'd heard someone . . . no, *him*. I'd heard *this guy* say *those words* before . . .

The second man moved closer, peered in the window tentatively, and laid a hand on his partner's shoulder. "Come on, dude, I don't think she's looking for a photo op right now. Just leave her alone."

"Nobody's supposed to be here. I'm gonna go call Buddy Ray, have him come lock her up a couple days so she can't tell the whole world we're in town. The Sheriff's Department helps me out with the paparazzi."

"Come on. Don't be a jerk. It's no big deal."

The dark-haired man set his chin like a playground bully determined to have the monkey bars all to himself. "This is my town, Nate. These people can't just come and—"

"This is not your town!" For some idiotic reason, I reached for the door handle and sprung the lock, then pushed open the door, knocking both of them back a step. No matter what, I didn't want anybody calling Buddy Ray. The last, last, last thing I needed was Buddy Ray Baldridge reporting that Lauren Eldridge had just been found passed out in the alley behind the Daily Hotel. Police scanners would wake sleeping Dailyians all over town. Whoever these guys were, they apparently had hotel keys, which was good enough for me. One way or another, we were going to negotiate, and I was headed through that door and into Aunt Beulah's empty room upstairs. Everything else could wait until morning.

Snagging my purse and overnight bag from the passenger seat, I climbed out on rubbery legs and explained my situation in the fewest number of words possible, while standing pinned in a triangle of door, car, and annoying man who didn't seem to be moving out of my way. "My key wouldn't work. I'm going up to my room now. Thank you."

"There's not supposed to be anyone here," the dark-haired man insisted, crossing his arms over his chest so that the slinky fabric of his shirt pulled tight over pecs that looked like he put a lot of time into them.

"It doesn't matter," the other one said. His face was in shadow, the neon shining through his hair—light brown or blond, slightly long, curly and tussled, so that when it caught the neon it produced a lopsided green halo. "It's cool, Shay. Let it go. It's late."

Shay. The name slipped through my brain, and suddenly everything from the silk shirt to the Rambo impersonation and the sappy dialogue made sense. *"Just clear out and I won't call the police, sweetheart . . . you don't want that kind of trouble."* It was a line from some cheesy international action-adventure movie I'd watched on late-night cable. No wonder he looked so familiar. This was *the* Justin. Justin Shay. The celebrity customer Aunt Netta and everyone else in Daily catered to in every possible way. The talk of the town.

A potentially disabling heat crept into my cheeks, and I slapped a hand over my eyes. Aunt Donetta was going to kill me in the morning. She'd be completely aghast when she found out her prized guest had discovered me sleeping in the alley.

On second thought, I didn't want to imagine Aunt Netta's reaction. It was too horrifying for the middle of the night. "I'm just . . . going to go up to bed now," I muttered.

"Sounds good. Me, too," Green Halo Guy agreed. Moving

a step closer, he laid a hand on the movie star's arm again and attempted to shift him away from my car door. "You're . . . in the way there, dude."

Justin Shay was unconvinced. "Yeah? I let her in here, and she'll be in my face in the morning with a camera. Where's Fred? He's supposed to be doing security. I want him to check her duffle bag."

"I don't *think* so!" I protested. For one thing, my underwear and Pooh Bear pajamas were in there. For another, this was *my* family's hotel. I would have said as much, but the last thing I wanted was for anyone to call the management.

Hiking up my purse and overnight bag, I prepared to use them as weapons. "I'm not showing you what's in my duffle."

"She's not showing you what's in her duffle," Halo Man repeated. I was starting to like him better. Grabbing both of Justin Shay's shoulders, he shifted the blockage to one side so I could exit my car without causing anyone bodily injury.

"Thank you," I breathed, then kicked the car door shut.

Halo Man, my new hero, waved toward the hotel as if he were ushering Cinderella into the palace. "G'night," he said and grinned, his teeth white in the shadow.

"Thanks," I grumbled and hurried into the building before anyone could protest or decide to call Aunt Netta.

Familiar scents enveloped me as I headed upstairs and to the end of the hall—Suite Beulahland, the pair of rooms that served as the designated repository for treasures belonging to the woman I affectionately called my great-aunt Beulah, and also functioned as a visiting-mother-in-law containment area whenever Beulah showed up for the dreaded extended stays with Aunt Donetta and Uncle Ronald. Considering that Aunt Netta and her mother-in-law got along about as well as two alley cats in a toe sack, the Beulah room had probably saved lives.

I slipped the spare key from behind the sign on the door, where it was always stored, because Aunt Beulah could lose keys faster than any human on the face of the earth. Footsteps echoed on the stairs behind me as I opened the door, tucked the key back, and slipped inside, then stood leaning wearily against the jamb.

The strangest observation crossed my mind as I stood in the dim glow of the tall street-side windows, surrounded by Aunt Beulah's collection of Elvis memorabilia.

Halo Man had a really nice smile.

What a stupid thought.

Voices from the hallway seeped through the keyhole.

"She went in *that* room, dude. I'm telling you I just saw the door shut. Don't open it. I'll stay in a different one."

"I don't have the keys to a different one." The voice belonged to Justin Shay. "I *always* stay in *the suite*. There's no way Donetta would give it to anyone else. She knows I take *the suite*. The other rooms are just plain, but this lady named Beulah decorated this one. See the door?"

"Suite Beulahland."

"Yeah. Suite, like hotel suite, get it? This side's got Elvis, my side's got those little Precious . . . whatever they're called . . . statue things—those little statues like Mama Louise had in her dining room, remember?"

"You're sentimental for Mama Louise all of a sudden?"

"Yeah, right." Shay snorted. "I sleep on the Elvis side sometimes, but I wanted you to have that room. Remember that Elvis poster you used to keep on the wall at Mama Louise's?"

"Yeah, I remember." Halo Man's voice was momentarily tender. "Thanks for the thought, dude, but I'm too tired to care where I sleep. How many beds in your room?"

"One . . . I think. Yeah, one."

"All right, I'm *almost* too tired to care where I sleep. I'm not crashing in a bed with you, dude."

"There's a sofa thing. You can have the sofa thing. . . ."

The conversation faded as they left my door and entered the other half of the Beulah suite. Fortunately, the adjoining door was closed. Letting out a long sigh, I slipped on my Pooh Bears and melted into bed. In the morning, we could straighten out the confusion about the rooms. For now, I just wanted to catch a few hours' sleep before facing Aunt Netta, my father, and all the hometown folk. I tried not to think about how it would be, finally returning after so long away. "*Troubles look smaller in the morning,*" my father always said. Everything would look better in the morning. . . .

When I awoke Friday morning, the blackness in the room had turned to gray. I could feel, even without opening my eyes, that dawn was coming soon. I snuggled closer to the mattress, looking for that moment when I didn't remember where I was, not only physically, but in life. I loved that moment. I'd keep my eyes closed and enjoy it as long as possible. In those dawning breaths, I'd be back in my father's house—Kemp and me getting out the breakfast dishes while Dad burned the bacon and cooked the eggs until they were crispy around the edges. Outside, the horses were nickering in the barn, impatient to be cared for. The cows were calling from the pasture because the feed truck was still parked in front of the house instead of coming their way loaded with chow. In the pink light, the sunrise was a watercolor wash over the hills in the distance. There couldn't be anything wrong in the whole world. . . .

That moment of quiet peace eluded me when I awoke in Suite Beulahland. I knew where I was. I knew why I was there. Someone in the next room was snoring so loudly, I could hear it through the wall. The noise stole away any sense of morning tranquillity.

It also brought back the night before, and my mind began spinning toward the day ahead. Any time now, Aunt Donetta would open the shop. She'd want to know why I'd arrived last night instead of waiting until today. She'd tell me it was dangerous to be on the highway so late. She'd say I should have called her, so she could properly worry about me during my traveling hours. She'd ask why I hadn't come on over to the house last night when I got in.

At some point, she would hear about the fiasco with Justin Shay and Halo Man in the alley, and that would be a whole other discussion. Heaven help us when that got started. Like everything else in Daily, it'd be all around town by the time the morning coffee pot went dry at the café.

Did you hear that Justin Shay found Lauren Eldridge sleeping in the alley last night? Darned near scared her to death, poor thing. He thought she was one a them poppa-rot-sees, waitin' to take his picture.

Well, I heard he found her in the Beulah room, and she grabbed the alarm clock and threw it at him, almost hit him in the nose and broke a whole shelf of Beulah's statues. . . .

I heard it hit Justin Shay and broke his nose. He's down in Austin having emergency surgery right now. . . .

I heard Beulah's headed up from Tampa to look over the damage. . . .

I heard it hit the light fixture, and sparks about set the whole buildin' on fire. . . .

The possibilities grew in my head, expanding like a balloon. I wasn't sure whether to laugh or try to sneak to my car and head out of town before anyone saw me. A story could morph faster in Daily, Texas, than anyplace else on Earth.

The best thing to do right now was probably to get up, get dressed, and meet Aunt Netta at the door. If she heard about my presence from her other hotel guests, she'd be even more rattled than necessary. If they told her there was a strange woman occupying half of the Beulah suite, she'd have no idea who it was. Fortunately, judging by the snoring, there was no activity in the room next door yet.

It occurred to me that either Justin Shay, super-stud movie star, snored like a little old man, or else the guy with the cute smile did. There was something slightly vindicating about that. It's nice when people who look perfect don't turn out to *be* perfect, after all.

I climbed from the bed feeling surprisingly rested, considering. Maybe it was the hometown air, but by the time I'd showered, dressed in jeans and a T-shirt, put on makeup and combed my hair, I felt . . . well . . . amazingly good. I left my hair loose around my shoulders, where normally at school, I would have clipped it out of the way, because, even though it looked fine now, it would get bigger and curlier as the day went on. Aunt Donetta said I had exactly what every Texas girl wants—natural big hair.

After taking one last look in the *Blue Hawaii* mirror and towel rack, I headed for the door. Fear seized me as I gripped the handle. I paused, swallowed hard, and pulled open the door just in time to hear the *creak-snap-creak* of someone coming up the stairs. Undoubtedly, that would be Aunt Netta. I braced myself for the squeal, the hug, then the inevitable barrage of questions.

A hand slid over the banister—not Aunt Netta's hand. A moment later, *he* followed, Halo Man, holding a cup of coffee with a huge plate of sweet rolls balanced on top.

I stood blinking at him, in shock. Fresh sweet rolls could only mean Aunt Donetta had already come in. *Maybe he hasn't told her you're here,* the voice of panic whispered in my head. *There's still time to sneak out, jump in the car, book it out of town . . .*

Halo Man saluted me with the plate and the smile I remembered from last night. "Morning, Red Sofa," he said cheerfully, and I felt myself blush from head to toe.

Chapter 6

Nathaniel Heath

I've never been accused of being particularly smooth. In high school, Justin was the cool one, the football star, the ladies' man. I was the funny, scrawny kid who was behind the growth curve, so that I remained shorter than all the girls until my junior year. I was the guy the girls danced with when they were mad at their boyfriends, the one who was good for a shoulder to cry on and a laugh. Half the time, I wasn't going for a laugh; I just opened my mouth and something stupid came out.

Hence the Red Sofa comment. Some brain blips you never outgrow completely.

The girl looked confused and slightly mortified. I guessed she didn't have much of a sense of humor, but she also didn't have a camera around her neck, so at least there was the satisfaction of knowing I'd been right about her all along. She was just a hotel guest, going about her business with no particular interest in Justin. He'd hate that—it made him wrong and not the center of attention, all at once. There was an attractive female in the room right next door, and she wasn't waiting in the hall for an autograph. Ouch.

"You and Elvis sleep all right?" *Well now, Nate, that was stupid, too. You're zero for two this morning. Must be the lack of shut-eye.* Sleeping in a room with Justin was like curling up in a cave with a hibernating grizzly.

The girl blinked and blushed another shade. "I really apologize. I drove in late. This is my aunt's hotel, but I didn't want to bother her in the middle of the night. The hide-a-key wouldn't work, and I was just . . . well . . . stranded. I hope I didn't scare—" In the Precious Moments room, The Shay snorked, caught his breath, and let out a rumble that probably registered on an earthquake monitor somewhere.

"Don't tell the media," I joked. "The snore is an insider secret."

She smiled, so she did have a sense of humor after all, and a nice laugh. Beautiful eyes. I debated a minute on what I'd call that color if I were writing her in a story. Green, maybe hazel, with little gold streamers toward the center. She'd be the pretty freedom fighter in war-torn Greece or at the battle of the Alamo, the one with the olive skin and ringlets of dark reddish-brown hair, slightly ethnic in her features, a little vulnerable, naturally pretty but too preoccupied to flirt.

When Justin woke up, he would like her. He would want to know who she was.

It occurred to me that the early bird gets the worm, and thanks to Justin's snoring, I was the early bird. "Nate Heath," I said, by way of beginning introductions.

"Lauren Eldridge." She offered her hand a little tentatively, the way women do when they want you to know the boundaries right up front. I checked for a ring on her other hand. It's always reassuring when a purposefully noninterested woman is married. Then you know it's not *you* she doesn't like. The circumstances just are what they are.

I looked around for a place to set my plate or my coffee, or both. Lauren waved off the handshake. "Oh, hey, don't bother. It's all ri-ight." She had a nice little Texas twang—not the whole southern drawl thing like Amber's, but just the slight stretch of a few words here and there. Cute.

Justin snorked again. The sound echoed into the hall, and the building seemed to shift. The walls crackled, and a gust of air moaned in what I'd concluded was a dumbwaiter that went to the first floor. Downstairs, the turn-of-the-century lobby had been converted into a beauty shop and health club—at least that's what the sign on the front window said. *Daily Hair and Body.* There wasn't anyone to ask and the lights were still off, but food had appeared on the buffet table and the cookie basket was gone. After listening to Justin tell spooky hotel stories, I could only guess that the ghosts of bygone Dailyians had baked breakfast and left it for those of us who could still enjoy a good sweet roll.

Lauren gaped at the door to our room. "Does he always do that?"

"Pretty much," I said, yawning into my sleeve and blinking because my eyes were grainy.

"You must've been up all night."

"I slept quite a bit on the plane." Which was good planning on my part, because Justin talked half of the night, as usual, then when he finally decided it was time, he downed a couple of sleeping pills, conked out, and commenced snoring. I bedded down on the antique, stiff, and lumpy sofa thing, which incidentally was red, and lay there remembering the old days, when Justin and I shared a set of bunks at Mama Louise's. I kept a pile of things on the top bunk to throw at him when he got too loud, but most nights I gave up, and since the rules prohibited wandering around the house after lights out, I sat up with a book to read or a notepad to write on. I did most of my sleeping in math class, which was probably why I was now a writer and not an engineer designing the next international space station. "You get used to it," I said, patting myself on the back for being cavalier so early in the morning. No sense making her feel bad about stealing the Elvis room.

Her lips twisted to one side in a way that seemed mildly flirty. I experienced a blip on my man-radar. She had a cute little dimple when she did that.

"Okay, you don't really get used to it," I admitted. "I stayed up and read the rest of the script."

"The script? For *The Horseman*?"

Ahhh . . . she knew about the script. So she wasn't a completely disinterested party after all. The mystery deepened. Who was the cute girl from the Elvis room and why was she giving me the hawkeye? "That's the one." I stopped just short of adding, *Sure cure for insomnia, let me tell you. By five a.m. I could have drifted off with a freight train in the next bed.*

"You have the script?" Was it my imagination or was I suddenly twice as interesting? Maybe she wanted a part in the movie. She didn't seem the type.

"Yes." *If you can call it that.*

"Can I see it?"

"The script?" *All righty then, what's going on here, Nater? The random girl in the alley isn't so random after all. . . .*

"Yes." She glanced impatiently toward the room, where Justin had finally rolled over and quit snoring.

"It's not . . ." *fit for public consumption.* If the screenplay (with Justin's idiotic notes in the margin), in its present befuddled, impractical, confused condition leaked out, Justin would look like the world's biggest idiot. "It's . . . uhhh . . . it's in the process still. It needs . . ." *to be burned* "some work."

Lauren seemed to sense that there was something I wasn't saying. Odd, because I'd always been pretty good at keeping people from getting a read on me. Old habit from life with Doug, and a skill that had served me well over the years in LA. When ego is everything, it's best not to let people know what you really think.

We stood silent a moment, and I had the weird, uncomfortable feeling that the little Texas girl was tunneling right through me. Her lips pressed together in a skeptical line that wasn't unfriendly, exactly, but there was an astute look in her eye. The blip on my man-radar vanished like a ship in the Bermuda Triangle. Clearly, we were talking business here.

She barricaded herself behind crossed arms, and I sensed that we were about to level with each other. "Look, I don't mean to be rude," she said, which is usually what people say right before they're going to take a shot at something that isn't nice, either. "But I'm wondering what in the world is going on here."

"Here?"

"Here," she said, waving a hand to indicate the broader *here*, as in, *in the general vicinity at this particular time.* "With this whole . . . movie thing. Who would want to film a movie in Daily, Texas?"

"Good question." I liked this girl. She was just spunky enough to be fun, just confusing enough to be a challenge. What was her interest in the film, anyway?

"Why?"

"Why is it a good question, or why does The Shay want to do a film here?"

Her chin tilted emphatically. "Both."

Just to provide a moment of suspense, I pretended to be thinking about it. "No idea."

"How can you have no idea?" She edged up the volume as if

to tell me we weren't playing anymore. For whatever reason, Lauren Eldridge, whose aunt owned the hotel, was heavily invested in The Shay's filmmaking plans. But the less information floating around the better. When this harebrained project collapsed, as it inevitably would, and Justin had to renege on whatever promises he'd made to his new friend, Amber Anderson, and the rest of the locals, there would be less fodder for a lawsuit or a media smear campaign. Even now I could imagine the headline—*Heartbreak in the Heartland: Superstar Sells Big Plans, Leaves Behind Broken Dreams.*

"*Is* there going to be a movie?" Lauren met my eyes. I had that annoying feeling she was reading me again.

Maybe I didn't like this girl after all. She was . . . irritatingly direct, without really revealing her interest in the matter. This was much more than a casual inquiry, more like a grilling, actually.

The door to the Care Bear cottage opened and Justin stumbled out, squinting through one bloodshot eye, sporting a case of bed head, and wearing nothing but those girly-looking silk boxers he thinks make him look hot when the tabloids catch him in his underwear.

Lauren blinked, then turned away, either shocked, appalled, or amused, or some combination of the three.

Licking sleep-jam from his teeth and smacking his lips, The Shay scratched his stomach while trying to focus. "What's with the noise out here?" Funny question, coming from the guy who'd just been shaking the building off its foundation.

"Yeesh, Justin, go put on some clothes. You're in a hotel." Which wasn't to say that ever made much difference. Home, hotel, Malibu house with glass on all sides . . . Justin did pretty much what Justin wanted to do. Being the center of the universe has its privileges.

He shrugged and continued across the hall into what I'd figured out this morning was the bathroom, since there wasn't one in our room. Sort of an old-fashioned concept, but it's not every day you get to shave with a life-sized cardboard John Wayne for company. The Duke was a bit one-dimensional, but we looked great in the mirror together. I took a picture with my cell phone. I thought I'd show it to my landlord when I returned to Mammoth Lakes.

As soon as The Shay was gone, Lauren got back to the question at hand. "So, is all of this for real? There is going to be a movie?"

I knew that by not answering right away, I was answering. It would have been more convenient to just say, *Yeah, sure, of course. The Shay said we're going to film* The Horseman, *and we're going to film* The Horseman. *Yee-haw. Saddle up there, cowgirl.* But in the back of my mind, in the farthest reaches of my memory, there was my grandfather, sitting beside me on the farmhouse steps as my mom's car wheezed up the driveway with Doug, my stepdad to be, in the driver's seat. *Be a good boy, Nate,* Gramp said, just before I left the farm to move into Doug's house. *Remember your Sunday school lessons. Do the right thing, even if it's hard.*

The bathroom door opened, and Justin stuck out his head. He answered Lauren's question, saving me from an inconvenient moral dilemma. "You bet there's gonna be a movie." Was it my imagination or had he grown a Texas accent overnight? "Nate's gonna make this thing sing Golden Globe like you wouldn't believe. Aren't ya, Nate?" The door closed, and he popped out of the conversation as quickly as he had popped in.

Lauren turned her back to the bathroom door, waiting for me to answer.

"Hooow-dee!" a high-pitched, yet startlingly robust call

echoed up the stairs, and I seized the distraction. "Hey up thay-er, any-buddy hu-u-un-gree this mornin'?" The words stretched in the air, playing a twangy, tinny rhythm, like an old guitar badly out of tune and a little too lively so early in the morning. "Hel-lo-o-oh, every-buddy decent?"

The stairs squeaked, then stopped like someone was wait-ing just around the corner. When I glanced at Lauren, she was what Mama Louise would have called three shades of pale. She looked like she was considering making a run for the front stairs at the other end of the hall. What was up with that? Maybe all that jazz about this being her aunt's hotel *was* just a cover. Maybe she was an interloper—a reporter for the entertain-ment tabs, a mentally disturbed Justin Shay fan, a spy from Randall's office. That would explain all the questions about the film plans. . . .

The next thing I knew, she'd bolted through the door into Suite Beulahland, leaving me standing in the hallway, alone with my sweet rolls.

"All-ri-ighty then, last warnin'. Cover up, 'cuz there's ladies comin'." It occurred to me that the proprietors, and anyone else who frequented this hotel, had probably been treated to the startling vision of Justin in his silk boxers before.

There was chatter on the stairway. "Are you sure he's decent?"

"Well, he's up, Imagene, I know that. I heard water goin' down the pipes."

"That don' mean he decent." The third accent was foreign—Chinese, Japanese, Thai, something like that. "In Coli-forna they go to beach not decent."

"Oh, Lucy, for heaven's sake. They do not."

"I see it on TV."

"Pppfff! That stuff gives people ideas. Pretty soon it'll be everyone runnin' around in the altogether."

"Oh, for heaven's sake, Donetta. Lucy was makin' a observation. People in California do things different."

"Folks hadn't oughta run around the beach in the altogether. The other day I was showin' the Sunday school kids them websites about our cruise, and there was a woman in a *thong* bathing suit in the picture. Looked like a plucked turkey in a smokehouse hangar."

The stairway broke into a raucous chorus of giggles. I'd concluded there were three people around the corner—Donetta and Imagene, whose first language was Texan, and Lucy, whose first language was something other than English. "Oh, mercy, if that ain't a picture," Imagene said finally. "I think you need one of them swimsuits for the cruise, Netta."

"That'd clear the beach!"

"How'd we get to talkin' about the beach?"

"I can't recall, actually."

"We talk about Mit-ter Shay. He don'a look like pluck turkey. He look like *Yoga With Yahani* show."

The bathroom door opened, and Justin came out with a Jimmy Stewart towel wrapped around his waist. He was just in time to hear himself being lauded from the stairway.

He slicked his hair back and posed. "Good mornin', ladies," he called, then checked the towel. I guess he figured that was decent enough. "What's for breakfast?" Leaning close to me, he grinned. "I love this place. Isn't it great?"

"Are ya decent?" A nest of tall, red—really red—hair peeked around the corner, followed by a face that was a cross between Carol Burnett and Miss Kitty from *Gunsmoke*. "Well, mornin', mornin', morning!" Donetta topped the stairs followed by, presumably, Imagene and Lucy. Imagene, with roller-curled gray hair, round cheeks, and thick glasses hanging partway down her nose, awakened some memory of my grandmother I couldn't quite put a finger on. My grandmother walked like that, for one thing, sort of shuffling from one foot to the other with her head poked cautiously out in front.

Lucy reminded me of the lady who used to run the convenience store down the block from Mama Louise's. She was a nice lady—from someplace in the Philippines. When we tried to lift candy bars, or drink part of a soda, then top it off again, she ran us out of her store, cussing in a language we couldn't understand and wielding a broom, but she was kind enough not to call the police. She just wrote it down and charged us for it the next time we came in with money. "No flee-bie," she'd say and shake a finger at us. "No flee-bie. You owe, you pay." Good life lesson. I wondered if Justin remembered *No flee-bie*. I'd have to ask him the next time he was yammering on in the middle of the night about things that didn't matter.

Donetta (Miss Kitty) gave Justin a big smile. "Well hay thay-er. Ya brought yer friend. You two have a good ni-ight? Were the rooms all ri-ight and everythin'?" The trio proceeded up the hall. Donetta stuck out her hand and introduced herself to me. "Hi, hon, I'm Donetta."

"Nate Heath," I said, and she yanked me into a hug, then let me go, and held me by the shoulders.

"Aren't ye-ew just as cute as a speckled pup! Justin's just told us all about ye-ew. He says yer the best movie writer there ever was. He said you was gonna write the script for *The Horseman*, and when you get done with it, why, it'll be a sure-fire bet for the Academy Award. We sat right down there in the beauty shop and talked all about it, not . . . when was that, hon?" She glanced at Justin, who shrugged helplessly. For Justin, most things were a blur. "Well, not more'n a month or two ago, anyhow," Donetta went on. "Willie Wardlaw sent that script to my brother, Frank. Two of them are old friends. Willie's been tryin' to get it made into a movie for a while, and he thought maybe since Frank's helpin' with some of the work out at Justin's ranch, well, maybe he could get Justin to look at it. Frank ain't much of a reader, and he ain't the pushy type, either, but I don't have a problem with either thang, so when Justin called and said he was comin' last time, I had the script ready and a'waitin in the room, and the rest is history. It's a real good story, and the movie bein' made'll mean a lot to Willie, and to Daily. It's a real good story, don't you tha-ank?" She ended with a definitive nod, and I had the feeling I was being sold something—a bill of goods, deep fried with sugar on top. A script fritter, so to speak.

All three women stood with their hands clasped expectantly, waiting for me to say something.

No comment. "I haven't . . . read it . . . all . . . yet."

"Well, it's got horses, and a cowboy, and a lonely little boy with no daddy. He's autistic. And a love story, *and* a big horse race all in one. Picture shows don't get much better'n that. I got some ideas for ya, too, when yer ready, a'course. I spent a lot of hours lookin' in the shop window and thinkin' about some ways the movie write-up is different from the book, and I had a . . . well, sort of a revelation. Sometimes, when I'm lookin' in the shop window I have . . . well, I guess you'd call 'em visions."

Imagene nudged Donetta, knocking her off balance. "Donetta, for heaven's sake, you're gonna make him think we're all one biscuit short of a panful. I bet he knows how to write a movie, anyhow. That's what he does for a livin'."

"I was just bein' *conversational*, Imagene. He might like to hear my idea." Swiveling my way, she raised penciled-on brows, waiting for confirmation, or an invitation. "Now, I got a big table all reserved down at the café. Frank's downstairs, and

Willie Wardlaw and his girlfriend, Mimi, are on the way here. I thought we could go on over and get us a real breakfast before I open up the shop—have one of them Hollywood meetin's just like on that *Studio 20* TV show."

She glanced back and forth between Justin and me, waiting for an answer. Justin was preoccupied with something. He checked the hall over his shoulder, not seeming to have heard the question.

"Oh . . . uhhh . . . we're good," I said, figuring that, since we were traveling sans-entourage, it was probably my job to extricate The Shay from uncomfortable situations involving social invitations. Aside from that, we really needed to get out of there before they could further stroke Justin's ego and convince him that *The Horseman* would be good because it had horses and people in it.

I held up the plate of sweet rolls. "These look great, though. Thanks." My stomach growled in a low, primordial voice, saying, *Give me sweet roll. Yum . . .*

Donetta snatched the plate from my hand. "Oh, hon, these were just a snack in case y'all got up early. A growin' boy needs protein—eggs and bacon and stuff."

The Shay was in his own universe, as usual. He studied the room doors, frowned, then asked, "Wasn't there a girl here a minute ago?"

"What?" My mind was a little slower changing tracks. It was probably the writer in me, but I tended to stick to one plotline at a time. Right now, we were trying to politely decline a breakfast meeting with fans of *The Horseman* at the local café. Pay attention.

"The girl. Where'd she go?"

"What girl?" It occurred to me that if the girl, Lauren, wanted to be seen, she probably wouldn't be hiding in the room right now. Interesting, considering that a minute ago, she was in my face, trolling for details about the film plans. Hmmm . . .

"The girl that was in your room last night."

"Girl?" Donetta gasped.

"Good heavens!" Imagene scanned the hallway from end to end.

Surprisingly, Justin felt the need to explain himself. "No . . . ummm . . . I mean the girl. When we got here last night she was . . . umm . . . sleeping in her car, I guess, and umm . . . she stayed in the Elvis room . . . the girl." He frowned at me. "Where'd she go, Nate?"

Something crashed inside the room, and all five of us turned to investigate.

Chapter 7

Lauren Eldridge

Why is it you never quite feel grown up in your hometown? Hiding from Aunt Donetta was the most juvenile thing I'd done in years. It wasn't intentional—it was an instinctive maneuver, like muscle memory. One minute, I heard her coming up the stairwell, and the next, I was bolting into Aunt Beulah's room like a two-year-old caught stealing cookies. My heart fluttered against my ribs, and I actually caught myself looking for a place to hide and thinking, *Just open the window and shinny down the drainpipe to the awning, then climb down the pole. You can do it.* The idea was crazy, but for a moment, I considered it. Kemp had used that escape route countless times during childhood games of hide-and-seek. I hated it when he did that, because I never had the guts to try.

You've lost it, Lauren. You've absolutely lost it this time.

I found myself fervently praying, which probably surprised God as much as it surprised me. For the past two years, He and I had been on uncertain terms. *Please don't let them find me. Please, please, please. I'm not ready. I just need a little longer to get it together....*

In the hall, Justin Shay was telling the story about some

strange woman sleeping in her car last night and then stealing one of his hotel rooms.

Shut up, shut up, shut up. . . .

Aunt Donetta and the girls were confused and mortified. They couldn't imagine who else would be in the hotel.

Turning to press my ear closer to the door, I knocked a pair of polyresin blue suede shoes off the wall. They clattered to the floor, and I knew that was it. I was had.

"What in the name'a Pete?" Aunt Donetta's voice pushed through the spaces around the jam. She was right outside.

Taking a deep breath, I grabbed the handle, jerked open the door, threw my hands in the air and said, "Surprise!" It was the best thing I could think of on the spur of the moment.

Aunt Netta screamed so high and so loud wine glasses and punch bowls probably shattered for three blocks. The next thing I knew, she'd tackled me with one of the near-strangulation hugs the guys on Kemp's high school baseball team always made jokes about. Whenever they won a game, Aunt Netta stood at the exit gate and hugged everyone she could get a hold of.

She screamed again, then I felt Lucy and Imagene join the hug, and we rocked back and forth in a wiggling, squirming reunion dance. I closed my eyes and abandoned myself to it, remembering all the times when those four-way hugs had comforted scraped knees, nursed failed dreams, and repaired broken hearts. In spite of all the hard-to-answer questions that would inevitably come later, it felt good to be home, to be wrapped in the arms of the three women who had mothered me after my own mother was gone.

Finally the knot loosened, and Aunt Donetta held me at arm's length, just the way she did in the old days when I came home to visit during college. "You've lost weight," she said, and I couldn't help it, I laughed. My first time home in two years, and Aunt Donetta was worried that I hadn't been eating enough. She solicited confirmation from Imagene and Lucy. "Don't y'all think she's lost weight? What in the world've you been eatin', hon? We need to get you on down to the café and feed you up a little."

"Aunt Netta, I'm fine." After years of being Aunt Donetta's favorite food sampler and little chubby bunny, I'd finally realized that diet and exercise do matter. Sometime in college, I'd worked my way down a couple of sizes, which Aunt Donetta still found highly disturbing.

When Danny and I were married and living in my grandparents' old house on the ranch, Aunt Netta dropped by at least three times a week with casseroles, desserts, leftover fried chicken, and pecan pie from the Daily Café. *"They were throwin' this out next door,"* she'd say, which we knew wasn't true, because Bob never threw away perfectly good food, especially not pecan pie. Aunt Netta went over there and bought lunches she didn't want and pies she didn't need so she could bring them to us. Her greatest fear was that having forgotten to eat for reasons no one could explain, we would inadvertently starve to death. She didn't want something like that on her conscience.

"I'm the same size I was when . . ." Minor slip. I'd almost said, *When I got out of the hospital.* If I'd said that it would have cast a pall over everything. "I've actually gained a little, I think."

Aunt Netta looked skeptical. She stroked my hair and fanned it out over my shoulders. "What're you doin' here, anyhow? You said you weren't gonna be in Daily till this evenin'. I hadn't even put Mr. Ham in the oven yet. Now, I don't want to hear any arguments about supper, y'hear? Everybody's just dyin' to see ye-ew, darlin'. Does yer daddy know you're here? What time'd you get in? Why didn't you call?"

I didn't worry about which question to answer first. If you gave Aunt Netta a minute, she'd fill in the blanks with the answers she wanted.

Her brows rose and knotted in her forehead. "Oh, hon, you shouldn'ta spent your first night back home in this drafty old place." I guessed she'd forgotten there were customers right behind her. "You shoulda come on by the house. I had the bed cleaned off in the sewin' room."

"I didn't want to scare everyone to death in the middle of the night," I told her. It sounded better than *I was reserving the right to make a quick getaway, and I almost shinnied down the drain pipe a minute ago.* If the blue suede shoes hadn't foiled me, I might have done it. I could have spawned yet another ghost story for the Daily Hotel—a female companion for the Confederate soldier who roamed the halls, when he wasn't busy counting gold in the underground tunnel.

"Lauren Lee, you could get mugged, sleeping in your car like that." Aunt Netta pointed a finger at me, and Imagene nodded in punctuation. "And out in a back alley, no less. Good gracious! I bet those boys scared you half to death when they came in."

Nate caught my eye and laid a splay-fingered hand on his chest, looking offended.

I laughed, as much at his expression as at the idea that I'd be the first-ever reported mugging in Daily, Texas. "I think I scared them worse than they scared me."

Nate nodded. "She did. Something about a red sofa."

I blushed, picturing myself half awake, muttering nonsense, with hair like the bride of Frankenstein. "I was having a strange dream when they came in."

Aunt Netta's lips parted in understanding. Sidestepping, she laid a hand on Nate's arm. "Oh, hon, good thing she wasn't dreamin' about something worse. She's been known to get up and walk all over the place in her sleep. One time, the night before the county fair when she was ten, she pulled her little brother outta bed, wrestled him down, and tried to truss him up with a shoelace. She was dreamin' about the goat tyin' contest."

Justin Shay gave me a wary look that said, *Look out. Crazy woman on the loose.*

Nate didn't seem worried. "Good thing there weren't any goats in last night's dream, huh?" His gaze caught mine, and his eyes reflected the light, turning the soft color of melted chocolate with a little caramel in the middle. A tiny jingle bell shivered in my chest as Aunt Netta assured Justin Shay that I'd outgrown the sleepwalking, and he didn't need to worry about hotel security. I *was* family, after all. I could be trusted not to attack him with a camera *or* a shoelace, or to reveal his presence to the masses.

From the corner of my eye, I saw Imagene glance back and forth between Nate and me. She nudged Lucy, and Lucy looked at us, too, rubbing the locket around her neck speculatively.

I moved so that I was farther away from Nate. No sense giving Aunt Netta, Lucy, and Imagene any ideas. Between the three of them, there was always some ongoing plot, which they understood and the rest of us suffered through. They were known for matchmaking, letters to the editor of the local paper, attempts to even the odds in the Daily Little League association, and passive-aggressive acts of civil disobedience when they didn't agree with the latest resolutions adopted by the city council or the school board. Once or twice, they'd even gone after the county commission and the state senate, with a fair degree of success.

It occurred to me that if I could convince the three of them to help my father get out of this movie deal, we would probably pull it off. When the girls of the Daily Hair and Body made up their minds about something, you could pretty much bank on it happening.

Aunt Netta went on talking about me. "Anyhow, sorry for all the confusion. Lauren's harmless, though, I promise ye-ew. Although, one time when she was sleep walkin', she did fill up this pail of water, and . . ."

"Aunt Netta," I preempted. "Isn't it time for breakfast?" With my family, the best means of self-defense is usually redirection. "Everyone looks hungry." Aunt Donetta could never resist people in need of food. Feeding people trumped even sharing embarrassing family stories with strangers.

"Oh goodness, of course y'all are." She addressed Nate and Justin Shay again. "Y'all just go on and git ready. We'll take Lauren out of your way, then Elena can just slip on in here, change the sheets, and move Lauren's things out." She herded me toward the stairway as if I were an escaped piglet rooting up the neighbor's flowerbeds. "Come on, darlin'. Your dad is gonna be so excited to see ye-ew. You hadn't ought to of sneaked in like that, though. He's not gonna be happy when he finds out I got the first hug. You know how he is about that kind of thang."

I grimaced. Always, there was the simmering brother-sister rivalry between my father and Aunt Donetta. Over the years, Kemp and I had been wishbones in their silent tug-of-war. Aunt Donetta wanted a quiet, stable upbringing for us in which we went to bed by nine on school nights and nine-thirty on Saturdays so we could be bright-eyed for church on Sunday. At ten o'clock on any given night, Dad was apt to have us bedded down in the pickup, on the floor of the announcer's box at the rodeo arena, at the auction barn—wherever he happened to be. There was no telling where we'd end up on Sunday mornings. If we passed a church, we might stop in for the service, we might not. It depended on what mood he was in. If he was thinking about Mom, he'd stop because he knew she would have wanted it that way.

Imagene stepped into the middle of the latest potential argument, as she so often had in the past. "Just don't say a word about it, Donetta. Frank's probably down at the café by now. Lauren, honey, you go on down there and surprise him, and he won't know a thing." She cleverly rescued me from Aunt Netta by asking for a hug. "Go see your daddy," she whispered before letting me go.

Aunt Netta looked a little disappointed as I headed for the stairs. Fortunately, Nate distracted her by telling her not to worry about the Elvis room—I could have it, and he'd take one of the others. "Oh, good heavens no, darlin'. Justin wanted you to have that room. He asked for it special 'cause he thought you'd like it. You gotta have plenty of space to get that script ready before them producers and directors and camera people and all the rest come in, right?"

"That's right," Justin Shay confirmed.

Nate remained mute, as if the question had skewered him like an arrow.

A queasy sensation started in my throat and slid slowly downward. Even I, who knew almost nothing about the movie business, knew you didn't start working on the script one day and fill up the hotel with cast and crew the next. Something here didn't add up, and I had a feeling Nate knew exactly what it was. If he was the one working on the script, how could he not? Behind the red sofa jokes and the laid-back California attitude, he was hiding secrets, and in order to get my father out of this mess, I needed to know what they were. I planned to begin ferreting out information at breakfast.

I was oddly nervous about seeing my father again, but when I walked into the café, he was so preoccupied with Willie Wardlaw that he barely noticed me. They were deep in conversation about Willie's washed-up racehorse, Lucky Strike, and how they would make him a star. Willie's bikini babe girlfriend, Mimi, lounged in a chair at the end of the table, looking like a bored beauty queen in her designer cutoff denim shorts and a tight-fitting bandanna halter top. Her long blond hair fell over her shoulder, silky and straight like the hair I'd always wished I had. Frowning, she gave the café a disdainful surveillance sweep as I walked in.

The old men of the Countertop Coffee Club sat a little straighter and smiled as her gaze passed by. She didn't seem to notice. Outside the window, three adolescent boys on bicycles stopped to peer in like they'd stumbled on a real-life episode of *Baywatch*. Mimi smiled at them and gave a little twinkle-twinkle finger wave, and their mouths dropped open. Passing by with the coffee pot and a breakfast platter, Imagene motioned for them to move on. Mimi was disappointed when her audience picked up the bikes and skulked away.

Her attention shifted to me as I crossed the room and stood by the table, waiting for a break in the intense conversation between my father and Willie Wardlaw.

"How's Lucky Strike doin'?"

"Flighty, still. Mostly just paces the stall—back and forth, all day long." Willie Wardlaw looked exactly the way I remembered him, except that now his hair and his thick mustache were gray instead of brown, and time had drawn deep, yet dignified, lines around the corners of his mouth and eyes. He was still tall and slim, a commanding presence making the café chair seem undersized, his broad shoulders and straw cowboy hat towering several inches over my father's, his long gray ponytail making him appear younger than he was.

"You turn him out in that round pen by the barn?" My father rubbed his chin, perhaps considering the difficulty of settling a young race-bred horse in a new environment.

"Yeah, but he ain't takin' to it too well. Hope he don't try to jump the fence."

"Aw, he'll be all right. He ain't stupid."

"I hope he ain't. . . ."

For some reason, they both glanced at Mimi, who'd just been served coffee by Imagene. Mimi was frowning into the cup. Willie passed the little plastic boat with the cream and sugar packets inside, saying, "Here, darlin'."

Mimi peered into the cream and sugar holder, the side of her lip curling almost imperceptibly. No telling what was in there—probably bits of dried-up French fries, salt and pepper, a dead fly or two lying belly up after having gorged on spilled sugar and ending up trapped. On a rainy day, when insects lounged by the hundreds under the awning outside, Mimi would have been treated to a flyswatter right along with her meal so she could protect her food, or have a little sport, or both.

Pushing the coffee away, she gave me a cat-eyed look. No doubt, she wondered what I was doing, standing there over my father's shoulder.

Willie paused in the conversation and tipped his head up so he could take me in from under the brim of his hat. His eyes were still the startling blue I remembered from years of watching him in bit parts on TV. "Well, butter my backside and call me a biscuit, is that little Lauren? Good gravy, if you didn't grow up into a dandy. Your dad and I was just talkin' about you." He stood and hugged me across the table as my father was unfolding from his chair. Something tipped and clattered against the tabletop, and I felt the warm splash of coffee splattering my jeans. Mimi squealed indignantly.

My father hugged me when Willie got through. He held on while Imagene mopped up the mess. I was filled with a warmth that had nothing to do with the coffee. "Hey, Dad," I whispered.

"Hey, yerself." His mustache scratched my cheek as he head-locked me and gave me a kiss before letting go. The feeling was so familiar, I could have been any age from eight to thirty-one.

By the time we all sat down again, Mimi was pouting in her chair with her arms crossed.

"Sorry about the spill," I said, then introduced myself to her.

Mimi gave a little wave rather than shaking my hand. "It's okay." The words ended in a sigh, as if all of this was far too much trouble, and she was hoping to move on to a restaurant where the coffee came in styro sippy cups. "Willie, honey, can you tell the lady to bring me some more? A mocha latte with calorie-free sweetener this time? You know I don't take it black."

My father frowned at the plastic boat with the cream and sugar packets in it, bemused. Willie hopped up and went to the counter to procure a proper cup of coffee for his girl-toy. In the prep area, Bob left the fry grill to personally fill Mimi's order.

My father chattered on about the movie project as we waited for Willie and Bob to figure out how to make a mocha latte from coffee, hot chocolate mix, and milk. When they were finished, they topped it off with a scoop of meringue from one of Imagene's famous mile-high lemon cream pies in the cooler.

"There ya go, Mr. Wardlaw. Just like one'a them fancy Starbucks," Bob pronounced as he handed over the coffee. "Who says we don't have culture in Daily, Texas?"

Something was burning on the fry grill. Imagene shoulder-butted Bob as she slipped behind him and turned the food. Bob barely even noticed. He was busy watching the presentation of his newly invented mocha-lemo-choca-lattachino as it crossed the room to Mimi. The Countertop Coffee Club turned to observe as Mimi dunked the meringue blob with a fingernail, studied it sideways for a moment, then skimmed a few lumps of cocoa mix off the top with a spoon before bringing the cup to her perfectly lined lips. Bob's brows rose as he leaned over the counter and breathlessly awaited her approval.

Swilling the first sip, Mimi considered the taste, licked a tiny bit of meringue off her lip, then purred, "Mmmmmm. That's good," as if she were screen-testing for a commercial somewhere.

The Countertoppers broke into applause.

"Well, th-there ya uggg-go, B-B-Bob," Doyle Banes said, his stutter slowing the sentence to a crawl, as usual. "Y-y-you done invented somethin' unnn-new, invented somethin' new. You ummm-might wanna uggg-go into business, mmm-maybe. Get-get you a wagon at the s-s-state fair, at the state fair." The thing about Doyle was that whenever he opened his mouth, you could always count on something positive coming out. Perhaps because the words were so much effort to produce, he was careful how he used them. Leaning forward on his stool, he peered over the counter at the leftover mocha-lemo-choca-lattachino supplies. "I ummm-might want one'a th-th-them myself."

"No, sir," Imagene said as she slid past Bob and rescued the slightly damaged lemon pie. "Y'all already ruint a pie."

"It ain't ruint," Bob protested, only now considering that perhaps the price of the doctored coffee wasn't worth the cost of the pie. "Just smooth it back over that spot. It'll be all right." Looking concerned about the loss of confectionary profits, Bob glanced at Mimi again. She'd set down the coffee and pushed it away, begun toying with a sugar packet, looking bored again.

Imagene was miffed about the pie. "Nobody's gonna want to eat that piece with the coffee and chocolate all dripped in it and a big hole in the meringue." She piled pancakes onto a plate and filled three cups of orange juice while keeping the debate alive. During my teenage years of working at the café, I'd concluded that both things were second nature to her—serving up food and arguing with Bob. They'd been at it since shortly after Texas applied for statehood.

Bob flipped the food on the grill, then peered at the cooler, considering the pie quandary.

"I'd-I'd-I'd eat it," Doyle chimed in.

"Oh, for heaven's sake, Doyle, that don't count. You'd eat anything." Imagene grabbed a tray of food and headed for the dining room while Bob took a wet knife, moved to the cooler, and began pie reparations.

At the countertop, the conversation turned to politics, then fishing, and grazed briefly over the price of feed, which ping-ponged the topic to livestock and the cost of horses at last month's auction.

My father leaned over, slipped his arm around my shoulders, and whispered, "Did'ja miss this ol' place?"

My heart filled with an unexpected rush of emotions. It was nice to be home, where everything was familiar, where nothing ever changed, where the café and the customers could be counted upon to be the same today, tomorrow, a year from now. Here in the café, I felt like a child again, basking in the privilege of being late for school while Dad lingered with the men, discussing his latest plan to strike it rich in cattle and used farm equipment.

So far, everyone was so preoccupied with Mimi's presence and the movie plans that they'd barely noticed Puggy was back in town. Maybe Imagene had told them not to make a big deal about it.

"Yes, I did," I said, and circled my fingers around Dad's, leaning my chin on the hand that had held me through the loss of my mother, through childhood hurts, through the long, painful days of recovery after my accident. Tears prickled in my nose. "I really did."

Clearing his throat, my father rubbed his free hand back and forth across his mustache, squeezed my fingers, and then let go and turned his attention to Willie and Mimi's questions about the menu. His voice quivered as he began making breakfast recommendations, then he cleared his throat again.

I relaxed in my chair, listened to the hum of conversation around me, and exchanged a few greetings with the counter-toppers, basking in the feeling of being back home in Daily's community kitchen. For as long as I could remember, we had been connected by this building. This was the place where news was spread, engagements and births were announced, recipes were shared, vacation adventures were recounted, and pictures of new grandchildren and high-school graduates were pinned to the bulletin board for all to see. The photos remained as the colors paled, children grew up, married couples fell into middle age, and family vacations faded into history. They collected the fine, fragile patina of memory until seemingly by happenstance, someone told a story from days past, and the pictures were awakened and brushed off, the colors polished to a luster beyond the original.

In my childhood, I'd loved this place. I'd loved the stories, I'd loved the people. The last two years, I hadn't realized how much I'd missed it.

"Hey, P-p-puggy, you gon-gon-gonna go out to the Anderson-Shay ranch'n train the hors-horses for the ummm-movie, for the movie?" Doyle's question sliced through my reverie. Suddenly, all the attention was focused on me. There was a pregnant anticipation in the air—round, and heavy, and bloated with water weight.

At one of the tables, someone whispered, "That's down past the low-water crossin'. . . ."

I felt the blood draining from my body, seeping into the silence. The moment seemed to stretch, growing larger, more potent.

My emotions swung violently, reminding me of all the reasons I'd stayed away. I'd been avoiding this very thing, this very stitch in time. With one seemingly harmless question, we'd all been brought back to the reason I'd left.

"I think I'll have an egg white omelet with green pepper, onion, and just a sprinkle of Swiss," Mimi announced, setting down her menu, then giving Willie a perplexed look when no one in the room responded. "Willie honey, I said I think I'll . . ." She trailed off as the door burst open and Justin Shay strode into the café with Aunt Donetta and Lucy trotting proudly behind him.

Aunt Netta did an under-the-lashes surveillance sweep, checking to see who was present to witness her entrance in such auspicious company. No telling what sort of mileage she'd get out of this at the next meeting of the ladies Bible study or the Civic Improvement Society.

Judging from the look of things, she might be able to claim title as not only hotel owner to the stars, but wardrobe mistress, as well. From head to shiny metal-tipped toe, Justin Shay was dressed in brand-new cowboy duds—crisp Wrangler jeans, a Texas flag–patterned western shirt with twin Lone Stars on the plackets, a blue bandanna neatly tied at the neck, and a black felt cowboy hat, which any cowpoke with sense would have known better than to wear in the summer in Texas. Justin Shay looked like what Aunt Netta always called a K-Mart cowboy, which wasn't an insult, exactly, just a name for someone with too many new western clothes all at once. Aunt Netta loved K-Mart.

Nate stepped through the door wearing a faded Hard Rock Café T-shirt, khaki shorts, and a pair of flip-flops, with an expression of complete embarrassment. He looked like he wanted to be anywhere but there, posing with the K-Mart cowboy while the pillars of Daily society stood up and took notice.

Chapter 8

Nathaniel Heath

Breakfast at the café was like a scene from that old Jim Carrey flick *The Truman Show*, where the main character, Truman, is living in a twenty-four-hour reality TV program, but he doesn't know it. Everything around him is part of a giant film set—the all too perfect island of Seahaven, the plucky townspeople, the Technicolor food. Each event in Truman's day is scripted. Even the weather is controlled, manipulated to keep Truman content and happy, oblivious. To keep him playing the game. Only he doesn't know it's a game. He thinks it's real.

This town was Justin's Seahaven. It encased him in militant goodwill. During breakfast, friendly neighbors admired his new cowboy shirt, stopped by the table to ask about construction at the ranch, offered to supply him with laying hens when the chicken house was ready, slapped him on the back and told him they were glad to have him in Daily. He was fitting in here just fine.

The weird thing was, he ate it up, along with a gigantic platter of over-easy eggs, French toast, and bacon. When he was finished, the horse wrangler, Willie Wardlaw, handed him the toast basket and said, "Here, son, yer leavin' the best part. Sop up that egg yoke and bacon grease. No self-respectin' ranchman throws out the drippin's. Hard day's work ahead.' "

Willie's bombshell girlfriend rolled her eyes, crossed her arms over her tiny waist, and sulked against her chair. She was tired of all the breakfast food and chit-chat, and displeased that after the initial introductions, The Shay had shown much more interest in the food than in her. She'd tried to draw attention away from the ranching talk and the breakfast platter. It just wasn't working.

Frederico wandered by the front window of the café, looking lost and slightly dazed, as if he couldn't remember how he'd awakened in Seahaven, and he was wondering how to get out. Doyle, the stuttering guy who'd just exited a counter stool, stopped to hold the door open as Fred peered through the glass, hoping to find someone familiar. "Come-come on in, uhhh-fella," Doyle offered. "Unnn-nice morning, ain't it?"

Fred scratched his head, blinked at Doyle, nodded uncertainly, then came in the door. He crossed the room without glancing right or left, like a stockbroker with a flat tire in the wrong part of town, afraid to look the locals in the eye. He was just in time to observe Justin sopping up a week's worth of trans fats and cholesterol while Willie Wardlaw and Lauren's father, Frank, cheered him on.

"Good stuff, ain't it?"

"Cowboy fare."

Willie slapped Justin on the back, and I thought Justin was going to choke on his toast. "Didn't know what you been missin', right son? That's real food."

Sometime after the initial introductions and before the grease sopping, a strange quasi father-son dialogue had developed between The Shay and Willie Wardlaw. There was lots of laughing and backslapping and talking about *the cowboy way*. Willie called Justin *son* and *young fella*, and Justin didn't seem to mind. He actually listened as Willie went on and on about his reasons for wanting to use some broken-down racehorse named Lucky Strike to play the equine lead in the movie. Right before the sopping began, he'd been warning Justin that the horse had been through a traumatic time with a broken leg and could be difficult to handle. This would be no problem, Willie assured him, because Frank's little girl was just about the best horse trainer around. He reached across the table and patted Lauren's hand when he said it, and Lauren returned a half-hearted smile that spoke volumes. She didn't want to be here any more than I did.

Frank Eldridge supported Willie's recommendation by promising everyone that his daughter could practically read an animal's mind. "Why, Lauren could train a goat to wear a neck tie and use a table fork," he added. "She's got a magic way with animals, always has."

As the conversation quickly moved on to other subjects, Lauren rested her elbow next to a basket of Texas toast and rubbed her temple with two outstretched fingers. She observed the sopping and the new cowboy mentorship while bracing up her head, as if all of this were too heavy to hold. I knew exactly how she felt. This was what my grandfather would have called knee deep and rising.

Frederico leaned over the table and seized Justin's empty platter, widening his eyes at the soupy mixture of grease and egg yoke. "This is *not* on the diet." Frederico, being fitness guru to the stars, was as mellow as a lap cat until it came to calorie consumption and calorie burn. Then he was a drill sergeant.

Justin paused, confused by Frederico's presence. He'd probably forgotten kidnapping Fred from LA the day before. Actually, so had I.

Justin observed the dripping half-eaten piece of toast in his hand, trying to decide whether even The Shay dared consume such a thing right in front of Frederico Calderone.

"Who's this fella?" Tipping back his hat, Willie Wardlaw took in Fred all the way from Nike track shoes to rumpled Under Armour workout shorts and day-old spandex tank top. Fred always looked like he was ready to step into a Bowflex commercial.

"My trainer." Justin set down the piece of toast, aware that the food party was over.

Willie scanned Fred again. "Horse trainer? Because we already got one of those. We got Lauren Lee."

"*Personal* trainer," Fred corrected, with a hand braced on his hip in a way that added, *to the stars, thank you very much.*

"What d'ya train?" Lauren's father broke in, and Lauren slid a hand over her eyes.

"People." Fred was indignant.

"To do what?"

"To *eat*."

Frank looked perplexed. "'Round here, folks just learn that natural, son."

Frederico raised an eyebrow, turning his nose up slightly before clarifying. "To make *good* food choices."

Willie threw back his head and laughed. "Well, yer in the right place. This food is goo-o-ood. Stick to yer ribs."

Setting the greasy platter out of The Shay's reach, Fred glared pointedly at his prize customer, the one who'd dragged him all the way to Texas. For months, Fred had been trying to help Justin take off the flotsam of too much catered food, alcohol, and a growing consumption of antidepressants, sleeping pills, and antianxiety meds, which tended to leave behind weight gain. Couple that with turning forty, and Justin was having to work to maintain the necessary physique. Sometimes I actually felt sorry for Justin. Nothing in his life was his own. He couldn't put on a few pounds without Randall and the studio on his back and the paparazzi taking long-range pictures of him on the beach, putting him on cellulite watch, and theorizing that he was on the way down—caught in an unbreakable web of depression, drugs, erratic behavior, and party nights.

It occurred to me that despite the insanity of Justin's plans here, it was too bad the tabloid reporters couldn't see him sopping up eggs and talking cowboy talk with the regular people in small town America. It was only nine in the morning, and he was once again up, dressed, and communicative. For the second day in a row, breakfast was real food, rather than the usual pill or two with a chaser of whatever mixed drink was by the bed.

Today, he looked alert and . . . well, enthusiastic. Both eyes were focused in the same direction. He listened with interest as, behind the counter, Bob the cook took a phone call from a reporter who was trolling for information about Justin's whereabouts.

"Hadn't seen hide ner hair of him." Bob winked at Justin, and Justin held up the high sign, while Bob hammed it up a bit. "Heard he was in that there Riviera someplace, livin' it up, but I don't know for sure. No . . . no, ma'am, I hadn't heard he's got any plans to show up here in Daily anytime soon. . . . Nope, hadn't seen Amber Anderson, neither. Reckon she's still out in California. . . . Sure, sure. Sorry I couldn't be more help. Y'all just feel free to call up the Daily Café anytime, y'hear." Bob hung up the phone, and Justin rewarded him with a round of applause.

Swiveling toward the door, Justin clapped his hands once more, catching the attention of everyone at the table. "Well, we should get out to the ranch." He rubbed his palms together rapidly. "Give Amber a call and tell her we'll pick . . ." The sentence drifted off as he realized there was no Marla hovering over his shoulder. "We'll just go by there . . . on the way."

"I'll call over to Amber's house and let her know you're comin'," Imagene offered from behind the counter.

Justin gave her the thumbs-up, then stood squinting through the windows, probably searching for the limo. No Marla. No limo. Difficult adjustment.

"Your new truck's parked out back," I reminded him.

"Right." He raised a finger and turned toward the counter. "Does this place have a door that goes there?"

"Right through the kitchen, here, Mr. Shay." Fry-cook Bob scrambled to move a bus cart of dirty plates out of the way. "You just come on in. Past the sink, down the hall, and you'll be in the alley. You need any help, now—caterin' for the movie, old time cowboy-type recipes, someone to play a ranch cook on screen—you just let ol' Bob know, y'hear?"

Justin didn't answer. He was busy lifting a contraband tidbit from a biscuit basket while Fred's back was turned. "So, uh, Fred can ride with you guys." He indiscriminately indicated anyone at the table and didn't wait for an answer. "Nate and I'll pick up Amber."

"Sure," Lauren's father obliged. "There's space in the truck with Willie 'n Mimi 'n me. You can ride with us, too, Lauren. It'll be a tight fit but we'll make it."

Fred looked frightened. "I can certainly wait in the hotel room." His slight Italian accent made the words sound like a poetry recitation. He frowned, probably realizing he had no idea where the hotel room actually was.

"Hey, no way, dude" was Justin's quick over-the-shoulder reply as he headed for the kitchen. "We're gonna build a gym and exercise center for the foster kids, and basketball courts. I want you to see the plans."

Fred stood a little straighter, having just been promoted from food police to foster shelter consultant. "Only certain types of exercise are appropriate for the developing body."

Justin waved over his shoulder. "Right, yeah. Exactly. You can talk to the guy about it." He'd disappeared through the kitchen door by the time I got out of my chair and waited for everyone else to rise and filter in separate directions. I caught a bewildered look from Lauren on my way past. *Someone please tell me what's going on,* the look said. Not a good indication, considering she was the one in charge of getting the horse to wear a necktie and use a table fork.

If only she knew how typical all of this really was. "Take good care of Fred," I whispered, leaning close to her ear. "He doesn't get out of LA much."

"I kind of guessed that," she admitted, then sidestepped so Fred could pass by. The two of us stood temporarily pinned in interestingly tight quarters. Her gaze found mine, and the space suddenly felt just right. "Is it just me or is all of this a little nuts?"

"It's just you," I said, and won a reluctant smile. For a moment, I had an odd kind of tunnel vision. I sort of . . . forgot there was anything else in the room but her.

My mind went adrift, as the writing mind is often prone to do. I was thinking there was something . . . different about her, and I couldn't quite figure out what it was. The question piqued my curiosity.

Then again, maybe she just had pretty eyes and a great smile and I'd been living in a cabin in the woods for too long. . . .

"Hey, y'all," Frank called as he pushed a chair under the end of the table.

I was suddenly aware that everyone had moved toward the door and I was still standing there with Lauren. We were just . . . looking at each other.

I blinked, pretended to be busy fishing out a tip and tossing it on the table for Imagene. My hair fell in my face, and I combed it back. I needed a haircut. Lauren probably thought I looked like a beach bum. "Uhhh . . . see ya back at the ranch." *That was smooth.*

We went in separate directions as Lauren's father, Willie, and Mimi started out the front door with Fred trailing uncertainly behind, like the Incredible Hulk awakening in a John Wayne flick.

Passing the cash register, I entertained the random thought that Justin hadn't done anything about paying for the meal. "I'll get the bill."

Imagene waved me off. "Oh, hon, don't worry about it. Bob'll just put it on Justin's tab. Won't ya, Bob?"

Bob grimaced and cleared his throat. "Uhhh . . . sure." The meaning was pretty clear. Justin probably already had a huge tab here, and most likely at other places around town, as well. No doubt it hadn't occurred to him that if he was going to sneak off without his personal assistant and live like regular folk, he'd have to pay his own bills. "I'll remind him about it," I said, then headed out the back door to catch up.

Leaving town, I pointed out to The Shay that, normally, business owners expect to receive money before the customer walks out the door.

"Yeah, that's what Marla's for," he said, his attention largely devoted to keeping the monster truck in one lane as we turned onto a gravel road near the Buy-n-Bye convenience store. On the rough surface, the balloon tires bounced and ricocheted, so that we moved along like a giant Super Ball. Any traffic going the other way would be in mortal danger—if there were any traffic, which there wasn't. Lucky thing.

"Marla's not here. You left her at home, remember?"

Justin ground it into third gear. "I brought *you*."

"I'm not your PA, dude." Sometimes he could be incredibly annoying. "I listened to you snore all night, and that's as far as I go. You can pay your own bills."

He shrugged. "It's okay. They love me here." Strangely enough, he was right. The people in this little town did seem to have a genuine affection for The Shay.

"Wake up, Justin. People need you to pay your bills."

He lowered his eyelids, giving me the look that sent assistants, sycophants, makeup artists, and grips sniveling from his presence. I really didn't care. If he wanted to get mad and tell me to blast off his planet, then fine. "Don't chap me. I'm having a good morning."

"People need the money," I said.

"If you need money, Nate, all you gotta do is tell me." The engine revved as he hit the gas and we rocketed down a hill and toward a creek, where a culvert covered by a lumpy strip of pavement provided a one-lane low-water crossing barely wide enough for Justin's new ride. We went airborne as the truck bumped onto the makeshift bridge, bouncing both of us toward the roof, then back down. "This thing is so cool." Justin ground the gears, throwing gravel as we hit the end of the crossing.

"I don't need money, Justin." Talking to him was like trying to carry on a conversation in a foreign language. The words never meant what you thought they would mean.

"Well, dadgum, then what are you on my rear about?"

I was stunned. *Dadgum* and *rear*? What was with all the G-rated language? Normally, Justin specialized in the hard stuff. "You know what, I'm just trying to help you out. People need you to pay for things when you get them. Not everybody's got a pool of cash sitting around. They need the money for stuff so they can buy more stuff to sell to other people." *So turn the wheels of commerce, big fella.*

The Shay seemed to have a moment of dawning awareness. Other people in the world have needs, too. Focusing on the truck temporarily, he reached into the console and pulled out an envelope with an auto dealer's logo on it. "Remind me to call the guy about the truck." He handed the envelope to me, then added, "Okay?"

"All right." Apparently, the Horsemanmobile wasn't paid for, either.

We drove along in silence as Justin contemplated the idea that *They love me here* was a two-way street. "Nate?" he said finally.

"Yeah?"

"Thanks for doing this project with me."

"I'm not committing to doing this project. I'm just here." The one thing I'd never done was lie to Justin. I'd kept my mouth shut a lot of times when I should have said something, but I'd never flat-out lied to him. "I think the project is a mistake. You'll never get the studio to go for it." *And when this thing falls through, all these people who love you now won't love you anymore, and you'll hit bottom so hard I'm afraid you won't get up.*

"I'll get the studio to go for it." If he was the least bit shaken by my lack of confidence, it didn't show. "I've got M. Harrison Dane coming here a week from Monday. Once he sees the project, and the place, and me with the horse, he'll agree to take it on. With him attached as director, the money men will be in the bag."

My mouth went dry. M. Harrison Dane? *The* M. Harrison

Dane? Four-time Oscar winner, who hadn't done a project in five years because nothing was worthy of his time, M. Harrison Dane? "You've got *Dane* coming *here*? How'd you manage that?"

"I called in a few favors."

"Those must have been some seriously huge favors."

He shrugged as in, *No problem for me, I'm The Shay.* "You just gotta speak people's language, Nater. That's how it's done."

Speak people's language? Since when did Justin bother to speak anyone's language?

He slowed the truck as we neared an old-fashioned white clapboard church that was tucked into a grassy valley beside a creek. "I need a detailed treatment to put in front of Dane— key scenes, synopsis, character cast, you know the drill. Not all of it. Just the proposal and maybe some of the scenes with the whisperer and the horse. Maybe the big love scene with the chick, and the one where the autistic kid gets lost before they go to the big race." He stared at the church, thinking heaven knows what. Maybe he was praying for a miracle, since that's what was needed here.

A fine sweat broke over my body. *M. Harrison Dane. M. Harrison Dane.* The name repeated over and over in my mind, growing louder and louder. I was going to write horsey scenes that would be placed in front of M. Harrison Dane. If they weren't right. If the dialogue didn't ring. If the action was flat, the characters plastic, the motivations contrived in any way, he would spot it immediately.

If I didn't believe in what I was writing, how could I make someone like Dane believe it?

"I know you can do it, Nate." Justin's voice came from somewhere beyond the storm of self-doubt. I was vaguely aware that the truck had stopped in front of the church. The engine rumbled at idle as he looked at me. "You're a lot better writer than you give yourself credit for. This time, the whole world's gonna see it."

Call me a wimp, but I didn't share his faith—in the project, or in what I could do with it. Maybe somewhere in the world of literary genius there was a writer who could make magic from *The Horseman*, breathe life into it, perform script CPR, but I wasn't the guy. I couldn't even create a magnum opus while sitting in a cabin in one of the most beautiful spots on earth, with all the time in the world, no restrictions and no pressure. How could I possibly put together something that was good enough for M. Harrison Dane . . . in a little over a week?

Deep down, I knew it was futile even to try. When you took away the royalty checks and the glitzy premiers, the nice cars and the A-list parties, I was just a guy who got lucky because I knew the guy who hit it big. That kind of loot trickles down. It gets you into restaurants without standing in line. It makes you look like *somebody* when you're not. Underneath it all, I was exactly what Daddy Doug always told me I'd be—a pain in the butt my mama didn't really want, a kid who'd never amount to anything. A loser.

You hear it enough times, it's in your brain, no matter how much you try to block it out. It's part of your DNA. I had about as much chance of writing an Academy Award–winning screenplay as Justin had of getting nominated.

"Big ideas get you busted down"—direct quote from Doug. *"Sooner you learn that, better off you'll be."*

". . . get out there and put my tools back where they go."

". . . I say you could touch my stuff?"

". . . touch my stuff again, I'll break your arm, you little brat."

"... What? You think you're somebody special? You gonna cry to your mama now? Come on, stand up and act like a man. Take a swing. I'm right here, you little snot-nosed son of a ..."

Doug faded as we moved on to the next place past the church, where an aging house trailer sat in the shadow of a new home being built. The trailer looked like someplace my mother would have lived. Last time I saw her, she was shacked up in the back of an RV park and working at a convenience store next door, while Doug collected workman's comp—something to do with a leg injury. I asked her if she needed anything. Doug told me to buzz off, more or less, and she just stood there. I hadn't been back since.

Amber came trotting out of the trailer with a half-grown boy following her. They slipped out the yard gate, shooing away chickens, a couple of lambs, and a few dozen cats. Except for the under-construction new house in the background, she seemed about as far from *American Megastar* as she could possibly be.

The little boy, Amber's brother, judging by the family resemblance, dashed past her and climbed up to the driver's side door as Justin rolled down the window. He wanted to see the truck. Justin was quick to oblige. He popped the hood and hopped out to show off the engine.

I exited the truck and helped Amber climb in. "Thanks, Nate," she said cheerfully. "How're you this mornin'?" We exchanged a few niceties during a search for the middle seatbelt.

While we waited for Justin, she talked about the recent *American Megastar* tour and the difficulties of adjusting to life on the road. She wasn't complaining, really, just stating facts. It was hard making the transition from small-town girl to up-and-coming singing sensation. She missed her family, her youngest brother in particular, Avery, the one now making engine talk with The Shay.

"Justin's been a real good friend." Amber leaned down to

peek through the gap between the truck and the hood. "I can call him from wherever I am and get advi-ice, and sometimes he'll just hop in the plane and fly there. One time, he went by Daily and picked up my family and brought them all the way to New York so they could see the *American Megastar* concert in Times Square."

"That sounds like The Shay." Justin was known for lavish, though often impractical, gift giving. "In Morocco, he bought me a water buffalo."

"He's been just like a big brother to me." Amber smiled fondly in the direction of the engine.

"Justin's not really the big brother type." It sounded harsh, but I felt the need to warn Amber that this good-behavior period with Justin wouldn't last. "When he spends time with someone, Amber, it's because he wants something. I'm not knocking him, but that's the way he is."

Amber turned pointedly to me. "People can change."

For the space of an instant, gazing into her wide blue eyes, I almost believed it. I could see why Justin was enamored with her. She had the mesmerizing glow of a true believer.

"That's why I asked him to think about makin' *The Horseman* instead'a that Davis VanHarbison movie his manager wants him to be in. Justin showed me the script for that movie when we met up in New York City. It's all about the worst things people can do to each other—shootin' and killin', and all the reasons people hate other people. If you watch enough of that stuff, you start thinkin' that's the way the world is supposed to be. You lose faith in people."

"The world's a cynical place."

"It doesn't have to be." The dewy look was gone from her eyes, replaced by a purposeful regard. "Justin needs ye-ew to believe in this movie, too, Nate. He knows you're the only person he can count on to really tell him the truth. All the rest of them people—Marla, and that manager of his, and the so-called friends he hangs around, they just want him to make money so they can get some of it. They don't care if he gets drunk all ni-ight, pops pills to sleep, and pops more pills to wake up. They buy it for him and wave it ri-ight in his face."

I suddenly felt trapped in a place too small. I'd been down the rehab road with Justin before—so many times I couldn't count. Each ended in a painful crash landing. He always found someone—his personal assistant, the janitor at the rehab center, the limo driver—to get him what he needed. "It's been that way a long time."

"That doesn't make it ri-ight." Amber's words had the lofty idealism of youth.

"True," I agreed. "But it is reality."

"Don't you think that way deep down he wants somethin' more?" The question burrowed in, unearthing the lost remnants of a dreamer I thought I'd buried years ago. "Don't you want somethin' more *for* him?"

"He doesn't want anything more for himself." I felt slightly unsteady, as if I were being dragged out to sea inch by inch and I lacked the strength to fight it. I didn't have the reserves to mount another campaign to save The Shay from himself. I was busy trying to get my own life straight.

"He doesn't drink when he's in Daily," Amber said. "Not a drop."

The hood slammed shut, Amber's little brother trotted back to the yard gate, Justin rejoined us in the truck, and my conversation with Amber ended abruptly. Both of us cast embarrassed looks in Justin's direction, but he didn't seem to suspect that we'd been talking about him. As Amber waved good-bye, Justin began cheerfully briefing her on the plan for the day.

"Guess what," she said when he was finished. Her eyes were bright with anticipation. She looked like a little girl waiting to announce that the tooth fairy had just left a dollar under her pillow.

"Hmmm?" Justin was preoccupied with trying to get the truck into reverse.

Amber paused to show him how it was done. "This way." She pushed the stick over and down. "We had one like this at the feed store once. Anyhow, guess what."

"What?" I said, when Justin didn't answer right away. Something about Amber pulled you in, whether you wanted it to or not.

She shifted so that she could swivel back and forth, delivering news in both directions at once. "I just talked to my friend J. Carter Woods down in Austin, and he's willin' to write some songs for the movie. Isn't that great? With him writin' the songs—oh my gosh—the sound track'll be so big. Country songwriters don't get any hotter than him. He's headed off to Acapulco to get married next week, but he said send him a script and he'll get busy as soon as him and Manda come back. Isn't that awesome? If I'd called an hour later, he woulda already been on the plane, headed for Acapulco, but I caught him at just the right time, and he said yes. I truly believe God's been pavin' the path for this movie every step of the way."

Fortunately, Justin answered before I had to. "Cool," he said, then put the truck in forward gear, and we rattled off in the Horsemanmobile, three peas in a pod, headed for a movie miracle, or an inevitable disaster, depending on who you asked.

Chapter 9

Lauren Eldridge

I opted to drive myself to the ranch rather than cramming into the back seat of my father's crew-cab pickup with Willie's girlfriend and Justin Shay's Italian exercise guru. Mimi and the personal trainer had struck up a conversation on the way to the car, and I didn't want to be the third wheel while they discussed abs, buns, and body mass index. Mimi was proud of hers. Frederico invited her to come along next time he did an on-air exercise segment for *LA Morning*. Mimi was thrilled.

My father didn't want me to make the trip to the ranch by myself. The look on his face told me why. He was silently worried that I'd get to the low-water crossing and have a breakdown—the emotional variety, not the automotive kind. He wouldn't say it, of course. The low-water crossing and everything tied to it were taboo subjects. Rather than mention what was really bothering him, he tried to talk me into the back of the truck by saying there was no sense in wasting gas, there was plenty of room for me, and Mimi would probably like some female company. Mimi was already in the back seat, holding her hand over her nose to filter out the auto-shop aromas of must, dust, and fifty years of axle grease. Frederico was patiently holding open the pickup door, waiting to help me in, as my father and I engaged in debate.

"You can ride up front with us," Willie offered and started moving a pile of beef jerky wrappers, work gloves, smashed soda cans, tools, and greasy shop towels.

"No, really, I'm fine," I insisted. The last thing I wanted to do was revisit the low-water crossing trundling along between my father and Willie, or Mimi and Frederico. "My Durango is right in back of the shop. I'll see you all at the ranch." I started mentally calculating the time it would take me to go around the long way, so as to avoid Caney Creek altogether. I didn't want to be reminded that, on a calm day, it was a harmless-looking little trickle of water, both serene and beautiful. I didn't want to pass the tree line of the Hash-3 or see my father's house in the distance, and across the field, the tiny stone cottage Danny and I had lived in when we weren't on the road trying to make it big. I couldn't predict how I'd feel, passing those places again. In one way, that life seemed like it was never real, and in another way, it seemed like yesterday.

My father, as always, read my mind. "Well, listen, sis, you might want to go around the back way, all right? There's pretty good potholes in the ol' crick road." *Old creek road*—my father's attempt at a harmless euphemism. Normally, he would have just called it by its name, Caney Creek Road. He was afraid even that would upset me. "And don't hurry, neither. We're gonna do a little sightseein' ourselves on the way." He pulled out his pocket watch and checked it. "It'll take us probably . . . ohhh . . . thirty minutes to get out there."

From inside the truck, Willie gave Dad a confused look but didn't question him. No doubt he knew that the Barlinger place was only fifteen minutes away.

"All right, Dad," I said, and hugged him. He held me tightly, as if I were setting off on a long journey rather than driving a few miles out of town. A lump rose in my throat as he kissed me on the top of the head. In the hospital, he always did that before he left for the night.

"I'm glad you're here, Pug," he whispered, then let me go, cleared his throat and rubbed his mustache, and climbed into the truck.

I headed out to the car, wiping my eyes and swallowing a spiny cocklebur of mixed feelings. It burned and prickled on the way down, a partly warm, partly painful sensation. On the one hand, it was good to be here, to make my dad happy. It was probably the best time to have come. With everyone so preoccupied with the movie, my return had barely even caused a ripple in the Daily radar.

On the other hand, I felt like I was walking on thin ice, just waiting for the moment the fragile surface would crack and I'd fall through into the raging current beneath. Sooner or later, no matter how far I drove to circumvent it, the low-water crossing on Caney Creek would rise up and find me. I would cross paths with Brother Harve, Miss Beedie, Otis Charles, Miss Lulu, or someone else from the congregation of the little African-American church just beyond the crossing, and we wouldn't know what to say to each other. In the space of an instant, we would all relive the day when one lapse in judgment, one five-minute delay for brisket sandwiches, one warning not heeded, one in a string of immature marital arguments, one time I shut up and gave in when I shouldn't have, led to the loss of not only the man who drove into the water, but the man who tried to pull us out—a beloved son, good father, treasured nephew, faithful church member, public servant. A good man who was just doing his job, on patrol on a bad night, bringing out the road cones to block off the crossing so no one would drive through it. Only someone already had.

It wasn't like we didn't know better; that was the worst of it. We knew that creek, that crossing. Old Mr. Fuller warned me about it again, frowning from behind the counter at the Buy-n-Bye, as my husband hunkered in the rain outside, putting enough gas in the truck to get us home. In the trailer, the horses kicked and squealed impatiently, restless in the storm, tired from the long trip.

"Better go the long way around, Puggy," Mr. Fuller said, moving lazily to the deli case. I'd ordered a couple of sandwiches, because after all evening on the road, Danny and I were starving. "Gully washer like this, the water'll be over the low-water crossin'."

"Might be," I agreed, squinting toward the window, watching the rain slash splinters of water on the glass. I waited, leaning drowsily against the Icee machine while old man Fuller pulled a hunk of brisket from the deli case and made our sandwiches. *He always takes forever,* I thought. *I shouldn't have ordered anything.* But it was late, and Danny was mad because he'd missed his calf and hadn't won anything, but I'd placed in the barrel racing. I was hoping the brisket sandwiches would cheer him up. He honked impatiently as Mr. Fuller took out a butcher knife. The metal caught a flash of lightning, then sliced through the beef, juice oozing out over the cutting board, dripping onto the floor. . . .

My body rushed into the memory and my mind turned hazy. I felt water all around me. The brisket juice turned to blood. I tasted it dripping into my mouth, blocking out the air, choking me.

The horses were screaming, thrashing desperately against the trailer. I felt the seatbelt tight against my throat, the water swirling over my legs, sucking the truck downward. The floor-board shifted, metal groaned, a tree limb pushed through the window, scratched my face. The seatbelt slid free. Danny hollered something over the rushing water. I grabbed the tree limb, tried to pull myself up.

The horses kicked and struggled, their voices a chilling, terrible sound. The truck lights blinked, then fizzled. Everything was impossibly dark. The seat jerked sideways, slamming my head against the side of the truck. I screamed for Danny, felt the force of the water separating me from the vehicle, dragging me through the window with the branches. Something in my arm snapped and I screamed again. I couldn't hear Danny or the horses. I couldn't hear anything but the water, terribly cold, impossibly fast, wicked and determined, filled with debris. I couldn't feel anything but wave after wave of pain.

I saw a flashlight beam just before I lost consciousness. . . .

Blinking hard, I pushed the sensations away, brought myself back to the alley, to a sunny summer day without a drop of rain in sight. *It's the past*, I told myself. *It's over. It happened. Let it be.* But my eyes burned. I felt it as if it were yesterday. Danny was mad about the sandwiches. The last thing he'd said before driving the truck into the current on the low-water crossing was that if I hadn't waited around for stinking barbecue sandwiches, we would have gotten there before the water topped the pavement. If, if, if . . .

Let it be. Let it rest. Let them rest. I tried to banish the memory as I left Main Street and circled the long way through the hills on roads that were familiar, a part of me like the lines on the palm of my hand. As the scenery passed, I relived the memories of places I'd worked in the summers, cutting and hauling hay with my father, combining oats, working to help neighbors bring in cattle for vaccinations, worming, weaning, and sorting. They were good memories, those mornings we rose early and loaded horses or tractors in the cool predawn air. I slept on my father's shoulder while we drove to wherever we were going. When we got there, the sun would just be coming up, and we'd go to work. We'd ride horses, or drive tractors, or load hay wagons all day, then go home hot, and tired, and dust covered, but it was all right because we were with Dad. Anything Dad did, we wanted to do.

I could still see Kemp, too small and stringy to pick up a bale of hay, grabbing the wires and dragging the bales to the trailer, because he didn't want Dad to think he couldn't help. That was the year Mr. Hill, who owned the Hilltop auction barn, had his second heart attack. My father took over his hay crop and took on auctioneering three nights a week. Kemp and I survived on concession stand hamburgers and Wacky Wafers, but we didn't mind. We played on the top of the tall bleacher-like seats around the auction ring until we were dirty from head to toe, sweaty, smelly, and exhausted. Aunt Donetta wanted us to come stay with her after school started in the fall, but Dad wouldn't hear of it. He knew Kemp and I would do our homework up on the top bleacher, then eventually spread the saddle pads, or horse blankets, or an old slicker, curl up in a fine layer of dust, and drift off. The rattle of the auction call, the sharp cries of the bid spotters, the plaintive cries of weanling calves separated from their mothers, the occasional tap of the gavel would sing us off to sleep like a lullaby. We'd wake in the morning, having been driven home and put in bed without knowing it. Once in a while, if we were lucky, Dad would need us in the hayfield the next day, and we'd get to miss school. *Assignments can be made up, after all*, my father insisted, *but a hay crop waits for no man. . . .*

The sheen of good memories settled over the road, and I rolled down the window, let the warm breath of summer flow over me, took in the scents of cedar and juniper, prairie grasses and caliche dust from the road. The thick, sturdy leaves of live oak trees rustled slightly in the breeze as I passed under their yawning arms. I remembered their music. How many times had I lain down in their thick shade and drifted to sleep listening to them sing? The sound of them, the feel of them was home. It was shelter and comfort. Peace. Relaxing in my seat, I let the drive be what it was—a journey through a place I loved and memories I'd kept packed away, like a box of mementos forgotten in the back of a closet.

By the time I reached the heavy piled-stone corner posts that marked the boundary of the old Barlinger ranch, now the Anderson-Shay project, I felt good. The day was bright, the sky an endless blue that seemed filled with possibilities. On the horizon, the hills basked in the uneven light of sun and shadow, dotted with live oak groves and scrappy cedars, feathery mesquite trees and squatty thickets of the prickly pear cactus that gave shelter to jackrabbits and roadrunners and, as my father had always warned us, rattlesnakes.

Ahead, a fencing crew was repairing the tumbledown gateway, the laborers cleaning old mortar from the limestone blocks and putting them back together like giant puzzle pieces, while a crew foreman ran a string from one guidepost to the next and squinted down the line, checking for plumb. I recognized the crew boss. Pearly Parsons had been building fences for as long as I could remember. When he finished here, this gateway would be ready to go another hundred years, and the fence would be as straight as an arrow, as tight as a fiddle string. The posts would be so even you could use them to count the seconds as you drove past.

My father admired Pearly, even though Pearly was rumored to have only made it through the sixth grade in school and did most of his fencing math by a system no one understood. My father said that if Pearly wanted a post hole four feet deep, and he ran into a rock at three feet six inches, he didn't cut off the post, he broke up the rock. More than once, when people made jokes about Pearly's hand-written advertisements on the bulletin board at the café, my father confronted them. He said that any man who thought less of Pearly because of his lack of education had only to look at one of the fences Pearly built. Those fences would be there long after the achievements of most men had faded away.

Pearly himself thumbed his nose at the educational issues. The cab of his flatbed truck and his ads at the café always read:

Pearly Parsons, PHD
Post Hole Digger
Fencing, welding, post drilling
The harder the ground, the bigger the shovel
Every fence true and straight
Fair prices
Nothing wasted

It was a good motto for life, my father said. When we complained that a school assignment was too hard, whined that we were being picked on, or said we couldn't do something, Dad quoted Pearly Parsons. *The harder the ground, the bigger the shovel. . . .*

I stuck my hand out the window and waved at Pearly as I turned into the driveway. Pearly tipped his hat without taking his eye off the string.

Ahead, the old Barlinger headquarters looked more like a construction site than a ranch. The cavernous limestone home that had been the site of haunted houses, teenage parties, and more double-dog dares than I could count was now surrounded by scaffolding. A painting crew was scraping window frames and eaves as a workman in white coveralls carried new panes of glass to the wide double doors. A drilling truck was at work on the well, and high atop the third-story roof, a chimney sweep in a black stovepipe hat stood against the sky, slowly moving his brush three stories up and down.

As I drove closer, I could see that the barn and corrals had also been cleaned and repaired, and behind the old orchard, areas had been leveled for new construction. The extent of the work was awe-inspiring.

Passing by the house, I considered the almost frenzied effort to reclaim what the grass, and the mustang grapevine, and the mesquite thickets had all but absorbed into the land. The money and sense of purpose involved here were staggering. For years, everyone in Daily had assumed that the remnants of the once-grand Barlinger ranch would remain in financial limbo until finally falling beneath the grass and the brush and disappearing altogether.

My father had once told Kemp and me that only a miracle could bring the place back to life, but apparently the miracle had arrived. Who could have predicted that the little girl from the trailer house down the road would win a TV talent contest, make big-money friends, and come back to reclaim the homestead that had been left for dead?

Drifting through the barnyard, I looked for my father's truck or signs of Nate and Justin Shay. There seemed to be nobody around but the work crews. Apparently, my father and Willie hadn't made it there yet. There was no telling where

Nate and Justin Shay had ended up. Maybe they were lost somewhere in the backcountry. Once you were a mile or two out of town, all the roads looked the same and only half of them were marked.

Movement by the barn caught my eye. I parked the car and climbed out, then walked around the corner. A black truck with monster tires and a ridiculous airbrushed paint job touting *The Horseman* was parked near the corral gate. I remembered it vaguely from my not-quite dream last night. Beside the truck, Nate and Amber Anderson stood shading their eyes, looking at something in the corral. Squinting into the sun to see what was happening, I moved closer. The corral gate was open, and in the pasture beyond, several horses bolted wildly from fence to fence, cavorting and kicking up their heels. From the look of things, they'd just been let out the gate by Justin Shay, who stood seeming somewhat bemused in his K-Mart cowboy getup.

I had a bad feeling one of the horses was Lucky Strike. He was running up and down the far fence alone, gliding over the ground on the long, graceful strides of a Thoroughbred, covering the rough terrain at a blinding pace, completely oblivious to rocks, mesquite bushes, jackrabbit holes. No doubt he'd never seen a barbed wire fence, either. An alarm bell rang in my chest as he skidded to a halt just before crashing into the corner, then did a ninety-degree rollback and dashed up the side fence whinnying and snorting, head high and nostrils flared. The other horses caught up to him finally, and he wheeled and kicked, then started running again.

Justin Shay stepped away from the gate, moving into position to head off Lucky Strike when he turned the next corner.

"Hey, don't . . . get back!" I hollered, but my voice was lost in the noise.

Amber screamed and covered her mouth as Lucky Strike barreled toward Justin, who seemed to be under the mistaken impression that a cowboy hat waved in the air would stop a twelve-hundred-pound racehorse, running wild after having been turned loose in a pasture, probably for the first time in his life.

"Justin, watch out!" Nate's warning carried into the field. Scaling the fence in a move worthy of an Olympic athlete, he ran across the round pen with Amber and me only a few paces behind. Lucky Strike saw us coming and shied away at the last minute, missed Justin, and left him in a cloud of dust next to the fallen cowboy hat. Spitting out a string of profanities, Justin jumped up and down on the hat, picked it up, and ring-tossed it into a tree, then cussed when it hung on a branch and wouldn't fall back into his hands. He looked around for something to throw at it.

"Leave it," I said. "You'll stir the horses up even more."

Ramming his hands onto his tightly packed abs, he glared at me. "This is idiotic!" he roared, stabbing a finger into the air. "That horse isn't trained. He attacked me in the corral, and then when I ran out the gate, he nearly mowed me over."

"You shouldn'ta opened the gate," Amber muttered. Being a country girl, she probably knew that if a very large animal wants to get out badly enough, it's not going to care whether one itty-bitty human is standing in the way.

Justin opened his mouth and raised a finger to defend his position, then gave me a bewildered look and said, "I just came out here to show Amber and Nate the horses." He flailed a hand impatiently in the direction of the gate. "When Willie was here yesterday, he just opened some gates and shook a bucket, and they came in."

"I don't imagine Lucky Strike was in the round pen at the

time." Judging from his current behavior, Lucky Strike wasn't the docile, come-to-the-bucket sort.

"Well . . . no he wasn't in the corral yesterday." The faraway image of Lucky Strike running wild reflected off Justin's mirrored glasses. "But I didn't know he was going to, like, mow me over. I told him to back off."

Behind me, Nate snorted. "He's not a dog, Shayman."

Justin jerked upright, his chin dimple disappearing into the made-for-Hollywood bandanna he'd tied loosely around his neck. "You know what, Nate. You been nothin' but a pain in the rear this whole trip. You can either get on board or hit the road."

Nate threw his hands in the air and backed off a step, refusing to be baited into an argument.

"It was my fault," Amber said, stepping in as a scapegoat. "I'm sorry, Lauren. We shoulda just waited for everyone else to get here. I know better. My peepaw taught us kids not to go messin' with a horse we don't know."

"That horse is an idiot." Justin's cheeks boiled red and a sardonic puff of air burst from his mouth. "You know how much we're paying to put that animal in the movie?" He wagged a finger toward me and then toward Lucky Strike. "He needs to do what I say."

Nate turned and walked a few steps away, shaking his head as Justin ranted, "I'll call and order a new horse. I don't have time for this."

Me, either, I thought. *There isn't enough time for this. It's impossible.* On the heels of that realization came the memory of my father telling me that Willie Wardlaw's last dime, and my father's, were riding on this film and Lucky Strike's future. If the horse broke a leg out there, my father and Willie would be in even worse shape than before.

I took a halter and a lariat rope from the corral fence. "The first thing to do is get your costar back in the round pen before everyone else shows up." If my father and Willie Wardlaw arrived and saw their prized racehorse running loose inside a rusty barbed wire enclosure, one or both of them would probably have a coronary.

Justin considered the idea that, so far, only the four of us knew he'd let the horse escape. "Yeah, I guess so." Pulling his sunglasses down, he squinted at me over the top. "How do we do that . . . exactly?"

I attempted to quickly think it through. How, indeed? "You go around to the left, and I'll go around to the right, and we'll see if we can pen him in the corner by the two metal gates long enough to get a halter on him. The main thing is not to push too hard. Horses are like people—they don't like to feel trapped or pressured. You pretty much get out what you put in." *It's all in the script—didn't you read it? The horseman works* with *animals, not against them. Negative input equals negative output. It's all very Zen.*

The K-Mart cowboy pushed his glasses back into place, uncrossed his arms, and clapped his hands. "Let's go. I'm in. We'll go this way. You go that way." Without waiting for a reply or checking to see if anyone else was following, he started off across the pasture. Amber jogged a few steps and fell into step beside him. Her hands gesticulated wildly as they walked.

Nate followed me. There was the barest hint of a smile on his lips as we left the round pen behind for mission racehorse roundup. "Good job with The Shay," he complimented, giving me a wise look.

I caught myself studying him a little more intensely than I meant to. "Why do you let him talk to you that way?" As if I didn't know. Stars wouldn't be stars without the hangers-on who tolerated divalike behavior.

Nate shrugged. "He talks to everyone that way."

"He shouldn't."

"Yeah, maybe. It's Hollywood. Attitude goes with the territory."

"That doesn't make it okay."

Squinting at Justin and Amber in the distance, Nate acquiesced with a noncommittal shrug, then changed the subject. "So you're not worried that when we start to crowd our friend, Lucky Strike, he might try to go over the fence or one of us?"

"I am worried about it." *Hmmm . . . the guy in the flip-flops and shorts knows more about equine behavior than he's letting on.* "So, you have some experience with horses, I take it?"

"Nah . . . not really," he answered evasively.

"Seems like it would be tough to write the script, then."

"Writing a screenplay is like riding a bicycle—you just get on and pedal—inciting incident, midpoint crisis, culminating crisis, act one, act two, act three. They're all pretty much the same."

"That must make it difficult to get inspired."

"Sometimes," he said, and there was a flash of emotion in his face that was difficult to read. His eyes, framed with thick, dark lashes, met mine very directly, and I felt the inconvenient tug of curiosity. *Who is this guy and what's his story?*

The contemplative look faded and he stopped to pull off a flip-flop, then hopped along on one foot while picking spear grass seeds from between his toes. "Guess I didn't dress for ranch work," he joked as he replaced the shoe.

"Where's your new cowboy suit?" I slanted a glance across the pasture toward Justin Shay, whose silver-toed boots were flashing Morse code in the sun.

"Missed the memo on that one." Nate grinned and winked, and something fluttered in my throat.

"Next time, wear boots." *Next time? Did I say next time? As in, we'll all be doing this again in the future?* What was wrong with me?

"I'll remember that." He grinned again, and I felt my body go hot and flush all over.

Chapter 10

Nathaniel Heath

Operation roundup looked more like the Three Stooges, plus one—two, if you factored in the horse. Lucky Strike had figured out the trick, and he was having fun with it. Every time we cornered him, he wheeled around, sized up the line of us, and bolted past Justin—practically right over the top of him. The horse was as fast as greased lightning, and apparently a fair judge of character. He knew Justin was afraid of him.

In the back of my mind I remembered my grandfather, taking me out in the pasture to help separate an ailing cow from the little herd of Guernseys he and my grandmother kept for their small dairy. *"Never let them get a bluff in on you, Nate. They'll run right through you if they know you're afraid,"* he said as we herded the bellowing cow into the barn. *"If you want to win against something that's bigger than you, you've got to have confidence and show confidence."* Perhaps when he said that, he knew my mother and Doug would be coming for me soon, and I'd need that pearl of advice. At ten, I was ninety pounds of stick-armed self-confidence. A few months after we moved in with Doug, I told him if he ever laid a hand on me again, I'd go straight to school and tell everyone about it. He never hit me after that—until I got big enough to hit back. I guess by then he figured it was a fair fight.

Lucky Strike had a look in his eye I recognized—a look that said if he backed down even for a minute, something bad would happen. Despite Lauren trying to soothe him and Amber murmuring sweet nothings in her sugar-coated country drawl, the horse figured he'd be better off anywhere we weren't. We chased him around and around until he was lathered up, Amber was winded, and Justin had doubled over, trying to catch his breath.

My feet felt like slabs of raw meat, thanks to the flip-flops, but I noted with some satisfaction that even if I didn't have a personal trainer, I was in better shape than Justin. To make matters worse, a storm had started to brew on the horizon, and the black clouds billowing over the hills gave everything a new sense of immediacy.

Finally, Lauren uncoiled the rope on her shoulder. The next time we went through our routine with Lucky Strike, she made a lasso loop as he trotted into the corner. Three swings over her head like Roy Rogers, and it was zinging through the air. The loop sailed forth like the rim of a flying saucer, circled the horse's head as he prepared to make another escape, then dropped into place before he, or any of the rest of us, knew what was happening.

The horse panicked. Lauren tightened the rope as thunder rumbled on the horizon, and for a moment all of us stood frozen. Justin started toward the horse, and Lauren waved him off. "Don't move," she said, keeping her focus on her captive. We watched as she let him run backward until he bumped into the gate. She waited patiently for him to settle there, then reeled him in with a slow tug and release on the rope, allowing the animal to come to her, rather than forcing it.

I was intrigued, impressed in a way I hadn't anticipated—not only with the lasso throwing, but with the measured, patient process that came afterward. It reminded me of something, but the thought was evasive, like a picture through a foggy window. I watched the curve of Lauren's body, the slow, patient movement of her hands as she fed the rope through her fingers, then took it in, took it in, took it in, let go a little. By the time Lucky Strike was within reach, he'd lowered his head, stopped snorting, and started licking his lips contentedly. He rolled a concerned eye toward the rest of us, but seemed completely comfortable with Lauren, as if some silent agreement had been formed between them, a bond only she and the animal understood.

Lucky Strike let out a long sigh as Lauren buckled a halter around his head and started to lead him toward the corral. The dull sound of applause reverberated from across the pasture, where a group of construction workers were watching us.

"Hey, Amber, can we have an autograph?" one of them hollered, and Amber trotted ahead to oblige. I fell into step beside Justin, following Lauren and the horse.

"That was good, the way she did that," Justin mused, swiping a hand across his forehead and tossing his hair as he checked out the oncoming thunderheads. "It was like the horse whisperer in the script."

"True," I agreed. Justin was right, but there was still a misty association to something else in my mind, and it irritated me that I couldn't put my finger on it. What did that scene, watching Lauren work the horse closer and closer, remind me of?

Justin went on talking. "When Dane comes here on Monday, we show me doing that stuff, and we'll have him in the bag. He sees how good that'll look on film, he won't be able to say no."

"You're going to learn to do that in a little over a week?"

I had a feeling skills like that took a lifetime to develop, and most people could probably work at it forever and never get it right. A big part of it was probably innate, a natural ability to understand the fears of a frightened, displaced, powerless creature, to see beyond the bluster, the self-defense mechanisms, and to understand—as *The Horseman* script poorly put it—that all communal creatures have an instinctive need to belong.

Looking ahead as Lauren led Lucky Strike through the gate into a round corral, where high pipe fences would safeguard the horse from further danger, I realized in a sudden, startling rush, why the capture scene had fascinated me. It reminded me of Mama Louise's house. Kids came in wild, defensive, hard, afraid down deep. They fought becoming part of the family because life had taught them, as it had taught Lucky Strike, that trust was to be avoided. Where relationships tended to end painfully, it was better to keep a safe distance.

From the moment a new kid came to Mama Louise's, she was there. She never laid on the pressure in a way that made you aware of it, that made you feel the need to run from it, but it was always present. A kind word, a pat on the back, a one-armed hug, a school paper taped to the refrigerator, a parent-teacher conference she showed up for, a basketball game in which you could see her waving a handmade sign with your name on it.

You'd never had a sign with your name on it before. . . .

A gentle tug on the rope, a beckoning that brought you out of the dark corners into the light of your own possibilities.

Suddenly, I wanted to call her, even though I hadn't talked to her in years. I wanted to tell her again that I was sorry Justin and I had taken off with the Comet the day after graduation. I wanted to tell her it wasn't because she'd failed with us, but because she'd succeeded. Without Mama Louise, I never would have had the courage to head for California and try to become a writer in the first place.

"You know, I was thinking maybe it'd be cool to name the basketball courts after Mama Louise," Justin said, and I had the eerie sense of having my mind read by Justin, of all people. If The Shay and I were thinking in parallel, then I needed a good shrink. "Remember how she used to make all those signs and go to the games?"

A disquieting déjà vu slipped over me. I'd just been thinking about the signs. "You hated it when she went to the games," I pointed out. Of all the kids I'd seen come and go through Mama Louise's, Justin was the least susceptible to her Mama magic. Justin just wanted to be left alone. A solo entity, too cool for school and just about everything else. He wouldn't have made it through his senior year at all if Mama Louise hadn't finally started walking him in the school door and following him around to his classes until she made her point. He could finish on his own, or he could finish with her on his tail.

He finally settled on a plan to have me complete most of his homework, which I did. The homework was easy, and I had to do my own, anyway. I figured what the heck, help a buddy out.

I never thought that twenty years later we'd be sharing the same brainwaves. Scary thought.

"I didn't really hate it when she came to the basketball games."

Justin had never admitted that before, at least not to me. Occasionally, I suspected that he might have told Stephanie things he'd never confided to anyone else. Before they split for good, Stephanie seemed to know quite a bit about our time at Mama Louise's. "I just . . . didn't want to get used to that kind of stuff, you know? I figured sooner or later she'd drop me off at the mall and never come back."

I stared at Justin, dumbfounded. I'd never, ever heard him admit that anything he did, any of his life patterns, might in any way be connected to the fact that his mother had abandoned him in a video arcade on his tenth birthday. The way I overheard it, she dropped him off with two dollars in change, told him she was headed to the store to get a birthday cake, took off with his little sister in hand, and never came back. He hung around all day waiting. At closing time, someone called child protective services, and that was that. He bounced around in foster kid limbo five years before ending up at Mama Louise's.

"She'd like it if you named the basketball courts after her," I said, and there was a weird tickle in the back of my nose. I pretended to study the oncoming storm, but found myself thinking ahead to the future of the ranch, to what it might mean to some kid who needed a safe place to be. Mama Louise would love it. "You ought to call her and tell her about it."

Justin nodded. "I thought she might like to fly out here— maybe pull the cover off the sign or break a champagne bottle on the fence—something like that. I could get her a plane ticket. I bet she's old by now, though."

I calculated the years gone by. "Well, about sixty-five, I'd guess. That's not so old."

"She's probably big as a house."

"She always was."

"Remember that red sweat suit she used to wear to the games? The guys used to sing 'Attack of the Killer Tomatoes' when she came in."

"Yeah, I remember." I could still picture Mama Louise decked out in her wind suit, out of breath from hustling across the parking lot, her caramel-colored skin glistening with a fine sheen of sweat beneath neatly-braided rows of hair that were gathered in the back and tied with a huge bow in our school colors. On game nights, she burst through the door like a force of nature, poster boards in one hand and an air horn in the other, yelling, *"We gonna play some basketball tonight! Where's my kids?"*

"I don't know why she did all that stuff." Justin cast a perplexed expression, as if he were earnestly trying to decipher something for which he had no frame of reference. We drifted to a halt by the big live oak tree, and he stared longingly up at his suspended cowboy hat. "I mean, CPS was gonna send her checks every month whether she put on the red suit and came to basketball games or not."

I guess she really cared, ran through my mind, but it sounded sappy, sentimental, and unmanly, so instead I said, "She probably wanted to make sure you were at the game, not out behind the gym lighting up."

"Yeah, you're probably right." Justin chuckled, and I was kind of glad, because this conversation was starting to feel mushy and vaguely uncomfortable. I wasn't used to seeing Justin so somber and reflective, so . . . serious. I was ready to move on to the pipe-fenced corral, where Willie Wardlaw, Frank, Frederico, and Mimi had gathered after getting out of their vehicle. Mimi frowned at the darkening sky, smoothing her silky hair with trepidation as the others watched from outside the fence. Inside, Lauren released Lucky Strike, and he ran back and forth along the opposite perimeter, staying as far away from the people as possible.

Bracing his hands on his hips, Justin sighed at his hat in the tree, then took in the horse and everything around him. "This place could be like Mama Louise's, only bigger." His shoulders rounded forward as if he felt the weight of the dream, and it was too big, too heavy. I knew that look on him. It was the look of moving out of a pie-in-the-sky manic phase and crashing back to reality. A binge of all things destructive and mind-numbing usually followed. Sometimes the low ride lasted a few days, sometimes it lasted a few months. Sometimes he landed in the hospital, and sometimes he came out of it on his own.

How many times had I told myself I wouldn't go on this ride with him again? Hence, the cabin in the mountains, the new and quiet life separate from the roller coaster ride that was Justin Shay. I didn't want to watch him try to blow himself up again. "Hey, you know, one step at a time," I said. "You've got to make friends with the horse first, right?"

"Yeah." I was hoping for another laugh, but I didn't get it. "I figure with all the publicity from the film, it won't be any problem to get people to donate to this place. We can put together a trailer about the foster shelter, attach it to the publicity, maybe have it roll after the credits. I want the ranch to have plenty of backing, you know, to keep it going in the future. I don't want it all to fall on Amber. She needs her money for her family."

A sense of disquiet settled in the corner of my consciousness, rumbling like the thunder. "Why would it fall on Amber?" As in, *Where will you be?* With Justin, you have to be careful how you ask questions if you want answers that are real and not pulled out of some past script somewhere.

He stared off into the distance for so long that I thought his thoughts had drifted off. "I just think one of these times I'll go down and maybe I won't come back."

Something clenched in my gut, because I knew exactly what he meant by *go down*. He meant that one of these days he'd take a ride on the party train and not get off. The textbook reaction from my end would have been to say something like, *Don't talk that way*, but there wasn't any point. Justin was going to do what Justin wanted to do, no matter what anybody said. "Let's focus on today," I urged, and I had the disturbing sense that this crazy project, *The Horseman*, the foster shelter, Mama Louise's basketball courts, was his way of trying to *keep* from going down—one final last-ditch effort. A commitment so huge, so important he couldn't bail on it. So insane, it couldn't possibly happen unless he held it together. "You've got a lot of work to do here. You have to build those basketball courts for Mama Louise."

Nodding, he straightened and took a breath, then glanced at Amber, who was headed our way across the pasture. "Guess we better get on it."

"Guess so," I agreed, happy to be back in safer territory, even if it did include one large impracticality in the form of *The Horseman*. How could I, in good conscience, continue encouraging him to believe this film was a good idea? Then again, how could I not? "Justin?" I said. When he turned my way, some idiotic comment about checking into rehab was on my tongue. Rehab never worked for him, because he didn't want it to. Most of the time he was more stoned in celebrity rehab than he was outside it.

"Yeah, Nate?"

"If you know you're going down, you tell me. Don't go there by yourself." So much for swearing off. So much for telling myself that no matter what, I wouldn't sign on for another one of Justin's frenetic roller coaster rides—up, down, up, down, then eventually off the edge, wherever the track ran out. I was right back there with him, climbing into the front car so I could pad the landing when he hit bottom.

The last time I tried to get between Justin and self-destruction, I ended up wrapped around a guardrail on the Pacific Coast Highway. I still wondered if the only reason he hadn't gunned it off the edge was because I was in the car with him. He wasn't looking to commit murder, just suicide.

A plethora of talk show truisms about codependency and destructive relationships ran through my mind. Dr. Phil would probably accuse me of being Justin's enabler, but Justin was perfectly able, all on his own. He was going on this trip, even if I didn't. The only question was whether I would opt for potential destruction or self-preservation.

Then again, what was there to preserve, really? A life in which I sat in a cabin, surrounded by pristine silence, trying to write something that mattered, but ending up with stuff that went straight in the trash? Afternoons spent with Oprah and Dr. Phil filling the room with white noise, so I could avoid the larger question that had whispered in my ear as we teetered on the guard rail, looking down at the ocean from what was left of Justin's slick red Ferrari.

Why am I here? If there isn't more to life than this, then why bother?

Yet, even as I was thinking it, I was trying to wake Justin and pull him from the car. I was thinking, *Just a few more minutes. Hang in there, buddy. I'm not ready to go yet.*

In my head, as those frantic seconds stretched out, Mama Louise was quoting bits of Scripture. I was surprised how clear they were when it really mattered.

Mama Louise was a firm believer. All those years ago, when I called to tell her I'd be sending her the money for the Comet, a little each paycheck, she said she didn't care about the money. She wanted me to repent in prayer, because she'd already forgiven us both.

She told me again I should stay away from Justin—the things that were broken in him could only be fixed by someone bigger than me.

At eighteen years old, the greater implications of that went right over my head. When I repeated the conversation to Justin later, I said she gave me some God talk, and the good news was that she hadn't called the police about the car, and she didn't intend to. We were in the clear, but I was going to send her five hundred for the car. He snorted and pointed out that the car had been just sitting beside the driveway doing nothing, until the two of us got it running. We did her a favor hauling it off. . . .

Amber caught up with us under the tree. "Looks like we mi-ight be in for a little weather." When no one answered right away, she shot a quizzical look back and forth between Justin and me, her brows lifting curiously over wide, blue china-doll eyes. "Is everythin' all ri-ight?"

"Yeah, fine," Justin said, then flashed her one of his hunk-o'-the-year grins the girls all loved, and added, "Come on, babe, let's go see the stupid horse." He looped an arm over her shoulders, and she didn't seem to mind, but she didn't snuggle in, either. She just tucked her hands in her pockets.

"You finish signing autographs?" he asked.

"I did," she answered. "I felt kinda bad, though. I meant to bring some tour T-shirts and CDs and stuff with me this mornin'. I forgot to grab the bag on my way out. Those guys work so hard all day."

Justin glanced down the fence toward the group of construction workers, now headed back to the ranch buildings. "They get paid. Man, I can't believe how much it costs to pay all of them. Let 'em buy their own CDs—we'll get some of it back."

Amber pulled away, frowning at him as if she wondered whether he meant it. She didn't know him very well. He meant it.

"That's not very ni-ice." She motioned in the direction of the departing workers. "The man in the red ball cap, Osvaldo, he's got a little girl in the hospital with cancer, and she's a big fan. She likes you, too. You could send her some of your movies, and then she wouldn't be bored all day long, layin' there in chemotherapy."

"Yeah, sure," Justin said. "No problem."

"I don't guess there's probably DVD players in the hospital, though," Amber observed as she and Justin started toward the gate, her petite red cowboy boots falling a little heavier under the weight of Justin's arm, or the DVD question, or both.

"We'll send her a DVD player, too," Justin offered.

Amber was pleased. A bouncy mass of blond hair twirled over her shoulder as she smiled up at him. "That's a super idea. One of those little kind from Wal-Mart you can use in your car or anyplace. I got my baby brother one for his birthday."

"Cool," Justin said.

Amber glanced over her shoulder, like she'd just realized I wasn't following. I was standing under the tree, watching the interaction between the two of them and thinking that she was way too nice to get involved with The Shay. He'd destroy her before all of this was over.

"You comin', Nate?" she asked.

I waved an affirmative and started toward the round corral, where Lucky Strike was galloping along the pipe fence, alternately pinning his ears and charging at the spectators. Lauren stepped toward him, and the horse reared onto his hind legs and pawed the air. I found myself quickening my pace in spite of the pad of burrs now compacted into the soles of my flip-flops. It didn't seem like Lauren should be locked in with the horse when he was in a mood like that. Now that he was trapped and separated from the other horses, Lucky Strike was even more agitated than before. With his dark brown coat sweat-streaked and foamy, he looked like the dangerous renegade from some late-night western rerun—*Fury* or *The Black Stallion*.

This would be the scene where the man-killer horse injured its inadvertently trusting trainer. . . .

Lauren didn't seem worried.

Taking a spot on the fence with the rest of the group, I studied the details of the scene as Lauren slowly worked the horse toward submission. I took in the horse's eye, the trainer's eye, the slight movements of her body, the responses of the horse, the silent way she guided and directed the animal's actions, built a bridge of communication where there had been fear. I took in the coppery glint of sunlight on Lauren's hair, the sheen on the horse's coat. Overhead, clouds blotted the sun as the minutes ticked by. Shadows slid over Lauren's skin, skimming her shoulder, her arm, her waist, soundlessly circling her, stroking the horse with silent fingers, pulling them closer, as if neither felt the wind rise or heard the thunder rumble, as if there were nothing in the world but the two of them, and all that mattered was unity.

Watching Lauren slowly break down the barriers, I understood the magic that the screenplay had tried, and failed, to convey. Together, she and the horse were poetry in motion, a carefully composed sonnet of shadow and light, of breath and body, fear and trust.

When Lucky Strike came to her in the center of the ring, this time with no lariat, with no restraint of any kind, a collective hush fell over the onlookers. Even Mimi stopped prattling about having felt a raindrop and gasped, "Oh, look."

I hadn't even realized Mimi was talking until she stopped.

Frederico muttered something in Italian. I didn't know what it was, but in my mind it translated to, *Wow, that was incredible.*

As quickly as the moment came, it was gone, fleeting like something so bright and clear the eye shouldn't take it in for long. A streak of lightning split the sky overhead, the horse bolted, and rain started to fall in earnest. Our first lesson in horse whispering was over almost before it began.

Willie, Frank, and Lauren took the horse to the barn, and the rest of us scattered to our respective vehicles to wait out the rain. I took shelter in the Horsemanmobile with Justin and Amber, although after the fact I wished I'd made another choice, because when the rain persisted and we left the ranch, I became a hapless prisoner on an unlikely mission to the nearest Wal-Mart to purchase DVDs and DVD players for children in a nearby cancer ward. After a few rather strange phone calls and an extensive buying spree at several stores, we burst into the children's wing like Santa Claus after a technology conference. We surprised Osvaldo's daughter, then handed out DVDs, equipment, and autographs up and down the hall before gathering the children in the rec room to sing several songs.

When the fun was over, and the children—including Justin—were tired, we headed back to Daily. We ended up at Frank's ranch with Willie, Mimi, Frederico, and Frank. Frank burned hamburgers for us, and we talked horseman talk as the storm rolled away, leaving behind a sunset that was bigger than life. While the others stood on the back porch enjoying it, I perused the living room, taking in dusty picture frames with rodeo championship belt buckles inside, and a collection of award saddles perched here and there around the room like furniture. One of them had Lauren's name on it—*1989 Daily Goat Tying Champion, Won by Lauren Eldridge*. A picture of Lauren hung on the wall above. She was mounted on a big gray horse, a little girl with a big smile, a smudge of dirt across her nose, and curly ponytails. She was wearing pink chaps and a big cowboy hat, holding her leg out of the way to display the printing on the saddle. There were similar pictures throughout the house, sprinkled among dusty haphazard displays of rodeo memorabilia, outdated calendars, and family photos. But the most interesting thing about the house wasn't so much what *was* there, as what wasn't.

Even though we remained through supper and for several hours afterward, Lauren never showed.

Chapter 11

Lauren Eldridge

I couldn't face driving the road to my father's house, especially with a storm brewing overhead, so I did the grownup thing and made excuses when our first session with Lucky Strike rained out. Yelling through the rain with my car window down, I told Dad I was going to visit with Aunt Netta and Imagene for a while, then I drove away before he could protest. By the time I got back to the hotel, he'd already called Aunt Netta to see if I'd "made it home all right," but what he really meant was that Aunt Netta should baby-sit me through my first thunderstorm back home. No doubt he was afraid I'd suffer some kind of sad flashback to the night of the flood and feel the need to run away again.

Actually, it turned out to be a good afternoon. Any afternoon spent in the Daily Hair and Body with Aunt Donetta, Lucy, and Imagene was guaranteed to be a good one, and entertaining, which was the reason I went there in the first place. We visited with the regular Friday cut and curl customers, ate pecan pie Imagene brought over from the café, did yoga with a hunky on-tape muscle man who looked like Frederico, and spent the remainder of our time discussing whether or not to cancel tonight's big feed at Aunt Donetta's place, due to the weather. After the decision was made, along with a number of cancellation phone calls, Uncle Ronald was instructed to pull Mr. Ham from the oven and turn off the timer, and the big feed was delayed until tomorrow, which was just as well, because that would give us a chance to call even more people. With no plans for the evening, we went to Imagene's house to admire her vegetable garden in the rain, eat leftover pork chops, and watch tapes of *Dancing With the Stars*—a girls' night, Aunt Netta called it.

When it was over, Aunt Netta shuttled me back to the hotel, rather than to her house. "We just went ahead and moved yer stuff to room 5. There's no sense you stayin' with all that junk in my sewin' room when we got empty space at the hotel." I smelled a rat, because she scanned the alley as we passed and muttered, "Now, I wonder where those boys are. . . ."

"Probably still at Dad's," I answered, and hopped out of the car before she could proceed with instructing me to look after her celebrity customers, or whatever else she was cooking up. "You know Dad. He'll keep them up all night, telling rodeo stories."

Aunt Netta frowned, showing obvious displeasure. "I hate for you to be stuck here alone. . . ."

"Aunt Netta, I'm fine," I said quickly. "In fact, I have some grades to finish up and post online, so I can use a few hours of quiet. Thanks for the girls' night." We shared a hand-hug through the window, and I trotted into the hotel, waving a quick toodle-oo to let her know I'd be just fine on my own, no matter where *those boys* were or when they returned to the hotel.

I spent the evening listening to the whispers of the old building while finishing my grade book online and then crashed early, dead to the world—a victim of a short night and a long day.

On Saturday morning we repeated the procedure from the day before—breakfast meeting at the café, drive to the ranch, unsettled horse in the round pen while the would-be horseman looked on sourly, Willie touted the horse's potential, and Amber murmured encouragement.

Just as Lucky Strike was beginning to settle in to our work-out, Aunt Donetta's voice squealed through the barnyard and sent the horse skittering to the far side of the enclosure. "How-deee! I canceled some wash-and-curls so I could come watch. Did I miss anythin'?"

She appeared at the fence in a flurry of bright clothes and big hair, and trailing a cloud of perfume that remained potent even in the open air. Aunt Donetta never made a subtle entrance anywhere she went. When she showed up at the last minute for Sunday services at Daily Baptist Church, the organist usually just stopped playing prelude music, because the fact was that no one could meditate while Aunt Netta was on her way up the aisle shaking hands, kissing babies, and inquiring after the health of people who had been on the prayer list.

Eventually, Brother Ervin would move to the pulpit and make some joke like, *Well, Donetta's here, now we can get started.* Aunt Netta would laugh and bat a hand, like she couldn't imagine what he was talking about, then she'd slip into the Eldridge pew, third row on the left, all the while explaining over the heads of Betty Prine and the sour-faced old ladies of the Daily Literary Society why she hadn't made it to church until the last minute.

She always had some wild story—stray kitten in the ditch by the road, downed electric line she had to report, old Mrs. Kaufer's house still dark at ten-thirty in the morning so Aunt Donetta thought she'd better stop by and check on things, the mayor's basset hound, Flash, on the lam around town again, a rattlesnake in the truck engine, which buzzed all the way to town and scared Aunt Netta so bad she had to exit the cab via the ventilation slider in the rear window. Halfway through her escape, she thought she'd end up wedged for good, but prayer and the sound of that snake propelled her past the impossibly small opening and into the bed of the truck. It was a Sunday morning miracle, and sure enough, when Brother Ervin and the men went outside, there was a six-foot rattlesnake, looking strangely addled and oddly biblical, there on the church lawn. Baily Henderson, Tam Moody, and my brother, Kemp, captured it in a trash can, and Aunt Donetta won the rattlesnake roundup at the Daily Reunion Days the next week. The sign on her entry read,

Division: Largest Individual Snake
Submitted by: Donetta Bradford
Capture method: Pickup Truck

It was Aunt Donetta's first and only time to be awarded the Daily Rattlesnake Roundup badge of honor—a custom-embroidered ball cap, a recycled trophy that had a cow on top, and a new .22 rifle, courtesy of Barlinger's Hardware. Aunt Donetta gave the ball cap to Kemp because it wouldn't fit over her hair, and she traded the rifle (over Uncle Ronald's protests), for a new Salad Shooter and a gift certificate. She kept the trophy and displayed it on a shelf in the beauty shop as a conversation piece.

"How's everybody doin'?" she inquired as she elbowed her way up to the fence beside Mimi. Nate moved to let her have his spot, but she insisted they all snuggle together in the gap between posts. "Oh, hon," she said to Nate. "You don't want to miss any of this. The things Puggy can do with a horse are just . . . well . . . amazin'."

I had the mortifying realization that she'd just used *the nickname*. Right there in front of everyone. Good gravy. Next she'd be telling the potty training story.

"Puggy?" Nate repeated, and I realized the subject wasn't going to die a quick and painless death.

"Oh, sure." Aunt Netta was happy to strike up a conversation, even at my expense. "When she come out of her mama, her poor little face was all flattened up and she had a cone-shaped head, bless her heart. Her daddy looked into that hospital bassinet and said, 'Kind of a pug-nosed little thing, ain't she? Hello there, little puggy.' She was cute as a bug, looked like a little pink baby piglet, and the funniest pug nose, just like this." My attention ricocheted from the horse as Aunt Donetta provided a visual aid, of all things. "But she grew out of it just fine. The nickname stuck, a'course. She always was a big eater, so it kinda fit, even after the nose got normal."

Please, embarrass me a little more. Blood rushed into my face, and the muscles in my arms tensed. The horse shifted away, sensing the change.

"She doesn't look like such a big eater," Mimi said. Apparently, now that the subject had turned to diet and exercise, she was willing to join in.

I tried to focus on the horse again. I could feel the rapport breaking down, his body stiffening, preparing for flight. His ears flicked toward the side of the corral, where Mimi had started chronicling her fitness regimen.

"Well, hon, some people just get high metabolism right outta the gate," Aunt Donetta remarked. "I was always thin, until I got old and fat."

"I have a protein supplement and a workout routine that is very good for the mature woman," Frederico offered.

"Well, sugar, sign me up!" Aunt Donetta clapped her hands

together enthusiastically, and that was all it took—Lucky Strike shied away again, practically ran over me, and proceeded to the opposite fence, where he began pacing back and forth.

"See, that's what he does," Willie complained, slapping the pipe fence in frustration. "All day long, all night unless he's dead asleep, or you put a halter on him and tie him up. In the stall, he weaves back and forth, back and forth. You put him in a pen, he runs his legs off, up and down the fence, up and down the fence. He don't ever settle. I ain't never seen a colt so bad. It's no wonder he couldn't go back on the track. He's always sore in the front end from pacing his fool head off all the time. I didn't know those things when I bought into the horse. They had him so drugged up, he was just standin' there in the stall, asleep on his feet."

I stood watching the animal's behavior, getting a dismal sense of the possibilities ahead. Lucky Strike was what horsemen call *a weaver*. He repeated the same pattern over and over and over, his eyes slowly going glassy, his countenance numb. Finally, he stopped calling out to the other horses, but continued pacing up and down the fence, repeating the pattern like an autistic child self-stimulating in an effort to block out everything else. At this rate, and having already shown a propensity for bone injury, he would eventually do enough damage to his legs to make himself completely nonfunctional. He would end up where useless but well-insured horses tend to—mysteriously dead in his stall, so that a hefty insurance claim could be filed.

There was no telling what had been done to the horse to keep him racing after his body began breaking down. Some techniques used with racehorses were gruesome and borderline inhumane. No wonder he didn't like people. The trick now was to convince him that it was safe to trust, to move beyond the trauma of the past.

Such a hard lesson to convey, coming from someone who didn't believe it anymore.

Glancing at my father, I shook my head, but he only nodded encouragement and gave me the thumbs-up. Dad had always specialized in lost causes of the animal sort. The horses in the trailer the night of the flood were the offspring of a little gray mare my father bought at the auction barn. She staggered into the sale ring on her last legs, just a yearling, so thin and sick even the slaughter buyers didn't want her. My father wasn't sure Maggie would survive the ride home, but when she did, he charged Kemp and me with her care. He said if she didn't make it, she at least deserved the dignity of dying with someone stroking her head and speaking softly in her ear—it wasn't right for a creature to leave this world without ever having known kindness.

Maggie recovered and carried me through the 4-H horse shows and trail rides of my childhood, and when I went away to college, my father sent her with me so I wouldn't get lonely and decide to drive home every weekend. He had no idea that, with Maggie staying at a stable near the college, I'd eventually fall for a boy who liked to compete in rodeos and rope calves, and one thing would lead to another. It wasn't a problem until Danny's application to veterinary school was denied, and he decided that he really wanted to do rodeos, anyway. His plan was to hit it hard, try to make the finals and get some endorsement deals.

After a short hesitation when his parents told him they wouldn't be sending him any more money if he didn't pursue a degree, he did what he wanted to do. One thing about Danny—he was never afraid to go for it. That character trait drew me in like a fly to fresh honey. There was always in me the latent sense that life was on a short timeline, perhaps because our years with my mother had come and gone so quickly. Now, having already passed the age at which she died, I was realizing that you don't live your parents' lives, you live your own. . . .

As Lucky Strike weaved back and forth along the opposite fence, it crossed my mind that even while I was away, I'd imagined the events that might eventually bring me back to Daily—a funeral, the big family reunion Aunt Donetta always claimed she was going to plan one of these days, a health problem with Aunt Netta or my father, maybe Kemp finally finding the right girl and planning a wedding.

The filming of a movie wasn't anywhere on the list. Any minute now, I would come back to reality and realize I was daydreaming in my office. . . .

The idea wore a prickly coating of disappointment. I didn't want to wake up at my desk, spend the day cooped up in a classroom. As strange as it seemed, given my feelings about coming home in the first place, I wanted this to be real. It felt good to be in a place where the rocks and the trees, the scents and the sounds, the buildings and the people were familiar. I knew these horizons—the jagged hills, the spiny yuccas and prickly pears, the prairie grasses that hid the scattered seeds of bluebonnets, which would provide the first colors of spring next year. I knew the hidden places that sheltered neighbors' ranch houses and old pioneer farms, now crumbling with age and sinking into the landscape. I knew where the thunderheads would blow over the rim when fronts came in, where the wet weather creeks would form, how quickly they would rise up . . .

I stopped before moving through the thick, dark pool of self-recrimination that told me I, of all people, should have known how quickly Caney Creek could take in rainwater off the hills, grow, and become deadly.

Don't do this. Just enjoy the day. Stay focused.

I took in a breath, exhaled, thought only about what was inside the round pen, not what was outside. *Only this moment. Nothing beyond . . .*

Moving toward the fence, I began to slip into a rhythm, maintaining a comforting calm that drew the horse closer. I was aware of Willie outside the fence, calling Justin over to stand next to him, then explaining the process of resistance-free training. "Now, you see, young fella, that horse—even though he's lived all his life in a stall—somewhere inside him, he's got the instincts of a herd animal. See how Lauren's pushin' him away each time he don't act right? That's what a mare will do to a bad-behaved colt, or a herd sire will do to a unruly yearlin'. Horses'll isolate one of their own to punish him for not behavin' in a good way. They know the worst kind of punishment for most any critter is isolation. See, Lucky Strike don't like that, because his instincts are tellin' him he ain't safe out there on his own. In the wild, a horse knows that if he's by hisself, he's vulnerable. He needs the rest of the herd to survive, to be safe from mountain lions and other predators and all forms of danger."

To my complete surprise, Justin Shay began to ask questions. "Is she making him move up and down the fence now, or is he doing that on his own?"

"Nah, that's her," my father said, joining in the horse-whispering conversation. "Watch how she steps toward the front of him just the littlest bit to bring him around and head him the other way. She's lettin' him know who's dominant here. She's makin' it a lot of work for him to stay out there on the fence, pacin' back and forth and lookin' off at nothin'."

"Like the guy in the script," Justin observed. "But in the script, he just does it once, and then the horse starts following him around the corral."

"Real life ain't as easy as the movies," Willie pointed out. "Some indavi'jals are smarter than others, some more stubborn, and some's been through more trauma in the past. Sometimes a creature's been hurt so bad he figures it'd be better to run hisself to death than to let anybody get close to him again. It ain't much different between horses and people, when you get right down to it, son." Willie's usually gruff voice grew soft, almost tender, strangely wise. "We're all products of our experiences, see? We do according to what we've learnt. Every livin' creature is born with a need to trust and a need for self-defense. Which one wins out depends on how that animal gets treated by life and by people. Once them habits are formed, they're hard to break, but it ain't impossible to change. A good horse whisperer don't have an agenda. He lets the horse progress at his own pace. That's the difference between a horse trainer and real horseman. A real horseman don't want to break the animal, he wants to win it over."

"That needs to be in the script," Justin murmured contemplatively. "Nate, that needs to be in the script."

"Yeah," Nate muttered. He'd moved to the other side of the corral, so that he was standing by himself, his arms hooked loosely on the fence. I could feel him watching me, studying the process, the movements of the horse, then me again.

I glanced over my shoulder just before Lucky Strike finally stopped pacing and dropped his head. My eyes met Nate's and I felt the intensity of his gaze travel through me like an electrical current.

I turned back to the horse. *Stay focused. Stay focused.* . . .

"Watch this," my father whispered as Lucky Strike turned toward me again. The pride in his voice made me swell inside. I had always wanted, above all things, to make my father proud.

"Wow," Amber whispered.

"We need that in the screenplay, Nate," Justin said again. "Nate?"

Nate didn't answer. I didn't have to look at him to know why. I could feel his gaze in every part of me. I could feel him searching, thinking, wondering. When Lucky Strike disconnected and moved away again, he moved in Nate's direction. I lost track of the horse, found myself looking at Nate instead. I wondered what he was thinking. Was he considering the scene, imagining how it would play out on film, calculating stage direction, and camera angles, and dialogue, or was he thinking about something else?

I wanted it to be something else. I wanted the way he studied me to be something more than writer's curiosity.

The thought surprised me, and as soon as it solidified into something I could identify, I chased it away like a stray dog on the porch. What was I thinking? What was wrong with me? Had anybody else noticed me staring at him?

"It's a God-given gift." Aunt Donetta was on the ragged edge of tears. She'd moved around the perimeter to stand by Nate. "It's so good to see Puggy with a horse again. Ain't she amazin', Nate? Ever since she was little, she could make friends with any livin' creature, no matter how scared it was, I'll tell you. When the sheriff had a stray dog he couldn't catch, you know who he'd come get. . . ."

My stomach twisted into a slipknot. Aunt Donetta had seen. She'd picked up on the look between Nate and me. She'd sniffed it out like a fox scenting fresh eggs. Now she was up on her tiptoes tracking down the source so she could burrow under the fence, get inside, and find something meaty.

I tried to ignore the spectators and concentrate on the horse, but all I could hear was my aunt giving a resume of sorts. Nate was getting the short course in Eldridge 101, with an emphasis on Puggyology. "Puggy's so good with horses . . . why, she was toddling out to the horse pen before she could even talk . . . Even when she was up in middle school, all she ever wanted to do was hang around the barn with her daddy. We wondered if she'd ever figure out she was a girl. She was such a cute little thing, but you couldn't melt her down and pour her into a dress. Just jeans and boots. We thought she'd never take an interest in boys, but . . ."

"Aunt Netta!" I protested under my breath. "You're distracting the horse."

"Oh," she whispered, as if she didn't know people in the next county could hear. "Sorry, hon. I just thought Nate might want to use some of that background in his movie writin'. You know, a good horseman's born, not made, my granddaddy always used to say. That's sure true about Lauren. . . ." Aunt Netta went right on talking.

Nate listened and occasionally asked questions.

I gave up and went back to working with the horse, moving him up and down the fence again and getting him to stop on command. Things were looking up—until Justin Shay decided we'd wasted enough time tinkering. Stepping into the round pen, he smacked the gate shut behind himself and sent the horse into another tailspin. Lucky Strike proceeded to shy away and weave up and down the opposite fence at a gallop, blowing and tossing his head.

Justin flashed a hand in the horse's direction. "Why's he doing that? I thought you had him calm."

It seemed like we'd been through this question several times before. "When you came into the round pen, the stimulus changed. He reacted. Part of building rapport is learning to anticipate the effect your actions will have on the horse."

Justin Shay's mirrored sunglasses swiveled slowly in my

direction, and his mouth dropped open, silently saying, *Somebody tell this . . . this person who she's talking to.* "I don't have time for this idiotic . . . shhh . . . stuff."

"It takes time," I admitted. "Habits don't change easily. That's why they're habits. You have to remember that the horse can't talk to you and explain how he feels. Animals show feelings through body language."

"I don't have time for someone else's feelings!" he exploded, and if the hideousness of that statement struck him at all, it didn't show. It struck me, but not in a way I would have predicted. I was taken aback by the realization that those words had been quietly cycling through the back of my mind for two years now, only I hadn't really heard them until Justin Shay put a voice to it. Since the accident, my existence had been a carefully executed strategy of insulating myself from everyone else's needs so I could focus on my own. I didn't want to deal with anything beyond my pain, my guilt. In the process, I'd made my world so small that there was nothing else in it—just me in a condo, going through a routine that seemed undemanding, yet felt exhausting. No energy for family, friends, relationships, even for the students I professed to care about. I showed up for class, gave them what my contract stipulated, then crawled back into my hiding place and went numb.

On the fence, Willie was worried about the ongoing breakdown in communication. "Now, son," he soothed, perhaps concerned that Lucky Strike was once again about to be fired. "Anything worth doin' is worth puttin' time into. Just give Striker some time. He'll make a horseman out of 'ya, if you'll let him."

Justin seemed to consider the comment, and there was a sense of collective breath holding among the audience, a realization that everything hinged on the whims of a temperamental superstar who was more unpredictable even than the horse.

Finally the would-be horseman took a breath and let it out slowly. "Tell me what I'm supposed to do."

I paused to confront a minor internal conflict over whether I wanted this project to fail or to succeed. Maybe it was best to convince Justin Shay that he should move his production to Hollywood and hire a stunt double to play the horseman. With a snap of his fingers, he could probably buy out my father and Willie. Dad would be safe, and everything could go back to normal.

Back to the way things were . . .

The way things were seemed impossibly small now, like a suit that had shrunk in the wash, so that it didn't fit comfortably anymore.

"Watch his ears. The ears will always tell you where his attention is. Body language doesn't lie," I heard myself say.

"Okay, watch his ears. What else?" The movie star rubbed his hands together impatiently, ready for the next step. Unfortunately, Lucky Strike wasn't in agreement. Justin was quickly frustrated again, and the horse went back to pacing the fence.

Over the course of the next two hours, it became clear that Lucky Strike's personality and Justin's were very much alike. Progress was one step forward and two steps back. Somebody was always mad at somebody else.

By lunchtime, all of us were ready for a break. I was glad when Joe, who lived in an apartment above the barn and looked after the horses at night, informed us that lunch had arrived. We were all happy to halt the horse-training lesson and proceed to the open-air tent, where food was being set out for the construction crew and volunteers.

My father and Willie led the way, muttering and talking

among themselves. Amber lagged behind, compelled, as usual, to cast a little ray of sunshine on the seemingly hopeless situation. "That was so interestin' to watch," she said as we crossed the barnyard. "All that stuff you said, too. I think every bit of that should be in the movie."

"Thanks," I said absently. I was focused on a sky-blue minivan bouncing up the driveway with a cloud of caliche dust billowing behind like white smoke.

"I think *you* did real good, too, Justin," Amber went on. Justin didn't respond, so she turned her attention to the minivan. "Oh, there's Mrs. Doll. It's so nice of her to come deliver the drinks and desserts every day to go with the stuff the churches bring out. The food oughta be super good today. It's from Caney Creek Church. Those ladies can put together a feed. When I got up this mornin', Pastor Harve already had the smoker goin' down there. I could smell it all the way from my house. Peepaw took some vegetables from his and Mrs. Doll's gardens and went down to help do the cookin'."

Amber continued on with some story about Pastor Harve's barbecue, but I didn't hear it. My mind had hopscotched to a screeching halt on the words *Caney Creek Church* and *Pastor Harve*. Suddenly I couldn't breathe.

Ahead, Imagene pulled her van up to the tent, and members of the little African-American church on Caney Creek came out to help her unload coolers and pie boxes. The blood drained from my head and my body went cold. I found myself searching, almost frantically, for Pastor Harve, for his wife, Miss Beedie, for Teylina and Otis Charles. If they saw me here, how would they feel? What would they say if they walked out of the tent, on a perfectly beautiful, perfectly normal day, and saw the person who was responsible—as responsible as anyone—for the loss they had mourned for two years now? A son taken away from a mother and a father, a husband taken from his wife, a father taken from his son and daughter. Harvard Jr. never had the chance to see O.C. suit up with the UT football team. He missed watching Teylina cheer on the sidelines of the high school games. He wasn't there to walk her across the field at homecoming, all because he came to block off the low-water crossing five minutes too late.

If they saw me here, they would be reminded of that night. . . .

"I need to . . . do some things . . . in the barn." The words were cottony and rough in my throat. I didn't wait for an answer—just turned and hurried off, feeling sick. Amber said something, but I couldn't hear her, couldn't process the words. Blood was pounding in my ears, and all I could do was keep walking—escaping, just like Lucky Strike, to the far side of the world.

Inside the barn, I leaned against the wall, closed my eyes, pressed a hand over the hollow place in my chest, tried to catch my breath. *Calm down, calm down,* I told myself. *It's been two years. . . .*

But in my mind, it was yesterday. I could still see Harvard in his deputy's uniform, a big man silhouetted against the head-lights as he tied a rope to his waist and secured the other end to his cruiser. He seemed to move in slow motion, my vision of him dimming behind a haze of pain. I was so cold, so tired.

He lifted a hand, shouted something I couldn't hear, then he started toward me. I watched him come closer, his body rocking as he struggled against the current. In a flash of lightning, I saw his face, felt comfort, felt hope. I knew he wouldn't stop until he'd gotten me out. Finally, I could hear him calling to me to hang on, hang on, just a little longer.

And then, in a swirl of water and a mass of debris, he was gone. I clung where I was, searching as the creek churned in the sheen of the cruiser's glow. There was nothing. Nothing but a slice of water in the headlights, darkness beyond, rain, noise, thunder. A siren wailed out of view, its voice struggling to rise over the storm, growing closer until a fire truck flashed against the sky. . . .

Stop, I told myself. *Stop.* Tears filled my eyes as I tried to push the scene from my mind, to step back into the present. *It's over. You can't go back and change it.*

I knew it in my head, but my heart wouldn't resign itself.

Footsteps on the gravel outside the barn pushed into my thoughts. I wiped my eyes, pinched color into my cheeks, and grabbed a halter off the wall, mentally preparing an excuse for skipping lunch. *Oh, I wasn't hungry. . . . I don't feel so well. . . . I wanted to work with the horse while things were quiet. . . .*

The footsteps continued past the barn door, and I heard a corral gate open, then close. Setting down the halter, I went outside.

Nate was trotting across the pasture in his flip-flops. Curious, I slipped from the barn, moved silently through the gate to the small square corral beside the round pen, then stopped at the pasture fence. Nate paused beneath the big live oak tree. Bracing his hands on the droopy waistband of his shorts, he stood looking up into the tree or at the sky, I couldn't tell which.

He turned and saw me there, and I was caught surprisingly off guard. *Say something, Lauren.* "Is . . . uhhh . . . everything all right?"

He nodded toward the tree. "Thought I'd get the Shaymeister's hat down." He smiled, his teeth straight and white against a California tan. "He keeps looking over here. I think he figures the horse might like him better with a cowboy hat."

I laughed, thinking of how the hat had ended up in the tree. "Well, you know what they say—the hat makes the man." At this point, anything was worth a try. "There's probably a ladder in the barn."

"Hey, no need."

The next thing I knew Nate was climbing an overhanging branch, like Tarzan. I stood there playing Jane, dumbfounded as he made it to the trunk of the tree, shinnied to the other side, shook the branch that held the hat, and succeeded in knocking it free. As the cowboy hat drifted to the ground, Nate traversed the downward arch of the branch like a gymnast on a balance beam. Finally, he jumped to the ground in a maneuver that looked fairly insane, but which he actually did very well.

"Previous circus experience?" I asked as he completed the rescue and joined me at the fence.

Chuckling, he dropped the hat over a post, then rested his elbows on the rail a few feet from me, shaking his head. "Nah, saw it on a TV western once." He winked, and I felt something inside me quicken. "Don't tell The Shay who got his hat down, all right? Wouldn't want him to think I'm getting soft."

"Your secret's safe with me." I met his gaze, wondering at the relationship between the two of them. They were more than just writer and actor, star and groupie. No matter what bill of goods he and Justin Shay were trying to sell my father and the rest of the Dailyians, there was more going on with this *Horseman* project than met the eye.

Chapter 12

Nathaniel Heath

Puggy was looking at me in a slightly discerning, slightly curious way that made me feel vaguely uncomfortable. In general, guys don't like it when a woman looks at them like that—all right, maybe some sensitive, post-modern, in-touch-with-the-feminine-side guys do, but I don't. Guys like me like girls like Mimi, who look at you with the dewy eyes of a Rodgers-and-Hammerstein starlet and bat long lashes as in, *You're my hero. Sweep me away with your manly brilliance, big boy.*

Lauren didn't appear to be swept away. Considering that I'd just done a pretty impressive job of tree-climbing *and* rescued a stranded hat, that was a little disappointing. I liked her better early in the morning, when she was still a little groggy, distracted and off her game. Here in the horse corral, she was in her element, and unfortunately, I wasn't. I had the feeling she was working me like she worked the horse, maneuvering toward some goal I wouldn't figure out until I'd already stepped into the trap. She wasn't just here to play horse trainer to the stars. She wanted something.

"Guess we should proceed on to lunch," I said. "The food

looks good over there. By now, the line should be winding down." When I'd walked over with Justin a few minutes before, it was crowded under the tent with all the workers, plus a dozen or so volunteer servers from the little church next to Amber's house, and their leader, Pastor Harve.

Justin hadn't seemed to mind the crowd in the tent. He enjoyed the unqualified adoration of the masses as the workers offered handshakes and the serving ladies asked him to autograph napkins donated by the Hungry Hog. In between signing napkins, he used a pallet stack near the food table as a stage and proceeded to salute the hard work everyone was contributing, thank the church and Imagene Doll for the food, and introduce the crew of *The Horseman*, as if he were M. Harrison Dane himself. He referred to me as "Nathaniel Heath, who writes the screenplays that make all us actors look so good."

The crowd cheered, and I felt like a sham. A big woman in a bright red muumuu pushed her way through the commotion and introduced herself as Miss Lulu. She told me she was the choir director at Caney Creek Church, and if I needed a choir in the movie, she could supply one. Then she bear-hugged me in a way that performed some sort of chiropractic miracle, because when she set me down, the tightness in my back was gone and I was an inch taller.

The old pastor was a friendly guy—hunched over with age yet with a deep, resonant voice that sounded like Mufasa from *The Lion King*. Thinking of *The Lion King* reminded me of the old movie and Broadway show tapes Mama Louise liked to play for the kids. That thought reminded me that she never let us touch a meal before she said grace over it. Realizing that made me wonder how many meals I'd eaten in the past twenty years that hadn't been properly graced . . . three times a day, times three hundred and sixty-five days per year, times twenty years . . .

When Justin finished his speech, Pastor Harve blessed the upcoming movie production, Justin for bringing such a fine thing to Daily, Texas, and Justin's friend (me) for taking time out from Hollywood to come here and write a film that would make a difference to Daily, the foster shelter, and probably the whole world. I had this weirdly guilty feeling that ruined my appetite, and when I opened my eyes, every one of those women in the serving line had Mama Louise's face. They were all looking at me, their eyes whispering with silent voices, *You're a liar, Nate Heath. You know this ship is headed for an iceberg, and you're just letting everyone party on until it hits. . . .*

I saw Donetta and Imagene headed my way, and I got out of there. I decided to rescue Justin's hat from the tree, on the vague theory that a random act of kindness might balance out twenty years of ungraced food and two days of misleading a bunch of very nice people into thinking their town would become famous.

It hadn't occurred to me that Lauren might be hanging around the barn until she caught me planning to climb the hat tree. Interestingly, she wasn't in any hurry to get to the food tent, either. She seemed more inclined to stand there talking.

"So, you're missing lunch," I observed, leaning on the fence next to The Shay's newly rescued cowboy hat. "Better hurry. That construction crew looks like it can put away a bunch of barbecue."

"I had . . . some things to do out here."

The evasive answer intrigued me. Why, I couldn't say. Maybe I wondered why she was hanging out at the barn instead of sharing in the festivities. "Anything I can help with?" Then again, maybe I was just hovering there because she was pretty . . . for a serious kind of girl.

She frowned at a bird skittering across the corral. I watched the way the light played on her skin, the way her eyelashes brushed her cheek. Her eyes flicked upward. They caught the light and turned the soft color of tarnished copper as she took me in. Then she turned to the bird again. "I don't want to keep you from lunch." For a nanosecond, I'd had the impression she was about to say something else.

"I'm scared to go back. I'm afraid Miss Lulu will hug me again."

She laughed, and I liked the sound of it. She was beautiful when she smiled. It didn't seem like she laughed enough. "You should see her at the Chamber of Commerce Christmas dance when they get out the eggnog and the mistletoe. Nobody's safe."

The mental image made me shudder. It occurred to me that even though Lauren seemed strangely uneasy here, she had history with these people. This bizarre, crazy, wildly friendly little town was her home. Watching her now, I wondered what that would be like. How would it feel to grow up in just one place—a place where everybody knew everything about everybody, where you knew who to avoid when somebody spiked the eggnog at the community Christmas shindig? "Thanks for the tip. If I happen by the Chamber of Commerce around Christmas, I'll be sure to avoid the mistletoe."

She gave me a surprised look. "Christmas?" she repeated, seeming incredulous. "You'll be working on the screenplay that long? My father gave me the impression they might start filming any day." She quirked an eyebrow in a way that reminded me of my high school principal, Mrs. Dickson. When Mrs. Dickson asked a question, you might as well have been strapped to a polygraph. She had a look that dared you to give anything but the truth.

For a girl who handled horses with such kid gloves, Lauren was pretty forthright when it came to people.

"Justin's . . ." *a moron entertaining an impractical cowboy fantasy that will soon enough lose its luster.* ". . . making it sound a little more . . . automatic than it really is. Putting together a deal, selling the money men on it, attaching the big names, and casting the talent takes time."

Lauren stiffened, her chin lifting. "So, this movie might never happen." It wasn't a question. It wasn't a statement. It was more like . . . an accusation.

I felt like a witness on the stand—the reluctant kind of witness who has to be subpoenaed, and still doesn't want to get involved. I was torn between being honest and just letting nature take its course. Who was I to say, anyway? In Hollywood, stupid projects got made all the time. "He has M. Harrison Dane coming to look it over." That wasn't really an answer, but it wasn't a lie.

Lauren's eyes widened. "*The* M. Harrison Dane? Coming *here?*"

"That's what I'm told."

"Wow." For the first time, she seemed as starstruck as all the rest of them. *Good job, Nate. Another boarding pass for the SS Disaster. Way to go, there, hero.*

Drumming her fingers on the corral fence, Lauren watched Lucky Strike pace a twenty-foot trench in the ground—up and down the fence, over and over and over, like a prisoner who'd been in solitary so long he'd lost his mind.

"Think you can make The Shay into the horseman by next week?" I asked, happy to change the subject to something that didn't require me to straddle a fault line of divided loyalty. "I got the hat down, that ought to help." Grabbing the hat off the post, I flipped it over and dropped it onto my head, testing it out for size. The Shay's head was bigger than most.

"I think we need to get him a goat," Lauren remarked.

"A goat?" I said, trying to imagine what The Shay would

do with a goat. I remembered goats from my childhood. My grandmother had one she milked to make goat cheese and soap. It climbed fences, ate flowers, stole the laundry from the line, and drank from slimy buckets of watery motor oil and never seemed to mind.

"For companionship," Lauren explained, and I was even more confused than before. "To help socialize him. Right now, he's socially handicapped. He doesn't know how to relate to his own kind, so he's acting out."

"True enough." She knew the Shay better than I thought. "I didn't know a goat could cure that problem." If so, we needed a whole herd of them in LA. They could replace Chihuahuas and sports cars for all the self-destructive show folk who couldn't settle into a normal, healthy life. All this time, I'd thought leaving Hollywood for a cabin in the mountains was the cure, and all I really needed was a pair of goats—one for me and one for The Shay. We could both be home with our goats right now, socially well-adjusted and content. "I think it's probably more than one goat can handle."

Lauren frowned. "What is?"

"What is, what?"

"What's more than one goat can handle?" She turned her attention fully to me, her lips twisting upward on one side and down on the other in a way that . . . well, made me think about her lips.

Suddenly, I couldn't focus. "Socializing The Shay," I muttered. "It's more than a . . . one goat . . . job." Every once in a while, you utter something, and it's not until it goes from brain to mouth, then back in the ears that you realize how stupid it sounds. I felt like the long-haired seventh grade nerd who couldn't string together ten coherent sounds in the presence of a cute girl.

Lauren's eyes widened and began tearing up, until finally she slapped a hand over her mouth, and laughter burst through her fingers. After politely trying to choke it back, she let her head fall forward and gave in to it, sagging against the fence and gasping out an occasional word, "You . . . thought . . . I . . . didn't . . . the goat . . . not . . ."

I laughed along, so that maybe she'd think I was in on the joke. "I was just kidding." It was a good attempt, but she knew. She could tell I'd been picturing The Shay driving down the Pacific Coast Highway with the wind in his hair and a goat strapped into the passenger seat.

"The goat's . . . goat's . . . for the . . . for the horse," Lauren coughed out between giggling and catching her breath. I'd almost caused her to choke to death, poor thing.

"I knew that," I said, and she laughed harder. "I just thought, hey, if the goat'll work for the horse, why not get two? It'll be a new form of . . ." I stopped right before *rehab* slipped off my tongue. The Shay and his rehab-of-the-week were a running joke—for the tabloids, for Randall and Marla, for everyone, actually. Even The Shay and I joked about it. Sometimes the things that are hard to face are easier to laugh about.

"Of what?" Lauren had a seriously annoying habit of picking up on the things I wasn't saying.

"Training. Maybe it'll help him . . . learn to be the horseman," I said lamely.

She rolled her eyes, then wiped her index fingers along the lower lashes, drying what Mama Louise used to call laugh tears. "Oh, wow, I haven't laughed like that in a while."

"Glad to be of service." I was relieved to have refocused the conversation away from the film project and onto goats. "Nice job with the horse earlier, by the way. It's an awesome thing to watch. Nice job with The Shay, too. He doesn't usually let people tell him what to do." I'd seen Justin be intractable to the point that he came within a whisper of collapsing multimillion-dollar productions. Between personality quirks, substance abuse, mood swings, partying with the crew, and general unreliability, it was only through sheer luck that we'd come out of Morocco with enough material to piece together into a film. It wasn't a good film, but considering that we'd almost ended up working the brick pits in a Moroccan prison, even a film that went rapidly to DVD seemed like a victory.

Watching Lucky Strike's pathologically self-destructive behavior made me think of Justin in Morocco. To get my mind off the subject, I asked a pointless question. "So why does a girl who's got the Snow White way with animals decide to give it up and take a desk job? Your aunt told me you teach college in Kansas now."

"Life changes." Her face tipped down, then away, her eyes hooded beneath thick, dark lashes. "It was time to grow up."

"You seem like the type who's always been grown up."

Groaning under her breath, she crossed her arms on the fence and rested her chin on her hands. Her body curved in a shapely S as she braced the toe of one boot on the bottom rail. "Yeah, I guess."

"It was a compliment," I told her. "I meant that you'd have to be fairly perceptive to do what you do—with the horses, I mean."

Shrugging, she lifted her chin off her hands and turned her head to check the food tent.

"The lasso thing was pretty impressive, too," I added. "Don't think I've ever seen anyone do that live and in person."

"*Lasso?*" She repeated, pressing a hand over her eyes. "Nobody says *lasso*. Didn't *The Horseman* script teach you anything, cowboy?" She motioned to my borrowed hat, and I felt obliged to drop it back on the fencepost.

"It says *lasso* in the script." Mama Louise loved old westerns, especially the really old singing kind that teenage boys couldn't stand. I could still hear Roy Rogers yodeling about his saddle and laso-o-ooh.

Lauren giggled. "That's, like, an old movie term. Real horsemen just call it a rope or a lariat rope."

I pulled an imaginary pencil from behind my ear and made a note. "Thanks for the tip."

"What else is in that script?" Lauren pressed.

"You probably don't want to know."

"Can I see it?"

"The script?" I said, even though I knew what she was asking. Showing her the script probably wasn't the best idea. As soon as she saw it, she'd realize what folly all of this was. Then she would look at me, the guy who didn't know a lasso from a lariat rope, and she'd see there was no way I'd be any good at reinventing some touchy-feely lonely-cowboy-meets-down-and-out-horse-owning-chick screenplay.

Maybe it'd be best if she figured it out now. Maybe it would be good to have full disclosure and be done with it.

The truth was on the tip of my tongue, but I looked at Lauren and didn't speak it. I fell into her eyes, and the answer bounced across my mind like a flat rock skittering over the water's surface.

"Mm-hmm." Her voice seemed breathy and intimate . . . or was that my imagination? "If I saw it, maybe I could . . ." She blinked hard, her cheeks flushing a most becoming shade of crimson. "Maybe I could help you . . . with it. The horse . . . ummm . . . related details, I mean."

I felt her leaning closer, or maybe I was leaning closer. Her shoulder touched mine and I was acutely aware of the contact point. If I'd been writing it in a scene, the male lead would have experienced a jolt of undeniable attraction.

"I just thought . . . it might . . . be good." I watched her lips form words, heard them just barely.

"It might be good." My mind went haywire, concocting a dozen different ways things might play out from here. That's the trouble with a writer's head—you can imagine possibilities that are a long way from reality.

"Maybe we could talk about it during lunch," I offered.

The suggestion seemed to fall over her like a bucket of cold water. "I'm skipping." She cleared her throat, then added, "Lunch. I'm skipping lunch."

"Guess you'll be hungry by supper then." *That was smooth. Man, are you out of practice at this. Loser.* "If you'd like to join me."

"Guess we . . ." I couldn't tell whether she was about to say yes or no, but I was surprisingly invested in the answer.

"Hey, are y'all hu-u-un-gry?" Donetta Bradford's voice burst into the gap between *yes* and *no* like the squeal of brakes, and I heard the pitter-patter of shiny silver cowboy boots tapping rapidly across the driveway.

Chapter 13

Lauren Eldridge

I t took a minute for Aunt Donetta's voice to penetrate the fluffy, floaty fog in my head, which is saying something, because Aunt Netta's voice is a force of nature, like Superman's X-ray vision. It can breech the six-inch stone walls of the Daily Hotel and still be as clear as a bell. Folks next door in the café always know when someone comes into the beauty shop, because they can hear, *How-deee! Be there in just a little ol' minute. There's coffee in the pot. . . .*

For some odd reason that I couldn't explain, her greeting bounced off the misty observation that Nate was taller than I'd thought. There was a little cleft in his chin that was . . . was . . .

"Yoo-hoo . . . y'all two are missin' lu-unch." The words were like the annoying buzz of a horsefly, circling incessantly, determined to land. I wanted to swat away the noise, think about the dinner invitation. What if I said yes?

Was it more than a dinner invitation?

Did I want it to be?

What was I thinking?

"Y'all come on over to the tent and—" Aunt Netta's aborted sentence was more disturbing than whatever she'd been about to say. She'd stumbled onto something worthy of a short silence, which was unusual. Now she would cogitate about what might have been going on before she entered the barnyard.

Oh shoot, was the only thought I had time to form before Aunt Netta went to work. "Well, goodness, y'all two are busy talkin' out here." She pretended not to notice that she'd just caught Nate and me in a moment of . . . whatever just happened. "I didn't mean to bother ye-ew te-ew," she stretched out the words, coated them with honey butter so they'd slide down all sticky-sweet.

Nate broke the invisible link between us, glancing at Aunt Donetta. "I was just trying to talk the horse whisperer here into taking a look at the script with me this evening."

Having no experience with Aunt Donetta and her legendary penchant for matchmaking, Nate was unaware that he'd just dropped a big wad of stinkbait into the catfish pond. Mama fish would be all over it quicker than I could say, *There's nothing going on here, Aunt Netta. The guy in the flip-flops and I were just talking . . . about horses and scripts. You know I'd never be interested in a guy who wears flip-flops.*

I wouldn't.

Ever.

My father made fun of guys who wore what he called *them beach shoes.* His contempt harkened back to the infamous years of the hippies. He said men should wear a man shoe—cowboy boots in general, slippers after hours, tennis shoes only after major surgery, or for the church softball game and occasionally donkey basketball. When my father took us to Corpus Christi as kids, his idea of beach attire was rolled up Wrangler jeans and tube socks, which was just as well, because my father's legs hadn't seen the sun since he quit the 1959 Daily High track team to spend more time rodeoing.

He had thoroughly warned me against hippies and all manner of men who didn't dress to make an honest living. He liked the fact that Danny wouldn't have been caught in anything but proper cowboy attire, but in the long run, he didn't like Danny.

Aunt Donetta wasn't bothered by Nate's choice of footwear. "Well, isn't that ni-ice?" She laid on the charm. "Way-ul, like I said earlier, there's not anyone that could tell you more about the way a horse thinks than our Puggy. Why, back when she was little, it was all we could do to get her to put on clothes before she headed out to the horse pen in the mornin'. When she was four, her mama told her to stall up her little pony and come take a bath for her birthday party. Next thang they knew, there was Puggy, all stripped down, sittin' in the horse trough. Figured she'd found a way to get a bath *and* be with the pony. Her mama got the Mane and Tail shampoo from the tack room, just dumped it right in the horse trough, and washed her and the pony both. Puggy's mama was a kind-hearted woman that way, rest her soul." Laying a hand over her chest, Aunt Donetta laughed. "I still got a picture somewhere of that mop-headed pony drinkin' out of one end of the trough, and little Puggy, naked as a pink piglet on the other, bless her heart. She was just the cutest little . . ."

"Aunt Donetta." I stopped her before she could describe in detail little Puggy in the birthday suit, sharing bathwater with Tootsie, the mop-headed pony. Somewhere in the back of my mind, though, I was fascinated with the story. I'd never heard it before, but now I thought I had a vague recollection of it. I thought I could remember my mother laughing as Toots lowered his mouth to the water's surface, snorted and blew spray in my face, then raised his head and curled his lip because the water tasted like soap.

"Look, Mama, him laughin'! Tootsie laughin'!" On the

fence, Kemp squealed, reaching toward the water. My father held him as his chubby two-year-old legs bounced up and down on the railing.

"Oh, let him come in," Mom said. "Might as well wash the whole family at once." She took Kemp as my father lifted him over. My father smiled at her adoringly, kissed her across the top rail. . . .

"She put Kemp in there, too," I muttered. I had the sudden sense of missing my mother. Even though I'd been without her most of my life, the loss still hit me at the strangest times. If she was still alive she would never have let my father risk the ranch and the shop building in some insane scheme to make a movie.

"She probably did, knowin' your mama," Aunt Netta agreed. "You'd have to ask your daddy for sure about that. The picture I have's just you and the pony. I'll have to look around and see if I can find that picture. That'd be cute on next year's Hair and Body Christmas card." Aunt Netta poked a long red fingernail carefully through the translucent web of hair and scratched her head, concocting a plan to make me next year's Christmas star. Last December's picture was of Kemp and me in a boat with my father. Kemp was about three, crying and pitching a fit because I'd caught three fish and he hadn't caught any.

"You should put Kemp on there again," I cleverly suggested. "He was a cute baby."

"You were cute." Aunt Netta never let me suffer criticism, even the self-inflicted kind. "After you outgrew the little puggy nose . . . well, when we could clean you up enough. Half the time, you looked like one a them poor little orphan kids on the Feed the Children commercial—grass matted in your hair and all covered with dirt."

Aunt Netta addressed the next comment to Nate so he wouldn't feel left out. "Puggy was such a little tomboy. She played baseball on the boys' team till she was twelve. She woulda took up football, too, but her daddy wouldn't let her." Fanning a hand against her chest, Aunt Netta laughed. "Puggy, remember when you sneaked off and entered the kids' steer ridin' over at San Saba rodeo? You were gonna show your daddy that just because you were a girl didn't mean you couldn't become a bull rider instead of a barrel racer."

Something between a groan and a laugh pressed my throat and Nate raised a brow in curiosity, or admiration, or both.

"I remember," I admitted. My steer riding career lasted about two and a half seconds. They had to drag my contorted body out of the way to close the chute gate. After that, I listened to my father and began resigning myself to the fact that I probably wasn't bull riding material, like it or not.

"She always was stubborn." Aunt Donetta was talking to Nate again. She slid a shrewd look back and forth between Nate and me. "Say, Nate, you make sure to come on over to the house and have dinner with the rest of us this evenin', y'hear? Got a bunch gonna be there—the more the merrier, we always say. Willie 'n Mimi, and Frank, a'course. Ye-ew bring Justin and that Fred-a-rica fella, too. You boys could probably use some real home-cooked food after livin' out there in Hollywood. Our whole family's horse folk, and any of them'd be happy to answer questions for the script."

As much as I loved my family, I blanched at the idea of Nate and Justin Shay among them. They probably would find fodder for their next movie—a western version of *One Flew Over the Cuckoo's Nest*. "Aunt Donetta, I don't think—"

"That sounds great," Nate answered. "I'm working on getting an ear for the local dialect."

"Oh, hon we got all kinds'a that, and good pie, too." Aunt Netta swatted a hand enthusiastically. "Ye-ew can have all you want. Puggy can tell ya how to git there, right Puggy? Why don't y'all two just walk over from the hotel together? It's a nice little stroll."

The insinuation of an arranged date was so thick, I could have cut it with a butter knife. I said the first thing that came to mind. "Aunt Donetta, I need to go get a . . . goat this evening."

She cocked her head and blinked at me like I was the crazy one.

"For the goat . . . I mean horse. A goat for the horse," I stammered. "To settle him down. I thought I'd go by Uncle Top's place. He's probably got something we could use for a few days."

"Uncle Top's gone to the stock show." Aunt Netta mused momentarily on the goat issue. "I'm sure he wouldn't mind if y'all went by and borrowed a goat, though. He's got so many. Why don't you get Nate to help you, then y'all two can come on over for dinner . . . say about six-thirty?"

"Sounds good," Nate agreed amiably. He was either unaware that he was being railroaded toward *date with Puggy* or he didn't care.

Aunt Donetta patted him on the shoulder, then squeezed his arm as if she were testing a side of meat. "Wonderful! It'll be good for Puggy to have a strong young man along. In case there's any trouble with the goat." She pretended not to notice Nate's shorts and flip-flops. Hardly goat-wrestling attire.

I gave up my end of the debate. There was no point. Aunt Donetta could talk the warts off a toad. Unless a tornado swept through town before six-thirty, Justin, Nate, Willie, Mimi, Frederico, and I were going to eat at Aunt Netta's house, along with whomever else she could gather up. Entertainment reporters and paparazzi all over the country would probably pay millions to crash this little shindig. It would be one of those cases in which truth was stranger than fiction—Tinsel Town's favorite party boy settled in on Aunt Netta's old harvest-gold sofa with a ham dinner in his lap and professional bull riding on TV. The newspapers would have to provide pictures in order to get the public to believe it.

"Well . . . good!" Aunt Donetta turned an ear toward the driveway, where Imagene was headed in our direction.

"Land's sake, Donetta!" Imagene called across the empty space. "Get over here. We got pies to cut!" One thing about Imagene Doll—she didn't believe in standing around talking when there was work to be done. For Aunt Netta, talking took priority over everything else. She always said, *"The dishes wait, but the folks move on."* You had to visit when you got the opportunity.

"On my way!" Aunt Netta called, happy to head out now that dinner plans had been sealed. Turning back to Nate and me, she flashed a self-satisfied grin. "Now, you te-ew just go on with what ye-ew were doin' before I got here. I didn't mean to git in the way." Her words stretched around us like taffy, pulling us together. "Y'all just go ahead and chat. I'll bring ye-ew some lunch plates over in a bit." With a little finger wave, she trundled off looking well pleased, having successfully arranged the evening and all.

When she was gone, I turned to Nate to apologize. A smile was cracking the sides of his mouth, and I couldn't help it, I started to laugh.

"I think we've just been shanghaied there, Puggy," he said in a deliberate and fairly good imitation of Aunt Netta's twangy Texas drawl.

"You think?" I had to give Nate credit for being, perhaps, the most tolerant guy I'd ever met. Every time Aunt Donetta had tried to railroad Danny like that, he'd gotten irritable. "You really don't have to show up for supper with my family. I can just tell her you all had other things going on."

Nate quirked a brow, and I felt a surprising sting of disappointment at the idea that he would take the out. *He probably only said yes to avoid hurting Aunt Netta's feelings.* That in itself was sweet. Nate, while possessed of questionable fashion sense, was an extremely nice guy. In the pairing of him and Justin Shay, he seemed to be the responsible one, the nurturer who patiently tried to steer around the pitfalls and clean up the messes.

I was once again curious about the relationship between the two of them. "I could meet you after supper to look at the script."

Taking the hat from the fence and attempting to straighten the mangled brim, Nate laughed. "Are you kidding? I'm gathering dialect and *y'all* have all kinds of it . . . and pie, too, remember? Besides, I'm looking forward to seeing the picture of you and Tootsie in the bathtub, and then there's goat wrestling. . . ." Grinning, he fanned an eyebrow. "You'll need a big strong man for that."

I felt that grin somewhere in the pit of my stomach. "You're not dressed for goat wrestling."

He took in his bare feet, then held one up and studied it. "Maybe I can borrow them-there fancy steel-toed boots from The Shay."

"Please don't," I said, and both of us laughed. I had the odd sense that I could have stood there with him all day, talking about nothing in particular and enjoying it. "So, have you ever lived in Texas? You do the accent pretty well."

The personal inquiry surprised him. "No telling. We moved around a lot. I wasn't always sure where we were."

"No, seriously." As soon as I said it, I realized he wasn't

joking. Was it possible to move around so much you didn't know where you were?

"Seriously," he confirmed, dismissing the answer with a shrug.

"That must've been strange." I wondered if that was why Nate seemed comfortable, quietly confident, in a situation that should have been foreign to him. "Were your parents in the army?"

"Gypsies," he answered with a straight face. For a milli-second I was fascinated. I'd never met a real live gypsy before. "We traveled around selling homemade soap and fresh honey. We had a big red-wheeled wagon pulled by a pair of goats."

I felt myself smiling, saw him grin in return. "It must have been hard to get the bees to follow along . . . to make the honey, I mean."

"We tied little strings to their feet." Pinching his fingers to-gether, he mimicked the motion of tying a tiny bow.

"I bet they didn't like that very much."

His warm brown eyes sparked with a hint of appreciation for the fact that I was playing along. "The trick is to roll them over and scratch their little abdomens. They enjoy that."

"No doubt. I guess you'd have to turn them loose to go col-lect nectar, though."

"Only a few at a time. The rest have to hang around and fan the soap trays and pat out the bubbles with their tiny feet."

"Wow." I could understand now why he was a writer. He almost had me picturing the gypsy wagon with the soap molds in the back. "Sounds like a business I need to look into. The bees do all the work."

Nate nodded. "My mother was always in favor of someone else doing the work." Even though he tried to make it sound like a joke, a part of the story, there was a flash of emotion that told me that bit was real. I wasn't sure how to respond. I wanted to know more, but something told me I shouldn't ask.

We stood suspended in awkward silence for a moment before he motioned toward the serving tent. "Looks like lunch is on its way."

Imagene was headed our direction. Carrying a shallow box, she chatted with Miss Beedie, who was ferrying two drinks with a pie pan balanced on top.

At the sight of Miss Beedie, something painful slammed my ribs, then constricted. I couldn't breathe. My mind raced ahead, imagining what I might say when, for the first time in two years, I was face-to-face with the mother of the man who was dead because of Danny and me. When Pastor Harve and Miss Beedie buried their son, Harvard Jr., I was in the hospital in Austin, in a quiet, medically induced sleep. I should have gone to them when I was finally back on my feet. I should have told them Danny didn't drive into the water accidentally. He did it because we were arguing, and I told him to go around the long way, and he wanted to prove he didn't have to.

When I woke up in the hospital, my father said no one blamed us for what had happened. It was dark. It was raining. The water over the road was hard to see. It was an accident. Some sad, guilty part of me felt relief. It seemed like it would be easier for everyone not to know that Harvard had died because of a stupid, careless mistake, an immature, childish argument that was one of a long string of arguments.

I couldn't make myself call Harvard's family and tell the truth, but I couldn't call them and lie, so I just didn't call. I sent a card, a tree to be planted at Caney Creek Church, and a plaque. I let time go by.

I'd created a chasm for which there seemed to be no easy bridge. Miss Beedie was crossing it in her slow bowlegged shuffle with two glasses of iced tea and a pie pan, her mocha-colored skin warm in the midday light. She and Imagene were busy talking, seemingly unaware that they were closing a gap I'd worked hard to maintain.

"I . . . left something," I muttered to Nate, then turned and hurried toward the barn.

Chapter 14

Nathaniel Heath

L unch turned out to be a quiet affair. By the time Lauren reemerged from the barn, Imagene and her helper, Miss Beedie, had delivered the food and then left in a hurry to finish serving pie to the workers. They asked where Lauren was, and I said I didn't know exactly. It didn't take a rocket scientist to figure out that she was avoiding someone or something having to do with lunch. When I was new in LA, I dated a game show model with an off-and-on eating disorder, so the vanishing mealtime companion wasn't completely unfamiliar. For a minute, I thought the farm dogs and I would be divvying up Lauren's plate.

When she came out of the barn, she was hungry, though, and we ate in a hurry before The Shay and crew returned to proceed with the horsemanship lessons. I was curious about our disappearing horse trainer, but I didn't ask. Sometimes it's more productive to study things, gather information until you can draw your own conclusions, or at least know the right questions to ask. If Lauren were a character onscreen, she would have been the gorgeous yet wounded and vulnerable small-town prodigal hiding some deep, dark secret beneath a pragmatic

197

exterior. This place, these people, the family gatherings and funny childhood anecdotes seemed to fit her like a comfortable old pair of shoes. Yet I got a sense that she was limping, carefully feeling her way through every step, afraid that sooner or later she'd come down on something sharp.

The more time I spent around her, the more interested I was. One of the drawbacks of a screenwriter's mind is that such characters fascinate you. You feel compelled to figure them out, understand their motivation.

Beyond that, the whole cowgirl thing was hot. My interest wasn't completely academic.

I caught myself losing track of everything else and just watching her as the afternoon wore on with little discernible progress in the horse whispering department, as far as The Shay was concerned. I had to give Lauren credit for tenacity. She was trying, but Justin's patience was minimal and his relationship-building skills were so thin even the horse could see right through them.

Our crowd of onlookers at the fence dwindled as the day grew hot and muggy. Amber had to leave for an interview with a radio station in Austin. Mimi got a headache from the heat and the dust, and Frederico secretly confided that he was allergic to both horses and hay. He and Mimi caught a ride back to town with Donetta. Even the barnyard dogs got bored with the activity and wandered off to lie in the shade, while Willie Wardlaw, Lauren's father, and I watched Lucky Strike pace the same twenty feet of ground, looking for a way out of the corral.

By the end of the day, gains were limited, but Justin had learned that every time he lost his temper and threw his hat in the dirt, it took a half hour to settle the horse down to a walk again. Animals don't react as understandingly to anger management issues as do grips, studio interns, and paid personal assistants.

Before calling the day a wrap, Lauren caught the horse and forced it to stand still while Justin petted it. By then, Justin was tired, frustrated, dust encrusted, and uncharacteristically defeated. He didn't like the horse very much and he was afraid of it. As Lauren led it away to the barn, Willie tried to console The Shay with the fatherly assurance that no ordinary man ever became a horseman in one day, and anything worth doing was worth working at. He gave Justin credit for grit. Willie had worked a lot of movie sets over the years, he said, and he was glad to see Justin was a man's man, not a little "snot-nosed, cotton-tailed wimp like most of 'em."

Justin was pleased. Bracing his hands on the undoubtedly sore abs Frederico had been helping him tone for months, he stretched his back and nodded, saying that he took commitment seriously, and he wouldn't let Willie down.

"I know you won't, son. When a cowboy takes on a job, he'll either git'r done or die tryin'." Willie slapped an arm over The Shay's shoulders, and they stood around engaging in horse chat and other cowboy talk with Frank and one of the barn-yard dogs.

Frank eventually suggested they go back to his ranch, relax, have a glass of tea, and catch up with Mimi before heading over to Donetta's for supper.

Justin checked his pocket and said he'd probably better drop by the hotel a minute to shower and put on some clean clothes. I knew what he was looking for in the pocket. The little packet of Vicodin he normally kept with him was in the duffle bag back at the hotel. Before we left in the morning, he'd tucked it into his jeans, pulled it back out, put it in again, then finally tossed it in the suitcase with a look of disgust and walked out the door. By now, he was probably cramping up and had a raging headache, and he wanted the Baggie.

"You comin', Nate?" Justin glanced back at me, as if the pills and I were somehow connected in his mind. Maybe he wanted me to be there to tell him it *was* a prescription, after all. It's not like he was actually using something illegal. Or maybe he wanted me to be there to flush his little Baggie down the toilet and tell him no—the way Stephanie used to back when they were together. Stephanie had spent most of her time searching for hidden stashes, flushing Baggies, and pouring flasks of vodka down the drain. She was always afraid the kids would get into the pills and eat them. When the older boy, just a preschooler then, finally did, that was that. Stephanie was gone. She didn't even come back to the house for her things—just went straight from the hospital to a new life. The family court judge had no problem terminating Justin's parental rights when he learned Justin was stopped for driving under the influence shortly thereafter. Justin didn't fight the ruling, really. Even through the haze, he realized that life with him was a sort of poison, and he couldn't control where the drops would fall, or who they'd hurt.

"I'm catching a ride with Lauren," I said, and Justin gave me a confused look that said the name didn't register. Names were on Justin's *why bother* list. Normally, he had Marla or Randall to handle such details. "The horse trainer," I added.

The Shay gave me an irritated look because I wasn't at his heel, like I was supposed to be. Aside from that, the horse trainer was more of an irritant to him than anything else. She had the nerve to tell him he wasn't doing things right. "Yeah, fine," he said, as if he'd decided to be magnanimous and let me do my own thing. "Whatever." Turning away, he sagged and rubbed his temples, his silver-toed boots dragging in the gravel as he headed toward the Horsemanmobile.

Despite my determination to stop being The Shay's handler, mommy, and part-time enabler, I felt guilty. Now he would probably overmedicate and make an idiot of himself at Donetta's house.

A real friend would stop that from happening.

Wouldn't he?

Wouldn't he?

I vacillated between babysitting Justin and going through with my plans to hang out with Lauren and the goat, which would probably be fun, and undoubtedly interesting.

Willie slapped Justin on the back again, and Justin's head rattled. "Aw, don't worry about the hotel. Cowboys don't mind a little soil. A man ought never be ashamed of the dirt from a good day's work. Besides, I want you to see them deer come out on Frank's place. On a clear afternoon like this, they wander right up in the backyard, and you can feed 'em out of yer hand." As Justin fished for his truck keys, Willie went on talking about showing Justin the deer and seeing how Mimi was doing with her headache. Justin seemed effectively distracted. I wondered if Willie knew about the stash at the hotel or if he was just in a hurry to make sure there wasn't something brewing between his girlfriend and Frederico, which was entirely possible. Fred was known for being good with the ladies.

I resolved to let Justin go. He was a big boy, after all. *You promised yourself, Nate. You promised yourself you wouldn't get involved the next time he started into one of his random bursts of insanity. But here you are again. You know this horseman thing is going to crash and burn. Let it. It might as well be tonight as later on. . . .*

Lauren walked out of the barn, and a comic-book-sized superhero hovering by my ear said, *She's worked really hard today. You wouldn't want her to be disappointed, would you?*

You wouldn't want her family to be embarrassed. You should go with The Shay, make sure he doesn't have anything stashed in the truck.

The villain hovering by my other ear looked at Lauren and said, *Go with the girl. She's cute.*

By that time, the Horsemanmobile had already roared off down the driveway, followed by Frank's pickup. I settled for calling Justin's cell phone while Lauren was busy cleaning fast food containers, junk mail, and file folders out of her SUV passenger seat.

Surprisingly enough, The Shay answered his phone. "Nate?" his voice was cutting in and out. "That you?"

"Yeah, of course it's me. Who'd you think it was?"

"I was afraid it was Marla," he said, like the walls had ears. "This thing must have been ringing like crazy in the truck all day. There's, like, eighty-seven calls on it from Marla and Randall . . ." His voice faded, then returned. ". . . need me to come back and get you?" He wanted me to say yes. Justin never traveled anywhere solo.

"No, but listen. Stay off the stuff tonight, okay?"

". . . can't hear you, dude. You're . . . aking up."

Yeah, I'll bet. "You heard me, Shay. Have you got anything stashed in the truck?" He didn't answer. I wanted to reach through the phone and grab him by his new bandanna. The connection fuzzed and came back. "Justin." The word was more of a threat than anything. "You screw this up, and I'm catching the first flight back to LA. You show up stoned tonight, you're on your own."

"Dude, I'm clean. Didn't you hear Amber? I'm, like, getting religion and stuff."

"Yeah, that's why you were sticking a bag in your pocket this morning."

More fuzz, and then, ". . . at's prescription."

Somebody please tell me, do I have STUPID *tattooed on my forehead?* I could have responded with quotes from the family visitation sessions of several rehab stints, but what would have been the point, really? He probably didn't remember the sessions. He was stoned at the time. "I'm not kidding, dude."

He waited so long to answer that I figured he'd hung up, which was what he usually did when he didn't like what he was hearing. "Geez, Nate, when did you go and turn all holy? You sound like somebody's mama."

"Just don't go by the hotel, all right?"

"Yeah, all . . ." The call faded and didn't come back, which was probably just as well. This way I could leave for the goat wrestling with only a modicum of guilt. The Shay had it all under control.

I made a conscious effort to switch focus as I joined Lauren. Some things in life are beyond your control, and there's no point obsessing over those. I learned that on an episode of *Dr. Phil* when I should have been writing.

Lauren tossed a few more fast food containers and a stack of notebooks into the back seat as I opened the passenger door of her Durango. "Sorry," she said, embarrassed by the mess in the car. "It's usually just me in here."

I cataloged that bit of information. *Hmm . . .* "Hey, you should see mine," I offered, and found myself feeling an unexpected comfort level. It was nice to be with a woman who wasn't afraid to live in her space. My former fiancé, Nicole, was a neat freak, and my car made her so nervous, she couldn't stand to ride in it without cleaning it up. Every time we went somewhere, she fed her compulsive need for order by picking up loose bits of paper or soda straw wrappers and tucking them into empty cups, or dabbing discarded napkins with bottled water and wiping the dash or the console. *"You're such a slob, Nate,"* she'd say. *"How in the world can you think in this place?"*

What she didn't realize was that bits and pieces of thought were attached to the junk in the car—little scraps of memory I'd jotted on napkins, newspaper margins, the backs of sugar packets. Ideas I wanted to remember for later, and little human dramas I'd come across on the sidewalk or standing in line at Starbucks—the way a little boy looked when he tugged his mother's hand and asked for a doughnut and his mom said yes, two college kids sitting under a tree on the lawn at Berkeley, a pair of lovers strolling on the beach, a boy throwing the football with his dad in the park—things I thought I might write about someday, if I had the time. If I jotted those things down, the observations that seemed valuable at the moment, I wouldn't lose them. They would be waiting when I had time to dredge them up again and examine the meanings.

When Nicole tossed them out, it seemed like she was probably right. It was all just junk, and letting it rattle around in the car was a bad habit I'd picked up during my mother's pre-Doug transient years. Back then, the notes in the car were a way of trying to hang on to people and places I'd probably never see again.

I had the fleeting thought that Lauren would understand that, if I told her. Then I decided it was stupid. I'd sound like one of those morons on *Jerry Springer*, whining about my childhood as a way of making excuses for where I'd ended up. Lauren had lived her whole life surrounded by family, safely entrenched in this quiet little town where everybody knew everybody. She wouldn't be able to relate to living on the road, not knowing where you'd stop next or how long you'd stay.

A couple mystery objects rolled from under the seat and hit the backs of my feet as we tooled past the last of the construction workers, who were packing it in and heading toward a group of camping trailers on the other side of the house. I leaned over to grab the rolling thing and something metallic that was wedged between my heel and my shoe. I came up with what looked like a thigh bone and a small hand saw. "Something I should know?" I asked. Now, this was an interesting girl. I'd never gone goat wrestling with a girl who carried bones and a saw in her car before.

Lauren glanced at the bone, flushed red, then took it from my hand and tossed it in the back seat, where it bounced off a cardboard box and landed in an open tote bag. "I teach anatomy."

"Oh . . . good," I said, using my fingertip to test the sharpness of the saw. "For a minute there, I was thinking serial killer."

Lauren laughed. "You're safe, I promise."

"I wasn't worried. At least not until the bone saw. That's not your standard everyday under-the-passenger-seat item."

She quirked a brow, seeming surprised that I knew what the tool was for. She glanced at my hand on the wooden grip. "Well, now you have *me* worried. You look like you've seen one of those before."

"My grandparents had a farm." I tucked the saw behind the seat, next to a box piled high with file folders and textbooks.

She blinked as if she were seeing me for the first time. "Really? I hadn't pegged you for the farmboy type."

"It's been a lot of years. They had to sell the place and move to a nursing home when I was thirteen." Taking in the horizon, I thought of my grandfather's dairy, of the little white house and native stone barn tucked among the soft green hills of northern Arkansas. It was like a picture postcard in my mind, a place that always seemed comfortable and safe. Every time my mother and I drove up the lane, I felt like I'd been holding my breath since we left, and now I could finally let it out. During the transient years, I knew that after the obligatory arguing,

Mom would settle into the front bedroom and I would curl up on the Murphy bed on the back porch, where my grandmother kept the nurse bottles for motherless calves and the cream separators. In the morning, my grandfather would wake me early, and we'd head out to bring in the cows as if I'd never left. He wouldn't ask where we'd been or how we'd been living. He would just lay a hand on my head and say it was good to have me home. After my mother and I moved in with Doug, I lied and tried to make Joplin sound better than it was. By then, my grandparents were old and frail, and I was afraid Doug might do something to them if I started trouble.

"What kind of farm?" Lauren's voice came from somewhere outside the swirl of memory.

"Dairy," I answered, and the next thing I knew, I was telling her all about the place—about the land that had been in my grandfather's family since before the Civil War, about the little dairy barn, where my grandfather did the morning milking before heading off to work at the post office. "The place was pretty much heaven on earth for a little boy." I finished, leaving out the smarmy details about my mother, because there seemed to be little place for them in the picture.

"Sounds beautiful," Lauren mused. Her green eyes were soft and filled with thoughts, making me wonder what was on her mind.

"I'd like to go back and see it someday," I admitted. "See if everything's still there."

"Why haven't you?" She watched me closely as we drifted along a winding gravel road with the windows open.

For a fraction of a second, I wanted to tell the whole story. I hadn't had that urge in years—not even with Nicole. The farm, Doug, Mama Louise were ancient history. Buried and forgotten. "Long story," I said, because oddly enough, I didn't want to whip up a convenient lie that wouldn't ring true later. I realized vaguely that I was thinking ahead to future conversations, more days spent with Lauren, goat wrestling or whatever came up.

"We've got time. It's a little trip out to Uncle Top's house," she offered in a way that made me want to divulge things.

"Nah. Tell me about life around here." I waved vaguely out the window. "Some background might come in handy with the script."

Lauren proceeded to give me the tour as we drove onward to Uncle Top's place, winding up steep hills and through canyons where live oaks and sycamores stretched lazily in the evening light. The branches fanned cool shade over streams of clear water that flowed through smoothly polished floors of buff-colored gravel. Outside the window, the air held the quiet scents of midsummer, of moist soil and grasses basking in long hours of sunshine while slowly dropping seeds into the wind.

Lauren talked about her family. The Eldridges were pioneers whose origins could be traced back to a pair of brothers traveling to Texas to find adventure. Instead, they landed among the sparks of revolution as Texas sought independence from the armies of Santa Anna. In the end, the brothers fought in the battle of San Jacinto and were given the adjoining land grants on which Lauren's father still lived today. "Which is one of the reasons I'm so concerned about this business with *The Horseman* movie," she finished, bringing the conversation back around, as always, to the practical. As far as I could tell, Lauren wasn't much of a romantic. "Apparently, my father co-signed on some loans for Willie. He used the ranch and the building downtown to secure the loans."

The larger-than-life story of the two brothers and the battle of San Jacinto popped like a soap bubble. "Why would he do that?"

Lauren sighed. "I think he felt he owed it to Willie. Their

friendship goes back a long way. Willie helped my father out when he needed it in the past. My father lives by the cowboy code. He won't leave a debt unpaid."

"Ughhh," I groaned, not because of the cowboy code but because, in this case, it was seriously inconvenient. There was more at stake here than just potential hurt feelings and the mass letdown of a town full of very nice, well-meaning folk who believed in Justin Shay.

Lauren combed dark curls away from her face, bound them in the back with her fingers and rested her elbow on the door frame. "If I'd been here, I don't think he would have done this. I think he figured if he got involved in this movie, I'd have to . . . come home and . . ." Something darted out of the bushes in front of us, and Lauren hit the brakes. The truck vibrated to a stop as a doe and two fawns skidded to a halt in the road. They remained frozen temporarily, then moved on.

Whatever Lauren had been about to say had been lost by the time we started up again. She seemed to shake off the melancholy mood. "There's Uncle Top's place." She pointed ahead, and then we turned into a hodgepodge entranceway made of dented chain link and shipping pallets strung together with wire, bungee cords, and what looked like a faded dog leash. Just past the gate, a hand-lettered sign read,

No trespassing
If you can read this
U R in range

I rolled a questioning look at Lauren.

"It's a joke," she said. "Uncle Top is harmless . . . mostly." Her lips quirked to one side, forming an adorable little dimple that made me wonder what *mostly* meant.

A collection of dogs barked lazily from the porch as we passed a ramshackle farmhouse then continued to a barnyard, where groups of goats wandered among corrals constructed of everything from more shipping pallets to what looked like highway guardrail metal.

After surveying the barnyard, Lauren backed the truck up to a converted U-Haul flatbed that had a cage welded on top. When the truck was in place, Lauren hopped out, so I did, too. In an enclosure nearby, goats began milling around, excited by the new activity in Uncle Top's barnyard. A fairly large goat with woolly white dreadlocks put its front paws on the fence and made goat noises at me. I reached over and scratched its head, remembering the pet at my grandfather's farm. This goat was larger and hairier, but it brought back memories.

"We have a volunteer," I said, but Lauren didn't seem properly impressed with my choice.

"I had something smaller in mind." She proceeded to attach the trailer to the truck.

"He's friendly." Not that I really cared, but this goat did have personality, and unique hair. The rest of the herd had moved to the opposite side of the corral and didn't seem interested in the prospect of a future movie career.

Lauren was unconvinced—stubborn girl. After hooking up the trailer, she backed it to the corral and opened the gates so as to create a loading corridor. "We'll sort off one of the young ones and run it into the trailer," she said as I climbed over the fence, thinking that real shoes would be a good idea right now. "That's a *she*, not a *he*, by the way."

As Lauren headed off across the corral, my she-goat followed me. I walked to the trailer. She came along. I walked in. She walked in. It may have been my charming personality, but the capture couldn't have been easier. "I got one," I called, and

Lauren turned around, then lifted her hands palm-up, seeming shocked and impressed.

I exited the trailer and triumphantly closed the door. "Just call me the goat whisperer," I said, and Lauren chuckled.

With goat procurement easily accomplished, we closed the corral gate, started the truck, and rattled back down Uncle Top's driveway with the newest member of *The Horseman* crew now safely in tow. I couldn't help patting myself on the back and thinking that some days, things just work out even if you don't have on the right clothes.

Chapter 15

Lauren Eldridge

Everything about Nate Heath intrigued me. He wasn't at all the hapless, shaggy-haired celebrity hanger-on he appeared to be. He was actually a thinker, a contemplative type who noticed the little nuances of the people and interactions around him. Goats liked him. People liked him. Uncle Top's Angora nanny seemed inclined to follow him anywhere. As we headed back to the ranch, we talked again about the farm Nate remembered from his childhood and how much he missed it when he and his mother moved away.

"You know, for years I wished I could remember it better," he said, the words filtered through thought. "If I'd known it was the last time I'd ever see it, I would have really looked, made sure I knew exactly how everything was."

"Isn't that one of those life paradoxes—if you knew it might be the last time, you'd fully live the moment? Carpe diem?"

He turned an appraising look my way. I waved off whatever he was about to say as we turned into the Anderson-Shay ranch and rolled up the driveway. "Sorry. I sound like a sappy internet chain letter." The construction site was quiet as we passed, and I could hear Lucky Strike in the barn, whinnying frantically and kicking his stall. He had probably paced around in circles all evening. "So, why didn't you ever go back to your grandparents' farm?" I asked as we rolled to a stop near the barn. Maybe I shouldn't have pressed, since he'd dodged the question the first time, but the look on his face when he talked about the place made me curious. I had the feeling there was a lot going on in Nate's head that he didn't share.

He reached for the door handle. "My mother's boyfriend didn't like my grandparents, my grandparents didn't like Doug, Doug didn't like kids. I didn't like Doug. Doug and my mother only liked each other some of the time. After a while, my grandparents started asking too many questions. My mother knew they'd eventually figure out what was going on and they'd call Social Services. Then my grandfather's health declined, and they moved to a nursing home, and the farm was gone. The school called Social Services eventually anyway." He stopped talking when he realized I wasn't getting out of the car, but just sitting there watching him, taking in the story. He shrugged as if it didn't matter. "You know how family stuff goes sometimes," he said, then got out and shut the door.

The truth was I couldn't imagine a family situation like that. My family had always been solid and consistent. We gathered for holidays, birthdays, Sunday dinners, weddings, and funerals. The only one missing was my mother, and there was nothing anyone could do about that. After she was gone, Aunt Donetta stepped into the gap and did everything she could to help raise us.

It occurred to me that it had been a long time since I'd been grateful, or maybe I never really had been properly grateful for my family. Ever since the accident, my thoughts had been on me, on rebuilding my own life, on nursing my own pain, on leaving the past behind. But in trying to move on, I'd moved away from the people who loved me most. Perhaps I'd felt free to do it because I knew that when I wanted them back, they would be there. It never occurred to me that family isn't something you put away in your pocket and just pull out when you're feeling needy. Family, a good family, is a gift not everyone receives. God gave me everything I needed to recover from the accident, to be whole again, but instead of trusting it, instead of letting other people hold me up as I found my feet again, I'd stumbled along on my own, disconnected, unhappy, ungrateful, unwilling to admit to anyone that I wasn't recovering.

When I got back to Kansas, I would turn over a new leaf, be more open to the people around me, be thankful for the things I'd been taking for granted, and stop wallowing in my own misery.

When I got home, things would be different.

You are home, a voice whispered in my ear. *This is home. Why wait? Start now. Start here.*

I stepped out of the car with the idea circling my head like a butterfly determined to find a sweet place to land. Looking around at the old Barlinger ranch, I took in, really took in for the first time, the scope of its resurrection. This place, which had lain fallow for so long, which had been useless and empty and broken, was being lifted up, given a new purpose. If such a thing were possible with old buildings, certainly it was possible with my life. This trip to Daily, this movie project, was an opportunity, and I should have been looking at it that way. I could have been back in my condo, where stuff was piled everywhere and there was nothing on the walls, because I didn't want to admit I'd be staying there. Instead, I was back home in Daily, taking on a challenge—creating a partnership between Justin Shay and Lucky Strike was definitely a challenge—but both Aunt Donetta and Imagene had always been confident that great things can come from humble beginnings. They'd painted that motto, along with others, over the tops of the beauty shop mirrors. *God uses small things for great purposes.* I'd passed that mirror a thousand times and never stopped to think about what the words really meant.

Nate was already unloading his new friend from the trailer by the time I rounded the truck. "You might wait until . . ." There was no point adding, *I can back the trailer up to the gate.* The nanny stepped out, looked around, then lowered her head and scratched her ears on Nate's leg.

"Guess we'd better put it in the stall, or someplace," Nate said, patting the goat's shoulder blades as if it were a big dog. He started toward the barn with the goat nibbling on the hem of his shorts. Nate pushed it away and quickened his pace. "Ouch, hey, there's skin under there. All right, this is getting a little weird." He moved into a jog. The goat bleated and trotted after him.

I laughed as the two of them disappeared into the barn, the goat crying out and Nate calling back, "Lauren? Hey! Lauren? Uhhh . . . Puggy, hurry up, all right? This goat's getting a little . . . uhhh . . . I think it likes me . . . Ouch! Cut that . . ."

When I entered the barn, Nate and the goat were playing tag around a pallet of feed sacks, while one of the barn dogs yipped and frolicked just out of reach.

"Open the door!" Nate had lost a flip-flop and was half running, half limping on the rough stone aisleway. In one graceful bound, the goat jumped atop the feed sacks, and Nate had nowhere left to go. He stopped, standing frozen with his hands palm out. "All right, open the door." He was focusing on the goat like an animal tamer keeping a lion on a pedestal.

"What's it worth to you?" I teased, and he cut a warning glance my way.

"Not funny."

"I wasn't kidding." I was, really, but the nervous, edgy side of Nate was something I hadn't seen before. He was always flawlessly laid back, at least on the outside.

"Puggy . . ." He pointed a finger at me while still giving the goat the one-handed stop sign.

"There's no one here by that name." Moving to Lucky Strike's stall, I pinched the gate latch between two fingers. The horse moved to the far end of the stall and continued pacing.

"Lauren. Open the gate."

"Ask me nicely."

"Lauren, darling. Pookie, open the gate now, and we'll let the little lonely goat go make a new friend. Won't that be nice?"

The muscles in the goat's haunches coiled as I slid the door latch and swung open the door. Nate bolted through the opening, closely followed by the goat, then performed a side pass worthy of a professional toreador. He slipped past Lucky Strike and vaulted over the rear gate and into the barnyard in one impressive acrobatic leap. I closed the door, flipped the latch, and only then considered the fact that if Lucky Strike didn't like the goat, things might get dicey.

Lucky Strike didn't seem to notice his new companion. He continued pacing along the far wall as the goat investigated the stall, then stood on her hind legs by the back door, searching for her flip-flop wearing new best friend.

Nate came around the barn, and we hovered at the front of the stall, watching for signs of goat-horse bonding. I was conscious of Nate's body close to mine, his arm warm and solid where it touched me.

The goat turned our way, stretched out her neck, and let out a long, bleating complaint.

Lucky Strike halted at the sound and stood frozen beside

the wall. He slowly swiveled toward the goat, lowered his head and took a sniff, then snorted, eyes wide and white-rimmed.

The goat was intrigued. Sticking out her tongue, she bleated at Lucky Strike, then moved in the horse's direction. The horse retreated, snorting and backing to the other side of the stall, then coming forward, then backing off again.

"I . . . dunno," Nate muttered.

"Give it a minute," I whispered. "At least the horse is reacting to stimulus. He's focused. That's good."

We watched as Lucky Strike and the goat circled the stall once, twice, again, again, again.

"Come on, come on," I muttered. If we were ever going to make a success of Lucky Strike in *The Horseman*, stopping the pathological weaving was a necessary first step. "Please . . ."

We waited as the moments ticked by, and then finally a minor miracle began to take place. Lucky Strike lowered his head to sniff in the nanny goat's direction, and the goat extended her nose toward Lucky Strike. The gap closed slowly, until finally only inches separated them. Lucky Strike nickered low in his throat, the nanny goat bleated softly, and then they greeted one another with a warm, wet nose rub. The bond of friendship progressed rapidly from there, horse sniffing goat and goat sniffing horse, until finally the nanny grew tired after her long evening adventure and moved to the corner of the stall, where she folded her knees and lay down in the soft pine shavings. Lucky Strike moved back to his pacing spot, and I held my breath, leaning closer to the stall door.

I felt Nate beside me, his body tense with expectation. "Come on, big guy," he whispered. Lucky Strike cocked an ear to the sound. In the corner of the stall, the goat gave a soft, beckoning call, and Lucky Strike looked back and forth between the goat and the wall, between a new possibility and an old habit.

Watching him, I recognized myself, stuck in one painful place, unable to take a leap of faith. *Please, please, please.* The prayer in my head was about more than the horse and the goat. *Stop.*

As quickly as the words went through me, the prayer was answered. Leaving the pacing wall, Lucky Strike crossed the enclosure, lowered his head to nibble gently on the ear of his new companion, then sniffed the ground, turned in a circle, and lay down like the lion beside the lamb.

Nate and I backed away from the stall, quietly triumphant. The barn was wonderfully silent, save for the muted strains of guitar music drifting from the stablehand's apartment upstairs and one of the dogs yipping at something outside.

"We did it!" I whisper-cheered, giddy with success.

"We did." Nate opened his arms, and suddenly, we were locked in a triumphant hug. He picked me up and twirled me down the aisle into the yard, and the next thing I knew, exuberance had turned into something else. Electricity crackled through my body like a lightning shower riding an oncoming thunderhead.

When he set me down, I was slightly dizzy and off balance. We stood in a pose that felt decidedly romantic.

"Sorry, I . . ." I tried to find my feet, or my head, or both.

He smiled slightly, his eyes a warm, rich shade of chocolate, and I felt myself tumble head over heels, until everything seemed unreal. *You're dreaming this,* some part of me said. *It's a nice dream. Just enjoy the moment. My gosh, he's gorgeous. . . .*

"Don't be," he said, and I couldn't even form a conscious thought. Somewhere in the distance, I heard the rising crescendo of music that could only lead to the long, passionate kiss that both the hero and the heroine had been trying to resist, yet both were waiting for, waiting for . . .

Yearning for . . .

A board or a ladder fell somewhere near the house, and I came to reality with a jolt. "Guess the . . . ummm . . . goat worked," was the only thing I could think of to say as we ended the romantic clutch.

Nate seemed temporarily tongue-tied. "Looks like it," he said finally.

"You lost your date." I motioned over my shoulder toward the stall, where things remained wonderfully quiet.

Inclining his head to one side, Nate gave me a slow, crooked smile. "Maybe not."

My mind once again began to spin possibilities, like a spider forming a web in which I'd soon be trapped, if I wasn't careful. Somewhere in my thoughts, a voice whispered, *Just leave this alone. You're not ready, and even if you were, he wouldn't be a safe choice. . . .* "Guess we should let sleeping goats lie."

"Guess we should," Nate agreed.

Despite the voice of conscience reminding me that I wasn't looking for any entanglements, I found myself analyzing the tone of his words, hoping he sounded a little reluctant to leave. As we closed the trailer doors and prepared to go, I felt his nearness, thought again about the fact that there was no one around for miles. Just the two of us. Except for Joe upstairs.

I struck up a conversation about *The Horseman*, because it seemed like a safe subject. Nate talked about various scenes in the screenplay, and which ones he thought might be good choices to present to M. Harrison Dane next Monday.

"I still can't believe M. Harrison Dane is coming here in a little over a week," I said.

"Me, either," Nate admitted. "I haven't had the chance to ask The Shay how he managed to swing that. It's a serious long shot to think Dane would attach himself to a project like this, but I have to give The Shay credit for smart thinking. With Dane committed, this project would be a whole lot closer to actually happening."

That uncomfortable feeling slithered up my spine again, creepy, like a deer tick under my clothes, looking for a place to burrow in. "You know, Willie and my father are under the impression that it's a done deal. So far, I haven't heard Justin Shay mention this thing in the *maybe* sense, even once."

Nate seemed to think carefully about what to say. I wanted to reach across the space between us, grab his arm, and shake him until the whole truth fell out. "Justin doesn't deal so much in practicalities." Nate's eyes met mine, and I knew he was finally going to level with me completely.

"The truth is that the numbers for his last film weren't good— over budget, poor performance at the box office, and onto DVD way too soon. His studio deal is in serious jeopardy, and with Justin's recent history, it's not likely the production company can put together independent money for something just because he wants it. The fact is that the studio deal is the only thing keeping his production company alive, and Justin's got to come through big this time. He's got to keep the studio happy, and they're going to want to do something close to home, where there's less budget and Justin's not so hard to insure. They'll want something they know they can sell—a typical Justin Shay flick. When he comes to the table with a tender cowboy story, they're going to laugh him out of the room. If Dane attaches himself to it, though, that's a huge push. Barring that . . ." Nate rubbed the back of his neck, shaking his head. "Without Dane, there's no way. It won't matter how cooperative the horse is or how well Justin learns to play cowboy. I'm sorry, Lauren, but if you want my honest opinion, I think Justin's fooling himself. It wouldn't be the first time."

I took a step away, studying him in a light that seemed too harsh for the late-day quiet. The hope I'd started to foster drained away, leaving an empty chill in its wake. "If you feel that way, then why are you here?" Maybe Nate wasn't the person I'd begun to allow myself to imagine. Maybe he was exactly what I'd thought he was to begin with—a celebrity hanger-on basking in the ambient light of fame while telling his benefactor what he wanted to hear. "Why are you letting Justin Shay mislead everyone into thinking you're going to write some Academy Award–winning screenplay that will make Daily famous? Don't you realize people are investing their lives in this—my father, Amber, everyone who's out here working on this place?"

Bracing his hands on his hips, Nate looked at the ground and let out a long sigh. A worry line—a first—creased the space between his brows, and I saw the truth even if he didn't want to speak it. He was afraid of this project. He was afraid to tell the truth. He was afraid not to. "Justin and I go back a long way. . . ."

"That's no excuse." The latent glow of passion whiplashed into anger. I focused it on him, even though I knew it should have been aimed in a dozen different directions—my father living by the code, Willie Wardlaw for taking advantage of it, Justin Shay for filling everyone full of lies, myself for beginning to hope. I should have been smarter than that. "My father invested in this thing. He has a right to the truth."

"You don't understand how the business works."

My spine went rigid, the old, familiar heat of indignation creeping through me. I hadn't argued like this with anyone since Danny. Danny was always so sure he was right about everything. He wanted it all *his* way. *His* plans were always the ones that would work out, if not today, then tomorrow, the next day. The rest of us were just supposed to keep hoping and believing until we were so far down a hole we couldn't climb out. I looked at Nate, and I saw Danny. Same operator, different clothes. "I may not be from Hollywood, but I'm not an idiot. I recognize a scam when I see one."

Nate's chin jerked up as if I'd slugged him. His jaw tightened and twitched. "It's not a scam."

"People deserve the truth. Even if it's not what they want to hear."

"There is no truth, it's . . ." He twisted away, took his frustrations out on a rock and watched it skitter across the gravel. "There's no way to know anything for sure until Dane comes. Strange things happen in Hollywood all the time." He blew into his fingers, his shoulders sagging as the air went out. "I'm not the one with the power to make or break this deal."

"But you don't think we can get Dane?" I felt my anger begin to go stale. This problem was so complex, it was hard to know who to be angry at.

Nate considered the answer for a long time, as if he were tormented by it, as if there were no good solutions. "I have no idea." He opened his mouth to say something more, but then thought better of it.

"What would it take to get Dane to commit . . . attach, or whatever you call it?"

Combing strands of caramel brown hair through his fingers, he squinted at the horizon, where the shadows of evening fell over the hills, slowly muting the colors, painting a watercolor wash of forest green, pale gray, and in the distance a soft, dark violet that blended almost seamlessly into the sky. "A good script that hasn't already been laughed at by everyone in the business, a lead with a name that brings in big box office. This is a character flick. The cast has to sell it."

"Justin Shay *is* a big name," I said.

"Not in this genre." Nate's brows knotted again, forming a long wrinkle in his forehead. "I don't know if he can do it. I don't even think he knows if he can do it."

I stood torn between hope and hopelessness. If the project remained a possibility, then everything might still be all right. If Nate was a sycophant merely hedging to protect his meal ticket, then all was lost. The options swayed like a tree in the wind. It was difficult to know which way to fall. "He seems confident."

"Justin's like that." Nate shrugged off the argument like a coat that was too heavy. He glanced toward my SUV, indicating that heart-to-heart time was over. "I guess we should get going, huh?"

"I guess," I agreed. The realities of *The Horseman* were best taken in small bites. Lumped all together, it was enough to choke a horse. *One thing at a time,* I told myself. *Get through the family dinner first, then let's have a look at this script, see how bad it really is. There must be a way to make all of this work out. There has to be.*

As we climbed into the SUV and left the ranch behind, I tried to leave off the analysis. There was no way of knowing where Nate Heath's loyalties really lay, and no reason for him to reveal them. Whether this project lived or died, his existence would go on as usual. He could afford to wait and see which way the ball bounced, but for Daily, for my father, this project was everything, which meant I couldn't just stand back and wait. If Justin Shay wasn't going to buy my father and Willie out of this project, I had no choice but to get behind *The Horseman* and start pushing. I'd been standing on the sidelines, letting life happen to me for too long now. I didn't want to be that woman anymore. I wanted to be the bright-eyed optimist, like Amber Anderson.

I used to be that girl, I thought. *I used to be the bold one.*

Somewhere in the chilling floodwaters of Caney Creek, that boldness had been washed away. Perhaps the part of me that died that night was still lodged in the rocks along the shoreline somewhere, like a long-lost artifact waiting to be rediscovered, rescued, and polished, if only I would come searching. . . .

Without consciously thinking about it, I pulled onto the county road and turned toward Caney Creek. When I realized what I'd done, a lump rose in my throat and my hands tightened on the wheel. I considered going on, driving past Amber's house, past Pastor Harve's church, continuing over the hill and into the next valley, slowing just a little as the truck splashed through the harmless trickle at the low-water crossing on the county road.

And then, despite all the bluster in my head, I couldn't do it. *If wishes were horses*, Aunt Netta always said, and I was only wishing. I didn't have what it took to go back to that place again, to face the pain and search for what was lost.

Stopping the truck in the middle of the road, I shifted into reverse, backed the trailer over a culvert by a gate, and headed around the long way. "Sorry about that," I said. "We'd better go around the other way. We'll drop the trailer back at Uncle Top's as we pass."

Nate nodded amiably, perhaps just glad to have the *Horseman* discussion over. If our conversation had offended him in any way, he didn't show it. Settling into the passenger seat and taking in the scenery, he probed the silence by asking harmless questions about local landmarks, jackrabbits, and a roadrunner that dashed by after we left the trailer at Uncle Top's house. The conversation slipped into a rhythm that was easy and nonthreatening. We talked about Daily and my years growing up here. As we drove into town and turned onto Main Street, I warned him about Aunt Donetta's gatherings and the fact that my relatives would probably force-feed him everything from grilled wild game to UFOs (unidentified fried objects) and a dozen varieties of pie. No shindig at the yellow clapboard house on B Street was ever complete without wild game and multiple desserts.

A low cloud of mesquite smoke hung over B Street when we reached it, and two blocks down, past an unstructured jumble of cars parked on the street, in lawns, and over ditches, actual flames were visible. A full-scale Donetta Bradford barbecue was underway. It looked like she'd invited half of the town, which was typical. Aunt Netta's plans always started small and grew larger, like the biblical ball of dough. Pour Aunt Netta into a situation, and it'd be leavened beyond manageable size before you could say, *Hold on a minute, maybe we should think this through*.

Nate poked his head out the window with a look of concern. "Smells like something's on fire."

"That's just my family cooking," I assured him, and he gave me a look of disbelief mingled with what was probably a healthy dose of fear. "Seriously," I said. "They've probably caught the fryer on fire again. Aunt Donetta usually feeds the volunteer Fire Department right along with the guests."

Nate rubbed his chin, which actually needed a shave. I noted, a bit reluctantly, that he looked good that way. For some reason, it was hard to think of Nate as potentially untrustworthy, potentially the enemy. I wanted to like him, even though I knew it might not be a good idea.

"Looks like The Shay made it here," he said, spotting Justin's ridiculous monster truck backed up to the carport, half on the lawn and half on the driveway. "I'll get the keys from him and move that thing out of there." Nate looked slightly embarrassed, as if he realized that parking on your host's lawn wasn't proper guest behavior.

"Oh, hey, don't worry about it," I said, wiggling my Durango into a spot behind a truck with a post auger dangling off the back. No doubt, Aunt Donetta had spotted Pearly Parsons working on fences at the Anderson-Shay ranch and invited him to dinner. "Everyone parks on the lawn here. We don't bother to mow the grass. We just drive over it until it dies."

Nate chuckled like he thought that was a joke, which it really wasn't. It occurred to me that compared to the manicured lawns and gardens of multimillion dollar Hollywood estates, Daily must seem incredibly redneck. Aunt Netta's house was anything but manicured. Around the porch, holly bushes and climbing roses had grown wild, so that the guests coming and going were forced to slip through a narrow opening in the foliage to reach the house. It wasn't much of an inconvenience normally, because everyone came and went through the carport door anyway.

At the moment, the carport was filled with coolers, two barbecue grills, a propane fish fryer, a smattering of mixed-breed dogs, lawn chairs of all types and the men who love them. It wasn't actually the fryer that was on fire, but a large barbecue grill, and trying to shut down the fire was, of all people, Justin Shay. Willie Wardlaw stood beside him, scratching his head and looking at an instruction book, and my father was dragging a garden hose across the lawn, shouting, "Ya want me to douse it?" Meanwhile, uncles, neighbors, and members of the local Sheriff's Department were looking on with interest, trying to decide whether to vacate their lawn chairs before the propane tank blew up.

The entire scene was a Norman Rockwell freeze frame. Next year's Christmas card in the making. *Happy Holidays from Daily, Texas!*

Despite the rising flames, which finally convinced several

dogs and a few guests to leave the carport, Nate waded into the fray and quickly involved himself in figuring out how to turn off the massive barbecue grill—a quandary, since the plastic control buttons had been melted by the flames shooting out. Justin held up one of the buttons to show Nate the problem, while Willie pointed out that in the picture, the grill had an emergency shutoff, but he couldn't find it. My father again offered to spray water on the grill, but there was a plate of freshly fried fish nearby, and the crowd was more concerned about the fish than our lives.

Finally Nate grabbed an oven mitt, took the perilous step of squatting down behind the grill and sticking his hand inside it, then closed the valve on the propane bottle. He came out shaking his hand wildly, then slung off the smoking oven mitt and checked to make sure he still had all his fingers. The mitt flew across the carport and landed on a sleeping dog, which jumped up, yelping, tucked its tail, and ran for daylight. My father went after the dog with the garden hose, just in case.

Uncle Beans, who'd been a latent observer until then, hurried to one of the coolers and pulled out a cold can of Dr. Pepper, which he shoved into Nate's hand. "Here, young fella. Hold that." Beans peered up from beneath the time-worn cowboy hat he'd had for as long as I could remember. His theory had always been that a man only needed one good hat in a lifetime, if he took care of it right.

Justin stepped toward the barbecue grill, and Nate slung an arm out like a mom protecting a toddler during a sudden stop. "It's hot." Nate moved the Dr. Pepper can around in his fingers. "Justin, what were you doing?"

"I bought a barbecue grill." Holding up the melted control knob, Justin motioned to a new red plastic cooler sitting beside the grill. "And some steaks, and all the stuff to grill it with."

From the cooler, he pulled out barbecue tools, a bottle of sauce, and a bag of jalapeños, and showed them to Nate. "Willie 'n me are gonna grill meat for everybody."

Nate's nose and eyebrows wrinkled together. "You're going to grill steaks?"

"That's what cowboys do. They grill meat." Justin glanced at Willie for confirmation, then added, "Come help us grill some meat, Nate."

Giving the barbecue tools a suspicious look, Nate scratched his ear. "Let me get this straight. You bought your *own* barbecue grill?"

"Sure," Justin chirped. "At the hardware store just now."

"You didn't stop by the hotel on the way there?" Nate leaned close to his friend, studying Justin's eyes in a way that was filled with hidden meaning. I wondered what was being said that wasn't being said.

Justin drew back. "No, I *didn't* go by the *hotel*. Willie 'n me were just talking about steaks on the way over here, and we stopped off to buy some stuff. I didn't know if Donetta would have a grill or not, so I got one. Don't be such a party killer, Nate." He ended with an irritated look, and Nate studied him a moment longer.

Justin turned his attention back to the cooler. "Hey, call that guy at the hardware store and tell him to bring us another grill. This one's screwed up. We've got meat to cook." He looked over his shoulder, then seemed to realize there was no one behind him with a notepad, taking orders.

"We can probably git this one workin'," my father said as he stepped in and took the instruction book from Willie, who was still looking for the page about what to do after you almost blow up your new grill. "Let me look them instructions over. I don't think you got this thing put together right." Sidestepping,

227

he moved closer to Nate. "You know anythin' about these gas kind, there . . . uhhh . . . Nate?"

"A little," Nate answered.

"I hadn't ever used anything but wood myself." My father turned the instruction booklet so Nate could see it, and Nate was quickly drafted into Project Barbecue, whether he wanted to be or not. Aunt Donetta called to me through the kitchen window, and I went inside to help.

In the house, Aunt Donetta had decided we were in danger of a pie shortage, so she and Imagene Doll were frantically defrosting packages of frozen blackberries and mixing up lemon pudding for an icebox pie. They were debating whether it would jell more quickly in the freezer. As usual, enough food for an army was already cooked, including a ham that was big enough to serve the town all on its own. The culinary conglomeration was slowly growing cold on the table and the old sideboard. In another half hour or so, while we cooked more food, we would begin alternately sticking parts of the original meal in the oven to rewarm.

Eventually, we would serve too much food an hour or so late. When we were finished, dishes and leftovers would be everywhere. We'd sink into lawn chairs around the dying barbecue grill, and the stories would start flying. We would laugh, in spite of the fact that we'd heard them all before. When we parted ways at the end of the night, we'd talk about what a good gathering it was, and how we had too much food, and how we didn't get together nearly enough. Even though I knew the routine, even though I could quote all the family stories from memory, even though I'd end up so full I'd feel guilty for a week, I found myself looking forward to every part of it.

The sights and sounds of Aunt Donetta and Uncle Ronald's house snuggled around me like a comfortable old quilt as we finished making the pies and began heating and reheating casseroles. By then, the pile of grilled and fried meat in the carport was monumental. Nate and my father had taken charge of the new barbecue grill, and Justin had settled into a lawn chair, where he and Willie were deep in discussion. Nearby, Mimi, Frederico, and Uncle Beans were sitting on the lawn furniture under the kitchen window. Their conversation drifted through the screen as Aunt Netta filled the oven with casseroles, stacked sideways and cockeyed, and I washed mixing bowls in the sink.

Frederico was explaining the concept of saturated fats and the unhealthy effects of consuming large quantities of untrimmed red meats. Mimi's comments showed rapt interest, while Uncle Beans's input testified to the fact that he'd left his hearing aid at home. He thought they were talking about today's menu.

"The greatest detriment is *cholesterol*." The words rolled together in Frederico's lilting Italian accent.

"What?" Uncle Beans cupped a hand behind his hear. "Why, a'course they're gonna *cook-it-all*. Smoked, smothered, or fried, son. Whatever's yer pleasure, we got it. Hooves, horns, and everythin' in between. You and the young lady can just take yer pick. Got plenty."

Frederico pinched his thumb and forefinger in the air, looking philosophical. "The red meat. It is difficult for the *digestion*."

"Well, I don't know which is the *best'un*." Scratching his chin, Uncle Beans pondered the growing meat stack. "Kinda depends on yer preferences, I guess. But you can try more than one. Load up. It's all good. Don't miss out on the fried catfish, neither. You ain't been to Texas if you hadn't ate fried catfish." Uncle Beans gave Mimi a gap-toothed smile. "You make sure and get you some too, young lady."

Frederico and Mimi exchanged bemused glances.

"In particular it is unhealthy for the *art-er-ies*," Frederico attempted once more, leaning close and speaking slowly. "The fried fish is greatly detrimental."

"Yep, them's my favorite, too," Uncle Beans agreed, because he couldn't even begin to make out *arteries* and *detrimental*. Slapping Frederico on the shoulder, Beans employed his usual strategy for parties without his hearing aid; he launched into a story so he wouldn't have to try to listen. "Now, back when I was a young chap like yerself, I was workin' for cowpoke wages on the King Ranch. I'll tell you right now, that was a life for a young man. We had a bunkhouse cook that could make the flank steak off a dry-grass steer taste like fillet mig-none. Big fella—German, as I recall. Couldn't understand a word he said, but . . ."

The story went on as Aunt Donetta and I rotated the casseroles through the oven and piled whipped cream on pies until finally, she, Imagene, and Lucy conferred and decided the most practical thing would be to move all the food to the carport. We dragged out yard tables, knocked off the dirtdobber nests, spread tablecloths in everything from lace to polyester print, and laid out enough provisions to feed the entire town of Daily, which was good, because by then Aunt Netta had invited everyone she saw and anyone who happened to phone in during the hours of preparation. We stopped just short of going out on the highway and flagging down passing cars.

Before dinner, we formed a gigantic circle on the front lawn, joined hands, and blessed the food. By then, Nate, Justin, and crew were practically part of the family. When the prayer ended, Aunt Netta took Nate and Justin by the arms and moved them to the front of the food line. She motioned for everyone else to follow, and our gathering began with the usual opening words, "C'mon y'all, I know you're hu-u-ungry!"

As the guests moved through the line, I stood back with Imagene and Aunt Donetta, taking it all in. Imagene hugged me to her side, and I laid my head on her shoulder. Aunt Netta squeezed both of us, then she hurried off to go make more tea, even though there was already a five-gallon bucketful on the picnic table.

Imagene was more inclined to stand still and just enjoy the moment. "It's good to have you back," she whispered, resting her cheek against my head.

"I should have come sooner," I said. "I'm sorry I wasn't here for Uncle Jack's funeral." Imagene's husband, Jack, had always been my favorite uncle, even though he was really just my father's longtime best friend. We weren't actually related.

She squeezed me harder, smoothing a hand over my hair in a way that was tender and comforting. "Oh, hon, you're here now."

"I've missed it," I whispered.

After supper, while Nate played horseshoes in the near darkness with my father and uncles, it occurred to me that I should probably make a quick trip back to the Anderson-Shay ranch to check on the goat therapy program. By the time I'd gathered my things and said my good-byes, Aunt Netta and Imagene had smoothly recruited Nate to go along with me, and they couldn't wait to pack the two of us into my Durango, along with some plates of leftover meat and Tupperware containing spare pies.

"Take these by the hotel buildin' on yer way back and put them in the storeroom refrigerator, hon," Aunt Netta instructed, making the pairing of Nate and me sound random and innocent. "And don't you worry about these dishes here, either. Don't bother comin' back here tonight at all, y'hear? Y'all two just go on about your rat-killin'. Imagene and me'll get the dishes cleaned up. Won't we, Imagene?" She elbowed Imagene, and Imagene nodded.

"Oh sure, sure we will." Imagene paused and yawned. "You kids just enjoy the rest of the evenin'. It's a beautiful night for a drive." She checked the sky, just to make sure the stars were in proper alignment.

I felt like I was back in middle school, having T.G. Taggert pick me up for the eighth grade FFA dance. T.G. and I were never more than friends who dated, but Aunt Donetta thought it'd be neat if an Eldridge eventually got hitched to a Taggert, since we were cousins way back. Why spread the DNA outside the family? When Danny came along, Aunt Netta tried in every way she could to steer me back to T.G. She always thought Danny was a bad choice—too wild and unreliable.

"Y'all two have fun, now," Aunt Netta chirped as she closed my door and waved us away. "See ya' in the mornin'. I'll have sweet rolls on the back buffet, ready and waitin' at six-thirty." She and Imagene backed up and stood shoulder to shoulder as we drove away. I could barely make out their silhouettes against the streetlamp in the rearview mirror, but I would have sworn they exchanged a high five and did a little victory dance, like football players watching the chains move downfield toward the end zone.

Nate and I sat in embarrassed silence, because we both knew what was happening. We'd been thrust together all evening at every possible opportunity. *"Here, hon, there's a chair next to Nate." "Why don't you see if Nate wants some more tea?" "Puggy, hon, you oughta show Nate the graveyard next door." "It's a pretty stroll when the jasmine opens up. . . ."*

On the way through town, Nate started asking questions about the old buildings to fill the silence. Since we were trapped in the car together, I sidetracked into the tale of the secret tunnel that, as Daily legend had it, began under the café and led to a hidden cave on the creek. "Supposedly, there's still a ghost down there counting Confederate gold. My father used to tell us a long story about how he was working cows down by the creek when he was younger. One broke away, disappeared between two cedar bushes along the bluffs, and never came out. When he rode through the cedars, he saw the cave." I lowered my voice to give the story an air of mystery as we passed through the bottom of a canyon where moon shadows cast eerie patterns over boulders and twisted oaks, bringing them to life. "His horse wouldn't go inside, so he got off and started in, but then he heard a strange growling sound, and it was black as pitch, so he left. He came back later with a flashlight and a gun, but he couldn't find the cave, and he never saw the cow again, either."

"You'll have to tell Justin that story. He was always into that kind of thing. He used to watch horror movies at Mama Louise's, then be too scared to go up to bed alone. He'd wait until I went up, because he didn't want the other kids to know he was chicken."

My mind was gathering bits of information like puzzle pieces. "So you and Justin grew up together?"

"For a few years. Through high school." Nate looked out the window, watched a pair of white horses doze in the moonlight, their coats illuminated like pearls.

"Are y'all cousins?"

Nate chuckled. "That's cute—y'all. I like the way you say that." He studied the world outside the window. "What are those tall things with the spikes on top?"

"Yuccas. You didn't answer the question."

"What question?"

"You and Justin. I wondered if you were family or just old

friends. You seem like"—*well, his parental figure, actually*—"you're close."

"I knew him when." Nate rolled down the window, and the soft, cool night air spun inward.

"When?"

"In the table-waiting, got no money, got no prospects years. We came out to Hollywood together after high school in Joplin."

"So, you're from Missouri?"

Nate didn't answer at first. In the darkness, I could see only the profile of his face. "Not really. Justin and I were in foster care together there. At Mama Louise's."

"Oh . . . I'm sorry." It was out of my mouth before I had time to think about it. When he'd said Mama Louise's earlier, I'd thought he was talking about a relative's house. "I mean, I wasn't trying to stick my nose into—"

"It's all right." His tone was tender, as if he didn't want me to feel bad for asking. "It was where I needed to be. Mama Louise was a good person. Before her place, I don't think I understood that the grown-ups are actually supposed to take care of you, not just let you stay around. She kept kids nobody else would touch. I wasn't really a hard case, but by the time she got Justin, he'd already been to juvie a couple times and he was about one step away from some real trouble. He'd been in foster care for a while by then. His mother dropped him in a video arcade with two bucks on his tenth birthday, and she never came back. Mama Louise understood those things, but at the same time she didn't let you use it as an excuse, you know? With Mama Louise, everything was about choices. Just because you had lousy parents didn't mean you weren't supposed to go out and do something with your life."

Nate motioned toward the house as we turned into the

Anderson-Shay ranch. "I think that's why Justin wants to put this place together. After all these years, he's trying to make things right with Mama Louise."

"Wow," I breathed, feeling guilty for my negative mental impression of Justin Shay. But for the grace of God, who'd dropped me into a good family, I could have been the kid growing up in foster care, looking for a place to belong. "Does he ever . . . ?" As we turned into the barnyard, the headlights swept the pasture. Underneath the live oak where Justin's hat had been wedged earlier, something caught my eye in a flash—something human, but not human. Something at least eight feet tall, covered with hair, standing in silhouette under the tree with its arms raised. The headlights glinted off its eyes as the beam skimmed by. "What was . . . Did you see that?"

"Back up." Unbuckling his seatbelt, Nate braced a hand on the door and shinnied halfway out the window to get a better look.

My heart hammered as I put the car in reverse, allowing the headlights to slowly sweep toward the live oak tree . . . closer . . . closer. A cottontail rabbit stood on its hind legs and froze in the glow as the lights cast an uneven sheen over the tips of the branches. A pulse fluttered in my throat as the beam reached the trunk, illuminated it, lit up the place where the man-thing had been. The spot was empty. I backed in a circle, Nate stretching further out the window, scanning the darkness. Finally, he slid back into the seat as the headlights shined toward the construction trailers by the house.

"What *was* that?" I muttered, my heart still gyrating and my fingers tight on the steering wheel.

"A . . . really tall, hairy . . . Confederate soldier-ghost?" I realized I'd known Nate would make a joke to lighten the situation, and I was looking forward to the comfort of it. "Or Bigfoot. It looked a lot like Bigfoot."

I couldn't decide whether to laugh or hit the gas and get us out of there. "Have you ever *seen* Bigfoot?"

"I worked on a documentary about it once."

"And did you see Bigfoot then?"

"In the dramatization, it looked exactly like that . . . the thing under there." Nate wagged a finger toward the live oak.

"That must have just been a shadow or something." I wasn't sure if I was trying to convince Nate or myself. "Look, the dogs aren't even barking." I pointed toward Joe's dogs, curled up like drowsy sentries flanking the barn doors.

"Right." Nate punched a fist into the air, punctuating my conclusion with a silent hurrah as we pulled into the barnyard and stopped, both sitting with our fingers on our respective door handles. Nate scanned the darkness. "You first, cowgirl."

"No way. You're the Bigfoot expert."

His soft, confident laugh echoed into the night as he opened his door, came around to my side, and opened mine. "Ready?" The word slipped over me like a flutter of warm breeze, seeming to mean something more than what it did. The clutch of fear loosened, melted into something tingly and warm. The sensation was heady and sudden, catching me unprepared.

"Sure." I slid to the ground, feeling unsteady, as if my feet weren't touching anything solid. The dogs rose and investigated us as we tiptoed to the barn and peered into the first stall, where Lucky Strike was settled peacefully in the corner, dozing on a bed of straw with his legs curled under him. The nanny goat stood happily nibbling hay nearby.

"Guess it's working," Nate whispered.

When I looked at him, his eyes were deep and dark. "Guess so." Somewhere in the distance, a whippoorwill called. I knew Nate was going to kiss me, and despite any and all reservations,

I wanted him to. *Keep your enemies close.* The words were rueful in my head. *Keep your friends closer.*

Which one was he?

Did it really matter?

His hand slipped into my hair, and I felt myself lean into him, our bodies connecting in a way that felt natural and perfect, electric.

His lips touched mine, lightly at first, then passionately. I fell into it, and there was nothing but the softness of the air, the scent of his nearness, the feeling of his arms lacing around me, the slight aroma of smoke on his shirt.

Every thought in my mind flew away on the call of the whippoorwill and there was only sensation, nothing else but Nate and me, and the night.

Chapter 16

Nathaniel Heath

The kiss wasn't premeditated, really. It just . . . happened. Afterward, I think we were both a little surprised. I had the sense that we'd just tripped over a line Lauren hadn't wanted to cross. Taking a step back, she turned her face away, her gaze fluttering off into the moonlight. With a nervous laugh, she suggested that maybe we'd better leave while the horse and the goat were peacefully sharing space, and before Sasquatch reappeared under the tree.

"Maybe he's looking for The Shay's cowboy hat. That thing would be worth some serious dough on eBay," I said to lighten things up, which was a technique I'd learned way back in the skinny middle school days. When you're potentially close to getting a reaction that might bruise your ego, make the girl laugh.

It seemed like she lingered there by the barn a moment longer, but that could have been my imagination. I got temporarily lost in observing the way the moonglow painted her cheek as she glanced toward the car, then back at me. Her gaze fluttered upward, met mine, her eyes deep and liquid. Her lips parted, and I halfway thought about kissing her again, invisible line or not. The other half of me said, *Don't be a doofus. She just said, Let's go.*

It's always hard to know which half has the better grasp on reality in a case like that.

A howling sound disturbingly close by convinced me that the truck might be a good idea. "What was *that*?" A chorus of eerie voices joined in and some primordial reaction made the hairs stand on end all over my body. The watchdogs barked and moved to the edge of the gravel.

"Coyotes." Lauren barely gave the noise a glance. "Don't worry. They won't come up to the barn. You don't hear coyotes where you come from?"

I knew there were coyotes where I lived, even around LA, because I saw complaints about them on the news. Periodically, one wandered into a park or a sidewalk coffee bar and gave the city dwellers an unwanted thrill. "I usually have the TV on."

Lauren made a soft *tsk-tsk* behind her teeth. "That must make it hard to write."

Ouch. Touché. She'd ferreted out one of my most counter-productive habits—using the TV for companionship and an avoidance mechanism. Brain anesthesia to keep my mind from wondering how I'd ended up thirty-eight, living alone in a cabin in the mountains. If I was there to create my magnum opus, why wasn't the room littered with shreds of genius and the computer filled with little opi just waiting to be strung together into a work that would add meaning to the world?

"Peace and quiet are overrated," I said.

She laughed again, and we got in the truck and drove back to the hotel. By the time we'd finished putting away the haul of leftovers from Donetta's house, Justin and Frederico came in. Justin was in one of his manic moods and wanted to hang out downstairs and talk horse whispering and foster shelters all night. Even though we'd all just eaten a week's worth of food, he was in favor of breaking out the leftovers and partying on. He called Amber to invite her over, but she was still on her way home from Austin. Lauren, perhaps noting that Justin was determined to get up a party, waved a quick good-bye and slipped off to her hotel room, looking tired. Frederico decided to investigate the exercise machines, which quickly drove Justin away because he didn't want to get roped into making up for two days of missed workouts.

Justin and I ended up together in Suite Beulahland, which I was enjoying much more now that Elvis and I had our own room. Unfortunately, Justin wasn't in the mood to sleep. He wanted to pull an all-nighter with the script and decide how we would put the proposal together for Dane before next Monday.

"So Dane's really coming here? In a little over a week?" I asked, wondering again if we were dealing in real reality or Shay reality here. It was possible that the whole Dane thing could be just another one of Justin's master-of-the-universe delusions, in which case I was (unknowingly or not) exactly what Lauren had accused me of being—a conman helping to perpetrate a really low scheme on some very nice people.

"Yeah, he's coming." The Shay stopped pacing the room and stood by the tall windows that overlooked Main Street. Hanging his arms in a gorillalike posture, he eyed me critically. "You know what, Nate . . . Why am I still getting the vibe that you're not on board here?"

Well, we've arrived, I thought. Moment of truth time. "You want me to be honest, or you want me to tell you what you want to hear?"

"Both."

Leave it to Justin to pick C when given a choice of A or B. "I think we're leading a lot of nice people down the yellow brick road, and when it comes right down to it, we won't be able to pull this thing off."

My point, whatever it was, whizzed over Justin's head like a bumble bee on its way to someplace else. "Don't worry, man, Dane's into me. With him on board, Randall and those stuffed shirts'll be falling all over themselves to do this thing."

There was no value in arguing with Justin when he was in a mood like this, and besides, I was tired. I wanted to close my eyes and sink back into that hospitable, homey feeling I'd had when I was enjoying the meat-o-rama and the ensuing horse-shoe game at Donetta's house. "How did you convince Dane to come here, anyway?"

He held up his palms as if it were elementary. "Hey, I'm Justin Shay."

Yeah, right. That doesn't count for much when you're practically uninsurable. In Hollywood, you're only as good as your last project. "Come on, everyone wants Dane. Nobody's been able to get him to work for how long now . . . five years or more? How'd you get him to come all the way to Texas to take a meeting?"

Justin crossed his arms over his chest, displeased with the fact that *I'm the Shay* didn't work as a passkey for me. "He owes me. I went to one of his kids' birthday parties."

"You went to a kid's birthday party?" The Shay didn't even like kids. As far as I knew, he'd never even been to his *own* kids' birthday parties. His personal assistant sent lavish gifts at the right times of year, but that was it.

"Yeah, his son's a big fan." He said it like it was the most natural thing in the world. "And Dane's interested in the foster shelter project. You know, he's got all those kids adopted from all over the place."

Ahhhh . . . now a few things were starting to make sense.

Dane and his actress wife were rapidly building a patchwork of family adopted from poverty-stricken orphanages all over the world. The tabloids and TV talk shows loved their mixture of glamour and humanitarianism.

The Shay grinned, seeming pleased with himself. "I told him to bring the kid out to the ranch, and I'd show him the horses and stuff."

"You used Dane's kid to try to get Dane on board for this project? At his birthday party?"

Justin's lip curled indignantly. "No. The kid'll get to see the horses. Willie said he'd even ask Frank to come up with a pony that likes kids." I once again noted Justin's obvious admiration for Willie Wardlaw. Such hero worship was completely uncharacteristic for Justin, as was taking advice—fatherly or otherwise—from anyone. Normally, Justin liked to be the alpha. Period. "He's a cute kid. I think he's about Brody's age. They got him from someplace that used to be the Soviet Union."

I was dumbstruck at the mention of Brody. Justin almost never mentioned either one of his sons. I wondered if he even knew how old Brody was at this point.

Justin's expression turned oddly pensive. He stopped moving and looked me in the eye. "Do you think Stephanie would want to bring Brody and Bryn here to see the ranch and stuff?" Maybe the question seemed more farfetched when he said it out loud, or maybe he saw my mouth dropping open, but he quickly added, "I guess it's a stupid idea."

"I think you . . ." I started to restate what we both knew by saying something useless and off-the-cuff like, *I think you've burned more bridges than Patton's army, where Stephanie's concerned.* Stephanie had spent thirteen years being lured by Justin's various attempts at rehab and normal family existence. She and the boys had been sucked in and spit out more times than I could count. After she moved out of LA and took the kids, I figured that was pretty much the end of things, which was probably for the best. Neither Marla nor Randall nor I encouraged Justin to complete the long to-do list required for him to get visitation again. He was mad at Stephanie at that point, and we all knew he wouldn't stick with it. Brody and Bryn needed to be safe, the dirt from the custody battle was slowly burying Justin's career, and aside from that, I remembered what it was like to live with the adults around you at war. No kid deserved that.

I'd always reasoned that some people just weren't meant to be parents. Now, face to face with Justin, and even though I knew this whole foster shelter thing was the brain child of one of his manic states from which he would eventually come down, I couldn't bring myself to tread on his fantasy. I just kept thinking, *You know what, Nate, if your mother ditched you in a video arcade, you'd be screwed up, too.*

"I think something like that's not going to happen overnight," I said carefully. I didn't want to cut Justin off at the knees, but I didn't want to blow smoke at him, either. "Stephanie's been burned a lot of times, and she's got Brody and Bryn to worry about. I think it's going to take baby steps, and the time to do it isn't when you're on a big high about a project."

The Shay frowned, rammed his hands into his pockets, and snorted sardonically to let me know that wasn't the correct answer. "I knew that's what you'd say. You're always so stinkin' careful, Nate. You're so worried about flying under the radar, you don't ever take off. It's like you're still afraid if you stick your head up, the old man's gonna knock it off."

The observation bit in a way I was completely unprepared for, and I couldn't think of anything to say at first. The *Shay* was standing here telling me *I* was a screw-up? It doesn't get

any more warped than that. "We're not talking about me."
Was he right? Did it sting because it was true? Was I living my
life in the safe zone, doing what was easy, always opting for the
sure thing rather than going after what I really wanted? Deep
down, in some disgusting, twisted, Freudian way, was I afraid
that if I tried something big, if I reached for the brass ring and
failed, a deeply buried, subliminal Doug would pop up and say,
*What'd you think was gonna happen, you little screw-up? Now
go out to the garage and get me a beer. . . .*

"You know what, Nate?" The Shay gave me a fierce look. I'd
rained on his parade with the Stephanie comment, and now he
was going to thank me by laying on the guilt and manipulation
with the old, *You're my brother, man. If you don't believe in
me, man, I might as well cash it in right now. . . .*

Every time I fell for that line, I got sucked into some form
of near disaster.

"Maybe we should be," he said, and I had to re-track, because the conversation had veered off unexpectedly. "Maybe
we oughta talk about you. Maybe we oughta talk about why
you're not on board with this project. You're just here hangin'
out, giving it lip service, waiting for it to crash and burn."

"I think I've been pretty honest about that," I said, and he
snorted again.

"I could make one phone call and have ten writers here to
take your place." Now *there* was The Shay I remembered—the
narcissistic, dictatorial, self-important action superdude who
made no apologies for occupying the gravitational center of
the universe.

"Why haven't you, then?" I remained calm only because I knew
it would annoy him. Justin hated it when the sycophants didn't
quiver in fear. "You could get someone who knows about all
this horse stuff, someone who's into emoting all over the page."

"I don't want someone who emotes! I want you!" he exploded. "I want this project for me and you, Nate. I want everybody to see we can do something more than another knife and gun car-chase flick. I want people to take us . . . seriously. I'm tired of walking into parties and knowing they're all thumbing their noses at us behind our backs. I want us to get respect. A man isn't anything if he doesn't have respect." The last part had an inflection that came straight from Willie Wardlaw.

Some long-ago comment from my grandfather about respect being something you *earn* came to mind, but I didn't say it. The Shay and I were in new territory here, and I wasn't sure where to go next. Maybe he was finally growing up. Maybe we both were.

"I'll do the best I can with the script." The words were out of my mouth before I had time to reassess the commitment I was making or the level of involvement required. Working with Justin on this project, particularly working in the disorganized, piecemeal, scrap-at-a-time way Justin operated, would tie me up for months. There would be no more long, lazy days in Mammoth Lakes. No quiet, contemplative walks in the woods. No afternoons with Oprah while the laptop quietly purred in snooze mode. Dr. Phil would miss me. . . . "I'll give it everything I've got, but you have to come through on your end. You've got to stay off the stuff, and I don't just mean the hooch, I mean the prescription stuff, too. After we finish this meeting with Dane, you need to do rehab—for real, this time. If you want to make a go of this project, if you want to get Stephanie to let you see the kids, you've got to keep your head clear and stay focused. This can't be another screw-up like Morocco. I'm not taking another ride to the bottom with you, Justin." I realized we were about as close to the bone as The Shay and I had ever been. Another road trip into unfamiliar territory.

He looked at me narrowly, and whatever he wanted to say—

probably some form of stock denial of his addiction and the fact that he'd almost killed us both the last time he went off the deep end—went unspoken. "I get it," he said flatly. "You just hook up with the horse trainer and give me a good proposal. She's hot, by the way. You should go for it. She's into you, dude." Without another word, he headed off toward his room, leaving me with a strange combination of lofty promises, relationship advice, and Elvis memorabilia.

A short time later, he was bored with rattling around the hotel, and he wanted me to, of all things, go down to the VFW hall and try to get in the poker game with the sheriff and some local guys, who apparently played at night. Picturing something like *The Dukes of Hazzard*, I politely declined. By then, I'd pulled out the screenplay and was looking it over again. Justin's feeling was that our Oscar run could wait until tomorrow. Right now, he wanted a poker buddy. In his room down the hall, Frederico was sacked out and unwakeable. Justin wasn't happy when I didn't cooperate, either.

"You act like you're old, dude. It's not even midnight," the bored, fun-seeking Justin complained, then he headed off to find the small-town party life. By the time I went to bed, he hadn't reappeared. I didn't worry about him. I figured available trouble in Daily, Texas, was limited, especially when your poker buddies included local law enforcement.

I woke up early in the morning listening to Justin snore on the other side of the adjoining door. Lauren was on my mind and I had the strange sense that I'd been dreaming about something, but I couldn't quite pull it out of the mist. The dream had something to do with Lauren—I remembered that much.

It had been a long time since I'd waken up in the morning thinking about a girl—since high school, probably, when

Jennifer Pope told me she'd go to homecoming with me next Friday. I woke up with her on my mind every morning from Monday until Thursday, when she canceled the date and broke my heart. She was nice about it. She made some excuse about her family having plans, but the truth was that her dad didn't want her hanging out with some foster kid from Mama Louise's.

After that, I joined the youth group at Jennifer's church. When her father figured out I was showing up there—mostly to see Jennifer—they moved to another congregation. That nixed my church career, except on Sunday mornings, when Mama Louise mustered us out of bed and dragged us three blocks down the road to the Victory Lane Fellowship, where the music was loud and you never knew who might get the Holy Ghost and dance in the aisles on any given Sunday. Justin used to make fun of that place when we lay in our bunk beds at night, but I didn't mind it so much. The preacher was high volume, but he said some things that made sense. He made me think of my dad. Even though by then I couldn't remember for sure, I suspected that my father had been a religious man. I had vague recollections of waking late at night and finding him praying over my bed. I liked the way it felt when he did that—as if he were weaving a net around me, and I could float away on it until morning.

Sometimes, after we were living with Doug, when the fights and the TV were at their max in the other room, I'd curl up in my bed and try to pull that net over me. I'd pray the only prayer I could remember—one my grandfather had taught me when I was sure there were elephants under the bed and monsters in the closet. *I will lie down and sleep in peace, for you alone, O Lord, make me dwell in safety.* Then I'd pull the pillow over my head so I couldn't hear anything. I'd try to remember the farm.

In the morning, Doug's house would be quiet, so you'd have to say the prayer worked.

I checked once to see where it was in the Bible. Psalm 4:8. When they asked us to name our most important Bible verse in Jennifer's youth group, I used that one because it was the only thing I knew off the top of my head, and I didn't want to look stupid in front of all the churchy kids. Besides, it had made a believer out of me. It always kept me safe until morning, and in Doug's house, that was a minor miracle in itself. At some point, I concluded that God was more powerful than Doug, which was good to know.

My mother didn't want to hear talk like that. She said all those church ladies sneering at her was the biggest reason she hated living at the farm. She never really complained about my father, just the family, and the farm, and the people in town. Maybe she even believed it was bad luck to speak ill of the dead.

I had the strangest urge to tell Lauren that story, but I couldn't fathom why. Perhaps just because she was in my thoughts as I woke up and took in anew the wonders of Suite Beulahland. Even Elvis watching me in all forms of Plasticine (and several colors of velvet) couldn't chase away the warm, slightly romantic notion that last night had been . . . well . . . special. Normally, I wasn't one to make a move when a woman appeared hesitant—after something like the Jennifer Pope affair, one never quite recovers—but with Lauren, it seemed worth the risk.

I had the urge to go knocking on her door, but I knew it was too early. The sky was just gaining a blush outside. I paced the room for a while, picked up the script and tried to concentrate on it, walked out into the hall with it, thought if there was a light under Lauren's door, I'd knock and say something suave and unobtrusive like, "I thought you might want to take a look at this before breakfast." Something that wouldn't indicate I'd been stalking her door.

The light was on and I almost knocked, but then I decided it was stupid. Of course she'd know I was stalking her door. It was six-thirty in the morning. She'd think I was one of those creepy obsessive types who called to phone-smooch ten minutes after dropping a girl off from a date. Women don't like men like that.

I hung around the hall waiting for it to get later, until finally the light came on in Frederico's room, and I figured I'd better head out before Fred drafted me into his morning celebrity boot camp. Last night at the barbecue, as Justin was slogging down coconut cream pie, Frederico had pointed out that tomorrow they must get back *on regimen.*

I heard Fred pass by in the hall as I laid the script on the table in my room and got dressed to go out for a jog. With any luck, I could get through the back door without Fred detection. A morning jog with Fred was like signing up for a challenge on *Survivor.*

Leaving my room, I moved down the stairs quietly, stopping at the bottom to listen for the hum and clink of exercise equipment in the lobby. The place was strangely silent, except for the moaning ghost in the dumbwaiter. Even the pecan rolls hadn't arrived yet.

Maybe Fred had left for a jog on his own.

Then again, maybe he was in the storeroom, with all the Styro-foam wig heads and the refrigerator where we'd stashed the leftovers last night.

Aluminum foil? Was that crinkling aluminum foil I heard?

I stepped down the hall and saw a fan of light coming from the storeroom door, warm and silent on the cool wood floor. A shadow moved in, materializing in the doorway inch by inch—

a foot stretching to a leg, a leg stretching to a torso, a torso stretching to an arm.

The shadow lengthened and came forward. I slid into the darkness by the wall, waited, watched Fred back toward the door. He moved carefully, hunched over like a cat burglar, his body shielding something. I had a feeling I knew what it was.

I smelled coconut cream . . .

And the unmistakable twang of barbecue . . .

I waited until he'd almost reached me, then I stepped out of the shadows and said, "G'mornin', Fred!"

Fred jumped three feet, squealed like a teenage girl at a slumber party, and threw his hands in the air. The pie flew skyward, did a double flip, and landed on one of the wig heads, giving it a pie in the face. "Mama mia!" Fred gasped, pounding a fist against his chest. "You surprise me!" Fred's eyes cut to the evidence, dripping wet and fluffy down the Styrofoam face as the pie pan slid free and clattered to the floor. It landed at Fred's feet, but he pretended not to notice.

"What'cha doin' there, Fred?" I asked. There was barbecue sauce on his chin, and he still had a fork tucked between his fingers. He held it up, as if he were considering offing the witness to cover the crime, then he shrugged helplessly and sighed out a long string of Italian that had something to do with nectar of the gods. With a quick swipe of the fork, he snagged a falling dollop of ambrosia, popped it into his mouth, and swilled it around, his eyes falling closed in a carbohydrate stupor. "Ahhhh, succulento . . . squisito, incredibile . . ."

"Enjoy there, big guy," I said, and left him to contemplate multilingual adjectives for the pie as he reached for another bite. In a way, it was nice to know that even Frederico Calderone wasn't immune to Imagene Doll's confectionary temptations.

The morning air was crisp and pure as I headed out for my

run. One thing about life in Daily, Texas—traffic wasn't a problem. The streets were especially dead this morning. Passing by a church in the predawn haze, I saw a preacher unlocking the doors and had the vague thought that it was Sunday already. The preacher watched me jog by like he was surprised to see anyone afoot this early, and as I continued on, the sheriff's deputy honked at me from his cruiser, but then he waved, so I think he was being friendly.

On my way past the local law enforcement headquarters, I stopped to admire the new cement culvert that had been erected in Marla's honor. Then I moved on, because I didn't want to think about Marla. By now, she and Randall were probably popping Valium like baby aspirin and calling out the National Guard. I was actually surprised they hadn't used some kind of satellite technology to beam the cell phones and track Justin down. He must have done an especially good job of leaving behind clues to lead them in another direction. Over the years, Justin had figured out how to disappear, when he wanted to. He usually surfaced among the high-priced party spots of Brazil, Mexico, Bali—anyplace he could get away with hanging out for a while and blowing some cash on mindless entertainment while Marla and Randall went nuts trying to discern where he was. I had to give him credit for having come up with a unique hideout this time. A quiet country town on Sunday morning was the last place anyone would expect to find him.

When I got back to the hotel, I found Lauren in the alley in her sweats, stretching like she was about to go for a jog.

"Headed out?" I asked, and she jumped.

"Looks like you've already been."

Was it just my male ego, or did I detect a note of disappointment in that observation? "Nah, I just got warmed up," I said, even though I'd been three miles around town, past the feed mill and the convenience store, through the park, and back. Undoubtedly, it showed. "Want some company?" I caught myself giving her the hopeful yet pathetic smile of a middle school nerd asking a cute girl if he could sit next to her in a cafeteria. What was wrong with me? "I mean, I'd like to do another mile or two." *What?* My knees protested. *Come again? You have got to be kidding.*

She glanced reluctantly toward the door, and I felt like an idiot. She probably liked her alone time in the morning. Maybe she was embarrassed about last night and didn't want to see me at all. Maybe she was on the warpath about *The Horseman* project again. Maybe she'd headed out the door so early because she was hoping she wouldn't run into me. . . .

I shut down the unproductive train of thought before it could get to the section of track where my manly self-confidence lay bound and gagged.

Maybe she was up early, like me, thinking about last night. . . .

"Sure," she said, and I let out an audible sigh of relief which I then cleverly covered up with a cough. "I'm more of a power walker, though."

My knees gave each other an invisible high-five. "Great," I answered, and we started down the alley.

Lauren's form of power walking turned out to be especially nontaxing. We strolled out of town to a trail by the river, listening as the water hummed a morning song beneath the crown of pecan trees and sycamores. High above, a summer sky burned red, then cooled to aqua. We stopped to tour the bluffs along the shore, where Tonkawa Indians had left a pictorial history of their passing, hundreds of years before.

"I guess it's a natural human thing," I observed as we knelt, shoulder to shoulder, by the drawings. "To want to leave behind something that lasts, I mean."

"I guess so." Her voice was soft, intimate. "I guess as a writer, you'd have that chance. I doubt anatomy teachers leave behind much of a legacy."

"Without anatomy teachers, there wouldn't be any doctors," I pointed out.

She frowned in a self-effacing way. "I teach pre-vet. My students are headed to vet school."

"Any veterinarians," I corrected, but she didn't laugh. Instead, she looked away, seeming a little sad. I slipped a finger under her chin, turned her face so that she was looking at me again. "Someone with your kind of talent shouldn't be just teaching anatomy," I whispered, and then I kissed her, because sitting this close, looking into her eyes, I couldn't help myself.

She didn't seem to mind at all.

Chapter 17

Lauren Eldridge

Just as Nate kissed me, the postman, Harlan Hanson, happened to be driving over the bridge. Somewhere beyond the swirl of wild abandon in my head, I heard the unmistakable rumble-cough-cough of the remodeled army jeep he lovingly called Bessie. Nate's lips parted from mine, and I looked up just in time to see Bessie creeping along the shoulder near the guardrail.

The fluttery feeling fell to the pit of my stomach like a lead butterfly. Harlan and Bessie were the Daily equivalent of an AP ticker tape. Harlan dropped the news at all the Daily hot spots, and then it multiplied exponentially, like jackrabbits. The area below the bridge, lovingly known as Camp Nikyneck, was one of Harlan's favorite targets of surveillance, because teenagers liked to hang out there doing . . . well, what teenagers do. When I was a kid, I thought Nikyneck was an Indian word, but once I hit middle school, I, like all Dailyians, learned the true meaning of the word.

I experienced an instant of panic as Nate and I climbed the hill to street level. We made small talk, but I couldn't focus and finally the conversation ran out. I was left alone in a tempest of thought to which Nate was, fortunately, oblivious.

What would people say? What would they think? I imagined them sitting in the café, whispering, bringing up the past, talking about whether it had been long enough since Danny's death. Betty Prine and the literary ladies would say two years wasn't enough time, considering. They'd turn up their noses, make snide comments that would embarrass my father, and bait Aunt Netta into an argument.

In Daily, even under the most normal circumstances, a budding romance was the meat of speculation, and my circumstances were hardly normal.

Budding romance? Had I said that to myself? Had I thought it? *This is not a budding anything. It's not.* Nate and I were working together on *The Horseman.* That was it. Period. End of story.

I repeated that mantra in my head as we walked back to town. *There's no place in my life for this. I'm not ready. It's too soon.* However painful, it was the truth. So much of my soul was still a watery wash of grief and guilt. It was all I could do to maintain a steady course. I couldn't allow anyone to jump into the pool—not Marsh and his daughter, Bella, and certainly not some slightly loony flip-flop–wearing California guy, who had a convoluted past and questionable motives, even if he was drop-dead gorgeous and a great kisser.

Oddly enough, the fact that I liked Nate was exactly what made me want to push him away. I was already floundering in an ocean of issues, and it wasn't a pleasant place to spend time. I wouldn't wish myself on anybody, at least not the way I was now. Maybe someday.

When? a small, lonely voice inside me asked as we crossed Main Street and angled toward the alley in back of the hotel.

How much longer? How long is long enough to erase those final angry words, to atone for Harvard's death?

"Everything all right?" Nate's question was filled with deeper implications, of which he was completely unaware.

"It's fine," I said. "Nate, I didn't mean to . . ." *lead you on* sounded like a line from a pulp novel. "There's not . . . I'm not . . ." I realized we'd stopped walking. Nate was standing by the back door to the Daily Chamber of Commerce, studying me, seeming confused.

"It was just a kiss," he pointed out with a grin that made me feel as if I were melting. "My fault completely. The aura of Camp Nikyneck overwhelmed me."

"You *know* about Camp Nikyneck?" I stammered.

"You hang around a place a little while, you learn its history," he said in a way that made me wonder how much Daily history he knew. "You find out a few secrets. Your dad told a story about the Indian paintings at the party yesterday."

"Ahhh." Back in the day, my father was famous for getting run out of Camp Nikyneck by the sheriff, and occasionally by the Baptist preacher, who was known to cruise the river bridge at night, tagging teenagers with his flashlight like a hunter spotlighting deer.

Nate laughed softly, and we started walking again. "Sounds like your dad had quite a reputation."

I nodded. "My father was one of Daily's wilder products. Legend has it that if he hadn't met my mom, he would have been lost to the evils of wild horses and wild women. He never gave up the wild horses, but he only had eyes for my mom. Even after she died, I can't remember him ever showing interest in anybody else."

"Ever wonder if that kind of thing just doesn't happen anymore?" Nate dribbled a smashed Coke can between his feet like a soccer ball, then kicked it down the alley.

"Sometimes." I felt a deep, painful tug inside. When I married Danny, I wanted the real thing so badly that I convinced myself to overlook the obvious and see things that weren't there.

"The concept keeps writers working, anyway," Nate mused, then he didn't say anything more. We came to the hotel, but neither of us reached for the door.

Tell him. Be grown up about this. I took a deep breath, felt him watching me. "Nate. I'm not . . . ready." He didn't try to interpret the vague revelation, just waited for me to define it. "For anything. I just . . ." Why was this so hard? Why did I feel like I was killing a relationship, giving up something that mattered? It was a couple of kisses. He'd probably think I was crazy for even bringing it up. "When I left Daily, I was . . . there was a reason. There are reasons I haven't been back."

Nate nodded, seeming unsurprised. "It doesn't matter." His gaze caught mine, gripped it tight. I felt a pull somewhere deep in my soul.

"But it does." How could I explain this? How did I summarize something I hadn't ever let myself put into words? "When I moved back here after college, I wasn't . . . alone. I was married. It wasn't . . . we were . . . we were just young, I guess. Impulsive. Danny and I had this plan to take a few years off school to travel and try to make the National Finals Rodeo. Two years ago, we were coming home from a show. The weather was bad. It was dark. There was water over the crossing on Caney Creek Road when we got there. We should have turned back, but we didn't. Danny thought we could make it through. It was stupid. It was a single careless moment. It cost his life, and the life of Pastor Harve's son, Harvard Jr."

A sad, rueful sound burned my throat, then escaped. "Harvard was there to put road cones up to block the low-water crossing before he went off duty . . . but he found us there. He should have waited for the fire trucks to come, but I think he knew . . . he knew I couldn't hold on much longer."

Nate sighed, and I felt his sympathy, palpable like a bitter scent in the air, making it hard to breathe. I didn't want sympathy. I didn't want to tell the story again. I didn't want to be the grieving widow who remembered those last angry moments, that final ugly meaningless fight I could never tell anyone about. I just wanted it all to be over.

Part of me knew it would never be over. This story, the past, would always travel with me. It would linger around every relationship, like a shadow only I could see at first. I'd always wonder how long to wait before revealing it, how much to tell, in what light to cast those who couldn't speak for themselves. I didn't want to be the one left to live with what had happened, left to tell the story. I wanted to have been swept down the creek, my last memory one of arguing over a barbecue sandwich and a crumbling life.

"I just . . . I'm not ready to move on," I choked out.

I didn't wait for an answer, just opened the hotel door and went inside. I stole quietly up to my room so Aunt Netta wouldn't hear me, then sat down on the bed and felt heavy, and sad, and lonely, and guilty. I was useless here. I was useless to everyone. I couldn't think about the future. I couldn't change the past. I was trapped, turning around and around in the same box, wondering why the scenery never looked any different.

On the deepest level, I knew I didn't deserve any better. I had no right to sculpt future plans or make peace with the past. Why should I have that right, when Harvard and Danny couldn't do the same?

Outside, the early bells rang in the steeple of Daily Presbyterian, and shortly after, the Daily Baptist bells chimed in, pointing out that on top of everything else, today was Sunday. I hadn't even considered going to church until now, or wondered whether, with all the movie excitement going on, Aunt Netta would have plans to round everyone up for church. There was no way I was ready to march off to Sunday service and sit there with all the hometown folks studying me, so I opted to do the grown-up thing and sneak out before the question could arise. After dressing in a hurry, I left behind a hasty note scratched on the back of a deposit slip from my checkbook, tiptoed out the back door, and headed to the ranch to check on Lucky Strike and the goat.

My father and the rest of the crew showed up at the ranch late in the morning, ready for another day of *Horseman* preparation. Nate wasn't among them. Aunt Netta said he'd decided to spend some time reading a copy of the novel on which the screenplay was based, and working on the script. I felt equal parts of disappointment and relief when he didn't show up.

He hovered in my thoughts as the day wore on. When I looked at the live oak tree, when the nanny goat rubbed her head against my leg to have her ears scratched, when Justin hung his hat on the fence right where it had been yesterday, I thought of Nate. I envisioned him dropping the hat on his head and smiling. I wanted him to be there to see that with the reassurance of the goat, the relationship between horse and horseman was beginning to progress. I wanted Nate to give me the thumbs-up, and wink, and point out that he'd been the one to capture the goat in the first place. I wanted him to laugh as he joked, *And you told me this one was too big. . . .*

The glimmers of triumph seemed incomplete without Nate.

As the goat rubbed against Justin Shay's leg, I backed away, allowing Lucky Strike to move closer . . . an inch, then another, then another, until Justin stretched out his hand. His eyes widened with a look of wonder as the horse breathed over his fingers. I imagined the little boy, abandoned by his mother in the cruelest of ways, finally reaching beyond his wall of self-defense.

From across the corral, my father smiled at me and nodded his approval. I realized I'd looked his way because I knew he would do that. Leaving Justin and the horse alone in the round pen, I circled the fence, slipped my arm around my father's waist, and laid my head on his shoulder.

He squeezed me in the crook of his elbow. I smelled the faint scents of grease and leather, livestock and hay. "What's that for?" he asked, his voice scratchy and rough.

"Just because you're a great dad." It was an unusually tender admission for the two of us. Love between us, while seldom spoken of, had always been understood, but I realized again how fortunate I was to have him. How foolish I'd been to isolate myself from his care.

"I think I got lucky," he said, and cleared his throat, embarrassed by the sudden display of affection. We focused on the corral, watching the horse-horseman-goat bonding continue as Willie gave instruction and Amber offered quiet encouragement and the assurance that she knew Justin could do this.

"I'll be dogged," my father said as Lucky Strike lowered his head and allowed the horseman to stroke his nose and scratch his ears. The horse blew out a long, contented sigh, nibbling tenderly on his goat's itchy spot, which made the goat close her eyes and bleat softly. "You worked a miracle," Dad added, as if he'd been worried it wouldn't happen.

"We're still a long way from being able to impress some director," I pointed out. For one thing, there was no goat in the script, and right now, the cooperation of the goat was essential.

"We'll get there," Dad assured. "You hungry? Lunch'll be ready soon."

"No," I said, which wasn't true, but I didn't know who was bringing lunch today, and I didn't want to risk running into Pastor Harve or Miss Beedie. "I think I'll just stay out here and work with the horse."

Sighing, Dad scratched his boot back and forth on the bottom rail of the fence. The sound traveled along the metal, a dull echo preceding his words. "Harve and Miss Beedie asked about you yesterday."

"I'm sorry I missed them." The words were tinny and false, like the sappy, electronic tune from a musical greeting card. "Tell them hello for me . . . if you see them, okay? Tell them . . ." A lump rose in my throat, and I pretended to be choking on dust. I could feel my father watching me, his expectation heavy.

"You might ought to tell them yourself." One thing my father didn't tolerate well was weakness. In the West, a man stood on his own two feet, even when the wind was stiff and the going was hard—likewise for a woman.

Every muscle in my body tightened, knotted with the familiar tension that, for the past two years, had accompanied the idea of being home. I knew sooner or later the honeymoon would be over, the welcome-home barbecues would end, and everyone would expect the hard work of healing to begin.

From the corner of my eye, I could see my father chewing his mustache, his jaw tightly set, his eyes narrowed against the sun so that they were barely visible, like pale blue marbles tucked amid crinkled old leather. "They'd like to hear from you."

"I'll go by Caney Creek Church when I get a chance." The lie tasted bitter coming out. That church was on the other side of the moon for me. I couldn't imagine stopping by the little white church, trying to make the idle chit-chat of survivorhood—
How are things? How are you? Are you feeling all right?
Harvard was such a good man.

How are your grandkids? I bet they miss their dad. . . .

We could talk about O.C.'s football games at UT, and how much Harvard would have liked to be there to cheer him on. We could talk about Teylina's college scholarship and how determined Harvard was that his kids would get out of Daily, go to college, work somewhere other than the Sheriff's Department.

Leaving the church, I'd pass the road to the cemetery, where the funeral took place as I lay in the hospital in Austin. Harvard's funeral there, and Danny's memorial service at his family's church in Dallas, were like fiction to me, stories other people told that weren't real, the details carefully manufactured.

If you never went to the final resting places, it was as if the funerals never happened. In my mind, I still expected to see Harvard duck and take off his hat as he walked into the café, all six foot six of him blocking the light from the doorway. I still expected to see Danny rattle through town with a shiny new pickup truck we couldn't afford, with a horse trailer behind. Danny never unhooked the horse trailer, whether he was hauling livestock or not. The trailer, boots, spurs, and cowboy hat were part of his identity. He valued being a cowboy more than anything.

He would have loved the idea of *The Horseman* being filmed in Daily. He would have hated that the leading role was being played by some down-and-out superstar who knew nothing about horses. Danny liked horses better than he liked people. He was a good cowboy.

I wished that had been the last thing I'd said to him. I wished my final words were something other than, *I can't do this anymore, Danny. I'm tired of fighting. I'm tired of living this way. . . .*

If only I could erase it from my memory as easily as I'd struck it from the public record. Surrounded by the flowers, and the condolences, and the sympathy, I couldn't reveal that our life had been falling apart before the flood. What would have been the point of letting everyone know that as Danny drove into the water, we were arguing about barbecue sandwiches and the fact that he'd signed the paperwork for a new pickup without telling me?

Life changes in the blink of an eye, and all the things you thought were so important turn pale. You awaken to what's left of the picture, trying to find something you recognize, something comforting.

Only there isn't anything. . . .

I left my father and walked to the barn alone. He went to lunch with the crew, then came back with a sandwich for me, and Aunt Donetta tagging along with a giant glass of iced tea. She was worried that I wasn't drinking enough and might become dehydrated in the heat. Dad pointed out that the Methodists had supplied lunch today. In other words, it would have been safe for me to go to the tent and partake with the rest of the crew.

We concentrated on *The Horseman* because the rest was too difficult to talk about. As soon as the remainder of the group returned from lunch, we went back to work.

By the end of the day, progress had been made, but I was boneless and exhausted. I had to give Justin Shay credit for his stamina and determination. After developing a rudimentary knowledge of how to move the horse around the ring, then bring him back to the center without the use of halters or ropes, he was like a kid with a new toy. Even when everyone else was ready to pack it in and head home, he wanted to keep going.

Willie finally entered the round pen and talked him into leaving. "C'mon, son," he said, resting a hand between Justin's shoulder blades. "Let's go to the house. You done a good day's work. I promised Mimi I'd be back in time to take her to dinner. She's pretty bored, settin' out there at Frank's place." He slapped Justin's back, and Justin seemed pleased. They wandered off shoulder-to-shoulder, Willie telling some tale about cowboys and chuck wagons, while I collected the horse and led him to the barn. The goat followed, snatching bits of grass along the way.

I lingered in the stable until after my father, Willie, and Justin were gone. Around the house, the workers had finished up and either gone home or moved to the construction trailers in the back yard. The stablehand, Joe, retired to his apartment and began cooking something that smelled good. My stomach rumbled, and I found myself wondering what Nate was doing for an evening meal and how the script was coming along. While she was watching us work the horse after lunch, Aunt Netta had mentioned (loudly enough to be sure I heard) that Nate was working back at the hotel, downstairs in the beauty shop, where the lighting was good and he could spread out his notes. She said she hoped he didn't get *lonely* down there later on. I pictured Nate among three decades of hair equipment, old cartoons torn from Farm Bureau calendars, and Aunt Netta's favorite mottos painted above the mirrors in her favorite color—red.

God uses small things for great purposes. It was a powerful statement if you believed it, if you could have faith in it. Without faith, it was just a bunch of letters strung together, meaningless.

I wanted to believe it again, to feel it.

I didn't know where to begin.

When I got back to the hotel, Nate was still downstairs surrounded by stacks of papers. He was sitting in one of the old vinyl chairs with his feet propped up and a fifties-style cone-shaped dryer above his head. He smiled as I came in. "Well, there you are," he said, as if this morning's conversation had never happened. I was relieved when he didn't bring it up, but in another way, I was disappointed.

"It got kind of quiet upstairs," he admitted in a way that hinted the script writing wasn't going well. "I thought a change of scenery might be good." He waved an arm vaguely toward the papers and sticky notes littering the room.

"Can I help?" I asked.

He studied me, seeming surprised, then smiled in a way that was open to interpretation. "I hope so."

"Let me see what you have so far." I felt the warmth of his invitation as I crossed the room and stood looking over his shoulder.

"Just a minute," he said, rising from the chair to retrieve something from the other side of the room. I watched as he gathered notes and scraps, which were tucked among the chairs, dryer bonnets, and wall shelves according to some organizational system only he understood.

Sitting down beside me again, he handed me the first newly rewritten scene, hastily scratched on notebook paper that looked like it had been in Aunt Netta's drawer since I graduated from high school.

"Don't expect too much," he said, seeming defeated.

"I'm sure it's better than you're making it sound." I looked up, caught the reflection of the two of us in Aunt Netta's mirror, read the lettering overhead. Someone had stuck a Post-It note over the *sm* in *small*, so that now it read,

God uses all things for great purposes.

Chapter 18

Nathaniel Heath

A strange thing happened as the week went by. I started to feel at home in the quirky little berg of Daily, Texas. I developed a routine that felt comfortable, and for the first time in a long time I was actually productive, in terms of writing. I got up early in the mornings, worked on the script, then went for a run before breakfast. The postman and the old gents waiting for the café to open began to recognize me and call me by name. Shopkeepers waved as they made ready to open their stores.

Once, a trio of little girls setting up a lemonade stand spotted me jogging past their house. "That's the movie guy," one of them whispered, then they got on their bikes and followed me down the street, asking questions about the film, but mostly, they wanted to know if there might be little girls in *The Horseman*. The inquiry was nothing new. Movie mania had gripped Daily. The postman, Harlan Hanson, thought there should be a postal representative in a scene or two. Donetta and Lucy thought a beauty shop would be good—everyone knew the beauty shop was the heart and soul of any Texas town with a population under two thousand. The principal at the high school offered to stage a Friday night football game, because it's not small-town Texas without Friday night football. The girls in the hardware store thought the horseman should come in for nuts and bolts, and the man in the feed mill was certain that, like all ranchers, the horseman would stop by for feed.

The Baptist preacher, Ervin Hanson, thought there should definitely be a church in the movie. Daily Baptist being the largest in town, it was the logical choice, of course. The sheriff's deputy, Buddy Ray Baldridge, wanted me to know he'd starred in Daily High School's production of *Grease*, and he'd be happy to arrest somebody on camera. Bob, the owner of the café and president of the Chamber of Commerce, was in favor of a café scene. The countertoppers even demonstrated their acting skills for Frederico when he went down to breakfast one morning. They wanted him to be sure to share the information with Justin, because Justin had started lying low after a few reporters passed through town in response to rumors of his presence there. To their credit, the Dailyians could keep a secret when they wanted to. They buzzed Justin on his cell when there were strangers nosing around, and everyone was careful not to talk *Horseman* talk if outsiders were near. When the coast was clear, the movie talk flowed like sweet tea at a Donetta Bradford picnic.

Including requests for bit parts, the film would be about ten hours long, depending on whether or not we included Miss Lulu's RV camp by the swimming hole at Boggy Bend and the Tonkawa cliff paintings. Lauren laughed when I told her that on one of our early-morning walks. She usually happened to be in the alley as I was coming in from my jog, and we power walked—more like strolled, really—while talking shop. We stayed away from Camp Nikyneck, though we did amble down by the river once or twice. We just didn't stop to look at the petroglyphs.

Lauren was hard to figure out. Given her reservations about *The Horseman*, she'd been surprisingly willing to take some vacation time from her university job to stay on in Daily to help. I tried not to take that as anything personal, but when we were together, we fit like Lucy and Ricky, without the romance. Every once in a while, in the middle of working or strolling and talking about horses and life, I'd look up and find her watching me. For a moment I'd be lost in the color of her eyes, the shape of her face, the smoothness of her skin. I'd never been lost in another person before, not even during the starstruck high school days of the Jennifer Pope affair.

It was a strange feeling—a little creepy, but not unpleasant, except for the fact that she didn't feel the same way. Occasionally, I thought she did, but she never gave any indication that she wanted to cross the just-friends line again. I could understand that, even if it was inconvenient. After something like what she'd been through, it would be hard to move on with life.

All the same, I thought about her when we were together, and when we weren't. When we were working, we'd laugh about something, she'd look at me and I'd think she was ready to let down the barriers. I'd gaze into her face, and I'd see her like Sleeping Beauty, locked in the tower. Then the window would close again.

I recognized myself late one night on the Discovery Channel's *Planet Earth* series. There was this bird of paradise strutting around with his feathers fluffed up, putting everything he had into the dance. Unfortunately, no one was watching. I empathized with the bird.

I resolved to quit thinking of Lauren in anything other than friendly terms. Hot pursuit wasn't my normal MO, anyway. I figured if a girl wasn't interested, she wasn't interested. End of story. Aside from that, what was I really going to do with some small-town Texas chick? Once Dane made his visit here and either rocketed *The Horseman* into reality or killed it, I'd be back home, and Lauren would be teaching anatomy to a bunch of college kids who probably would never know there was so much more than neck bone-connected-to-the-jawbone inside that pretty little head of hers.

Lauren was smart—really smart. She had an insight into people, both the fictional kind and real kind. She understood the deeper motivations of the horseman, Sarah, the female lead, and Sarah's autistic son. Sarah was a lot like Lauren—intelligent, perceptive, and beautiful but wounded after her gambling-addicted husband committed suicide and left her with nothing but a used-up racehorse and a mountain of debt. Sarah was trapped, afraid to look back, unable to move forward. The more I wrote Sarah, the more she became Lauren. Sometimes when we were working on the script, I thought Lauren noticed. Occasionally, when we were laughing about the latest Bigfoot sighting around town, and the growing volume of theories about the creature's identity, I thought she remembered that night at the ranch.

She was careful never to mention *the kiss*, even when Bigfoot came up in conversation. We talked, instead, about recent sightings from cars passing in the darkness on the rural road, twice by the postman on his route early in the morning, and once by Joe, the stablehand, who was burning candles near his Blessed Virgin statue and wouldn't come out of his barn apartment at night. Even the construction workers staying in the camp trailers near the ranch house were keeping their spotlights and weapons at the ready, but the creature was elusive.

Pearly Parsons had the distinction of having experienced

the closest sighting. According to Pearly, "It was standin' at the other end of the fencerow, near nine foot tall and covered all over with hair. It was tryin' to push down the top strand of barbed wire." Pearly went for his gun, but by the time he got it out and grabbed a flashlight, the beast was gone. Only a quiver in the wire remained to testify to its existence. Fortunately, a Pearly Parsons fence could withstand anything, even mythical man-beasts with a case of don't-fence-me-in.

"W-w-wonder how-how come it don't jus-just climb over, climb over?" asked Doyle. "Be-bein' nine f-f-f-foot tall." The creature was growing each time a new story came in.

"Maybe it ain't too agile," the Baptist preacher suggested. He smiled after he said it, to indicate that he was just playing along.

"For heaven's sake, all'a you hush up." Imagene, behind the counter, had heard enough. "You'll have Nate here thinkin' he's trying to make a movie in a looney bin." Smiling at me apologetically, she wheeled a finger beside her ear. "I been livin' not two miles across the field from the Barlinger place all my life, and never seen anything but farm animals, coyotes, jack-rabbits, and once in a while a fox or a bobcat or two. If there was a eight-foot-tall hairy man livin' around there, I believe I'd know it."

"Nine-nine f-f-foot," Doyle corrected, and Imagene smacked a plate down in front of him.

"Hush up and eat," she said, and hurried off to wait tables. I liked Imagene. She was practical and she cut the pie in large slices. She fell squarely in the Bigfoot-naysayer group, but that didn't stop the countertoppers from theorizing about the creature's identity. Having seen it for myself, I couldn't help pondering the question on occasion, even though I wouldn't have admitted it to anyone.

After almost a week of sitting in the beauty shop working

270

on the script with Lauren while platonically eating to-go food from the Daily Café, I was about a thin half-inch from either kissing her or saying something that would cause her to once again explain her tragic past and tell me she wasn't ready for anything other than friendship. To keep from losing my mind, I pondered the Bigfoot question. Finally, I suggested we go out to the ranch and see if we could spot the thing again.

Lauren frowned sideways at me. "We should stay here and work on this." She pointed to the disorganized jumble of papers. "We only have the rest of today and tomorrow before M. Harrison Dane shows up here on Monday."

I felt the crushing weight of expectations and the looming deadline, which was probably as responsible for my desire to go AWOL as anything. "We could have a month and we wouldn't be ready."

Lauren rolled her eyes, then blinked hard and rubbed them. She'd been putting in long days, leaving for the ranch early to work with Lucky Strike before Justin and crew showed up each day. Mostly, I stayed behind to continue my efforts at turning the script into a masterpiece, using a laptop and printer Donetta had borrowed from the local school. She had let me take over the exercise room and half of the beauty shop, so I could tape scene and sequel notes and character attributes to the walls, the front window, the exercise equipment, creating giant story-boards and character sketches. In the evenings, Lauren and I discussed everything from technical details to characters. Usually, Lauren fell asleep in the chair before I finished working. Sometimes I stopped and just watched her, and wondered what she dreamed about.

Tonight, I was feeling the pressure of Dane's imminent arrival, along with another more vague realization. My time here was almost up. Two days from now, Dane would have come and gone, and the string of long evenings in the beauty shop with Lauren would come to an end.

"Come on, Puggy," I urged. "Live a little."

She seemed to think about it for a minute, as if tempted by the possibility. The scene stole into my mind—moonlight, pretty girl, me, whippoorwills singing in the distance, the trees swaying slightly in the night breeze . . . Bigfoot. The tape screeched to a halt. Who was I kidding? Lauren was only interested in the script. That was it.

She seemed to come to the same conclusion. "I'm sorry. I know I'm not much fun. I'm just . . . worried about . . . my dad. I can't stop thinking about what's going to happen if this movie thing falls through, and . . ."

Swiveling my chair to face hers, I took her hand and held it in both of mine. "We'll make it work." I wasn't sure if that was confidence or delusion in my voice, but I noted dimly that I actually believed my own rhetoric. Somewhere along the way, I'd come to see the movie as a reality. Without consciously thinking about it, I was planning the next several months based on the project. I was envisioning trips back to Daily, home-cooked food, stays in Suite Beulahland, and Lauren. The project and Lauren were intertwined in my mind. I wanted both.

"It's not you, Nate." Her eyes were filled with a tender regret, a lingering sadness I wanted to wash away. "You're an amazing writer. The way you put words together, you've captured things I can't even solidify in my mind. If anyone can make this project work, it's you. It's just that there are so many variables, so many things that stand in the way of this ever becoming an actual movie." Her fingers tensed in mine. I laid them flat, smoothed a hand over them, tried to imagine how I would write this scene. There were a million things I wanted to say to her,

272

but no words seemed right. It's so much easier to write about emotions than to live with them.

"Lauren, life *is in* the variables. Things change. Things don't go according to the plans we make. There's a bigger picture, and it doesn't always make sense until you're looking back on it." Who was this Dr. Phil wannabe talking through my head? "When I moved out of LA, I thought the key for me was to leave it all behind—the movie business, the partying, Justin and the insanity he manufactures. I thought the solution was to take myself out of it, go someplace quiet where I could focus on writing something really good, something that would make a difference to people."

I remembered that logic now. I remembered the exact moment, the morning after Justin almost drove us off the cliff, when I woke up with an adrenaline hangover and the realization that, but for the grace of God and a good set of brakes, I could have been in a morgue with my watch and wallet in a Ziploc bag no one would pick up.

I packed my stuff and headed north that day, found Mammoth Lakes nestled in what seemed a safe place, miles from my old life. "But now I realize you can't impact something you don't touch. The world marches on, and to have input in the direction it goes, you have to join the parade. You've got to work with the instruments you're given. I've got The Shay, whether I want him or not. I've got the contacts in the business, even though they come with temptations attached. I've got the ability to write, despite the fact that I've been a sellout because the money's good. And I've got a history that makes me understand what that foster shelter could mean to the kids who come there."

Lauren's fingers tightened around mine. She watched our intertwined hands, then searched my face. I had the sense that she understood what was inside me, that she could relate to the yearning in a way no one else ever had. Her lips parted and I focused there, had a vision of kissing her to seal the bargain.

A door creaked and slammed shut upstairs, and the ghost knocked on the joists overhead. Lauren came out of her trance and glanced toward the stairs. Whatever she was about to say, whatever had been about to happen, evaporated like cooling steam.

"Guess we'd better get back to work," she said, the words accompanied with a resigned sigh. I felt the unmistakable chill of a wet blanket as she slipped out of her chair to cross the room. "How about a fresh Coke?"

"Sure." In the mirror, I watched her face as she put ice in the glasses and poured soda. I studied her expression, her hair falling over her cheek, the way it hid her eyes.

She's probably just trying to let you down easy, dude. Give it up. Don't be pathetic. You're not her type. She probably likes big, burly guys who can ride a horse all day and dance the two-step all night. Strong, silent types like the horseman. You're about as far from that as it gets. No woman dreams of falling in love with a writer. . . .

It occurred to me to wonder what her husband was like—if the horseman in the script reminded Lauren of him. There was a rather large black hole attached to that line of thinking, so I nixed it. Stretching back in my chair, I grabbed a stack of index cards and went back to work.

Lauren got tired early. After a period of watching her fight dozing off with her chin braced on her hand, I suggested she head up to bed, since it looked like I might be pulling an all-nighter. By tomorrow, I had to have a bang-up proposal in Justin's hands. By tomorrow night, we'd be e-mailing a proposal packet to Dane.

This was probably as good a time to panic as any.

Justin showed up shortly after Lauren went off to bed. He seemed a little less tightly wound than he had been the last several days, and maybe a little low, which worried me. For the first time since we'd come here, he wasn't trying to drag me out to some all-night poker game. I hoped he wasn't headed for a crash right before Dane was due in town.

"You okay?" I asked as he rummaged through the plates of homemade goodies even Frederico had given up trying to resist. Fred looked like he'd gained a few pounds since arriving in Daily, even though he'd taken up participating in the daily exercise class at the Hair and Body with Imagene, Lucy, and Donetta.

"Yeah," Justin muttered as he poured himself a soda. "Dane's had some scheduling conflicts. He'll be here tomorrow evening at five."

"Come again?" *Hold the phone. We're not really stepping up the time frame by fifteen hours, right?* "He's supposed to be here Monday morning, not tomorrow."

"Yeah, I know. His wife had something come up. They have to be back in LA on Monday. No big deal. E-mail him the proposal packet by tomorrow morning. He'll read it on the plane."

"No big deal?" A golf ball went down my throat and bounced around my chest at high speed. *Heavens to murgatroid, Batman, we're doomed.*

Don't panic. You'll scare the talent.

"You can handle it." Something in his tone stopped me just before I was about to say something dire. There was a flat, listless quality, a lack of enthusiasm in those words that brought back a host of dark memories.

"You okay?" I asked again.

"Yeah. Just wiped. Sick of looking at the rear end of a stupid horse all day. I'll be glad when Dane gets here and we bag this thing." It sounded simple when he said it. I didn't point out that after Dane came, if by some miracle we were successful in our newly shortened time frame, there would be weeks of meetings ahead, then months of casting and filming, most of which would involve horses' rears of different varieties.

"Lauren says it's going pretty well with you and the horse," I said. Justin looked like he needed some encouragement.

He shrugged. "Amber thinks so. She came and watched today."

"That's good." But it really wasn't. After a few days of being tied up with publicity, Amber was around town again. Justin was moody and distracted.

"Yeah, her stupid fiancé's coming Monday." Ah, bingo, the reason for Justin's melancholy state this evening. "He just gets in the way."

"Well, if I had a fiancée that looked like Amber, I wouldn't leave her alone too long, either."

The Shay flashed an irritated look at me in the mirror. Support for Amber's engaged state wasn't what he wanted to hear.

"You do anything about getting in touch with Stephanie?" *Time to redirect the conversation. Let's talk about Steph— the real reason you're mooning over some twenty-year-old girl who's engaged to another guy.*

"She's unlisted." He stirred his soda with a finger, watching the ice swirl around. "I e-mailed Marla for her number."

"You e-mailed *Marla*?" The security alarm went off in my head. The last thing we needed was for Marla to figure out where we were. She and Randall would crash our little party like warthogs at the ballet.

The Shay snorted. "Relax, dude. I didn't tell her anything. Marla'll never figure out where we're at."

276

"Okay." But the eerie sensation creeping up and down my spine said otherwise.

Justin stared out the window, the streetlights reflecting against his face. Directors would have loved that vulnerable, pensive, slightly broken look on him. "I'm going on to bed. I have to get up for church in the morning."

I almost choked on my drink. "Seriously?" *Although on second thought, prayer probably is a good idea at this point, since we need a miracle.*

"I missed last Sunday because we were busy with the horse." He gave me one of those looks intended to let me know I wasn't adapting fast enough to his latest personality change. "Amber's singing there tomorrow morning."

"Ohhh," I said. *I get it now. You're out to impress a girl.* Except for the years Mama Louise had dragged us down to the Victory Lane Fellowship, and a short stint of involvement with the new-age theology of Shokahna (which had also been about the pursuit of a girl), Justin hadn't ever been much of a spiritual seeker. Aside from that, he needed to be in his room studying what there was of the proposal packet and getting ready for the meeting with Dane.

"What's that supposed to mean?" He gave me a snarky sneer.

"What?"

"Oh-h-h." He did a melodramatic, and fairly lousy portrayal, of me. I hated it when he got in this kind of mood. Stephanie used to call it the *blue muggies.*

"Just that rolling out of bed on Sunday to go to church isn't normally your thing, and you've got the proposal packet to study."

"I go a lot when I'm here on Sundays," he defended. "It clears my mind. I'll look at the proposal after church. Dane's not coming till evening."

"Cool." I went back to my work, feeling a weird shift in the world I knew—not a bad shift, just weird. Still, this new reality seemed ominously positioned on a narrow pedestal, ready to come crashing down at the slightest change in the wind.

Justin walked a few steps away, then hovered by the exercise machines. "You can come if you want. To church, I mean."

"We'll see." I couldn't help recalling the time he'd tried to get me involved in his stint with Shokahna. It was rally day and he needed a prospective member to bring. "I've got a long night ahead. I'll have the rest of the treatment and some key scenes for you in the morning. I'll go over it with you, and then you need to make time to study it."

"Okay." Justin didn't sound too excited about getting the packet. "I hope Willie likes it."

I didn't know how to respond to that. Since when were we banking major decisions on Willie's opinion?

"See you in the morning," Justin said, and wandered off, leaving the conversation feeling unfinished.

I poured my attention into the script, keeping focused, like a college kid on the night before finals. Tomorrow was it. The big one. Do or die.

Sometime around four in the morning, I lay down on the Jetsons-era vinyl sofa by the exercise room and closed my eyes just for a minute to visualize a scene. As the floor joists overhead sang a chorus of creaks and moans, I felt myself sinking deeper. I knew I should get up, collect my papers, finish a few last edits so everything would be ready to email to Dane in the morning. . . .

I dreamed about the horseman. He stood at the center of a vast corral, his back to the camera. A white horse circled him, its mane and tail streaming, its strides light and free, its hooves barely touching the sand. It was a magnificent creature, strong, powerful, yet it had the wide, gentle eyes of a fawn. Suddenly, I was the horseman. The white horse circled and circled, never coming closer, never moving farther away, always watching. Finally, I held out my hand, and it drew near, blew softly over my fingers, its breath the breath of peace.

Along the fence railing, Mama Louise and all the little foster kids cheered. Pastor Harve and his wife, Miss Beedie, saluted me with an enormous platter of unidentified fried objects as Miss Lulu's choir rocked back and forth and sang "He Leadeth Me" in golden choir robes. Beside the old pastor and his wife, my grandmother and grandfather stood just as I remembered them. My grandfather smiled and waved. My father was with them. He motioned to me and called my name. For the first time in years, I could clearly see his face.

"Nate . . . Nate, hon. Na-a-a-te . . . hon? Wake up." My grandfather's voice turned high and shrill, took on a twang. "Yer just out li-ike a light. Did ye-ew sleep here all ni-ight?"

My eyes opened like window shades stuck down with goo. Donetta was a blur of tall red hair and bright crimson lips. She backed away a step as I sat up.

"You hungry this mornin'?" she asked as I tried to figure out why I was waking up on the beauty shop couch. My body ached in strange places, and a combination of pressure and sweat had plastered the clothes to my back.

"I'm not sure." A zap of adrenaline rocketed through me as I pushed what had become sandy-colored dreadlocks out of my face. "What time is it?"

"Oh, it's early yet." Giving my knee a reassuring pat, Donetta set a pan of pecan rolls on the counter by the coffee pot and started making coffee. "I just thought I'd deliver some rolls over before everyone stirred around. Justin said y'all would be up with the chickens, gettin' your script out to Mr. M. Harrison

Dane before church." She concentrated on measuring coffee, then added, "Did Puggy go on up to bed last night?" I caught a curious backward glance.

"Yes, she turned in early. Guess she was tired." There was more disappointment in that than I meant to convey. I was a little out of it this morning. The strange dream about the horseman swirled around my head, making everything else fuzzy. "There wasn't much more she could do, anyway. Last night was just a matter of fine-tuning some things and getting the proposal together."

"Oh, that sounds excitin'." Donetta sat on the sofa beside me while the coffee brewed.

"I can't wait to see the movie," she said finally.

Stretching the back of my neck, I chuckled. "It's a long way from film right now."

"You'll git there. Lauren says you're just an awful good writer."

I was surprised how good that felt. "The proposal wouldn't have come together without her."

"You two are a good team." Donetta stood up and walked to the coffee pot. "I haven't seen her so excited about anythin' in a long time."

"It's an exciting project." Surprisingly enough, I really felt that way, even on two hours' sleep, and with Dane coming this evening.

"I wasn't talkin' about the movie. I was talkin' about you and Puggy." I could feel Donetta watching me from the corner of her eye as she poured two cups of coffee and put the pot back to catch the sizzling stream. "I've got a sense when it comes to these things, hon." A penciled-on eyebrow rose over one eye, and she turned toward me with stirring sticks in hand. "Cream or sugar, darlin'?"

"No thanks." I sensed that we were about to get down to the real reason Donetta was hanging around this morning. I figured I might as well save her the time. "We had a talk about it. She's not interested."

Donetta's lips twisted on one side as she crossed the space and handed me my cup. "Oh, hon, she's interested." She sat down again, her long red fingernails tapping the handle of her mug. I felt like I was in the principal's office for having failed to complete an assignment. When Donetta Bradford got down to business, all the sugar crust disappeared. She was five feet eight inches of big hair and determination.

"Sometimes you just have to figure the chemistry's not right," I said.

"Nate"—lowering her chin, she peered at me over the top of her glasses—"you're old enough to know better than that. Anybody within six foot'a you two kids can see things cracklin' like fatback on a griddle."

"She says she's not ready." Now I knew how those talk show guests felt. Dr. Donetta was on to me, and she wasn't letting go.

"Honey . . ." Leaning back in her seat, she hitched up her glasses and gazed at the old, wavy plate glass windows as the sun slowly rose over Main Street and the long shadows faded in the light of a new day. "You can fool a lot of people, but you can't fool a hairdresser. I know who's got roots, who's got big ears, whose scalp's flaky, who buys cheap shampoo, and who's got lipstick on their shirt collar. I know when I spot a match, and I know Puggy. I hadn't ever seen her look at *anybody* the way she looks at you . . . *ever*. Now, sure, she feels like if she lets go the guilt about the accident, if she moves on and finds happiness again, it'd be wrong of her, but the thing is, her standin' with her feet in the mud isn't gonna change anythin', or bring anybody back. I know Harvard Jr. wouldn'ta wanted that, and I don't think Danny, as sorry as he was most of the time, God rest his soul, woulda wanted it either."

"Maybe you should try telling her that."

Donetta batted a hand and spat a puff of air. "Pfff. Hon, I have tried. A million times. That girl's stubborn as a sow and twice as hard to move."

The analogy made me laugh, but Donetta didn't laugh along with me. She was staring at the front windows, squinting as if she saw something in the play of light and shadow on the wavy glass. "You know, Nate. I'll tell you somethin' I learned a lot of years ago. If you wait for the perfect time, most often it ends up you waited too long. Sometimes God puts a new path under your feet, not because *you* think you're ready to walk it, but because *He* knows that's the way you need to go." Her lips curved upward into a smile, and she added, "She'll come around."

Chapter 19

Lauren Eldridge

The room was cool and shadowy. The last thing I wanted to do was get out of bed, but Aunt Donetta was sitting beside me, stroking my hair and trying to awaken me gently. I'd always loved Aunt Netta's tender morning voice. At home when we were kids, there was no ceremony with my dad. Mornings began with the sound of his boots echoing across the floor and the screen door slapping as he went out to dump yesterday's coffee grounds in the flower bed or bring in logs for the woodstove. If you didn't hop up by the time he finished putting on the coffee or stoking the fire, you were likely to get a cup of ice dumped in your bed. When we stayed over at Aunt Netta's, things were much more serene, and we could languish in a state of foggy bliss while the sweet scent of pancakes and bacon filled the house.

My mind sifted through childhood memories, sprinkling them over the pillow like white flour as she tried to rouse me. After a night spent pacing the floor, letting worry and frustration defy every sleep-inducing technique known to man, I was groggy and bleary-eyed. It took me a minute to realize I was in the hotel, all grown up, and Aunt Netta wanted me to rise for church. She'd brought an assortment of clothing, just in case I hadn't thought to pack church clothes myself.

Reality fell like a lead overcoat. Last Sunday, by sneaking out to check on Lucky Strike and his goat, I'd avoided the issue of accompanying Aunt Netta to Sunday service. Now that I'd been here over a week, the idea of my skipping out of church a second time was unthinkable, but the idea of going was unthinkable, too. I couldn't picture sitting in the third pew on the left, in the church where a small memorial service for Danny had taken place before his parents had his ashes transported to Dallas. If I'd been able, I might have protested their plans. Danny was the black sheep in his family. He hadn't spoken to his parents since he dropped out of vet school, took up full-time rodeoing, and married me. I didn't know how he'd feel about the big funeral in Dallas or the family cemetery as a final resting place. We'd never talked about anything like that.

By the time I was fully aware of things in the hospital, two weeks had passed, and it was already done. I was in too much pain to argue—physically and emotionally. Aunt Netta told me all about the memorial services. I guess she thought it would help me gain closure. If she could have suffered through the surgeries, the head injury, and the broken bones for me, she would have done that, too.

Which meant, of course, that there was no choice really, but to go sit in the family pew at Daily Baptist and try to focus on the sermon while friends and neighbors cast sympathetic glances my way. Afterward, we'd shake hands and they'd offer up kind words about Danny, and I'd act like we had been the happiest couple in the world.

You can't keep hiding forever, a part of me said. *It's time.*

The words were true enough. After coming upstairs early,

I'd paced the floor all night, frustrated with life, frustrated with myself, frustrated with my inability to move forward. . . .

Aunt Netta smoothed back my hair and kissed my forehead. "It's a beautiful mornin'," she said, then got up and opened the blinds, letting pink light spill into the room. "Start of a brand-new day. Rise and shine, darlin'." She bustled around, straightening things and dumping a half-used cup of water into the bathroom sink. "I just found poor Nate asleep on that hard old sofa downstairs. He'd been up workin' all night, bless his heart." She hawkeyed me when she mentioned his name. "He said you turned in early. You feelin' all right, darlin'?"

"Sure," I said, and then realized I'd just surrendered my last possible excuse for staying home this morning. I could hardly claim to be sick now. "Why?"

"Oh, no reason." Aunt Netta casually fluffed a heavy velvet drape that was dusty and crinkled with age. "Just if I were a single girl and I had a fella downstairs who looked like *that*, I wouldn't be calling it an early night."

"Aunt Netta," I admonished, but then I didn't know what to say next, what excuse to give. "He lives in California."

"So." She shrugged, arching a brow. "It's a smaller world all the time—I saw it on *Good Morning America*. These days, people meet on the intra-net, and they fall in love before they ever even seen each other in person. I did hair on a girl like that. She was just passin' through on her way from Austin to Omaha, Nebraska. She'd met a fella online. Wheat farmer. I gave her the Amber Anderson special. She wanted to look like a star when she met her beau."

"Nate and I are just working together, Aunt Netta," I answered flatly. With *The Horseman* preparations coming to an end, the Daily Lovelorn was getting desperate to make something happen before we all parted ways and returned to normal life.

Unfortunately, that very possibility was what had kept me up all night. I couldn't stop thinking that in a couple days, Nate would be gone and I'd be back at work in Kansas. I wouldn't wake up anymore looking forward to our walks together, or go to bed thinking about his silly jokes, trying to conjure the exact way he smiled—just a little twitch at one side of his lips that slowly spread until his eyes sparkled with it.

"Oh, they were, too—that intra-net couple I did the hair for, I mean." I had the feeling Aunt Netta was making up the story as she went along, but with her, you could never tell. The things that happened to her were often stranger than fiction. "They were working together for . . . well, some big comp'ny I can't think of right now. But that's how they met, and then they got to chattin' over the intra-net, and the rest is history. They fell in love. Isn't that just wonderful? Somethin' like that don't happen every day—you meet someone and just know it's right, I mean."

"I guess not," I said blandly. "I'd probably better get ready for church. I need to wash my hair this morning."

"I could do it for you downstairs."

I pictured myself getting my hair washed and fluffed amid the scattered flotsam of *The Horseman* script—a captive audience while Nate looked on and Aunt Donetta shared stories of inter-net romance and things meant to be. "That's okay. I don't want to take up your morning. I'm not going to do anything fancy."

Aunt Netta frowned. "You should let me do somethin' fancy. Fluff it up a little. You're such a pretty girl, Puggy, and it is Sunday, after all. The higher the hair, the closer to heaven."

I pictured myself going back to church with the Amber Anderson special, like the Austin girl on her way to meet her cyber Romeo. "I figured I'd just pull it back."

Aunt Netta snorted. "Let it curl up cute. Don't just put it

in a ponytail holder. You got such nice hair." Before I could escape, Aunt Netta had grabbed my hair and pulled out the band, spreading weary, dust-laden ringlets over my shoulders. "More like that," she urged. "Only clean, of course."

She slipped the ponytail holder onto her arm. Unfortunately, it was the only one I had with me.

"Aunt Netta," I complained, stretching for the hair band, which she held out of reach.

"See ya downstairs," she said. "Everybody's leavin' about ten-thirty."

Everybody? I thought. *Everybody who?* Most of the time, Aunt Netta went to church by herself, because Uncle Ronald wasn't inclined to attend.

Aunt Netta paused in the doorway. "Oh, and they had to step up the time frame for the movie project. Mr. M. Harrison Dane's comin' here tonight at five. Isn't that excitin'? It's a big day in Daily!" She flashed a huge smile, then disappeared into the hallway before I could process the news or ask any questions.

My mind spun as I got out of bed, showered, and prepared for church. Where was Nate? When did he find out about the change in Dane's arrival time? Was he finished with the proposal? Was he in a state of panic?

Behind that thought, there was another one that lay cold and heavy on my chest. By the end of the day, our work on the movie proposal would be over, for better or for worse. I could go home.

The thought scratched like a thorn in my skin as I finished getting ready. I tried to concentrate on the basics. I left my hair down, put on a blue summer dress—one of those light, filmy things from India you can wad up and stick in the suitcase at the last minute. When I was finished, I stood in front of the mirror. I didn't look too bad, which was inappropriate, perhaps. Maybe I should have brought a darker dress, something in the bland grays of grief. . . .

But it *had* been two years. Maybe it was all right to wear a floaty blue dress after two years. . . .

As soon as the thought crossed my mind, it was followed by the ravenous guilt that haunted every good thing, every pleasant thought, swallowed it whole and reminded me that I didn't have a right to anything good.

I stared at myself in the mirror. *How long until a blue dress is just a blue dress?*

The mirror couldn't answer. I knew it wouldn't. Mirrors only confirm what you already know.

I gave up and went downstairs. Aunt Netta was waiting in the back hall. "Everybody else went on ahead," she said cheerfully, then stopped to look me over. "Oh, Puggy, don't you look pretty!" Holding my face between her hands, she smiled from ear to ear. "There's my girl. I'd give you a kiss, but that'd leave a lipstick scar." Her eyes welled, and I fully understood how important this morning was to her. I was glad I hadn't done anything to spoil it.

We headed off to church arm-in-arm. On the way, she talked about the new carpet in the sanctuary and the ongoing debate over replacing the old theater seats in the back with pews. "Bob says it's too much money, because we got perfectly good seats already, but then Betty Prine and her bunch say if we don't get things updated, some folks'll head over to First Baptist, McGregor." Aunt Netta rolled her eyes. "By some folks, she means her and Harold, of course."

"I like the old seats," I said, picturing Betty Prine, her basset hound husband, Harold, and the rest of the Daily Literary Society cronies in the front rows. A cloud of dread formed over my head and started raining little black droplets. I wished they'd head over to First Baptist, McGregor *today.*

Fortunately, when we arrived at the church, Betty Prine and the Literary ladies were busy fawning over Justin Shay and Amber Anderson. They didn't even notice Aunt Donetta and me slipping through the crowded foyer, which I think was Aunt Netta's plan. We'd entered the sanctuary and settled safely in the third pew before Iris Mayfield pushed her walker in the back door, sat down at the organ, and began playing prelude music to call everyone to worship.

The Eldridge pew filled as my father entered with Willie, Mimi, and Frederico, who was wearing one of my father's old western suits and, oddly enough, looked good in it. Justin came down the center aisle shaking hands like a politician, hugging giddy women, and autographing church bulletins. Amber Anderson trailed along, seeming surprisingly embarrassed by all the fuss. She looked as though she wished she could just walk into church without generating an event.

As the crowd filed in from the foyer, the church filled to capacity and beyond. Aunt Donetta got up to usher someone into the seat next to me as Brother Ervin took the pulpit and greeters rushed to set up extra chairs in the aisles. No doubt, Brother Ervin wished he had the draw of Justin Shay and Amber Anderson every Sunday. Attendance was up by fifty percent, at least. Normally, finding a seat wasn't a problem.

"Packed house," the person beside me said, and I recognized the voice. When I turned around, there was Nate. He drew back, studying me, and said, "Wow. You clean up pretty well."

I was filled with sensations that had nothing to do with church. Fortunately, right then, the choir came in, and the service began with announcements. I felt people watching me as we stood to sing the first hymn, but then I realized they weren't watching me at all. Every eye in the room was focused on the little knot of visiting celebrities. Brother Ervin even offered them a special greeting, then explained that he was going to have Amber sing *after* the sermon, because Daily Baptist hadn't enjoyed a crowd like this in years, and he wanted to pretend that all the visitors were there to hear him talk. In the corner, a group of interloping Methodists jokingly pointed out that they'd gotten up and gone to early service down the road, and were on their second round for the day.

Across the aisle from us, Pearly Parsons, who was more likely to be seen on a fenceline on Sunday morning than in church, lifted his chin, smacked his lips, and crossed his arms over his chest, impatient to get on with things. This morning, he'd even brought his crew along. They were lined up in the pew beside him, looking confused. They were dressed for work and no doubt wondering how they'd ended up in church this morning instead.

As usual, there was a point to Brother Ervin's greeting. It led right into the sermon. "Yes, I've got to say I'm pleased to see so many Dailyians and guests in the Lord's house this morning', amen?" He gestured acknowledgment to Justin, Willie, and company. "We're all excited about this newest dose of fame for our little town. Why, between Amber's big finish on *American Megastar* and now Justin Shay comin' here, and this project out at the old Barlinger ranch, Daily hasn't had excitement like this since the bald eagles nested out at Boggy Bend. It's been something to see, especially for those of us who watched this old town go quiet, and the buildings close up, and the young folks move away."

Brother Erve gazed toward the back door as the crowd murmured in agreement, giving Justin and Amber appreciative looks. "It wasn't so long ago, Daily was a broken place, but now we got the café full of people, and trucks of construction materials passin' through on the way out to the old Barlinger ranch, and the new Amber Anderson souvenir shop open next to the washateria in the Prine building. Ol' Harold even put up the money to fix the roof that's been leaking for ten years, and that's pretty close to a miracle in itself." He paused, and the crowd chuckled. On the front row, Harold and Betty couldn't decide whether they'd been insulted or praised, but finally Harold lifted a hallelujah hand in acknowledgment as Brother Erve went on.

"Yes, there's been a sure-enough case of *Horseman* fever around town lately, everyone pitchin' in to bring food to the volunteers and construction crew at the ranch, and helping with the work out there. It feels good to do good, amen?"

Brother Ervin paused, taking in a round of amens. Reaching behind the pulpit, he pulled out a sack, and the crowd grew silent. There was no telling, on any given Sunday, what Ervin Hanson would have in his paper bags. Once, he came in with a live bull snake hidden inside. Sometime later in the sermon, when he pulled the bag out again, it was empty. Ladies screamed and little kids crawled onto the pews, but Brother Ervin's point was made. If we were half as worried about the lost people among us as we were about that snake underfoot, the church would be full to the brim every Sunday. Shortly before pandemonium broke out, he produced the snake, safely tucked in a glass container.

Today, Brother Ervin had a set of spurs in his bag. Since that seemed like a fairly benign item, the crowd leaned in as he began to talk. I studied the spurs with interest. They were antique, the worn leather straps cracked and crisp, the heavy brass rowels darkened with the soft patina of age, testifying to the fact that many years had passed since the pinwheel of sharp edges had touched flesh. The spurs were wicked looking instruments; the old-fashioned kind charros wore in Mexico. My father always said that if a man couldn't control a horse without using tools like that, he didn't need the horse. At the end of our row, Dad crossed his arms over his chest and frowned at the spurs.

Brother Ervin turned them over in his hand, touching a thumb to the ring of spines and appearing impressed by the sharpness. "Still pretty formidable, after all these years," he said, and chuckled, his round stomach shaking up and down where his polyester western suit hung open. "You know, I watched my daddy use these spurs on many an ornery young horse. He was a big man, served in the First World War, mounted infantry. Went off when he was just sixteen, because he felt it was what he needed to do. He was one of those old-time cowboys that don't hardly exist anymore—lived by the code. Make no excuses and take no excuses. He was hard on horses and hard on kids. There was a lot of years I resented that. I was angry with the kind of man my father was."

Scanning the crowd, he sought the faces of others who felt the same, then nodded meditatively, the wrinkles deepening around his eyes. "Looking back, I think he did what he knew. Most folks go through life that way, when you get right down to it—they aren't trying to hurt anybody, they're just doin' what they know. They learnt it from someplace, and they never thought about whether it was right or wrong. Mostly, what's done with us as a child is what we go on and do in life. My father's way got the job done. Many was the day he roped a colt, and if it fought, he just let the rope get tighter and tighter until the critter either gave in or choked down and fell to the ground. Sometimes, he used that old blacksnake whip and these spurs until there was hair and hide and blood all over the breakin' pen, him, the horse, and the rest of us." Flipping the rowel on the spur, he let it turn in the sunlight. The metal moaned softly and the jinglebobs chimed an eerie music as if they remembered the rise and fall of a boot.

"Watching him cured me of ever wanting to be a horse breaker. I figured if that was how the job got done, it wasn't for me. There's nothing easy about making a twelve-hundred-pound animal bend to your will." Down the row, Justin Shay nodded in agreement. Beside me, Nate grabbed a pencil and made a note on the church bulletin, and up front, Betty Prine glanced at her watch, giving the preacher a disgusted look. She hated it when Brother Ervin went off on a tangent. She wanted to get to the point, read Scripture, sing "Old Rugged Cross," and go home to Sunday dinner.

Brother Ervin pretended he didn't see her, as usual. "Now, back in them days, we still delivered milk and eggs around from our farm, and there was an old black man who lived on my route. A lot of you probably don't remember Hardy Pots, but he was the father of our Pastor Harve, out at Caney Creek Church. Hardy Pots was old and crippled up by the time I knew him, but he still broke horses for folks. I'd watch him sometimes when I passed by his place, and I never saw a whip, or a spur, or heard his voice raised when he was in the corral with an animal. Seemed to me like he didn't do much but stand there and let the horses run around him. It never occurred to me to really ponder the reasons for that."

Pausing, Brother Harve set the spurs atop the pulpit, where the colored light from the windows fell over them, bathing them in red. "It's been only just recently I finally understood why it was always so quiet around old Hardy's corral. You see, I been readin' the book on which the movie is actually based, *An Ordinary Horseman*." Taking the book from behind the pulpit, he held it up for everyone to see. "If you haven't read it,

I encourage you to. There's a few copies floatin' around town these days, and maybe even one in the library, if you're lucky. The book will help you understand the movie, but there's a deeper meaning here. This book'll tell you a lot about how we ought to be to each other, and how our heavenly Father is toward us."

Brother Ervin set the book aside and let the assertion—that something about God could be learned from a book about horses—settle. In the front rows, Betty Prine and the ladies of the Literary Society frowned back and forth at one another. They'd warned Brother Ervin in Church Council time and time again that examples should be strictly biblical.

Brother Ervin went on, "You see, there's a lot of us think God is like my father was. They think He just throws on the rope and keeps the pressure up until we choke down, and when we go the wrong way, He lays on the blacksnake and the spur." With a benevolent smile, Brother Ervin shook his head at the spurs. "But you see, that's not how a good horseman works. A good horseman is patient. He's quiet. He knows that the horse's natural state is to live in partnership. Deep down, way down in its instincts, that animal realizes that isolation puts it in danger, makes it vulnerable. The horseman sees that truth all the while the animal is circlin' the corral, squealing and kicking and trying to keep as far away as he can, and so the horseman just waits. He waits because he knows the nature of the horse. He waits when the animal does wrong. He waits when it fights and runs away. He just moves real quiet around the corral. He lets that horse run all it wants, wear itself out as much as it needs to. Eventually, the horse figures out things aren't good out there by the fence. It stops and turns to the horseman, and comes into the center, and sees that's where peace is. That's where safety is. That's where rest and comfort lie."

Taking the spur from the red light, Brother Erve covered over the rowel with his hand, so that the sharp points were no longer visible. "God is a good horseman. He waits while we circle the fences of our lives—whatever they are, whether it be a bad childhood, or a destructive habit, family problems, an addiction, a personal tragedy, an inability to forgive someone else or to allow ourselves to ask forgiveness, or believe we deserve it. The Good Horseman waits, and each time we turn and look at Him, He stretches out His hand, slow and quiet, until finally, sooner or later, we reach for it, and we come to the center with Him, and find that peace was waiting there all along."

Iris Mayfield struck up the music, and Amber crested the steps to the microphone as Brother Erve let the last words fade. He took the spurs of a horsebreaker to the altar of the Good Horseman and laid them down atop the Bible. I watched metal touch the worn leather cover, felt the preacher's hand move away as if it were my own.

Where there was pain, I felt the beginnings of release, and all at once I understood that the Good Horseman had been waiting for me for a very long time.

Chapter 20

Nathaniel Heath

When the service ended, a crowd of hand-shakers mobbed our pew, and we were trapped. Lauren must have seen it coming, because she slipped out during the closing hymn and disappeared through the back door as The Shay's admirers gathered around.

Justin was in his element. Compared to the usual throng of screaming fans and jostling paparazzi, the Daily Baptists were pleasant people—friendly, laid back, definite foodies. We garnered at least a dozen invitations to Sunday dinner, and Bob offered to feed us at the café for free. Justin seemed to be entertaining the offers, so I took the opportunity to play Marla and remind him that he needed to head back to the hotel and focus on the proposal. It was now noon, T minus five hours in *Horseman* terms. When Dane arrived this evening, we had to be ready to whisk him off into the sunset, impress him with cowboy magic, convince him that Justin could do a picture without guns and car chase scenes, and dazzle the Dane kids with pony rides until their father had no choice but to attach himself to the project. With Dane committed, Randall and the studio would be hard pressed to fight it.

I hoped.

They wouldn't say no to M. Harrison Dane, would they?

No. No one would say no to Dane. All I had to do was get Justin back to the hotel and get him focused. Why that was *my* job, I couldn't say. I wasn't the one who had wanted this project in the first place. I was the one who said it was a stupid idea, yet here I was, worrying about scheduling and other practicalities while Justin sailed around the crowd like a cuttlefish, handing out autographs, posing for photos with Amber and the Daily-ians, and acting like he had all the time in the world.

What's wrong with this picture?

He knows you'll do it, Oprah muttered in my head. *He knows you'll play the adult, which leaves him free to act like a teenager at the prom. You should just step back. Leave it to him. It's his project. This happens every time. He acts like an idiot, and you end up stuck in jail in Morocco.*

How's that workin' for ya? Dr. Phil added.

I pictured Dane showing up and Justin stumbling through the proposal materials, unprepared and bloated on chicken-fried steak and mile-high coconut pie from the Daily Café.

Not happening. Not.

I told Frederico we needed to get Justin out of there. Happy to oblige, Fred did a pretty good job of elbowing old ladies out of the way, gathering up The Shay, and clearing a path to the door, where we said good-bye to Amber, who was headed to some little town near Dallas for a fund-raiser but planned to be back in the evening before Dane arrived.

Justin was pouty about the idea. "I figured you'd come help me study the proposal, babe," he complained, his arm looped around her shoulder.

Amber's big blue eyes were filled with the self-inflicted guilt of a natural nurturer. "I'm sorry, Justin. I didn't know Mr.

Dane was gonna decide to come *today*. This fund-raiser's been planned for weeks. If I don't go, they won't be able to put together the money so kids can have coats next winter. I thought I told you about thay-ut." She probably had, but Justin only heard what he wanted to hear. Right now, with Dane coming in a few hours, he was feeling pressured and needy. He wanted to lean on someone, preferably someone cute.

Amber cast a desperate look toward a van with a radio station logo on the side, already waiting for her in the parking lot. "Justin, I've gotta go. I'll be back this afternoon before Mr. Dane comes. I promise."

"Yeah," Justin muttered, slipping into passive-aggressive protest mode as Amber kissed him on the cheek and hurried off. "Go ahead. I'll figure it out. If Nate hadn't taken so long to get me the proposal, we wouldn't be in a bind, anyway."

I gaped at The Shay, my sleep-deprived brain fishing for words. *Back up a minute. Let's review. I've been kidnapped and taken to Texas. I've been working like a word slave for days, up all night to pull this rabbit out of a hat for you. I got up and went to church instead of sleeping, because I figured we probably needed a miracle to pull this off, and now this mess is my fault?*

I'm going home. That's it. I'm going home. Let the horseman take care of himself. Whatever happens, happens. . . .

"*The Good Horseman is patient. . . .*" The words from the sermon repeated inconveniently in my head. "*The Good Horseman waits, and each time we turn to look at Him, He stretches out his hand, slow and quiet, until finally, sooner or later we reach for it. . . .*"

By the door, Willie laid a hand on Justin's shoulder, saying, "Now, son, calm down. You ever seen a Thoroughbred on race day? He's a ball'a nerves from the minute he hears the tractors draggin' the track. He'll pace, and chew the stall door, and act up. If you don't watch him, he'll burn up the energy he needs for the race, just worryin' about it ahead. To win, he's gotta keep calm, stay focused, so that when the time comes, he can git out there and do what he's meant to do." Willie's big hand squeezed Justin's shoulder and he leaned close, meeting Justin's eyes, horseman to wannabe. "You gotta stay calm. Keep focused. I'll help you read—" Willie paused to cough, and the coughing turned into a spasm that sent him staggering off the porch. Imagene and Frank hurried down to check on him as he caught his breath and stood upright again, looking pale.

"Everything all right?" Brother Ervin asked as he closed the church doors.

"Fine." Willie's voice was hoarse and sparse. "Think I swallered a gnat."

Donetta cast a concerned look at Willie, and by the car, Mimi stopped conversing with Fred long enough to notice that her boyfriend didn't look so well. "Everything okay, sweetie?" she called, and Willie waved her off.

We all stood for a minute, trying to figure out what should come next. Finally Donetta suggested that Willie go back to Frank's to rest for a while. Since the beauty shop was closed today, Donetta and Imagene would help Justin study the proposal packet, or practice lines in the sample scenes, or whatever was needed. "I got some actin' experience, and back when *American Megastar* did Amber's hometown show, Imagene got interviewed. On national TV."

Justin didn't protest. He wanted someone to coddle him, and now he'd found someone. I considered being a fly on the wall during this afternoon's script session, but really, I wanted to go find Lauren. I'd been thinking all morning about what Donetta had said when she woke me up earlier.

"Sometimes God puts a new path under your feet, not because you think you're ready to walk it, but because *He* knows *that's the way you need to go."*

Maybe Donetta was right, or maybe it was just wishful thinking on both our parts, but I wanted to further investigate the possibility before my time with Lauren was officially over.

"I think I'll head back to the hotel on foot," I said as the group moved toward various vehicles in the parking lot. It was a nice morning, the town quiet in the reverent way of little towns after Sunday service, when everyone moves on to dinner at Grandma's house or the local café. I felt good inside, like Sunday was more than just another day for once, and that was the way it should be.

The pastor's sermon replayed in my head as I walked, and I considered the time I'd spent circling the fences of my life at top speed, looking for a way to bust through, to break away from my mom, from Doug, from pointless leftover childhood questions, like, *If my grandparents loved me, why did they let my mother take me away time and time again? If my mother loved me, why was some guy she'd just met always more important? If my father cared about me, how could he die and leave me with my mom?*

If the people who raised me didn't care about me, then I wasn't anything special and I never would be. . . .

Doug was right. . . .

All these years, I'd been battering the same barriers over and over and over, thinking that the answer lay in breaking through and leaving the past behind. I'd looked for the answer somewhere outside—my work, my house, my car, my name in the credits, a paycheck, A-list parties, friends with big names. But every time, I came up empty. The answer wasn't there. On the way back to the hotel, it dawned on me: Maybe the answer isn't in getting beyond where you come from but in learning to accept the things that went into your making. Maybe the secret is in looking at the end product and figuring out what it's good for.

I pondered it as I strolled the long way home, past the feed mill, where my steps echoed hollowly against the tall grain silos, and I could hear the river floating by. *Maybe the point of life isn't in getting past it, but in making something of it.*

The new frame of thought took shape in my mind, and I realized that I wanted to share it with Lauren. I looked for her when I got back to the hotel, but there was no one around other than Frederico, doing thigh burners in the exercise room, while Imagene, Donetta, and Justin sat gathered in the beauty shop. They were sharing chicken nuggets and gravy as Donetta read the proposal aloud. They were impressed with my work, which was nice, but in reality I could see that, between the distraction of the two of them talking and people passing by outside the window, stopping to gawk or wave, Justin wasn't getting anything done.

"You'd probably better take that upstairs," I suggested, and he gave me a peeved sneer.

"I got it under control, Nate." Dipping a nugget in the gravy bucket, he leaned over and touched one of the pages, leaving behind a greasy smudge. I made a mental note to reprint a clean set before Dane arrived. No telling what shape these would be in.

"It's time to get focused." I sounded like somebody's mommy, but what other choice was there? For whatever reason, Justin wasn't getting down to business, and time was running short. He needed to concentrate, and generally, he only did that when there was no one around to play with.

Imagene regarded me in an acute way, then nodded as if she understood. "You know what, Netta. We should head on over to Frank's place and take them some of this pie."

Donetta straightened in her chair. "I gotta help Justin go over his script, Imagene. Besides, Frank took a pie home from the café yester-dey. They probably still got some left."

Imagene's eyes widened, and behind Justin's back, she thumbed insistently toward the door. Donetta ignored her and focused on the papers. Finally, Imagene grabbed Donetta's arm and tried to lift her out of the chair, and for a minute, I thought we were about to be ringside for a wrestling match.

"Uhhh . . . we can just go upstairs," I suggested, and got another annoyed frown from Justin. As long as there were people, and pie, and a constant stream of admirers passing by the window down here, he wasn't in the mood to leave.

"Nonsense." Imagene was a determined woman when she had her mind set. "We'll just head on out to Frank's and leave the buildin' quiet for you boys. We'll take Frederico with us. You can have the whole place to yourselves to get ready for this evenin' and such. Besides, Donetta and me ought to go check on Willie and make sure he's feelin' all right, shouldn't we, Netta?"

Peering up over the top of her bifocals, Donetta smacked her lips as if she had a bad taste in her mouth, but then finally acquiesced. "Oh, you're right, I guess we should. Knowin' Frank, he'll have Willie out in the pasture a'horseback. Somebody's got to take care of the poor man, him havin' that lung cancer and all. He—"

"Netta." Imagene pulled Donetta's sleeve, and it was clear to me, even if Donetta seemed oblivious to it, that a rather large cat had just escaped the bag.

"Well, it's not like you could count on that Mimi to do it." Donetta was completely oblivious to the secret now prowling the room. "You know, he hadn't even *told* her he has cancer, and her supposed to be his girlfriend and all. Can you imagine—"

"Netta!" Imagene's protest filled the space between us, and then everything went silent. "That ain't any of our business."

Donetta laughed, batting away the words with savoir faire. "Pppffff, I'm a hairdresser. Everything's my business."

"Maybe he don't want *folks* to *know*." Imagene cleared her throat, and from the body language I could tell she meant The Shay and me.

The hollow under Donetta's cheekbones went red. "Oh, gravy," she murmured, her mouth falling open. "I didn't figure it was a secret from *everybody*. I just thought he wasn't tellin' Mimi—that maybe he figured if she knew, she wouldn't stay around. She don't seem like the type to stick around, Willie bein' so much older than her, and his odds not bein' very good and all."

"Netta!" Grabbing Donetta's arm, Imagene hauled her to her feet, snagged a suitcase-sized red purse off the shelf, stuffed it into Donetta's hands, and said, "We're goin'. Y'all two just go on with what you need to be doing." She hustled Donetta out the back, the two of them arguing all the way. Frederico followed, looking confused.

When they were gone, I turned my attention to Justin. He was watching a family on the sidewalk, each of them carrying a bag from the Amber Anderson souvenir shop across the street. They peered in our window and waved, but Justin just stared at the glass, unfocused.

"Shay-man," I said, but he didn't react. "Hey, Shay-man." I flashed a hand in front of his face, and he blinked. "You all right?" I waved to the onlookers on behalf of The Shay, and the family moved on.

Justin started stacking up proposal pages. "Yeah, fine." He shrugged me off as if he couldn't imagine why I was asking. "Why wouldn't I be, dude?"

"I just thought maybe you'd be upset about Willie." I watched closely for a reaction. After all the times I'd seen The Shay and Willie arm-in-arm like family, I couldn't believe this would roll off so easily. Then again, Justin's ability to detach from things had often surprised me. After Stephanie took the boys and moved away, he never mentioned their absence. It didn't seem to bother him that one day Brody and Bryn were in his house and the next day they weren't. It almost seemed like he was glad. Family life had cramped his ability to party. With Stephanie and the kids gone, he could do whatever he wanted.

"Come on, Shay," I said. "You and Willie have been tight. You're going to tell me this doesn't bother you?" Of all the days for Justin to find this out, today was the worst possible one. The last thing he needed was another distraction or any more weight on his shoulders.

Shrugging, he gave himself a quick sideways check in the beauty shop mirror, his reflection casting a sardonic smile. "If we were tight, I guess I'd know he had cancer, wouldn't I? He didn't tell me because he didn't want me to drop his project. People tell you what they want you to hear, dude. You been in the big town long enough, you ought to know that. Everybody uses everybody. That's the way it works."

"That's a pretty cynical outlook on it."

The man in the mirror flashed a smile that worked on screen, but in actuality meant nothing. "It's real, dude. You gotta be real. Dreamers like you don't ever figure that out. Everyone wants somethin'. Mimi's out for a free ride wherever she can get it. Willie wants this movie made. Amber wants me to help her build that foster shelter. Frank wants to pay off a debt to Willie. You think you owe me, because we spent a few years in the same room at Mama Louise's and I gave you a break in the business when I got mine."

Shrugging, he smoothed back his hair, twisting his head from side to side, checking for perfection before turning away from the mirror. "We all got our own thing, and we look out for our own thing. And the world keeps turning. You gonna run with the big dogs, you gotta be ready to bite before they bite you. Law of the jungle, baby."

Stuffing the papers under his arm, he swiped a bite of pie up with one finger, popped it in his mouth, and started toward the stairs. "I'm heading up to get some work done. I'm sick of these people." He waved vaguely toward the room, or the plate glass window, or me. It was hard to say.

"Go for it," I muttered. Not that it mattered, because the Shay was halfway out of the room and probably not listening anyway. "You're on your own, dude."

"Yeah, well, that's nothing new." His words echoed after him, and I felt the usual cross between irritation and parental guilt. I hadn't really meant for him to hear that last part. Or maybe I had, in a subconscious way. What did it say about me that I'd spent the past twenty years baby-sitting a jerk who thought I was here because I owed him for giving me my big break in action-adventure screenwriting?

For about two and a half seconds I considered grabbing the laptop off the counter, going upstairs, chucking it in The Shay's general direction, and telling him what he could do with this project. Let *him* try to write it if he was such a one-man show. I could get on a plane, fly a couple of hours, drive a few more, and be right back where I started from.

Now, there's a cheery thought. Just me and Dr. Phil again, fixing broken lives one episode at a time.

Sitting down in one of the chairs, I pulled a hair dryer cone over my head and tried to focus. I thought about all the people who were counting on *The Horseman* and the foster shelter the project would help create. I thought about the kids who would eventually come there, who would figure out, the way I had at Mama Louise's, what it means to be safely home. Until I lived at her house, I had forgotten there were places where you could lay your head down and go to sleep and know you'd wake up all right in the morning.

I went back to work, determined that quitting wasn't an option. We couldn't drop this project. The Shay knew that, too, deep down. He knew it because of where we'd been together. In a couple of hours, he would descend the stairs, and he'd be ready. For once in his life, he would cowboy up instead of caving in. He knew how important this project was to everyone, how much this whole town, and all the kids who would come here later, were counting on it.

For an hour, I poured over the text, read through it again and again, printed out clean pages, got it perfect, made sure we had plenty of copies if Dane brought people with him. As the last file rolled off the printer, I fell asleep.

Donetta's voice was echoing in my ear when I woke up. She sounded far away. I opened my eyes, and everything was black. Small circles of light reflected against the darkness like fake stars in an old theater ceiling. A gonglike sound rang around me, and I clued into the fact that my head was inside one of the dryer cones. Donetta was knocking on the outside. She lifted it up, and there was light.

With the light came panic. "What time is it?" Blinking as my eyes adjusted, I tried to focus on my watch.

"Around three in the afternoon," she answered. "I wondered if Lauren had been by here. Nobody's seen her since church. She got in her car and left as soon as service was over. Didn't say a thing to anybody. It's not like Puggy to do that. Imagene and me and Frederico looked for her out at the ranch, and at

Frank's place, and I checked upstairs for her. There's no one up there, either, and—"

"Justin's upstairs," I said. "Maybe he saw her."

Donetta shook her head. "There's nobody upstairs. I checked Puggy's room, and I checked Justin's. There's nobody here but you. At first I thought there was nobody here at all, until I walked around the corner and saw you hangin' out from under the hair dryer. I thought maybe ya'll had . . . I don't know, maybe went out to the ranch and we just missed you on the road. Imagene and Frederico just headed out to drive around and look some more, and . . ."

I missed the rest of what she was saying. I was still stuck on *nobody's upstairs*. Nobody's upstairs? My mind zinged to a fully awakened state. If The Shay wasn't upstairs, then where was he? "Are you sure Justin's not up there?"

"Sure as a hot day in July. His truck's gone, too. There's papers all over the room up there—looks like a tornado went through while he was studyin' the script, and he left that mobile phone of his on the table. It's been ringin' like a church bell ever since I walked in here."

"Could he and Lauren have gone somewhere together—somewhere else?" I struggled to piece together some scenario that made sense. "Maybe they're doing some prepping before Dane gets here." I stood up and started walking toward the stairs with Donetta following me.

"I don't think so," she answered. "Bob seen that big four-wheeler truck roar outta here about an hour ago with only Justin inside, in a hurry and drivin' wild."

A sick feeling started in my head and worked its way slowly downward. As we crested the stairs, I heard Justin's phone ringing. I hurried to the room, checked the call.

Marla.

The list of recent calls was an echo.

Marla.

Marla.

Marla.

Justin had called her about an hour and a half ago.

I pushed the button and answered the call just before it could roll to voice mail.

Marla wasn't happy to find me on the end of the line. "What do you want, Nate?" she snapped.

"You're the one who called." I'd forgotten how much I loved talking to Marla. After almost a week surrounded by the slow drawl and pervasive niceness of the Dailyians, Marla's voice was like the annoying squeal of a car alarm.

"Put Justin on the phone."

"I would if I knew where he was." I had a feeling Marla knew. I had a feeling she had something to do with his sudden disappearing act. I pictured him on the plane, on his way back to California, slowly melting down, caving under the pressure, running back to Marla and Randall, who would pat him on the head, tell him what he wanted to hear, and feed him prescription anxiety meds to help him feel better about bailing on everyone here in Daily, Texas.

Would he really do that?

He's done it before. He's done it over, and over, and over again. Why wouldn't he do it now? Why were you stupid enough to believe this time would be different?

"Where is he, Marla?"

"None of your business, Nate." Marla's forked tongue whipped through the phone and gave me an ear lashing. "I'm on my way down to that stupid backwater little hole in the earth to pick him up, and he'd better be there when I get there. You can find your own way home."

"He's not here *now*," I pointed out. "What did he say when you talked to him?"

"Like I'd tell you."

"I mean it, Marla. He's somewhere, and he's bottoming out, and I need to find him." Across the room, Donetta gasped and mouthed *Oh my!* I could guess what was going through her mind right now.

Marla snorted into the phone. "Sure. Right. What are you—his keeper?"

"Why did he call you, Marla?"

"Why don't you get a life of your own, Nate? Oh yes, I remember, because without Justin, you're a big, fat nothing. How's that master work of yours coming along, by the way? Got a big shiny option contract yet? Guess not, huh? Wonder why that is?"

"Why did he call you?"

"Go to—"

"*Why* did he *call*?"

"He needed a prescription filled. I phoned it in for him."

I felt like she'd just hit me with a right cross through the phone. "Where? Where did you call it in?"

"I'm hanging up now," she sing-songed.

"Where!" My voice reverberated through the room. Donetta took a step backward, her long, artificially thickened lashes blinking open so that her eyes were white around the edges.

"Wall's Pharmacy in some town nearby," Marla huffed. "There's not exactly a chain store on every corner around there, you know."

"Where. What town?" Grabbing a pen off the nightstand, I snatched a sheet of paper off the floor, wrote *Wall's Pharmacy*.

Marla finally gave it up. "Killeen. Someplace called Killeen. I'm flying in lat—"

I didn't listen to the rest, just hung up and turned off the phone, then dropped it on the table. "How far is Killeen from here?"

Donetta pondered. "Way-ul, let me think." Her voice seemed to bend and stretch, each word painfully slow. "Less than a hour. Maybe forty-five minutes. You just turn left outta here, go straight down the highway, turn when you see the big green sign to Killeen. That runs right into town."

Glancing at the clock, I did a quick mental calculation. Forty-five minutes there. Forty-five minutes to return. An hour and a half. Dane was due to land at the Daily airport in less than two hours. I could make it there and back . . . if I could find Justin right away. If he wasn't strung out. If we didn't pass each other en route. There was no choice but to try. "Do you know where the Wall's Pharmacy is? She said Justin was headed for Wall's Pharmacy."

Donetta ruminated again. "Way-ul, let me think about thay-ut. . . . There's a Wall's Pharmacy right on 190 as you drive into town, but I think there's more than just one. I could call Brother Ervin and ask. His mama lives in Killeen in the nursin' home. She's a hundred and two years old. Real sweet lady, and—"

I didn't wait for the rest of the story. "I need you to do some things for me, all right?"

"All ri-ight," she agreed, a twinkle of intrigue in her eyes.

"I'll head to the pharmacy in Killeen." *What are the odds? What are the odds he'll be there?* "Dane is due at the airport in less than two hours. Make sure someone's there to pick him up. He'll probably have a number of people with him, as well as his family. If Justin and I aren't back when he gets here, take Dane's group out to the ranch. His kids want to ride a horse. Get someone to show them around the foster shelter and give them the tour. Find Lauren. Get her prepared to do a demo with

310

the horse—anything to stall for time until we can get there. If I can't find Justin, I'll come back by myself." In reality there was no way this thing would work without Justin. Without the horseman, there was no project.

Donetta stood at attention like a soldier receiving marching orders. "You can count on us. One thing about Daily folk, we know how to hand out southern hospitality. When that Mr. Dane gets here, he won't know what hit 'im."

That's what I was afraid of. If someone had told me a few hours ago that I'd be sending Imagene, Donetta, and Frederico to pick up M. Harrison Dane, I would have laughed the idea out of the room. Now I didn't have much choice. "I'll need a car."

For the first time, Donetta looked worried. "Imagene and Frederico took the van, and Ronald's gone fishin' in my truck. . . ." Tapping a finger to her lips, she considered the problem as we hurried down the stairs. "Pearly Parsons' flatbed is right there in the shop. Frank just plugged a tire on it. Pearly wouldn't care if you used it, bein' as it's a emergency and all."

I didn't argue. Right now, there wasn't time to be choosy. I followed her to the auto shop, helped her raise the door, and in under five minutes flat, I was sputtering down the alley, surrounded by a smell that reminded me of Lucky Strike's barn, and sporting the unlikely handle,

Pearly Parsons, PHD
Post Hole Digger
Fencing, welding, post drilling
The harder the ground, the bigger the shovel
Every fence true and straight

If I could make this situation turn out straight and true, then the PHD part would be well earned.

Chapter 21

Lauren Eldridge

The instant Brother Ervin finished the sermon about the Good Horseman, I knew what I had to do. When the service ended, I rose from my seat so quickly that people probably thought I was headed down front for the invitation. I rushed out the door as the closing hymn faded and people began zipping up their Bible covers and waking sleeping kids. I probably looked like a lunatic, but it didn't matter. I had somewhere to go, and I had to get there before it was too late or my newfound courage faded.

As I drove out of town, my hands tightened on the steering wheel, growing clammy even before I turned off Main at the Buy-n-Bye. The store was closed this morning, the squatty cement-block building basking peacefully in the sunlight under a sprawling live oak tree.

In my mind, it became night. I saw the tree shuddering in the rain, the branches swaying wildly, groaning in the wind. A flash of lightning lit the road, illuminated the snake of curves ahead, then died. In the trailer, the horses whinnied and kicked the walls, uneasy, anxious, as if they sensed what was ahead.

I could hear them as if I were there again, in the storm with Danny, lightning crackling inside the vehicle and out. . . .

I tried to push the image away, to bury it again.

The only dangerous demons are the ones you lack the courage to confront. I'd read that in a Campus Crusade pamphlet someone left sitting around the classroom building. *Courage,* it said, *doesn't come from an absence of fear, but an abundance of faith.* It was time to pull out my faith and acknowledge the fact that I hadn't been saved from the water so I could spend the rest of my life focusing on myself. There was work to do, and for me the work began here, where a single split-second decision went horribly wrong.

My heart beat faster as I drew close to the low-water crossing. Scenes from that night flashed by like bits of memory randomly torn from a scrapbook no one would want—trees swaying, wind buffeting the truck, the horse trailer fishtailing in the mud, Danny driving too fast, the trailer rocking back and forth, rain pounding the truck, so loud. The voices inside, even louder.

Topping the hill, I saw the headlights glint against the flooded crossing, the water churning behind the low-water bridge, building power, then rushing over the pavement. I told Danny to turn around, but he let the truck creep forward. He wanted to see how much water was coming over the top. I argued. He drove on.

I gave in. . . .

Forcing the memory to fade, I slowed the car, pulled in a breath, let it go, looked up and out. This journey was about moving forward, pressing through, facing the guilt, self-hatred, self-recrimination, finally pushing those things away after years of embracing them, feeding them, making them stronger, running from them only to turn around and embrace them again.

I saw the crossing as it was today—a quiet place, a lazy trickle of water winding over a bed of limestone the soft color of milky tea, the water narrowing to slip harmlessly through the culvert under the crossing. Trees lined the creek banks, the limbs painting a canvas of sunlight and shade. This was a beautiful place, a place I'd always loved. How many times had Kemp and I talked my father into stopping here so we could wade in the pool of water behind the culvert, hunt for fossils, chase dragonflies and catch minnows?

There were good memories here. I'd let them go, allowed them to be eclipsed by the blackness of a single terrible night. Time had moved the river onward, cleared away the debris and broken tree limbs, washed clean the mud-covered grass, planted a growth of sunflowers where they could lean over the water and watch their reflections passing by. God had made this place whole again. The brokenness remained in me only because I had clung to it.

I stopped the car, got out and stood at the crossing, gazing down the river. My mind thumbed through images of Kemp and me wading in the water, Danny and me crossing over the bridge coming and going from the ranch as we chased impractical hopes. Things weren't always bad. We were happy in our own way. We were young, and starry-eyed, and foolish. We grew up and began to outgrow each other, and I think we both knew it. Rather than address the real issues, admit our mistakes, we pressed onward, pushed harder, pursuing an immature dream that, in the end, died painfully.

Time had moved on in this place, and I had to, as well.

Taking in the sweet scent of noonday, I let go of the idea that regretting what had happened would ever change it. I cast the burden of it to the wind like a dry leaf, allowed it to float away on the water. I watched it disappear into the distance, growing smaller and smaller until the image of what had been was replaced by the realization of what could be. Life held so many possibilities now. But there was one more thing to do. One more place to go.

As I left the crossing behind, I felt a lightness settle over me, an acceptance of what had happened, of being the one who was saved from the water.

The parking lot was just beginning to clear at Caney Creek Church when I pulled up and stopped under a tree near the road. Sitting in my car, I watched from a distance as Pastor Harve shook hands with the brethren at the door. Miss Beedie was handing out roses from a bucket of blooms she'd probably clipped from her garden. Miss Beedie's flowers were legendary.

When the crowd was gone, Pastor Harve turned back to the door to lock up, his movements slow, his body hunched over as he struggled with the lock. The heavy bar of guilt lay over me again. Pastor Harve and Miss Beedie would spend their last years without their son to tend them. That responsibility would fall to the grandkids, O.C. and Teylina. Things could have been so different. . . .

Miss Beedie looked up from her flower bucket as I let my car drift across the parking lot. Shading her eyes with her hand, she tried to see who was inside. She called over her shoulder to Pastor Harve, and together they squinted toward my car.

They didn't react at first when I opened the door and got out. The sun was behind me, and perhaps they couldn't tell who I was. My heart pounded in my throat, grew large and painful and heavy with tears. I didn't want to cry. I didn't want to inject sadness into their day. I just wanted to say I was sorry, and to tell them that when I saw Harvard coming across the water toward me, it gave me the courage to hold on. He was a remarkable man, their son, a hero.

But when I reached Miss Beedie, the dam burst, and all I could do was let the tears come. Setting down her bucket, she said, "Why, it's Lauren, Harve." Then she stretched out her arms and took me in.

"I'm sorry," I sobbed, holding tight, circling her thin shoulders, surprised by the strength there.

"Oh, honey," she whispered, and the two of us rocked back and forth, joined in shared grief, locked in a painful reunion that seemed to last far too long. Finally the tears faded, and she let go. We stood for a moment near the church steps, none of us knowing what to say.

"I should have come sooner," I whispered, my voice gravelly and rough.

"It's no matter." Pastor Harve laid a hand against my cheek, swept away a tear with his thumb. "You're here now. Harvard would like that. He always loved you a lot. He loved all you kids he taught in the 4-H."

I nodded, knowing it was true. Throughout the years of my childhood, Harvard had been the one who had shown up in the heat, the cold, the rain, to teach 4-H horsemanship, to help kids trim show steers, and clip sheep, and build transport cages so bunnies and chickens could be taken to the county show. No matter what the weather, how difficult the project, or how overstressed and mouthy the kid, Harvard could be counted on to be there, dealing out lessons in animal husbandry and proper 4-H behavior.

Miss Beedie picked up her flower bucket again. "I was just gonna take these to Harvard." She looked toward the tree line, where an old wagon road led up the hill through the pecan trees to Caney Creek Cemetery. "This bucket's heavy, though."

"I'll carry it." I reached for the handle, then hesitated. Perhaps this was a private time. Maybe they wouldn't want anyone along, especially not me. "If it's all right." I waited for the answer, feeling breathless, telling myself I would understand if they asked me to leave.

Miss Beedie nodded benevolently. "Why sure, sweetheart." She handed the bucket to me, and the three of us started along the path—Miss Beedie walking with her cane, me carrying the bucket, and Pastor Harve with his elbow crooked in mine. We moved slowly over the uneven ground as the sun grew high and hot overhead. On the hill, Caney Creek Cemetery cradled aging monuments beneath a pecan grove. The aromas of honeysuckle and antique roses hung in the air, a comfortable blanket of scent that, were it visible, would have been soft shades of gray and blue, with lacy calico around the edges.

"Harvard's over there by the big tree," Miss Beedie said, but she needn't have told me. I could already see the climbing roses growing over Harvard's resting place, a rich spray of green and red twining over the milk-colored monument and spilling onto the ground, searching for new places to take root. When we reached the graveside, Miss Beedie picked up a vase of daisies that had wilted in the heat. I replaced them with the bucket of fresh flowers.

"There you go, love," Miss Beedie said, then slowly bent and kissed Harvard's monument. My eyes burned and spilled over. How hard must it be for them to come to this place every week, leave flowers on Harvard's grave and miss him over and over again?

"I'm sorry," I choked. "I'm so sorry. I wish I could . . ." My voice snapped like a twig under too much weight. *I wish I could go back and change things. We shouldn't have driven across. It wasn't worth it. I should have stopped Danny, made him turn around. . . .*

I felt myself sinking, returning to the black space where the *what ifs* overshadowed everything, where the guilt made surviving just that—surviving. Nothing more.

Brother Harve took my hand, encased it in a circle that trembled, yet was strong. "Harvard's work was done." His voice was low and soothing, confident. "He's up there, singin' with the angels. He don't hurt, and he ain't tired, and he ain't sad, and he ain't ever gonna shed another tear. You know that, Lauren Lee."

I nodded, because I did know. I believed it. I had faith in it, yet at the same time, I wanted things to be different. I wanted Harvard to be here with his parents, with his children. I didn't want him to miss what was here for him on Earth.

"Only our heavenly Father knows our time to go," Pastor Harve went on, and I wondered if he was talking to me or to himself. "He who loves, and hopes, and forgives. You know you been forgiven, Lauren. You know you been forgiven by the Lord and by this man layin' here in the ground. Harvard loved you so much, he walked into the water for you. If it was you or him, he woulda chose to go. He wouldn'ta wanted to live knowing he couldn't save you." He squeezed my hand, brought it to his lips, and brushed my fingers with the gentle kiss of forgiveness, then let go. He and Miss Beedie turned away and started down the hill arm-in-arm, leaving me there to make my peace with the man who'd given his life to save mine.

I sat down beside Harvard's grave, said good-bye, whispered a thank-you that seemed inadequate. Then I closed my eyes, let forgiveness wash over me and drive away the voices that came from all the darkened corners of my soul. So many times, I'd tried to come to this point and failed. I'd tried to forgive myself for what had happened. But sitting by Harvard's grave, I finally understood. It wasn't within my power to forgive myself. I'd already been forgiven. All I could do was accept it.

The trees cast long afternoon shadows over Harvard's resting place as I took two roses from the bucket and left the cemetery behind. Driving home, I stopped at the low-water crossing again, stood in the current and let it wash around my feet. I kissed the roses, smelled their scent, then lowered them to the water and let them go. They floated away like tiny ships on a journey to someplace new.

Leaving the crossing behind, I felt my lungs fill with breath, become buoyant for the first time in a long time. The day seemed bright, and perfect, and filled with possibility. I took my time driving back to the hotel, just enjoying the feeling of being back in this place I loved, of embracing it again, of finally being home.

My reverie lasted until I reached the Daily Hair and Body. Aunt Donetta, Imagene, and Lucy were waiting there. Before I was even in the door, Aunt Netta captured me and began relating the latest *Horseman* drama, and the fact that they were to meet "M. Harrison Dane himself" at the Daily airport and entertain him until Nate could find Justin and get back to town. So far no one had heard from Nate, and Dane was due in less than thirty minutes.

"You better run up and get changed!" Aunt Donetta fanned her hands in the air, then waved toward my soiled church clothes. "Land's sakes, Puggy. Today wasn't the day to take off wanderin'. Let's go. Imagene, get the pecan pie. Lucy, you better grab a brush, a comb, and a wet rag . . . and an extra cowboy hat, just in case we need it. Let Bob know to get the barbecue out there. And call Harlan. Tell him Kemp's back in town, and he said he'll drive the school bus."

I didn't even bother to ask what the bus was for, or how my brother had somehow become involved. I just hurried off to my room to change clothes before Aunt Netta could blow a gasket. I'd tell her about my visit with Pastor Harve and Miss Beedie later. Right now, there was business to tend to, and somehow it involved pecan pie, barbecue, and a cowboy hat. In Daily, pretty much everything did.

Twenty minutes later, we were ready for the trip to the airport. My Durango was second in line after Imagene's van, and behind us the squatty half-sized school bus the Dailyians lovingly called the Bean rumbled and whined in idle protest at having been awakened on a Sunday afternoon for special duty. The Bean was covered with finger-in-dirt graffiti after having been at baseball camp all week with Kemp and his team. Behind the wheel, my brother looked like a deer in the headlights. "You just don't know what you've missed around here this week," I told him, and he shook his head ruefully.

"Looks like it," he said, his dark eyes droopy and tired as he watched Aunt Netta and Bob load the last of several coolers into the van. "What's the food for?"

"You probably don't want to know." As far as I could tell, part of Aunt Netta's plan was to ply the M. Harrison Dane contingent with country cookin' and lots of pie if we couldn't produce Justin Shay.

"I probably don't," Kemp agreed, pulling off his baseball cap and scratching his head. "Tell me why we need the bus again?"

Aunt Netta was passing by and answered the question. "You know them Hollywood types. It's just like on TV," she said, then buzzed away to make sure the pecan pies were securely positioned.

Kemp shrugged helplessly and relaxed in his seat, letting the chaos continue around him. Having been involved in a few Donetta Bradford schemes before, he knew it was usually better to sit back and keep your head down than to try figuring things out.

By the time we headed for the airport, Aunt Netta's face was covered with perspiration, she and Imagene weren't speaking, and Lucy was pointing and hollering at everyone in Japanese. Luckily, they departed for Operation Dane in three different vehicles—Imagene in her van, Lucy with Bob in the Daily Café truck, and Aunt Donetta in the Bean, which meant there wasn't much chance of Kemp falling asleep behind the wheel.

When we arrived at Daily Air, Dane's plane was just turning the corner by the hangar. The stairs came down, and a man who looked like a pro wrestler squeezed through the opening. He descended to the tarmac and checked out the lay of the land, his burly arms akimbo, as if he thought he might need to put someone into a chokehold. He seemed surprised that there was no gaggle of press and paparazzi on the runway—just a ragtag group of Dailyians gathered outside the Bean and several interested Herefords looking on from the pasture next door.

A little Asian girl appeared in the doorway of the plane. Seeing the Bean, she pointed and tugged someone's arm, trying to get down the stairs to the big yellow vehicle. The arm led to Dane's wife, Monique, whom I recognized from countless movies and magazine covers. She was smaller than I thought she'd be, slender and willowy, dressed in a silk tank top, loose cotton pants, and sandals. A spray of long dark hair swirled in the breeze of the dying engines and circled her shoulders. She smiled as the girl pulled her down the ramp, then at the bottom, Monique scooped her daughter up and listened while the child chattered. Three more Dane kids of varying sizes and different nationalities, several nannies, more security, and various other personnel followed her off the plane.

Dane exited last. He was more unassuming than I'd expected, dressed in a T-shirt, jeans, sunglasses, and loafers. A blond-haired boy of about seven walked beside him. I'd seen the boy in a *People* magazine article about Dane's family. He was their eldest, adopted from an orphanage somewhere in the former Soviet block. He held his father's hand and looked timidly around the airport, his gaze settling on the wandering welcome committee of Hereford cows, then snapping toward us when Aunt Netta called out a greeting.

"Howw-dee-ee-e!" Her voice echoed across the empty space and reverberated off the buildings, causing the Dane babies to swivel in the arms of their nannies, following the sound.

Completely unintimidated by the gaggle of security, Aunt Netta marched across the tarmac and performed the Daily, Texas, version of a Hawaiian welcome, handing out kisses and handshakes. Instead of dropping leis over the children's heads, she crowned them with Amber Anderson souvenir cowboy hats. While the stunned group tried to figure out how to respond, Aunt Netta waved toward the Bean with a grand flourish intended, I guess, to present our redneck limo with some amount of flair. "We brought along some transportation we thought the kids'd get a hoot outta. Y'all come right on, y'hear? We'll just pile in like nuts in a squirrel hole. The more the merrier. Welcome to Daily, Texas!"

Chapter 22

Nathaniel Heath

If not for the teenage clerk at the Wall's Pharmacy counter, all hope would have been lost. There was no sign of Justin when I got to the store, and the clerk rolled her eyes when I asked if a prescription had been filled for Justin Shay.

"Yeah, right," she said. "George Clooney was in here a while ago, too. It's been a big day."

I told her Justin Shay was my uncle who had dementia and wasn't supposed to be out alone, and yes, I realized he had the same name as the famous guy.

Her mouth opened in a silent *Oh*. She took pity on me and made some phone calls, then located Justin's prescription at another store on the other side of town. He hadn't picked it up yet. She was even kind enough to draw me a map. I gave her the number to my cell phone, even though the low-battery indicator was beeping. She said she'd call me if she heard anything more about the prescription.

I tried not to theorize on why Justin, who was an hour ahead of me, hadn't picked up the meds. Maybe he'd changed his mind . . . maybe he was lost or stuck in traffic, maybe he'd stopped off for a burger, maybe he was headed for the airport, maybe the Horsemanmobile had broken down. . . .

Maybe he'd found enough pills in his luggage to zone out completely. Maybe he was passing out behind the wheel somewhere right now. Maybe he was about to drive off another cliff. I wouldn't be there to stop him this time.

I pictured the monster truck lying in a ditch, a heap of twisted, smoldering metal.

He wouldn't do that. He'd do what he always did when life got too heavy for him. He'd medicate himself until he couldn't feel anything.

What if this was the time he took one pill too many and didn't wake up?

The PHD truck belched and wheezed, zipping through neighborhoods and around cars like a stunt vehicle in an episode of *Miami Vice*. A metallic squeal announced my passing as the post drill created a pendulum above the bed, causing other drivers to move out of the way and gape in sheer amazement.

I rocketed over a hill and saw the second Wall's Pharmacy ahead, as my phone rang. "Hey." The girl from the first store reported, her voice high and excited, "Your uncle just picked up his prescription. It showed up in the computer as filled. I called the store, and they said he used the drive-through."

"Thanks." I hung up and stepped on the gas. The truck coughed and flooded out, then roared back to life with a screech of tires and a rattle of tools. *One more block, just one more block . . .*

Please, I know he's an idiot, but let him be all right. Make him stay put until I get there. Send down a flat tire. A flat tire would be good. I realized I was talking to someone. God, I guessed. He was probably shocked to hear my voice coming

324

from the PHD mobile, but then, He was probably shocked to hear my voice at all.

I checked the clock. Dane would be arriving anytime. The phone beeped a low-battery warning, then died, as if to punctuate the thought that there was no point calling home base to see what was happening. So far, I didn't have any good news to report.

The truck sputtered again as I rounded the last corner. There in the parking lot, in all its airbrushed glory, was Justin's vehicle. Even though it was hard to miss, towering over normal cars, I blinked, and blinked again, afraid it would disappear like a mirage. I felt a rush of gratitude, which quickly ebbed, leaving a mixed debris of anger and desire to drag Justin out of the truck and lay a right cross on him. *Idiot. Jerk. Moron. Loser* . . .

Murderous impulses replaced the fluffy benevolence of prayer as I skidded to a halt, trapping Justin's truck between a lamppost and my vehicle. The PHD truck coughed and sighed, sounding exhausted as I turned off the engine.

I was out of my ride and climbing up to the cab of the Horsemanmobile before my truck could sputter into silence. Justin barely reacted when I yanked open the passenger side door. He wasn't doing anything, just sitting there with the prescription bottle and his hand full of little white pills.

"Stop it!" Leaning across the seat, I smacked his forearm, sending everything skittering through the truck. The bottle collided with the dashboard, and pills rained against the seat and the floor like hailstones. "You idiot! What are you doing?"

He sat staring at his hand for what felt like an eternity. *Maybe he's already too stoned to know I'm here.* . . . I pictured sitting at the hospital while the doctors forced charcoal down his stomach and pumped it out. You'd think once or twice through that routine would be enough to cure a person.

"Hey!" he complained in delayed reaction, his head swiveling to take in the potpourri of pills. Leaning toward the gearshift, he picked up the bottle and started putting the pills back in one by one.

"Leave it." I snatched the container from his hand and tossed it over my shoulder, sending it clattering into the parking lot. "How much did you take?"

"I didn't take . . . anything." The standard denial came in a slurry mix of emotion and indignance as he stretched toward the floor. Air escaped his body in a long sigh, and he hung hunched over his legs like an underinflated superhero balloon. "I just want . . . wanted one to . . ." The sentence collapsed, unfinished.

Grabbing the back of his shirt, I pulled him upright. He was dressed in his horseman clothes, as if at some point he'd intended to actually go through with the day as planned. "How many did you take?" I demanded again, as his head thumped loosely against the back window glass. His eyes popped open, then fell closed. His cheeks were wet with tears and salt, his mouth tight. "Look at me, Justin." I shook him, trying to see how dilated his pupils were. "Open your eyes and look at me."

"I didn't have . . . take . . . any, Nate," he sobbed. "I didn't take . . . I just wanted one to . . . smooth the edge . . . off. I flushed the stuff I had at the hotel. I flushed it the other day." His shoulders rose and lowered, and he seemed like he was falling asleep.

"You're not doing this." Doubling his collar in my fist, I yanked him off the seat with a force that rattled his head back and forth.

"Get out!" he roared and aimed a sloppy right hook in my direction. "Get away from me!" He followed with a jab I barely had time to deflect.

"You're not doing this again. You're not bailing out on this project," I said as the punch collided with the steering wheel and the horn blared.

Through a haze of moisture, Justin gave me a vicious look. "This project was a stupid idea. You should have told me that, Nate. You're like all the rest of them. You just want something. Everybody wants something. Everybody uses everybody. That's what Mama says."

I wasn't sure who "Mama" was. His mother, maybe? In all the years I'd known him, he'd never mentioned her. I only knew about her because I'd overheard a social worker talking to Mama Louise when we were young.

"Mama knows." He punctuated the words with a rueful laugh. "She knows you're just a stupid, worthless little . . . She knows." He let his head fall against the window again, stared at me from beneath lowered lashes. "She knows how people are."

It occurred to me to wonder if Justin was having a complete emotional collapse, a nervous breakdown. I'd seen him close to the edge before. I'd seen him topple over it with the help of booze or pills, but I'd never seen him like this. Sober, yet drunk with emotion, incoherent.

I leaned over, tried to get him to focus on me. His eyes were glassy and dull. "Come on, Justin. You can't buy into that stuff. At some point, you've got to turn off the voices in your head. You know those people in Daily believe in this project. They believe in *The Horseman*. They believe in *you*." Somehow, in the space of a week, we'd come full circle. Now I was the one begging him not to let the project die.

"You're such an . . . stupid, Nate. They're just like everybody else. Big town, little town. It's all the same."

"You promised them something." From the corner of my eye, I caught the time on the digital clock. Dane would be there by now. "The whole town is counting on you. They're counting on this project."

Justin's head rolled side to side. "Randall's got a project for me."

"Randall's got garbage for you!" My voice reverberated through the truck. "He's got junk, and he'll bury you in it until you can't get up again. Come on, Justin. This is our chance to do something that matters. Think about all those kids who'll come to that shelter and get to run around in the grass, and breathe fresh air, and know that life doesn't have to be bad. Think about the people who'll see this film and maybe stop to think about what they're doing to each other. We all get the scars because someone put them there—just like Lucky Strike, right? Just like the horseman. This story means something. It's the start of something. M. Harrison Dane agreed to look at it, for heaven's sake. We've got to be there to show him what this project can mean."

Justin didn't answer, just sat staring out the window, his eyes reflecting the pharmacy billboard and a passing cloud.

"It's time. It's time to change things."

He took in a breath, held it, let it out, his stare still glassy and unfocused. "Amber wants . . . she said I should go to . . . to some rehab . . . some . . . stupid place to do rehab and pray. I called her on the . . . with the pay phone. . . . I asked her to go back to LA with me, and—" he laughed ruefully, shaking his head—"she told me I didn't need her—I need God . . . and . . . and more stupid rehab."

Good for Amber. She was smarter than I'd given her credit for. She knew enough to realize that fixing the broken parts of Justin Shay was a job for someone bigger than she was. "I think she's right," I said flatly. "After we convince Dane to attach himself to this deal, there's going to be lag time while we

Lisa Wingate

work on the studio, assemble the production team, and finish the script. I think you need to spend that time in rehab. The first step toward getting your life right is getting off the pills."

"Pppfff!" He spat. "You sound like her. You gonna pray for me, too? That's what she said—that they'd all pray for me here."

"I think they will." If Daily prayers weren't answered, I couldn't imagine what kind might be. "These people love you, Justin. They care about you. I care about you. I don't want to see you flush your life down the toilet. I want to see you give this project all you've got. I want to see you get in touch with Steph, see about Brody and Bryn. They deserve to know they've got a dad out there who cares about them enough to get off the stuff, make a decent life. You can't keep running out on them like your mom ran out on you. You can't. You know, and I know, if you keep doing what you're doing, sooner or later you'll check out—with the pills, in the car, whatever—and you won't be here for them at all. Deep down, you know that, or you wouldn't have left LA to come here in the first place."

Justin rolled his head to the side, turning his face away. Folding his hand into a fist, he tapped his knuckles against the bridge of his nose, slowly, rhythmically, as if he were trying to block out everything else in his head. Finally, he stopped, and I was afraid he'd fallen asleep. Then I decided that might be a good thing. I could stuff him in the passenger seat, head for Daily, and hope a little rest and a forty-mile drive would put him in a better frame of mind.

He muttered a few words I couldn't understand, and then, "My truck won't . . . It won't start. I think it's out of gas."

I felt something between a laugh and a sigh of relief, and then the vague realization of an answered prayer, however strange. *That's what you get for praying his truck would break down, doofus.* "We can go in mine." *I hope. I hope the PHD mobile's got enough fuel for a return trip.* On the way down, I'd discerned that the truck ran on a propane tank in the bed. I had no way to put fuel in it, nor would I have known how.

"I left the script back at the hotel."

"I brought another one for you." After the dramatic conversation, it was a surprisingly nondramatic ending. "Let's go."

Nodding, Justin took the key from the ignition, then looked around at the pills. I waited to see if he would grab one or two. He seemed to think about it, then finally just brushed them out of the way and climbed down from the truck, little white pills falling off of him like rain. I met him at the PHD mobile.

"You came in this?" he asked, eyeing the giant corkscrew suspended over the flatbed.

"It was all I could get on short notice."

"Is it gonna make it back?"

"I hope so." Climbing into our ride, I turned the key and the engine wheezed, wheezed, wheezed, then coughed, squealed, and grumbled begrudgingly to life. "Buckle up." I grabbed the proposal packet from the dash, where it rested on a pile of receipts and some drawings of Justin's ranch gateway. "This is going to be a wild ride."

We returned to Daily in record time, considering that the truck took forever to rev up to third gear and was moody about going into fourth. We didn't talk. I didn't want to, and Justin was occupied with the proposal—getting focused, I hoped. I left him alone, kept my complaints about the traffic and the truck to myself, because I had a sense that any little thing could upset the horseman's tenuous return. I hoped that, when we got to the ranch, he was up to the task. He was going to have to sell Dane on the project, and to do that, he needed to be fully lucid, on top of his game.

When we rolled through Daily, the place looked strangely deserted. The stores were closed, which probably wasn't unusual on a Sunday, but even the Daily Café had shut down. The lack of atmosphere on Main Street was disappointing. I wanted Dane to see Daily as it really was. In the treatment, I'd set several scenes in town.

"Who died?" Justin poked his nose out of the script long enough to look around.

The horseman, I'm afraid, I thought, but I didn't say it. A haunting possibility formed in my mind—one in which Dane, upon arriving in Daily and finding The Shay conspicuously absent, had gotten back on the plane and taken off. Now everyone in town was at home, mourning the demise of the film project.

I left off considering the worst case scenario as we sped through town and took a left before the Buy-n-Bye. The post truck blew smoke rings, the gears grinding and the auger swinging in a squeaky pendulum, ticking away the minutes like a giant clock. I tried to think positively, to believe that Dane, now in Daily for almost an hour, was happily enjoying a tour of the ranch, so enthralled with the ongoing construction and plans for the future foster shelter that he hadn't even noticed his host was nowhere to be found. Maybe Amber had made it back from her publicity trip and she was crooning a little southern gospel to entertain everyone.

It was a nice scene, charming to imagine, if hard to believe.

My knuckles drummed impatiently on the steering wheel as we skidded around corners and chugged up hills, me downshifting repeatedly to make it to the top and Justin shooting me irritated looks because he was trying to study the packet.

"I think I'm sick," he complained as we bumped through a low-water crossing, the back and forth motion making the post drill almost turn a three-sixty.

331

"Don't you get sick in here," I said, as if by threatening him I could prevent it. "I mean it, Shay. You keep it together. We're almost to the ranch."

The little church and Amber's house whizzed past the window. A couple miles farther, and we'd find out if there was still a chance or if all was lost.

Justin swiped an arm across his forehead. "Oh, man, I'm gonna hurl. Stop here."

"*Hold* it." I wondered if he had any concept of the dire nature of our present situation. We were ridiculously late. We had only about two daylight hours left to woo Dane, if he was, by some slim chance, still present and even remotely woo-able.

What were the odds of that?

"Stop the car!" Justin demanded, slamming his fist against the door. "I said I don't feel good."

"I don't care!" *One more mile, just one more mile.* "Cowboy up, already." I was surprised to find myself spouting the cowpoke code, but at the moment, I was willing to try anything.

"You sound like Willie."

"Well, Willie's right." I shored up the crumbling walls of Fort Hope as the ranch came into view. "And by the way, cut the guy a break. If you had cancer, you might not want to broadcast it to everybody, either."

Justin curled his lip. "He should have told me."

"Everything's not *about* you." I swung the truck wide into the gateway to keep from downshifting. "Maybe he didn't do it *to* you, maybe he just did it. You ever consider that? The man probably has his reasons."

"Yeah, whatever," Justin muttered. "He . . ." The sentence faded as he leaned close to the window, squinting against the evening sun. The field near the old house was filled with cars, pickups, horse trailers, farm trucks. There was even a team

332

of mules pulling a hay wagon across the driveway, and people riding on the hay. They were laughing and making gestures in the air, as if they were doing some sort of organized cheer together. . . . No, not cheering . . . they were singing . . . "Old MacDonald." I rolled down the window, and over the rumble of the engine, I could hear the words.

"What the . . ." Justin and I exchanged bewildered glances as the hay wagon passed on its way toward the gate. There were kids on board, lots of kids, and a few men and women, too. I thought I recognized Dane's wife among them, perched on a bale of hay, laughing as she bounced a baby on her knee. In the back of the wagon, I caught a glimpse of Amber with a guitar . . . or at least it looked like Amber. Her face was hidden beneath a pink cowboy hat, so I couldn't exactly tell.

"What's going on?" Justin pointed at the house. On every level, from the roof to the front steps, people were working—sanding, painting, sweeping, nailing, washing windows, repairing shingles. By one of the chicken house foundations out back, a group of men were raising a new wall. I recognized them—Bob from the café, and the countertoppers. Outside the food tent, Pastor Harve and crew were cleaning up the leftovers from a meal. They waved at us as we pulled in. Justin waved back, and the two of us shared an exchange of complete confusion as we got out.

From the shadows inside the tent, I heard Willie and Frank telling some story about taking horses from a kids' riding stable in Texas, trucking them to California, and renting them to movie studios for five times the price, back in the days of the big westerns. "Yeah, by gosh, I figured if Girl Scouts could ride 'em, they'd sure enough do for actors!" Willie exclaimed, and laughter drifted into the open air.

As we stepped inside and my eyes adjusted to the light, I saw

M. Harrison Dane, *the* M. Harrison Dane, in the flesh, along with Willie, Frank, Imagene, Donetta, and Brother Erve from the Baptist church chatting it up at a picnic table made from an old electrical cable spool. The table was covered with paper plates, Styrofoam cups, blueprints, and pieces of paper, which I recognized as bits of *The Horseman* treatment. My blood, sweat, and tears lay mixed with used napkins and spatters of barbecue sauce, like so much trash. Not a good sign.

Donetta was the first to greet us. "Well hoowww-do!" She stood up and crossed the tent with her arms outstretched and a smile that seemed like it went from fingertip to fingertip. "Y'all come right on in hay-er. We were just finishin' up some good ol' Texas pork ribs. You hun-greee?" She hugged Justin, then me, the volume of her voice growing ear-piercing up close. "I was just tellin' Mr. Dane it was a lucky coincidence he got here on the very day we were havin' a party to celebrate the foster shelter plans. Isn't that the luckiest thang?" Widening her eyes at Justin and me, she nodded meaningfully.

"Sshhhure," Justin stammered, slowly beginning to bob his head as if it were rubber banded to Donetta's. "Sure is . . . good he . . . came during the . . . party?" For an actor, he wasn't very convincing.

Donetta winked like she had a tic in her eye. "Well, come on over and say hi. I told Mr. Dane you were tied up a bit earlier, but it was fine, because it gave us all time to tour the ranch, look at all the plans for the foster shelter buildin's, visit and talk about the movie and have some fun with the kids. It's just fascinatin'—about the movie, I mean, and they're sure cute—the kids. I'll tell ye-ew, I don't believe I ever saw such a cute bunch, and that oldest boy! He just can't get enough of them horses. Why, he's down at the barn with Lauren right now. Reckon we ought to go down there and y'all can take a look at Lucky Strike, or do you two boys want to talk here first? We still got Imagene's gen-u-ine Daily apple pie ready to serve up. You hadn't lived till you had Imagene's apple pie. She's gonna be on *Good Mornin' America* with that pie one'a these days."

Imagene blushed and batted a hand, shooing away the compliment before it could land. "Well, it's real easy to make."

"Let's go take a look at the horse," Dane answered, and he immediately became the conversational centerpiece.

Surprisingly enough, he didn't seem irritated by our late arrival, just ready to get down to business. I'd heard that Dane was an impatient man, not given to chitchat. Sitting here in Justin's food tent, sopping up the last of his creamed corn with a half-eaten hush puppy, he seemed oddly relaxed. When he stood up, he bowed like an eighteenth-century courtier. "Ladies, that was delightful. I don't think I have space for apple pie, but the kids might like some when they get off the hay wagon."

Donetta smiled and began clearing the table. "Well, we'll fix them up just as soon as Kemp brings the hayride in. And we'll just cut ye-ew a piece to take home—a little souvenir from Daily, Texas. It tastes fine on airplanes, too. Oh, good gracious, look. We got ribs and sauce on yer papers here." Licking her finger, she began trying to wipe splatters off pages of script.

"No need." Dane gave the papers a dismissing glance. "I'm finished with those."

I took that as a bad sign. If Dane liked the proposal, he probably wouldn't leave it covered with barbecue sauce and used napkins. "Let's go see Corley and the horse." It occurred to me that perhaps this Dane family outing was mostly about entertaining the children. Dane was known for taking his kids on extravagant getaways.

"Sounds good." Justin finally seemed to be coming out of his fog. Stepping forward, he reached across the table and shook Dane's hand. "Great to see you again, Harrison."

Harrison? Harrison? I thought as Dane returned the greeting. They're on a first-name basis?

"I hope Corley's having a good time," Justin went on, and I recognized the rising gleam in his eye. It was time for negotiation, and Justin loved negotiations. Having people beg and offer him obscene amounts of money fed his ego. I wondered if he realized we were on the begging end this time. "Sorry I couldn't be at the ranch when you got here."

"Not a problem. Corley has hit it off with your horse trainer." Shading his eyes as we walked out of the tent with Frank and Willie, Dane looked at the hay wagon, where his kids were giggling and bouncing as the wheels bumped over driveway ruts. Next to Amber Anderson in the wagon, Dane's wife threw her head back and laughed, her long dark hair streaming out behind her. Dane stood at the edge of the tent, momentarily enthralled. As we walked toward the barn, he took in the ongoing construction, the pads for new buildings, the flags that marked areas for riding arenas, basketball courts, and playgrounds. His face straightened, becoming unreadable.

Justin seized the opportunity to press on with business. "This is my writer, Nate Heath." He introduced me as we crossed the driveway. "He put together the proposal packet, and he'll be working on the screenplay. I'm sure you've heard of him."

Yeah, right, I silently choked. *I think we sat next to each other at the Academy Awards last year.*

Dane was polite. "Nate," he said, and shook my hand, but that was it. As we neared the barnyard, his attention gravitated toward the little corral next to Lucky Strike's round pen. In the small enclosure, Lauren and a hairy gray pony were giving riding lessons to Dane's eldest. He was listening intently as she offered instructions.

"I think Corley's in love with the horse, or the trainer, or both," Dane commented.

Justin delivered a practiced laugh that didn't really mean anything.

"Puggy has that effect on people," Frank chimed in. "She always has."

"She's a good trainer," Willie added, trying to roll the ball along toward the topic of his horse and the movie. "She's one of the best trainers I ever did see. She and Lucky Strike got on with each other right away. 'Course, he's an amazin' horse, but she's an amazin' trainer, too."

"It's unusual to see Corley react so well to someone new," Dane observed, seeming largely immune to the conversation and mostly interested in his own agenda. "Corley came out of an orphanage in Poland. He's been diagnosed as mildly autistic. He loves movies, but real people aren't always so easy for him." He motioned to Justin. "He invited you to his birthday party because he's seen all of your films."

"Of course," Justin answered, as if he couldn't imagine that someone wouldn't have perused the entirety of his work.

"I appreciate the fact that you accepted the invitation. It was very important to Corley. He sometimes has difficulty discerning fiction from reality."

"Wouldn't have missed it." Justin's reply was completely plastic. Fortunately, Dane was engrossed in watching Lauren, the pony, and Corley. Lucky Strike's goat had wiggled through the fence to join them and was sniffing noses with Corley's mount. In the next corral, Lucky Strike remained surprisingly calm about his friend's absence.

We stopped near Lauren and the pony, and Dane leaned over

the gate, listening in as Lauren patiently showed Corley how to turn to the right and left. Lauren's back was turned, and she seemed completely oblivious to our presence.

"I'm interested in what you're planning to do here, with the horses and the kids. I've been doing some reading on animal-assisted therapy," Dane offered. "It's impressive what some of these programs can accomplish, especially with kids."

"Exactly." The only thing Justin knew about animal-assisted therapy was what little was in the script. "The original screenplay for *The Horseman* was ahead of its time, but the market's right for it now." Clever how Justin quickly turned the discussion to the film project. Clever, but maybe a little hasty. Dane looked displeased.

"The original screenplay was horrendous. Everyone knows that. The writer's sense of story and character was laughable—clearly a novice effort. It lacks inciting incident, shows no clear character development, the action's flat. What works in a book doesn't work on film. It's a different medium. Film requires an understanding of the visual and a compression of time frame. On film, there's only space for the things that matter most."

"Exactly," Justin said, as if he knew all about it.

A rope tightened in my stomach—something between one of the horseman's lassoes and a hangman's noose. I felt the boom over my head, waiting to fall. If Dane didn't like the original, what were the chances he'd like my partially completed rewrite? I was way out of my league here.

I heard the still, small voice of Doug, telling me I should have known that all along.

Dane opened his mouth to say something, and I thought, *Here it comes. He's going to tell us the new treatment is lousy, too, and there's no way he's getting involved in this thing.*

"Of course, what we e-mailed you is just a draft," I stammered, trying to delay the inevitable. "There's a great deal more to be done on the writing end, but we've had a limited amount of time to put a proposal together, and—"

Corley picked that moment to wave at his dad, and there wasn't any point in finishing the sentence. Dane's attention swung instantly. He was engrossed in watching Corley play with the pony. Lauren looked over her shoulder and smiled at us.

Justin used the conversational gap to move the negotiation from talk to action. "We've got a little bit of a demo worked out for you over there with the horse." He pointed toward Lucky Strike's corral, and I wondered if he'd even noticed that Lucky was sans goat at the moment. Justin had never succeeded at playing the horseman when the goat wasn't there, standing at Justin's feet, providing enticement for the horse.

Dane turned his attention to the round pen. "So that's the famous Lucky Strike."

"In the flesh," Willie confirmed proudly.

"I've seen him race. He's a beautiful animal."

"Yes, he is."

"Heard he's got a bit of a reputation."

"He did have. In the past."

"Shame about his leg."

"Yes, it is," Willie lamented. "But he's got a whole new career ahead'a him here in this movie. Won't hurt the movie a bit that Lucky had all that press back when his leg was broke, either. Had folks from Dallas to Paris sending him flowers and well wishes. The pile at the gates of the vet hospital built up so big they eventual' had to clear it out with a front-end loader. You can bet every one of his fans'll come see the film the minute it hits the screen. They'll all want to see ol' Striker back on his feet again. He's an eyeful. Just wait till you watch him in action."

Willie nodded to Frank, and Frank opened the gate to the

small corral, then went inside to take over the pony's reins. "Here, let me walk the little chap around," he told Lauren. "Y'all go on over to the round pen and talk movie talk."

Lauren obliged after giving Corley a few more instructions. She won his rapt attention and a smile, which seemed to fascinate Corley's father. "He never reacts to people that way," Dane observed as Lauren joined us and we walked to the round pen.

Lauren glanced back at Corley, a tender look in her eyes. "Animals have an amazing ability to reach beyond the barriers. That's the overriding message of *The Horseman*, I think— breaking down the fences, not being afraid to let someone in." Her eyes caught mine, and I experienced a sensation I couldn't translate into words. It was like nothing I'd ever felt before, as if I knew what she was feeling because I was feeling it myself.

The moment seemed longer than it was—like a five-second still shot, and then we were at the round pen, and Lauren went in. I stood on the rail next to Dane as Lucky Strike took notice of the fact that he wasn't alone anymore. He whinnied and bolted toward the fence, making a strafing run past Lauren, which she calmly sidestepped. The horse circled once, twice, pawed the fence that separated him from the pony and the goat, then circled again.

Lauren began explaining the process of resistance-free training, of building a bond between human and animal. Her body movements subtly propelled the horse away, pushing him along the fence, keeping him moving, allowing him to run and nicker, check the boundaries of the enclosure and search for an escape that would lead him to the pony and the goat. A sheen of sweat formed on his coat as five minutes passed, then ten. Lauren continued to move him, pausing occasionally to explain his actions and reactions and to describe the body language she was looking for—the displays of submission that would show a willingness to come to the center.

Dane began to lose interest, and Justin drummed his palms impatiently on the railing. I found myself fearing that this would be the one time Lucky Strike wouldn't cooperate. Maybe he'd become too attached to the goat. . . .

And then, finally, it happened—a lowering of the head, a softening of muscle and bone that rounded the animal's back. A long, slow sigh and a glance inward.

Lauren took a step back, and Lucky Strike stopped running, then came to her, finally lowering his head into her hands.

The moment was a postcard in my mind. Lauren, the horse, the sunlight falling over her hair, casting it in deep shades of red, her hands catching the shadows as she stroked the horse's muzzle, her face close to his. The animal relaxed, as if in that moment, there was perfect trust between them.

The bond broke as quickly as it had begun. Justin entered the corral, and the horse went berserk. Lauren stiffened, casting a worried look toward Willie and me.

"Now, you see, Lucky Strike, he's got a lot in common with the racehorse in the movie." Willie began explaining Lucky Strike's history of abuse and injury, of being filled full of drugs and forced to continue to run when he must have been in tremendous pain.

Dane watched with skeptical interest as Lauren whispered something to Justin and exited the enclosure, leaving him alone.

Willie went on, trying to thread together the story of *The Horseman* and Lucky Strike's past. "You see, any horse, even one raised in a stall like Lucky Strike, or the racehorse in the story, he's still a herd animal, at the instinctual level. He don't want to be out there on the fence alone. . . ."

Slipping in beside me, Lauren let out a long breath and

wrapped her fingers over the rail, holding on for dear life. Her lips moved almost imperceptibly, as if she were sending out signals, or praying for a miracle, or both.

I slid my hand over hers. Her eyes met mine, and I lost track of things until the horse bolted past, snorting and kicking. Dane took a step away from the rail, and Lauren closed her eyes, whispering, "Come on, come on . . ."

"Now, sometimes it takes a little longer for him to come around," Willie hedged. "Ol' Lucky, he's got a lot of bad past to overcome, but that's okay, because it makes it all look nice'n real. Too many movies out there use some old washed-up kid horse to play a youngster like Lucky Strike. It don't look real to anybody that knows horses. You want people to believe it, you gotta have a real runnin' horse. A blueblood like Lucky, and . . ."

The moments ticked by as Willie rattled on, trying to fill the time. In the corral, Justin looked confused, and eventually, frustrated. He yanked off his hat and slapped it against his knee, undoubtedly considering throwing it. Amber joined us at the fence, and Justin glanced at her for support. She flashed an encouraging smile, giving him the high sign. He grimaced, shaking his head.

"Calm down, calm down," Lauren muttered under her breath as communication broke down and Lucky Strike began to weave back and forth along one section of fence. "Keep him going forward," Lauren whispered. "Don't let him disengage."

Justin changed his position, forced the horse out of the repetitive pattern, pushed him along the rail.

"Good," Lauren whispered. "Good. Keep him moving. . . ." Justin looked at her, and she nodded almost imperceptibly, wheeling a finger, then turning her thumb upward and giving the signal for Justin to step up the pressure a bit.

Justin closed in slightly, focusing intently on the horse, pushing Lucky Strike harder, until the horse's coat was slick with sweat, foamy and lathered around his neck and shoulders. His ribs heaved with effort, and Lauren's hand tightened inside mine. I felt myself giving up, surrendering to hopelessness. *It's not going to happen this time,* I thought. *This is it. We're dead in the water.*

Across the corral, Amber closed her eyes, intertwined her fingers, and pressed them to her mouth. Her lips moved slowly, sending up silent words. Her face was serene, as if no matter how the evidence looked in the corral, she still believed in the horseman.

I reminded myself that we weren't finished yet. Dane was still present. There was still hope. Lucky Strike circled again, snorted at the dust swirling around his feet, coughed and tossed his head, then circled again. Justin yanked off his hat and I felt my teeth clench. *Don't quit,* I thought. *Give it a little more. Give it everything.*

Mopping his forehead with his sleeve, Justin squinted against the dust, pressed his arm over his eyes for a moment, seemed to consider whether to keep on or give up. An impossible silence enveloped the round pen. In the corral next door, Frank stopped walking the pony. At the house, the hammering and sawing halted. Overhead, the breeze stilled in the live oaks, and the cicadas fell into a hush, as if even they felt the weight of the moment, the breathlessness of anticipation. There was no sound, only the rhythmic collision of Lucky Strike's hoofbeats, the drawing and releasing of breath, the groan of flesh and muscle, straining to continue, fighting to keep running rather than giving in.

Then suddenly, there was a subtle sign—a slight lowering of the horse's head, the barest indication of surrender.

"Back off," Lauren whispered. "Back off." In the arena, Justin stepped back, not as if he'd heard, but as if he knew without being told, as if he'd felt the change in the horse's motivations, as if he were the horseman. He stopped pushing, let the animal come to him, seeking a partnership, a gentle communion, a place of safety. Justin stretched out his hands, and Lucky Strike lowered his head, moving tentatively forward, one step, then two, then another, until only inches separated them. Justin cupped his fingers, and the horse laid his muzzle inside them in an instant of trust between man and animal.

Justin looked surprised, amazed, relieved. Content. In that instant, he was the horseman.

Across the ring, Amber smiled, her cheeks wet with tears. Wiping her eyes impatiently, she silently pressed her hands to her face as if she were trying to still her joy before it could bubble into the round pen and disturb the silence.

Lauren's lips parted in a long sigh. I felt her body relax against mine. Her fingers loosened, and I realized they had been clutching mine so tightly I couldn't feel my hand.

"That's how it's done," Willie said. "A true horseman works with the animal, not against it. He takes the time to build a bond of trust instead of resorting to force. There's a good lesson in that for people. When you get right down to it, animals and people ain't that different. We're all workin' through the places we been, and we all need someone who's gonna wait for us till we're ready. This story'll help folks figure that out sooner in life, rather than later." He gave Justin a meaningful look as Justin stroked Lucky Strike's nose. "That's a good job, son. You're a fine horseman."

In the arena, Justin smiled to himself and looked into the horse's eyes with a sense of wonder.

Backing away from the fence, Dane dusted off his hands and stroked his thumb and forefinger along his chin, frowning. He studied Corley and the pony, seeming unaware that everyone was watching him, hanging in thin air while awaiting his reaction. He backed away a few steps, and for an instant, I was afraid he was about to walk off without saying anything. What did we do then? Follow? Leave him alone? Let Imagene and Donetta try to ply him with pecan pie and southern-fried conversation?

Maybe he'd head back to LA without giving us any indication of his feelings. Dane was known as an independent type, not the sort to be pushed into anything. If we didn't get an answer now, the wait would be agonizing. . . .

He cleared his throat, and the onlookers froze like kids engaged in a game of Mother May I. "I like it," he said, rocking to his heels and looking around the ranch.

On the driveway, Dane's family had finished petting the team of horses pulling the hay wagon. Monique was laughing and talking with the driver as he handed her one of a set of twins adopted from Africa. The rest of the kids dashed ahead to see Corley and the pony.

Dane watched them bolt toward him. "It's a good project," he remarked, as if we'd suddenly become an afterthought. "Good message. Well done." He turned and headed toward his family.

Lauren, Willie, and I exchanged glances, wondering, no doubt, the same thing: *Is that a yes, a no . . . a maybe?* I had a sense that the lot of us were still hanging in agonizing limbo— except Justin, who seemed content just to have finally succeeded with Lucky Strike. Laying his forehead against Lucky Strike's, he closed his eyes and traveled inside himself to a place that had nothing to do with the film. I stood watching him, taking in the moment as a look of peace settled over him. A soft breeze circled the round pen, ruffled the horse's mane, and caught

Justin's cowboy hat. Neither of them noticed as the wind lifted it and sent the crown of the horseman floating away. Justin only whispered something to the horse, and the horse nickered in return, and they remained in their weary embrace, finally in harmony with one another.

One of Dane's daughters, a stocky-legged little girl from some south-sea island, reached him, and he scooped her up, asked her if she wanted to go see the pony. They started off in that direction while the rest of us stood in suspended animation, wondering what to do next. Push for an answer? Wait longer? Follow along behind Dane? Give him some time to relax and entertain his kids?

The little girl put her hand to his ear, leaned close and whispered something. "Yes, we are," Dane said, then glanced back at me. "How soon can I have the remainder of the script? A month? Six weeks?"

"Your choice." I sounded amazingly calm, considering that my head was exploding and I felt like I'd just scratched off the million-dollar Lotto ticket. "You tell me. I'll get it ready." *If I have to glue myself to the chair and live on Starbucks and NoDoz, I'll get it ready.* It occurred to me that the magnum opus I'd started and restarted a hundred times, the piece I'd moved to the mountains to write, would have to wait, and I didn't care. My mind was filled with *The Horseman*, with all the lives it could touch, with all the people who believed in it. I saw them standing on the porches of the old ranch house—Donetta, Imagene, Lucy, Bob, Brother Ervin, Pastor Harve, Miss Beedie, the boys from the Countertop Coffee Club, and a few dozen more Dailyians, all looking our way, piling their hopes on the wind, waiting for a sign.

Tapping a forefinger in the air, Dane gave me an appraising look. "Give it the time it needs. It's fine work so far. Excellent sense of the character. Good writing. Keep on with what you've been doing."

"I . . . yes, I will." *Be calm, be cool*, I told myself, swallowing the seventy-six piece band in my chest. *Don't act like an amateur. Act like this happens every day.* "I'm pleased that you like it. Thank you for the vote of confidence." *Good job. Perfect. Friendly, but not desperate. Grateful, yet not groveling.*

"It's well deserved. You've dug down and found the heart of this story. That's a writer's job." Dane met my gaze very directly, giving the sense of a man much more complicated than the tabloid hype indicated. I had a feeling he was someone I would enjoy working with, someone who really could do justice to the story of *The Horseman*. "I've been waiting a long while for a project that seemed . . . worth the time."

"This one is," I said, and the words conveyed a belief I didn't have to manufacture.

"I agree." Dane put his hand out and shook mine. With a last glance toward Justin and Lucky Strike, he headed off to join his family, and I stood slightly numb, basking in the glow.

Doug was nowhere in my head. There wasn't a whisper of him, not even in the most remote corner, and suddenly I knew that was what I'd been seeking all along. I wanted to create something that was only good, that didn't come from fear or loathing, insecurity or financial need, self-recrimination or self-doubt, that had no part of the past in it, but came only from a hope of what could be.

The dark corners were gone now. There was no place for Doug to hide.

Lauren smiled at me, and I knew she understood. "I think that's a yes," she whispered. "He said to keep on with what you've been doing." Her eyes were the soft green of spring grass, dewy with joy, and I was lost in them instantly.

"I guess that means more late hours in the beauty shop," I answered.

"I guess so."

"And besides, there's still the Bigfoot mystery to solve."

"That's true."

"We might need to stake out the place. . . ."

"We might." Her lips spread wide in a smile that was dazzling, and for the first time, all the sadness in her seemed to float away. "You did it," she whispered, the words glittering with joy and pride that made me feel larger than I was.

"*We* did it," I corrected, and she threw her head back, smiling triumphantly, her hair swirling in the breeze. She opened her arms, and I took her in mine, lifted her from her feet as if she were lighter than air, and twirled her into the barnyard as she laughed.

If I'd been writing the scene for film, it would have been the one in which the music rose to a crescendo, and the boy knew this girl was different from anyone he'd ever met. His mind and heart and soul would tell him he was falling in love, and so was she.

The moment would be perfect, and the ranch would fade into the cool shadows of evening, and then the credits would roll, because there was nothing more to say.

Except, of course, that they lived happily ever after.

Chapter 23

Lauren Eldridge

As the world spun around me, I saw Willie punch a fist into the air in triumph. Applause and cheers erupted near the old house. I thought of Aunt Donetta, my father, Brother Ervin, Pastor Harve, and Harvard Jr.—all the people who had loved me since the day I was born. I thought of Daily, the place that had made me, and broken me, and waited patiently for me to stop clinging to fear, stop running, and come home again.

Nate set me on my feet as Amber ran squealing across the barnyard. "That was awesome!" She cheered, then tackled me with an effervescent hug, and suddenly, everybody was hugging everybody. My father hugged Nate, Willie hugged my father, my father hugged Amber, Amber hugged Willie, Willie and Amber hugged Nate in a three-way. Nate looked embarrassed. Amber took his hand and Willie's and dragged them off to the round pen to give Justin the good news about Dane.

My father slipped his arm around me as we watched them go. "That was somethin' to see," he said, then lifted a hand to give Aunt Netta the high sign. By the food tent, Aunt Netta held her hands clasped and raised them high in the air, like an Olympic athlete declaring victory.

"Yes, it was," I agreed.

"I wondered there for a minute," Dad admitted.

"I did, too."

Dad squeezed my shoulder, pulling me off balance so that I teetered on one foot, using him for support. As always, he kept me from falling. We stood for a minute, just taking everything in, then Dad nudged my shoulder and pointed toward the round pen. "Look there," he whispered, close to my ear.

I followed his line of vision to the fence, where Lucky Strike's nanny goat had spotted an abandoned Dr. Pepper atop a post. After eyeing it from several angles, she rose onto her hind legs, walked a few steps, then braced her front hooves on the corral fence, and stretched out her neck, trying to reach.

In silhouette, she was seven feet tall and hairy, manlike . . .

"Could be that solves a certain mystery," Dad observed, his mustache twitching upward when I looked at him.

"I guess it does." I felt a twinge of disappointment. "Too bad, though. There won't be nearly as much to talk about at the café now."

Dad chuckled, his body shaking up and down. "Well, we could keep it our secret a while. Just between you and me."

"We could," I agreed, thinking that Nate and I might get to have our stakeout after all.

"Shame to spoil a good mystery," Dad said. "After all, what's a little town without its secrets?"

"I'd hate to think."

Dad chuckled again, and I knew we'd entered into a silent pact. The true identity of the Daily Sasquatch was safe for now.

"Guess I better get back and give some pony rides," Dad said finally. He gave me another squeeze, and I wrapped my arms around his middle, holding on tight.

"I love you." The words trembled from my throat, weighted with emotion, heavy with so many other things I wanted to say, but I knew if I started, tears would come. This wasn't a moment for tears.

My father sniffed and rubbed his mustache, then cleared his throat. "Oh, I know it." His voice was hoarse, soft like the evening air. "I've always known that. You're a good girl. You never been a disappointment to me, ever, Pug. I want to tell you that. Your mama always said, *That Puggy can do anythin'*, and she was right."

I chuckled silently at my father's old habit of attributing compliments to my mom because he was embarrassed to deal them out himself. "Dad, Mom never called me Puggy." One thing my mother never approved of was the fact that my father had christened her little girl with such an unflattering handle.

"I know it," Dad chuckled, his chin gently ruffling my hair. "But you been my little Puggy since the very minute I first laid eyes on you. I'd never seen anythin' so fine in my whole life." He kissed me on the top of my head, then balanced me on my feet. Across the way, the Dane kids were impatient for pony rides. "Welcome home, Puggy."

I watched my father walk away to the small corral, where Justin had slipped through the fence to help Corley dismount the pony. My father entered the round pen, untied the pony's lead rope, and handed it to Corley. Grabbing one of the little Dane girls by the waist, my father swung her into the saddle. In my mind, I knew just how the motion would feel—his strong hands under my arms, the high swing through the air, the plop into the saddle, not hard enough to hurt but just enough to force a giggle out. And then the words, "There you go, young lady. How about a ride? Hang on now, cowgirl. He's a wild 'un." My father was never too busy to hold the rope while I rode around in circles.

"Guess that'll clinch the deal." I heard Nate's voice, and I turned to him.

"I guess it will."

He smiled slightly, his eyes catching the light of evening, turning warm brown. "I wasn't worried, were you?"

"No way."

Nate looked into my eyes, and all the other thoughts seemed insignificant. I knew he would kiss me, and I didn't care who was watching. A warmth slipped over me that made everything feel right, and perfect, gold and crimson and edged with pearl like the clouds in the darkening sky behind him. There was no need to hide any longer, no need to pull away. I abandoned myself to the kiss, let go of everything and just allowed myself to live fully in the moment.

When our lips parted, I was conscious of someone tugging at my shirt. I looked down, expecting one of the Dane children, but the goat was there, nibbling on my hem. Apparently, she'd given up on the Dr. Pepper. Laughing, I pushed her away, and she stood back and bleated at me, giving me a keen look, as if she knew I'd figured out her secret.

"Guess your girlfriend's worried," I told Nate.

Nate chuckled, then shooed her away. "I don't have a girl-friend."

"That's good to know."

His grin made something tighten and flutter deep inside me, and this time I didn't tether the emotion to the weight of regrets and sadness, guilt and apprehension. I let it take wing and soar. I allowed myself to feel it, to revel in it, to believe it was pos-sible for life to move from what had been to what could be—for

Nate and me, for Willie and my father, for Aunt Donetta and the town of Daily. I thought once more of Harvard Jr., who had saved my life and sacrificed his own. After all, what good is a life saved if you fail to live it?

Turning in Nate's arms, I gazed past the old house, watched it become a shadow as the horizon dimmed and the hammers went silent. I thought of all the lives that would intersect here, through film and through the children who would come to this place, and discover that no matter where you've been, or what you've done, or what has been done to you, it's all right to stop running and let yourself be loved.

It's more than all right. It is the thing that matters most. Peace doesn't lie in all that we run to, in the independence we struggle to maintain, in the things we embrace that don't embrace us in return. It is not in the noise of the world, but rests in the quiet place we last look. It waits until we stop running, stop battling the fences, stop searching outside and look toward the center. There, in the very heart of who we are and what we were created to be, we find it—the greatest thing in this world or the next, the very essence of God.

We turn toward the Good Horseman, and He opens His arms, and we come into His presence, where there is love enough to cover everything.

Discussion Questions

1. In the beginning of the story, Lauren ponders whether it's possible to ever really leave behind your roots. What do you think? Where are your roots and how have they shaped the way you live today?

2. Daily is struggling to retain its identity in the face of sudden fame. Lauren observes some changes when she arrives in her hometown. In what ways do fame or sudden prosperity change a community? Are these changes positive, negative, or both?

3. As Nate's story begins, he is struggling with the choice of continuing his destructive friendship with Justin or calling it quits. When we are involved in painful relationships, how should we make the decision between self-preservation and self-sacrifice? Is there ever a time to let go? If so, when? Why do you think Nate goes to Daily with Justin, even though he's told himself he won't?

4. Justin's friendship with Amber has changed his behavior in ways that are not typical for him. Have you ever experienced a friendship or chance encounter with someone who changed your way of thinking?

5. Amber and Justin have both experienced the mega-fame American culture seems to crave, yet they have responded to it very differently. Why? What things determine the choices we make in using the resources we're given?

6. Themes of guilt and forgiveness run throughout the novel. How can a failure to accept forgiveness trap us? Do you see applications for the sermon of the Good Horseman in your own life or the lives of people you know? In what ways?

7. Many characters in the story are in the position of Lucky Strike, struggling between a new option and an old habit. Have you or someone you've known ever experienced something similar? What was the result? What made the difference?

8. The nanny goat is integral to Lucky Strike's healing. Have you ever been given a "nanny goat" when you needed one? Who or what was it?

9. Lauren realizes that in pulling away from her family and friends and trying to control her own healing, she has weakened her ability to recover from her grief. How are our families, friends, communities, and church families integral to surviving difficult times? In view of this, why do we sometimes choose to keep our struggles to ourselves?

10. Nate begins to consider that the secret to life might not be in getting past previous traumas but in looking at how those traumas have shaped us for a specific purpose. Do you see ways in which your past experiences, good or bad, have prepared you for a specific purpose?

11. Late in the story, Donetta tells Nate that sometimes God puts a new path under our feet because He knows we're ready, even if we don't know it yet. Have you ever been pushed toward something you didn't think you were ready for? How did you react? What happened in the end?

Lisa Wingate is a former journalist, inspirational speaker, and *New York Times* bestselling author of thirty novels. Her work has won or been nominated for many awards, including the Pat Conroy Southern Book Prize, the Oklahoma Book Award, the Utah Library Award, the Carol Award, the Christy Award, and the RT Booklovers Reviewer's Choice Award. Her latest book, *Before We Were Yours*, was the winner of the 2017 Goodreads Choice Award for Historical Fiction. Lisa writes her stories at home in Texas, where she is part of the Wingate clan of storytellers.

Sign Up for
Lisa's Newsletter!

Keep up to date with Lisa's news on book releases
and events by signing up for her email list at
lisawingate.com.